Lov

Other books by Becky Barker:

Bedroom Eyes
Captured by a Cowboy
Dangerous
The Cowboy and the Cradle
Impossible Match
The Last Real Cowboy
Renegade Texan
Sassy Lady
To Trust Again
Western Dreams
Back in His Arms

Love in the Air
Becky Barker

WILDSIDE PRESS
Doylestown, Pennsylvania

Portions of this book have appeared elsewhere as etc

Love in the Air
A publication of
Wildside Press
P.O. Box 301
Holicong, PA 18928-0301

www.wildsidepress.com

FIRST EDITION

Author's Note

I first conceived the idea for *Love in the Air* while watching my daughter's high school basketball game. One of the opposing players had the name 'Sharla' printed on her jersey. I had never seen the name before and it intrigued me, as did the rhyming names of Darla and Carla. All three swirled through my creative muse, giving birth to the Prescott triplets.

I decided right away that they'd need unique professions, so I made them pilots. I set the Prescott Air Service on their family's Virginia plantation and my imagination took flight from there.

Born to Fly is Sharla's story. She's an exceptionally skilled charter pilot. She's also a strong, independent and self-confident woman whose love of flying comes second only to her love of family. Although a romantic at heart, she can't imagine any man becoming more important to her than career and family. At least, not until she flies US Marshal Reed Connors on a secret, cross-country mission.

Logan's Lady is Darla's story. You can call her Dee, and she'll win your heart with her tenderness and extrasensory perception. Her expertise is flight instruction. She's the epitome of patience with her students until she's hired to train the staff of Kentucky horse breeder Logan Bradford. She and Logan have a history, and it's not a good one.

Loving Carlie is obviously Carla's story. She's a cargo pilot and enjoys her work, but she's neither as confident as Sharla nor as gifted as Dee. A brief, disastrous marriage to an abusive husband has battered her self-esteem and left her emotionally insecure. She has no desire to become involved with another man, especially not her former brother-in-law, Michael Trehearn.

This series was a pleasure to write and I hope it will be a joy to readers, as well. I'm dedicating it in honor of one of my most treasured fans, my dad. (1929–2002)

The Prescotts are a close-knit family and the men in the triplets' lives are true heroes. I hope you'll love them as much as I do.

Happy Reading!

Born to Fly

One

The identical cheesy grins on her sisters' faces meant nothing but trouble, thought Sharla as she entered the reception area of Prescott Air Service and caught sight of Darla and Carla. They were looking altogether too cheerful for a Monday morning.

As one sibling in a set of triplets, she knew the odd man out was always at risk. She'd just returned from a rare four-day weekend — one she'd earned and desperately needed. Her sisters were envious, so she supposed they'd hatched some scheme to harass her. There was no doubt she'd been given a rotten flight schedule today. She loved her family, they were her life, but there were still times when she wished she could avoid their good-natured teasing. Today was one of them.

Dee and Carlie were sitting on the sofa, dressed much like Sharla in khaki jumpsuits bearing the Prescott emblem. The style was practical for the three pilots, yet the figure-hugging style left no doubt about their gender. Even though their chosen profession was considered a masculine domain, they thrived on the challenge without losing sight of their femininity.

"I hope my short vacation hasn't resulted in my getting last refusal on some stinky assignment," Sharla commented after wishing everyone a good morning.

Carlie was French-braiding Dee's waist-length hair. The triplets were identical in looks, with brilliant turquoise eyes and honey-blond hair. The only way to differentiate between them was their hairstyles. Dee's fell heavily to her waist, Carlie's was cut in a smooth pageboy with wispy bangs and Sharla's wind-blown, layered style draped her shoulders.

"You *are* the most rested of our staff," Dee teased, flashing a saccharine-sweet smile.

"The customer *is* one of your favorites," Carlie added, tongue in cheek.

Sharla wondered what those rare consecutive days of rest were going to cost her. "Who's the customer, and how bad's the job?"

"Sharla, dear, you shouldn't be that way about an assignment," admonished Belle, their mother, the family air service's receptionist and their schedule manager. "It's taken five years to establish our clientele, and you know we accept only the most respectable charters. Mr. Connors is a good customer, and he's brought us a lot of business."

Sharla groaned and felt tension creep into her body at just the mention of the man. "Connors?" she repeated. "Reed Connors, and I'm getting stuck with him? Why can't Dee or Carlie handle this one? I had him the last time."

"You know he likes you best," Carlie teased, her eyes sparkling with mischief.

All three sisters had flown charters for the U.S. Marshal during the past couple years. Dee and Carlie had even dated the man. Sharla was the only one he hadn't asked for a date, and she didn't mind one bit. Well, maybe a little bit, she admitted silently. She couldn't deny that his disinterest stung her pride. Thankfully, the man didn't elicit any deeper emotion.

"He wants someone to fly him from city to city for about a week, and we're just too tired. You're the only one rested enough to take on that sort of charter," Dee insisted. "Carlie and I are booked solid."

"Mother?" Sharla decided to ignore her sisters and concentrate on getting the assignment rescheduled. Reed Connors was a strain on her nerves for short periods of time, and she knew she had the same effect on him. They wouldn't survive an entire week together. "We agreed to take turns on Connors. I had him last. That means it's somebody else's turn."

The man in question wasn't a difficult or demanding customer. He was an enigma, and the strength of his presence could be unnerving, but Dee and Carlie didn't really mind working with him. Although they did more training and cargo than charters, they were perfectly capable of handling the assignment. They just knew she was reluctant and loved teasing her.

"Yes, dear, I know it's not your turn," Belle countered in the same soft, southern drawl she'd used to soothe the siblings for twenty-five years. "But Dee and Carlie have such tight schedules. It's too late to juggle assignments. Mr. Connors did apologize for the short notice, but you're the only one who can pilot for him."

Sharla dropped into a seat near her mother's desk and glared at her two sisters. The service had three types of planes. All three pilots could fly any of them, but each had a preference.

"I can handle Dee's schedule for the week," she insisted.

"You're not flying my plane," argued Dee. "I have to give lessons. Besides, I have next weekend off, and I'm not taking a chance of spending it somewhere in the wilds of the Midwest."

Sharla groaned and asked the dreaded question, "Where does Connors want to be flown?"

"His schedule includes a trip up to Pittsburgh, then over to Columbus. Later he plans to go from Columbus to Lexington and then to

Nashville. He's not sure of the timing, but he's made reservations for overnight stays in every city. He may come home with you on Thursday, or send you back alone. Either way, he's paying all the expenses."

Sharla stared at her mother in amazement. "You let Connors make arrangements for accommodations?"

"He said you'd be staying at the airport hotels."

"I object on behalf of taxpayers everywhere. How does a federal employee's expense account stretch to airport hotels and several days' charter flying?"

"I'm sure I don't know, dear," Belle replied. She came from a long line of southern aristocracy and had firm beliefs on what was proper and what wasn't. It definitely wasn't polite to ask a man about his finances. "But he promised quality accommodations."

"I don't like it," declared Sharla, "and I don't want to be Reed Connors' personal chauffeur for a week. Why can't he fly commercial?"

She ignored her sisters' exaggerated gasps of shock. They weren't really horrified by the suggestion of turning away a customer. They just wanted to annoy her some more. "Why can't we tell Connors we can't make the run? Tell him we can't fit him into the schedule."

"That's not the truth," her mother admonished in a tone that remind lying was a sin. Belle epitomized the socially and morally upright gentility. Despite the age lines on her face and silver in her hair, she was as beautiful as her daughters, and much more concerned with proper, ladylike behavior.

"I've already approved the trip," she informed her reluctant offspring, then glanced out the glass-paneled doors. "Mr. Connors is just arriving and is scheduled to leave in an hour."

"An hour!" Sharla exclaimed.

The man in question entered the office in time to catch the protest. He pulled off his sunglasses and shot a narrowed glance at her, but didn't ask the cause of her outburst. The room suddenly shrank and grew warmer. Reed Connors was the type of man who radiated so much masculine energy that his presence was felt, not just witnessed. He wasn't a particularly big man, yet he exuded an air of supreme confidence and capability.

"Sharla." He greeted her by name, nodded a greeting to her sisters, and then moved closer to Belle's desk.

Personally, Sharla thought the air around him was electrified to warn people to keep their distance. She heeded the warning, rose from her chair, and stepped away from the reception desk while he discussed business with her mother.

Dee was mouthing a silent message, "He always liked you best." Referring to the fact that Reed had spoken to Sharla by name. Even with different hairstyles, most of their customers had a problem telling them apart. Connors always managed to single her out.

"Shut up." Sharla was mouthing a response back to her sister when he turned and looked her directly in the eyes. His left eyebrow rose in arrogant query.

"Just a little discussion with Dee," she explained.

"Amazing," Reed drawled in his deep, soft tone, "I didn't even hear Dee speak."

Her sisters had the grace to muffle their laughter.

She didn't know what it was about the man that made her feel so belligerent, but she experienced ripples of annoyance along her nerves every time he leveled his golden brown eyes at her. Something very elemental in her seemed to have an adverse reaction to his proximity.

"Dee and I are very good at silent communication." The statement was made with little expression, but Sharla's eyes were bright with challenge as they tangled with his.

Connors returned her gaze steadily. She thought of her sisters' insistence that he was a real hunk and wondered why the description annoyed her every time it came to mind. He wasn't the tall, muscled type. He topped her five feet six by only a few inches. Dee called him lean and mean. Carlie thought he could double for movie star Don Johnson.

He wasn't gorgeous. Not really. Not movie star gorgeous. His hair was light brown, streaked with gold, and so were his eyes. His features would be considered average if it weren't for the sharp intelligence in his eyes and the strong, stubborn line of his jaw. Coupled with the aura of suppressed energy and raw sensuality, his penetrating gaze always made her wary.

He was dressed in casual slacks, a white shirt, and a light blue linen jacket. He obviously dressed for comfort and to please himself. She thought federal law enforcement officers were supposed to be button-down bland to blend into the scenery. Connors never did.

"Have you ever considered working for Uncle Sam?" he asked in a carefully measured tone. "We can always use people with special talents."

Sharla didn't have any fondness for federal agents, and Connors knew it. He liked to get in a few taunts whenever possible. The two of them kept a shield of subtle insults between them at all times. Innate feminine instinct urged her to keep an emotional distance between them.

"I'm sure our talents would be wasted as marshals," she argued, just for the sake of it. "We were born to fly."

Carlie interrupted their exchange, "Speaking of flying, Dee, we'd better get started. It's going to be a long day." She grabbed her clipboard, rose from the sofa and headed to the door.

"Aren't they all," Dee said, following her. "Of course, it might not be so bad if we had nice long weekends to play on the beach."

Sharla let the comment slide, but glared at her sisters. Good-byes were exchanged as the two left the building. The phone rang to distract Belle, and Reed turned his full attention to her.

"Are you just back from vacation?"

"I took a four-day weekend. They're in a snit because I spent some time with mutual friends, and they couldn't go."

"So that's how you got stuck with me twice in a row," he guessed, his eyes alight with the knowledge that she didn't want to go anywhere with him.

Sharla felt herself blushing. She hadn't realized he was aware of their "turn taking." Despite her reluctance to work with the man, she'd been raised to be more considerate. Belle never tolerated offensive behavior, and she wasn't sure how to make amends.

"I guess we wouldn't make very good feds after all," she commented.

A corner of Connors' mouth tilted in a grin. Sharla thought he had the most expressive mouth and eyes she'd ever seen, yet she knew he concealed a lot more emotion than he ever displayed.

"Is there somewhere we can talk?" he asked.

Her eyes widened in surprise. She couldn't think of any reason they needed more privacy. They weren't likely to be disturbed in the reception area, but the request made her curious. She glanced toward the hallway behind her mother's desk. "We can use Daddy's office, if you like."

Reed nodded and followed her to Harold "Bear" Prescott's private office.

Bear was a retired Air Force sergeant. His specialty was airplane mechanics. After retirement from the service, he'd developed his own air service on a small portion of the Virginia plantation his wife had inherited. Now he spent most of his time keeping Prescott's aircraft in superior condition.

Sharla opened the door to her dad's office, stepped aside while Connors entered, and closed the door again. Her feminine wariness intensified when the two of them were alone. The air crackled with tension, so she kept her back to the door while he began to prowl around the room.

"This office must not get much use," Reed commented. The room was sparsely furnished and spotlessly clean.

"Daddy doesn't work in here very much," she said. "Mother thinks the president of the company should have his own office, but he spends most of his time in the hangar."

An eight-by-ten photo on Bear's desk caught Reed's attention. It was of the three sisters. He imagined they'd been in their late teens when the shot was taken. They were dressed in matching outfits, their hairstyles and mischievous expressions were exactly the same, and it was impossible to tell them apart. Reed wondered how their parents had survived.

"Does your mother handle all the secretarial duties? I've never seen anyone else at the reception desk."

"For her, it's just an extension of southern hospitality. She wouldn't think of letting anyone else answer the phone or greet customers. This past year she hired some part-time help, but she likes being in charge."

Belle's organizational skills were legendary, but she'd always been utilized for social activities, her daughters' education, and taking care of her family. She'd surprised them all when she'd decided to put her skills to use in the business. She argued that if she ever wanted to see her loved ones, she had to live at the airstrip. They'd all come to appreciate the sharp mind behind her ultra-feminine facade.

"Your mother is quite a lady," Reed commented.

"That she is," Sharla agreed.

Connors rarely engaged in small talk. She knew he had something more serious on his mind, but she didn't have a clue. There was no use trying to press him. She'd have to wait until he decided to tell her.

"When I was checking some records, I learned that your dad is a licensed pilot, too."

Sharla frowned in annoyance. "Just your average record checking?" One of the things she disliked most about federal law enforcement officials was their ability to scrutinize people's personal lives without permission.

"The records are public knowledge," he drawled, giving her his full attention now.

"All of them?" she demanded, crossing her arms over her chest.

She didn't realize how much attention the action drew to the fullness of her breasts. Reed thought she was one beautiful woman, even when she was bent on antagonizing him. Indignation enhanced the brilliance of her eyes. Her defensive posture was more provocative than intimidating. She was an unwanted threat to his peace of mind.

"Would you trust your life to a pilot you didn't have investigated first?" he taunted, then mimicked her by crossing his arms over his chest.

"Thousands of people do it every day," Sharla retorted briskly. "It's called commercial flight. You don't even know the pilot's name unless he tells you."

"That's why I avoid it," Reed declared succinctly. He speared her with a sharp gaze and drew a deep breath. She wasn't going to be pleased with his request.

"I'd like to have your dad pilot for me on this assignment. I know it would be an inconvenience, but I'm willing to pay double your usual rates."

Sharla stiffened, taking his suggestion as a slur on her abilities. Prescott Air Service had struggled against prejudice for years. She and her sisters had been forced to prove their capabilities far more stringently than any man had to. The business had nearly been destroyed before customers learned to have faith in female pilots. She was shocked to realize that his attitude hurt as well as angered her. More tension coiled through the muscles of her body.

"If you don't think I'm qualified to pilot for you, then why the hell are you here?"

"This doesn't have anything to do with your qualifications," he argued.

"Convince me," she snapped. The very least he owed her was an explanation.

"It's the case I'm working on," he volunteered. "It's highly sensitive, and your dad has security clearance."

"So do I."

"That's not the point."

"Then what is?"

"The point is, it's a tricky case and something could go wrong. I don't want to put anyone at risk."

"You don't want to put a woman at risk," she corrected. "You obviously don't mind putting my dad at risk."

At the agency, Reed was notorious for salvaging bad situations, but his control was always faulty when Sharla was involved. Everything he said or did seemed to irritate her, and her defensiveness put him on the defensive. He decided to try another approach.

"There shouldn't be any problems. I just want to be careful."

"Well, you don't have any choice in the matter," she told him flatly. "Daddy has a minor heart condition. He's in good health and his license is valid, but our insurance company won't allow him to pilot for the service. I'm surprised you missed that in the records."

Reed's mood kept getting darker. He knew Sharla didn't like him very well. He was making matters worse, but that wasn't important. He didn't want to take a chance of putting her in danger. Normally he used Prescott's for routine work. This assignment was different, but he couldn't use another service without creating suspicion. He was stuck.

"If you checked your records thoroughly enough," Sharla continued, "you probably know that my sisters and I are trained in self-defense. I'll admit I'm not the best. Carlie has a black belt in karate, and Dee's the weapons expert, but I'm still better trained than my dad and most other men."

Belle had once told Reed that she'd done her best to raise her daughters as proper ladies should be raised. She'd insisted that they take dancing lessons, learn to play the piano, and cultivate knowledge of the arts. But the triplets had been Air Force brats, moving from location to location every few years, and sometimes to areas that weren't as safe as their permanent home in Virginia. Bear couldn't always be with his little girls, so he'd wanted them trained in self-defense.

He ran a hand through his hair and wondered how best to explain himself without divulging too many details of his confidential assignment. "I'm not suggesting that I might need a backup for protection," he insisted.

"You'd just feel safer with a man." Her tone was sweet, but her eyes flashed with indignation. How many times over the years had she battled that same chauvinistic, outdated mentality?

Her sarcasm annoyed the hell out of him. "I told you this has nothing to do with your qualifications as a pilot."

"Just my qualifications as a person?"

Reed had known she'd take his suggestion as a personal insult. He couldn't explain his crazy protective instincts where she was concerned. He didn't understand them himself. He never felt the increased tension when Dee and Carlie were piloting for him.

"Personality has nothing to do with this, either."

"I beg to differ," Sharla responded, wondering if he would have asked for another pilot if one of her sisters had been given the assignment. "I don't appreciate your non-too-subtle distaste for working with me."

Reed's temper escalated. She had a knack for undermining his control as few other people could do. "That's not what I said or meant. You're being even more difficult than usual!"

"And you're being stupid as well as difficult," she tossed back at him.

Every muscle in his body tightened in tension. He'd leveled men twice his size for lesser insults. "Stupid?" he repeated, his eyes blazing. She really knew how to get under his skin.

"You'd prefer to be piloted in a potentially dangerous situation by a man with a heart condition and very little experience rather than admit that a woman might be better qualified and more capable."

"I didn't say that," he argued through tight lips, "Don't put words in my mouth."

Tension crackled in the air between them. They glared at each other, both wondering how the other always managed to threaten their normal, civilized calm.

It was time to regain control of the situation. Reed raked a hand through his hair in agitation, and then took a deep breath. He hadn't planned to create so much antagonism with his request. "I just asked if your dad could pilot for me. You're the one who got all defensive and belligerent."

"I wonder why?" she grumbled.

He wanted to grab her and shake her. Or shut her sassy mouth with long, deep, hard kisses until she stopped challenging him at every turn. No other woman in his acquaintance filled him with such primitive emotion. He clenched his hands into fists, turned his back on her, and put the distance of the room between them. It didn't matter if they saw each other once a week or once a month, their reaction to each other was always the same volatile.

Sharla realized she was trembling. She drew in a long, shaky breath and forced herself to relax. She wasn't going to let Connors' attitude totally shatter her control. He'd already wreaked havoc on her confidence. Professionalism seemed her best defense.

"If you'd rather not fly with Prescott Air Service, my mother has a list of charter services that we call when we have more business than we can handle. I'm sure she can find someone who'll be able to help you."

Reed looked her directly in the eyes, and the tension between them thickened. He was tempted. It would be simpler to use another service and a less disturbing pilot. On the other hand, he knew he wasn't going to find a better pilot. Sharla was the best. She was absolutely awesome in the air. He had implicit faith in her skills. Dee and Carlie were good, too, but Sharla's affinity with her plane was amazing.

"Shall I have Mother check around for you?"

If he chartered with a different service, the word would be out in a matter of hours. It would cause suspicion and generate too much unwanted interest in his travel plans. He knew, had known from the beginning, that he didn't have any real choice.

"I didn't give you much time to prepare for a week of traveling," he said. "How long will it take you to pack and make arrangements?"

Sharla hadn't realized she was holding her breath until his clipped words forced her to exhale. His refusal to fly with another service was somewhat mollifying, and she forced herself to relax.

"We keep a supply of clothes here for overnight trips, and I can be packed in ten minutes. You're welcome to load your luggage onto the plane." She glanced at her watch. "I'll have my flight check completed within a half hour, and we can leave on schedule."

"Good," said Reed.

He moved toward her and all the air got sucked from her lungs. She didn't want him too close, so she abruptly turned, opened the door, and preceded him from the room without another word.

Two

Reed left the keys to his car with Belle; he usually left it parked on the lot while he was chartering a flight. Then he collected his luggage and headed for Sharla's plane.

Sharla went to the room she and her sisters shared for personal use at the terminal. They always kept a cosmetic case filled with the basic needs. She checked the contents, added a curling iron, and snapped it shut.

There were a dozen jumpsuits hanging in the closet, so she packed two extras for the trip. They could be cleaned if they were gone more than a couple days. She packed underwear, a pair of jeans, a knit top, and one cocktail dress. Her mother had taught her to be prepared for the unexpected. The only clean nightwear was a pair of red silk pajamas. Sharla frowned. She didn't like pajamas, so she just grabbed the top. It was thigh length and would be enough.

Thoughts of Reed Connors churned in her mind. Her body hummed with the tension she could only credit to being near him again. She resented the powerful physical impact he made on her. She also resented the fact that he could rattle her composure so easily. There had to be a way to deal with him in a sane, professional manner, she argued to herself. Whatever it took, however hard it might be, she was determined to get this job done. Then she'd absolutely refuse to work with him again.

After adding a handbag and shoes to her flight bag, she returned to the reception area. Belle gave her a copy of the flight plan, extra cash, and a farewell kiss for a safe trip. From there, Sharla headed out into the sunshine, and then strode across the tarmac to load her bags in the plane. Even though she knew Papa Bear never let a plane taxi down the runway unless it was totally air-worthy, she never skimped on her preflight check. Her life and the lives of her passengers were dependent on her ability to recognize and handle potential problems. She took those responsibilities seriously, shoving Connors to the back of her mind while she concentrated on the job at hand.

Once he'd stowed his bags, Reed crossed the tarmac to the hangar and greeted Bear with a handshake. No one who knew the older man would ever think he suffered from a heart condition. He was tall, robust, and energetic. There was just a touch of gray in his light brown hair, and the turquoise eyes his daughters had inherited were always keenly alert.

The two men discussed the perfect spring weather, but Reed's gaze followed Sharla as she checked her plane. He liked watching her — too much — which he knew was unwise. He didn't want this assignment complicated by raging testosterone. His body's quick response to her grace and beauty had to be fiercely contained. He willed his blood to cool and his pulse to stop hammering through his veins.

Bear watched Reed watching Sharla. He liked the man, and knew he could trust him to watch out for her safety, but he didn't like the ever-present risk of one of his daughters getting involved in law enforcement scuffles.

"You're not expecting any trouble on this one, are you?" He asked the younger man.

Reed had been asked the same question every time he'd flown with a Prescott pilot, but this time he wasn't sure of the answer. "If I run into any problems, I'll keep Sharla out of it and send her home with an escort."

Sharla called to Reed. It was time to board the plane. The two men looked at each other, gazes locked and steady.

"If you have any problems," said Bear, "you call me. I have friends who can escort her home."

"Yes, sir," Reed replied. He didn't doubt that the ex-airman had plenty of friends spread across the country.

"Have a safe flight."

He watched the younger man stride toward the plane and climb into the passenger side. A small grin touched his lips. His eldest daughter, by mere minutes, had met her match in Connors. She either didn't know it or she wasn't ready to admit it, but Bear could tell.

There weren't many men who could challenge Sharla on a personal and professional level. Growing up, the boys had always pursued her, but she'd changed boyfriends on a regular basis. She'd never had much patience with anyone who couldn't match her in courage, integrity, and intelligence. Few men could. Bear believed Reed was one of the few.

Sharla usually blocked all thoughts of her passengers once they were safely fastened into their harnesses. It wasn't easy with Connors sitting in the copilot's seat. All the little hairs on her arms tingled and the pulse drummed in her ears, nearly drowning out the sound of the engine. The cockpit always seemed smaller when he was aboard. Pilot and passenger were closer than she wanted to be to him, but she wouldn't allow anyone or anything to distract her when she was flying.

After radioing the radar tower for clearance, she prepared for takeoff. The Piper Saratoga was her baby. It was a direct descendant of the Piper Cherokee she'd learned to fly in, and her hands moved over the controls with comforting familiarity. The single engine's vibration sent its usual thrill through her as she scanned the runway, then taxied into position.

"Ready?" She tossed her passenger a cursory glance as she revved the engine to full throttle. She noted that his seat belt was fastened, his earphones in place and he appeared relaxed.

"Ready," Reed repeated over the increasing whine of the engine. He knew she wasn't overly concerned about him. Her attention was totally focused on the plane. He admired her ability to shut him out, even though it sometimes rankled. Better to worry about safety than ego.

It was her talent of concentration that made her an expert pilot. Sharla became part of the aircraft she flew — an attractive extension of the marvel in technology that allowed metal and man to soar the skies like birds. It never failed to amaze him. She was all woman, all soft curves and feminine allure, yet she instilled more confidence in him than any man he'd ever flown with, and he'd flown with some of the country's best.

He knew Sharla's delicate beauty was a deceptive facade for a fearless heart and nerves of steel. Any pilot who'd clocked as many hours as she had would have experienced some pretty hair-raising conditions, yet she had one of the finest flying records in the commercial air-charter service.

She made him proud, and that irritated him, too. There was no logical reason for him to feel pride in her accomplishments. They weren't even friends, and he didn't like feeling anything he couldn't logically explain. The physical attraction wasn't much easier to rationalize. He'd wanted her sexy body since the first instant they'd met, but he'd never felt the same fierce attraction to Dee and Carlie.

Except for hairstyles, the triplets were identical in looks, yet the chemistry was totally different. He'd tested the theory by taking first Dee and then Carlie on a casual date. He'd ended up more frustrated than appeased. Holding the other sisters in his arms hadn't been half as exciting as sharing a cockpit with Sharla.

"We're off," she told him as the plane cleared the runway, and they rose toward spacious skies.

An incredible rush of excitement swept through Sharla. Her heart pounded a little harder, and her pulse accelerated while every nerve responded to the unique thrill of becoming airborne. It was always the same, no matter how many hundreds of times she flew. For her, there was nothing in the world that compared to defying gravity and soaring into endless expanses of blue sky.

Reed felt the strength of Sharla's exhilaration. Her reaction to takeoff was always fascinating. It was the same every time he flew with her, and he wondered why she didn't grow bored or indifferent to her job. He felt a wild thrill at sharing a little piece of her excitement. His body hummed with excitement of a different nature as he watched her expressive features. She was never more beautiful than when she flew.

Once they were leveled off at sixty-five hundred feet and headed in a northwesterly pattern, Sharla adjusted to cruising speed and allowed herself to relax a little. She was as comfortable in the Saratoga as most people were behind the wheels of their cars.

The weather was gorgeous. Winter had been colder and wetter than normal, and she'd heartily welcomed spring. It had always been her favorite season of the year, and April was her favorite month.

Her only concern was that they were flying northward and to the Midwest where the weather patterns weren't as mild as those in Virginia, especially in early spring. She didn't want to get grounded for very long with her passenger.

As they rose to cruising level, Reed's attention drifted to the patchwork landscape beneath them, but when they leveled off, he returned his attention to Sharla. A grin tugged at his lips when he noted a slash of color across her right cheek.

"You have lipstick on your cheek," he commented, lifting his hand and brushing at the spot with his thumb. Her skin was as soft as it looked. It was a fact he hadn't needed to confirm, yet he couldn't resist another couple strokes of his thumb across her cheek.

A current of electricity shot through Sharla at his lingering touch. She held perfectly still while he gently rubbed her cheek, but her breathing faltered. Her reaction to the contact was slightly unnerving. She wasn't used to being so deeply affected by such a simple touch.

"My mother forgets about her lipstick when she kisses me good-bye. She wouldn't be caught dead with naked lips," Sharla explained, using a teasing tone to cover her sudden breathlessness. "And she wouldn't dream of letting me leave without a kiss."

For just an instant Reed let himself think of his mom. She'd never let him leave the house without a kiss, either. When he'd grown older, she'd been considerate and made sure his buddies didn't see her kisses, but she'd never stopped giving them. The memories were sweet, yet they inevitably brought pain and regret.

"I like your mother. Does she enjoy running Prescott Air Service?" he asked in an effort to dispel his own depressing thoughts.

Sharla was surprised by the question. She and Connors had flown together many times. He'd always kept conversation to a bare minimum, and had never engaged her in a personal discussion of any kind. She wondered if he felt the need to alleviate some of the tension that sizzled between them.

Maybe he had the right idea. She was usually more comfortable with men and felt less threatened by sexual tension once she'd gotten to know them better. Most of her princes reverted to frogs after a few dates. Her sisters accused her of being too critical and analytical when it came to her relationships with men, but her tactics had kept her wholehearted and fancy-free for most of her life.

"Sometimes I feel guilty for depriving my mother of her active social life," she confessed. "She used to love her afternoon teas, charity work, and bridge club, but she's never complained about our decision to start the service."

"Your dad got restless after his retirement and decided to start a family business?" he asked. He'd already heard some of the company's history, but he was interested in Sharla's role in the decision.

"It was the realization of a dream for Dee, Carlie, and me. Mother wanted us to attend Ivy League colleges, marry well, and produce lots of grandchildren. We hated spending the time and money on college when we already knew we wanted careers in flying."

"Must've been a blow to your mother."

"She fretted for months, but she was the one who ultimately suggested using a portion of the plantation for an airfield. She decided that our college funds combined with Daddy's retirement would supply sound investment capital. She really has a gift for business management."

"You went into business right out of high school? How did you convince people to fly with teenage pilots?"

"We didn't launch the business until two years after we graduated," Sharla explained. She made a slight adjustment of the throttle, and then gave him a quick smile.

"For the first couple of years we handled more cargo than people. Dee got a license to train and gave a lot of flight lessons. We did whatever we could to stay afloat. Once people got used to us, business improved considerably."

Reed had been using the service for a little over three years, and had seen the steady increase in popularity at Prescott's. Their airfield was within driving distance of DC, and a lot more government employees were taking advantage of the timesaving, quality service.

"So your mother decided a family business would have to suffice until you all decided to marry well, settle down, and give her grandchildren?" he teased.

"She stopped holding her breath a long time ago," Sharla informed him. "I told her she could adopt our clientele if she really wanted to enlarge the family."

"Did she come from a big family?"

"No. She's the only child. Neither of my maternal grandparents had siblings, but my great-grandmother was one of a set of triplets."

"A generation removed?"

"In our family, at least," she said.

"Have you ever worried about the odds?" Reed felt a strange jolt of emotion at the thought of Sharla carrying a child, but he swiftly stifled the feeling.

"I've never spent much time thinking about children," she confessed. "Getting married and having babies has never been high on my list of priorities. I don't think I'd want to take on such an awesome responsibility with three tiny lives at once."

Reed could identify with that sentiment. Love was a grim responsibility. Loving someone who was totally dependent on you was hell. He'd learned to protect himself from that kind of complication in his life by avoiding people who stirred his emotions.

Sharla couldn't help being curious about Connors' background, his family, even his love life, but she'd never felt free to ask questions. She wondered if he'd ever been married.

"Do you come from a big family?" she asked instead.

"No," was his only response. He shifted in his seat and slipped his sunglasses over his eyes.

He was letting her know that he didn't appreciate personal questions, but he hadn't hesitated to ask her a few, so she tried again, "Have you ever been married?"

Reed stiffened. He rarely discussed his past or his private life. His memories brought painful reminders of his inadequacies in the relationship department.

"I was married right out of high school," he told her in a flat tone. "It lasted two years, and they were the longest two years of my life."

So there. Sharla got the impression he was expressing a confirmed bachelor's opinion on the state of matrimony. Marriage wasn't a popular word in his vocabulary.

She wondered if he'd had a shotgun wedding. She wished she wasn't curious about his ex-wife. Had she been the passionate love of his young life? Had the passion burned itself out too quickly? Had she been beautiful? Why had their marriage failed? Had there been a child involved?

It was extremely bold of her to ask, but she couldn't contain her curiosity. "Any children?"

The question caused a brief stab of pain. Reed hardened himself against it. His response was totally lacking in emotion. "I don't have any kids."

She decided to drop the subject. Connors obviously didn't want anyone prying into his personal affairs. He struck her as a very self-contained, private person. She had hundreds of questions she'd like to ask, but had a feeling that the answers would never be freely given.

The cockpit grew quiet for along time with the exception of the droning of the plane's engine. Despite the fact that the physical awareness between them never lessened, they enjoyed a companionable silence. Reed was the first to speak again.

"I never thought to ask if this trip would be causing problems for you. Your mother said your flight schedule was clear, but she didn't mention any personal plans you might have to cancel."

"She didn't ask me if I had plans," replied Sharla, "but it's no secret that my work always takes precedence over my social life."

"No boyfriends who'll fret over your absence?"

"None that don't understand how important my career is to me."

"You must have some mighty understanding friends," he surmised. He knew it was irrational, but he hoped she didn't have any intimately close male friends.

Sharla shot a glance at her passenger. His features were relaxed and his eyes shielded by dark glasses. She wondered if he was criticizing her taste in men or just making a general comment. She decided to turn the tables.

"Anyone going to miss you terribly?"

Her tone was deceptively sweet. Connors' low answering chuckle sent a ripple of awareness all the way to her toes.

"Touché," he teased. "I'll promise not to ask any more personal questions if you'll do the same."

She smiled. "It's a deal, I guess — but I feel compelled to mention that I answered your nosy questions."

Reed chuckled again and stretched his legs, then settled more comfortably in his seat. "As one of Uncle Sam's most faithful employees, I'm completely devoted to my country and have no time for women in my life."

Sharla grunted indelicately. He might be a loner by nature, but he was also a very sexy man. She was sure he made time for women. He'd made time to see a movie with Dee and a baseball game with Carlie. The dates had been casual. The only real significance was that he hadn't asked her out, however casually.

Still, she was pleased to know that Connors could relax a little and joke with her. The rest of her family agreed that he had a sense of humor, but she hadn't encountered it until now.

"I think I'll take a nap," he said, shifting in his seat again.

He thought he'd better resist the temptation to continue chatting with Sharla. He was on assignment, and he couldn't risk serious distractions. The case involved a very special lady in the witness protection program, and he intended to ensure her safety.

"How long before Pittsburgh?"

"Another hour or so. Plenty of time to nap," said Sharla. She was a little disappointed that he wanted to cut their conversation short, but she wasn't offended.

"Will your business in Pittsburgh take all day?" she asked. She'd been so agitated this morning; she hadn't taken the time to discuss details.

"Probably not." Reed couldn't explain that he was acting as a decoy, and that it didn't matter how long they lingered in any of the cities he'd scheduled. Once he'd made a couple of phone calls and checked to see if he was being followed, his business would be finished.

"When we reach the Pittsburgh terminal, should I immediately request a runway for takeoff to Columbus, or do you plan to stay overnight in Pittsburgh?" Her mother had mentioned accommodations in every city.

"I made reservations at the airport hotel in Columbus for tonight," Reed told her. "If we can get approval for takeoff around five this afternoon, we should be fine."

"I'll make the request as soon as we're in radio range of the Pittsburgh's tower. There shouldn't be any problem."

Reed nodded, crossed his arms over his chest, and leaned his head back against the headrest, making it clear that he intended to sleep.

Sharla turned her attention to the cloudless blue sky and kept her eyes focused forward until she heard Connors' breathing grow slow and regular.

When she thought he was asleep, she took the opportunity to study him more closely. She'd never seen him so relaxed. Sunglasses shielded his eyes, but the rest of his face was softened by sleep. He was deeply tanned with features that held a unique appeal even though they weren't strictly beautiful.

Her eyes rested on his mouth. It was slightly parted and looked incredibly kissable. Sharla jerked herself to attention. She didn't need this kind of aggravation. It was going to be a long week. She had work to do, and she had no business entertaining thoughts about how Connors' mouth might feel against hers.

The man had made it perfectly clear that he didn't find her attractive or even as interesting as her sisters. It was probably just his aversion to her that prompted her interest. She'd always loved a challenge.

For some reason she didn't think he was a man who loved easily or superficially. He was too intense and complex. Her experience with his type made her believe that he would also be primitively possessive should a woman make the mistake of falling in love with him.

Three

It was just after noon when they touched down at the Greater Pittsburgh International Airport. The landing was smooth, and Sharla smiled with satisfaction. She always felt a thrill of accomplishment with each landing. Flying was the only thing that continually challenged her at a level that was necessary to her own personal satisfaction.

Reed had awakened from a deep sleep when they'd circled the airport in preparation for landing. It never ceased to amaze him. He couldn't manage even a catnap on a commercial flight. His complete confidence in Sharla's abilities allowed him to totally relax. He'd been putting in a lot of hours for witness protection, and the extra sleep was much needed. He noted his pilot's tiny smile of satisfaction as she made a faultless landing. Her eyes sparkled, and her pleasure was obvious. He found himself envious of an airplane. It just didn't make sense.

Shaking his head while stretching his stiff muscles. Reed released his seat belt and waited for Sharla to come to a complete stop. She taxied to the nearest fuel station.

"Will this be all right for you?" she asked. "I can get you an airport transfer if you'd like to get closer to the main terminal."

She preferred to refuel and have her plane checked in an area well beyond the main flow of traffic, but it wasn't always convenient for passengers.

"This is fine," he said. "All I need is to find a bank of phones, and the walk will give me a chance to stretch my legs."

"I've got a confirmed runway clearance for five fifteen this afternoon," she told him as she came to a stop and shut off the engine.

"Sounds good. What will you do until then?"

Sharla was a little surprised at his concern, but didn't hesitate to answer. "I'll file an official flight plan with the controllers, check the weather forecast, and make sure the plane is readied for the trip to Columbus. Then I'll probably grab a bite to eat and head back here."

"I'm picking up all expenses this trip," Reed reminded her. He reached into his pocket and pulled out a handful of bills, then tried to give her a twenty.

She ignored the money and gave him a bland smile. "Thanks, but think I can handle the bare necessities. I'm not even that hungry."

He frowned. "Keep the receipts, and I'll reimburse you." When she didn't look inclined to agree, he tacked on a threat. "I promised your mother I would take good care of you on this trip. If you don't want her wrath on your head, I suggest you cooperate."

Sharla couldn't help but laugh at his tone and his reasoning. She shook her head, causing a wealth of silky curls to bounce over her shoulders. "Heaven protect us from my mother's wrath."

Reed's eyes gleamed. He hoped she didn't realize how much pleasure he derived from just looking at her. He tucked a twenty into her hand, and she accepted it without further argument.

His smug grin delighted her. She could get used to the laughing, teasing side of Connors. It was a whole lot more appealing than his quiet, guarded side.

They both climbed from the plane. Sharla gave instructions for refueling to an airfield attendant and turned her attention back to Connors.

"I'd like to board the plane again about four thirty. Let me know if there's a change in plans or if we need to reschedule for any reason."

"Will do," he said, turning toward the terminal. "I'll be here at four thirty."

She didn't bother with a good-bye, but allowed her eyes to follow his retreating figure for an extended length of time. His long, confident strides quickly put distance between them and alerted any onlooker that he was a capable, self-assured man.

With a sigh, Sharla admonished herself to forget about Reed Connors and get on with her business. After making arrangements for the temporary care of her plane, she completed her other official duties and then had a light lunch in an airport snack bar.

Later, she contemplated the bookshelves in a gift shop and purchased a romantic suspense to help pass the time between flights. Then she headed back to the small aircraft area where her plane was temporarily parked.

Sharla made a habit of avoiding the lounge areas where commercial flight customers waited to board their planes. She made her way out of the terminal and toward the Piper. She'd learned that her Saratoga had the best seats in any city, and that she could get a lot more peace and quiet inside her own aircraft.

The Pittsburgh weather was sunny, but a little chilly. The cabin of the Saratoga was warm and cozy. She sat in the passenger seat behind the pilot's chair and propped her feet on another seat. She'd planned to read, but her eyes grew too heavy, and she dozed off to sleep.

Reed was alarmed when he returned to the area. He saw the Piper, but Sharla was nowhere in sight. A glance at his watch proved that he was right on time. She was never late. He surveyed the area again, but didn't see her.

Sharla was momentarily startled when the passenger door of the plane opened. The action jerked her upright in her seat. She blinked sleepy eyes, and then focused on Connors. He was wearing a deep frown that eased at the sight of her.

"I thought you'd gotten lost," he explained while appreciating her flushed, sleep-softened features. The muscles in his stomach knotted at the sight of her drowsy eyes and tousled beauty.

She gave him a lazy grin. "I never stray far from my plane," she assured him. "I hadn't planned on taking a nap, but I must have been more tired than I realized."

"Probably that four-day weekend catching up with you," he suggested, reaching out a hand to help her shift to the front of the cabin.

Sharla accepted his help, but swiftly retrieved her hand when his touch sent a quiver of heat up her arm.

"I didn't get much sleep over the weekend," she admitted while settling into the pilot's seat. "Those four-day weekends don't come around very often, and I didn't want to waste a minute of it."

"I thought you and your sisters took turns with the long weekends," said Reed, taking the copilot's seat.

"That's the ideal schedule," she explained, "but there always seems to be an emergency that interferes with ideal plans."

Reed concurred. The best of plans had a way of going bad. He hoped his boss' plan for protecting Sandy Rudolph went as smoothly as they hoped. She was a brave but very frightened lady, and she had good reason to be scared.

When he thought about Sandy's husband, John, he felt murderous. The man was a ruthless criminal, but he disguised his depraved nature with expensive living and suave charm. Rudolph was facing two consecutive life sentences in prison for murder, kidnapping, drug smuggling, money laundering, and a variety of other offenses.

He'd be appealing his conviction for several more years, but he had plenty of people still doing his dirty work. His wife had been the main witness against him in court. She'd discovered his illegal activities and collected enough evidence to send him to prison. John wanted her found. Reed planned to make sure she wasn't found.

The Saratoga was in the air again within minutes of the scheduled clearance time. Now they were headed in a southwesterly pattern to Columbus. Sharla noticed that Connors was deep in thought, and she didn't try to initiate a conversation.

She wondered if he was worried about his work. She wasn't entirely sure what U.S. marshals did on a regular basis. He seemed more preoccupied than be had earlier in the day, and she hoped nothing had gone wrong in Pittsburgh.

The flight to Columbus was a quiet one. It was shorter than their earlier trip, but not by much. Their wait to land was a little longer, and they circled the airport until a runway was clear for them.

The delay didn't surprise or concern Sharla. Business commuters were always the heaviest traffic at this time of evening, no matter where the airport was located.

It was after eight o'clock before she'd landed and made arrangements for overnight storage of her plane. Reed stayed close at her side until all the preparations had been made. Then he walked her to the terminal, insisting on carrying her bag as well as his own.

They wove their way through the crowds and headed to the main lobby of the concourse. The hotel where they had reservations was a half-mile from the terminal, so they took the airport bus to their final destination for the night.

Reed declined the assistance of a bellboy and stepped up to the reception desk to get them registered. Sharla didn't mind letting him handle all the details while she surveyed the hotel lobby. She was studying a particularly appealing piece of sculpture when she heard a familiar male voice behind her.

"Hey, you, Prescott person!" the newcomer called.

A grin split her face. She was propping her fists on her hips in feigned indignation as she turned to face the man behind the voice.

He was tall, dark, and extremely handsome in his navy blue pilot's uniform. His dark eyes sparkled with mischief and obvious delight in seeing her.

"Prescott person?" she exclaimed in disgust.

The man in question shoved aside her balled fists, grasped her waist, lifted her in the air, and then swung her around in a hearty welcome.

"Ugh" — he pretended to strain under her weight. "It must be Sharla"

She retaliated for the insult by pinching his ears until he begged for mercy. After a smacking kiss on the lips, he set her back on her feet.

They both spun in surprise when Reed spoke Sharla's name. His tone and expression weren't friendly. His jaw tightened when the other man slipped a protective arm about her waist.

Sharla was surprised at Connors' openly hostile attitude. "Michael, I'd like you to meet Reed Connors," she said in the way of introductions. "Reed, this is an old friend of mine, Michael Trehearn."

Reed set down the flight bags, exchanged handshakes with the other man, and muttered a greeting. The name Trehearn was familiar, but he couldn't place it immediately.

"Our rooms are ready," he declared tonelessly.

"Am I interrupting something here?" Michael wanted to know. He gave Sharla a questioning glance.

Her eyes widened at his obvious misconception. "Not at all," she hurriedly explained. "Reed is a regular customer of ours, and I'm just doing some piloting for him this week."

"Are you finished with business for the day?" he asked.

"I'm finished."

"Have you had dinner?"

"No."

"Then how about letting me take you out to unwind with a little dinner and dancing? I'm supposed to meet some friends downtown, and I'd love to have you join us."

"Just friends?" Sharla asked cautiously.

Michael gave her a reassuring smile. "Just friends, I promise. I haven't seen my big brother in months. I think he's doing a trans-Atlantic schedule again."

Michael's brother, William Trehearn the third, was Carlie's ex-husband. The marriage hadn't lasted a year, but it had been a brutally painful experience for her and everyone who loved her.

Michael had followed in his brother Bill's footsteps by becoming a pilot, but except for their good looks, the two men were as different as night and day.

At the mention of a brother, Reed remembered where he'd heard the name Trehearn. It had been in Carlie's personal file. She had an ex-husband. He'd sounded like a real bastard.

"How 'bout it?" Michael coaxed. "I promise the food will be the best in town."

Sharla grinned. She was hungry, but she wasn't sure about Connors' plans. A glance in his direction brought an instant invitation from Michael.

"Mr. Connors is welcome to join us," he insisted. "It's just an informal group of friends."

"Thanks, but I have some business to take care of," said Reed.

"How 'bout you, beautiful?" Michael teased, turning his flirting gaze on Sharla. "Did you bring a party dress?"

"I have one, but it may need to be pressed, and I'll need a shower."

Michael shot back his cuff and looked at his watch. "How 'bout I meet you back here in an hour? Will that do?"

"Make it a half hour, I'm hungry," she teased.

"You got it, princess."

The three of them parted company. Michael headed for the hotel lounge, and Reed led the way to the bank of elevators. They were the only people who entered the next car going up.

The ride to their floor was quiet. Sharla got the impression that he wasn't too pleased with her plans for the evening, but he had absolutely no right to complain, and they both knew it.

Reed found their rooms, which were side by side. He unlocked Sharla's door, dropped her bag on the bed, and then made a quick check of the room.

"We have adjoining rooms," he told her, his tone cooler than it had been all day. "You're perfectly secure, but I'll be next door if you need anything."

"Thank you," she responded politely.

"How well do you know this guy you're going out with tonight?" he demanded as he handed her the room's key card.

She was careful not to make physical contact as she accepted the key. She didn't know if Connors was concerned about her personal welfare or if he suspected that Michael might be some kind of threat to his assignment.

"He's a good friend of the family. I trust him completely."

"How late will you be?"

Sharla's gaze narrowed, and she propped her hands on her hips again. She resented his proprietorial attitude and the interrogation.

"I don't see that it's any of your business," she declared indignantly. "I'm finished working for the day."

"I still have to worry about your ability to function tomorrow," he drawled softly.

Her temper flared, and her reaction to his insinuation was clearly expressed on her face. She took a step to the door and held it open for him.

"You have my promise that I'll be alert and competent tomorrow," she snapped. "Now I'd appreciate it if you'd leave so that I can get ready for my date."

Their gazes locked for several pulsing heartbeats. A wealth of unspoken emotion passed between them. Neither of them chose to acknowledge the strength of it.

Reed walked out the door. He didn't want to, but there was little choice. He had no claim to Sharla's free time. That's how he wanted it — no emotional entanglements. He'd spent the last three years telling himself that he didn't want any personal involvement with the lady in question.

Sharla fumed all the time she was showering and changing for dinner. She couldn't understand Connors. He'd always kept a safe distance between them. Now he was acting as though she owed him some sort of loyalty. The only thing she owed him was a job well done.

So why did she feel guilty about going to a party and leaving him alone at the hotel? It was ridiculous. She was sure he could find someone to keep him company if he tried.

Temper kept her moving at a rapid pace. She showered, dressed, and restyled her hair within the half hour she'd allotted herself. After making sure she had her key, she left the room and headed for the lobby.

Michael was waiting for her. His bright smile and compliments boosted her morale. She promised herself to forget about Reed Connors and enjoy the evening.

She was partially successful. Michael's friends were other pilots and attendants who worked for his airline. They were a good-natured bunch that warmly welcomed her to their party. The food was delicious, the band was good, and the company was especially nice.

She ate, danced, and laughed a great deal, but she still didn't manage to put Connors completely out of her mind. Too often her thoughts drifted to him. More often than she cared to analyze.

The party broke up at midnight. Everyone hated to call an end to the evening, but they were all scheduled to fly out of Columbus the next day. Sharla left them with promises to keep in touch.

Michael hired a cab and took her back to her hotel. He escorted her through the lobby and punched the button for the elevator.

"I'll be happy to see you right to your door," he told her as they waited. "With just the tiniest bit of encouragement, I'd be willing to spend the night."

Sharla knew he was serious. It wasn't the first time he'd hinted at deepening their relationship. She knew it would be a mistake.

"I think I'd rather keep you as a very special friend," she declared, giving him a smile to soften the rejection. He'd loaned her his jacket for the ride to the hotel. She slipped it off her shoulders and returned it.

"We could always be friends and lovers," he insisted, returning her smile with an intimately warm one.

None of the Prescotts had been very fond of Carlie's husband, Bill, but they all adored Michael. Sharla loved him like a brother. Grasping his face in her hand, she scolded him affectionately. "You are so bad. You need to go to bed alone and get a good night's sleep."

"B-o-r-i-n-g! I hate sleeping alone," he insisted with a come-hither look in his eyes. The effect was spoiled when a wide yawn split his face.

Sharla laughed softly. "I'm really happy you invited me to join you tonight. I thoroughly enjoyed myself."

"Enough to thank me with a big, wet kiss?" he coaxed, wrapping an arm around her waist and dragging her close. His lips had just dropped to hers when they heard the ping of the elevator button.

Michael groaned and eased his grip on her as the doors slid open. They stepped apart when they realized they had an audience. Connors was the sole occupant of the elevator.

The sight of Sharla in an intimate embrace hit Reed like a ton of bricks. Every muscle in his body coiled in tension. His lungs constricted, and his temper flared. The hot flash of jealousy was more potent because it caught him off guard. It didn't help that he'd spent the last few hours wondering what she was doing.

"Going up?" He fought to keep all expression from his face and tone. He pressed his finger on the hold button and waited for Sharla to speak. He didn't trust himself to move. It took all the control to keep from reaching out and snatching her away from the pretty-boy pilot.

"Were you coming off?" she asked.

"I was coming to the lobby to wait for you," he said without apology. "It's getting late, and I wanted to make sure you made it safely to your room."

Sharla resented his cool, emotionless tone. She took offense at being treated like a bothersome piece of humanity.

"Because you promised my mother?" she prodded in her sweetest voice.

Her taunt drew a surprising reaction. She caught a glimpse of hot emotion in his golden eyes that made her regret taunting him. Then his gaze turned cool and detached, making her wonder if her own eyes were playing tricks.

Michael glanced from one of them to the other. The tension was thick enough to cut with a knife. He'd been forgotten. There was apparently more than a professional relationship between the two.

"I'd better say good night and let you get some sleep," he told Sharla.

She gave him a grin. "You need some sleep, too."

Michael grimaced and gave her a quick peck on the cheek. "Give my love to your family."

"I will," she promised. "And thanks again for a delightful evening."

"You're very welcome," he replied with a broad wink.

Sharla watched him stride across the lobby and then turned her attention back to Connors. She eyed him warily as she stepped into the elevator. He seemed more irritated than indifferent, but she couldn't understand why. She hadn't asked him to wait up for her.

As soon as the car was set in motion, she slipped off her shoes and reached down to massage her aching feet. The dancing had been great fun, but she wasn't used to wearing high heels for so many hours.

Until tonight, Reed had never seen Sharla in anything but her company flight suit. Except for thin straps, her neck and shoulders were bare. The smooth, shiny fabric of her dress clung lovingly to her figure and ended just above her knees, exposing gorgeous, shapely legs.

Reaching their floor provided him with temporary relief. He was fighting to subdue his violent reaction to her beauty, and it helped to get out of the elevator.

Sharla grabbed her shoes in one hand and fished her key card out of her handbag with the other. She put the key in Connors' outstretched hand and followed him to her door.

Reed motioned for her to stay just inside the door until he'd turned on all the lights and made sure the room was safe. After checking the bathroom and closets, he was satisfied.

Sharla dropped her bag and shoes, then leaned back against the door. She was tired. She knew her brain might not be functioning in high gear, yet she couldn't understand why he was taking all these precautions with her safety. She hadn't said anything when he'd done his search earlier in the evening, but she felt compelled to ask about a repeat performance.

"Are you expecting someone to break into my room, or are you always this paranoid?"

Reed stepped close enough to catch a whiff of her sweet, floral perfume. Her eyes were glittering green slits between heavy lashes. Her posture was languid and silky curls tumbled over her smooth, bare shoulders.

The combination of sensual delights presented him with the most brutal temptation of his life. It took all his willpower to resist pulling her sexy body into his arms.

"I'm always cautious," he told her in a voice that dropped to a deep, rough tone.

Sharla sensed a double meaning in his words, but she was too tired to analyze the possibilities. "Thank you for being cautious on my behalf," she responded politely.

Reed's lips tilted in a derisive smile. "You're welcome." He walked out the door, ordering her to secure the extra lock.

She grumbled about bossy federal agents, but she made sure the safety latch was in place. A short time later, she climbed into bed and fell to sleep as soon as her head hit the pillow.

Four

Sharla had the Saratoga in flight from Columbus to Lexington by ten o'clock the next morning. Reed hadn't spoken more than a few succinct sentences since checking out of the hotel. He wasn't rude, but his cool, distant manner curtailed any hopes for friendly conversation.

She wished his quiet, withdrawn mood didn't bother her so much. Today's all-business attitude was more like the Connors she'd grown used to working with over the past three years. It was a letdown after getting a glimpse of a much more personable man yesterday.

As a client, he'd never been as troublesome as some of their other customers. The reason she and her sisters had argued over who would pilot for him was based on altogether different reasons.

The triplets found his sexual magnetism a little disconcerting, and his normally imperturbable disposition could be annoying. The only time Sharla had ever seen him lose his temper was on this trip. Even after a date with him, Dee and Carlie hadn't felt much more comfortable in his company. He wasn't a man who let people get too close.

She knew her sisters didn't really mind working with Connors, but they knew she did, so they continued to give her a hard time about piloting for him. Her objection to working with the man was a fierce physical attraction for him that had no logical or emotional basis. Still, she couldn't easily ignore it, or the fact that he was oblivious to her feminine attributes.

She kept hoping the attraction would die a natural death, but so far, no luck. Maybe this trip would help destroy her irrational interest in a man who treated her like a necessary evil.

She wished he would display a few disgusting habits. Surely he had some, she thought. If she spent enough time with him, he was bound to do or say things that she'd find crude or offensive — maybe even totally repulsive.

As she piloted them through more clear, sunny skies, she imagined him guzzling beer and belching loudly. Then her imagination had him chewing and spitting tobacco. Maybe he was a total slob who threw garbage on the floor and let food crust on his dishes before washing them. Probably left the toilet seat up, too.

He probably hated children and pets, thought Sharla. She'd bet he'd never been a Boy Scout or helped a little old lady across a street. He might even hate music.

She spent quite a bit of their airtime thinking of the most unappealing characteristics she could credit to Connors. It was a silly game, but it helped pass the time. It also produced a wickedly amused grin on her face.

*R*eed had spent most of their flying time staring out the window at cloudless blue skies and trying to suppress his increasing desire to reach out and touch his pilot. The more time he spent with Sharla, the more acutely aware he became of her proximity. Just being confined in the cabin with her was slow torture.

Her scent teased him unmercifully. He knew he had to get control over this insane attraction or it would drive him out of his mind and shatter his concentration.

His sunglasses hid his eyes and allowed him to observe Sharla without openly staring. When her features slowly softened into a sweet, sexy smile, his gut knotted painfully.

She had to be thinking about her date last night. The possibility gnawed at him. Did she like the high life with constant parties and men drooling over her all the time? He knew she worked hard, but did she play just as hard? How many men were ready and willing to play with her? Was there one in every city?

Reed didn't like the train of thought. What Sharla did in her free time was none of his concern. He didn't want to initiate an affair with her, so he had no right to pry into her personal life.

If and when he wanted female company, he knew women who were willing to satisfy his needs with no strings attached. He trusted those women not to make demands he wasn't capable of meeting. They shared a good time without worrying about emotional commitments. The relationships suited them as well as him.

Any relationship with Sharla Prescott would mean complications, plenty of them. He wasn't sure how he knew that for certain, but he did.

"How long are you planning to be in Lexington?"

Sharla asked the question to dispel some of the tension mounting in the cabin. She was aware that Connors was studying her intently, and it made her nervous.

"I'm planning to spend the whole day," he said. "I've made reservations in Lexington for tonight, but I want to get an early start to Nashville tomorrow."

"How early?"

"By eight, at least"

Sharla didn't think that would be any problem. "I'll try to schedule a runway around seven — that way we should be in the air by eight."

"Sounds good."

"Will you be needing me for anything after we touch down in Lexington?" she asked.

Reed frowned, then spoke without considering how his question might sound. "Another boyfriend?"

Her eyes widened in surprise. Why should he care if she had twenty boy friends in Lexington?

"Are you afraid I might party all night and neglect my duties?"

"No." The word sounded like a dismissive grunt.

Sharla wanted to argue, but he turned his attention back to the sky.

Neither of them said another word until they were landing in Kentucky. Then conversation was limited to necessary details. Reed took care of their luggage and insisted on staying with her until she'd completed her arrangements for the plane and made all the necessary flight plans for the next leg of their trip.

Once inside the terminal, Sharla excused herself to make use of the restroom. She assumed Reed would need to do the same. He wasn't in sight when she left the ladies' room, so she waited for him, wandering a short distance to a window display in a gift shop.

She was facing the window when a large, masculine hand grasped her arm and turned her to face him. Her eyes widened at the sight and close proximity of a tall, broad-shouldered stranger wearing a cowboy hat.

"Dee?" The man's voice was rough with emotion. The brim of his hat shadowed his eyes, but Sharla could see a strained expression on handsomely chiseled features. When she didn't show any sign of recognition, he grasped both of her forearms and pulled her close to his big, hard body. His eyes darkened with emotion. "Damn," he whispered gruffly. "Don't do this to me."

Sharla wasn't alarmed by his actions. Her blank expression gave way to understanding when she realized he'd mistaken her for Dee. At the same time, she realized that this man had some strong emotional ties with her sister.

She was being bombarded with waves of intense emotion vibrating from him. The sensations hit her in an extrasensory fashion that she normally associated with Dee and Carlie. She was used to feeling any emotional upheaval they experienced, but never through a third person.

The man's gaze narrowed, and then his grip on her relaxed. "You're not Dee, are you?"

"I'm her sister," Sharla managed to explain. She was still reeling from the force of her reaction to a total stranger, yet she felt no fear or mistrust.

"A twin?" he asked in a rough tone.

Sharla managed a thin smile for him. His hands abruptly dropped to his sides as she reached into her handbag and pulled out a wallet. She found the most recent snapshot of her and her sisters.

"Actually," she told him as she handed him the photo, "there are three of us. I'm Sharla, Dee's in the center, and Carlie's on the right."

"Triplets," the big man mumbled in a low tone. He held the picture as though it were made of gold and studied it with quiet intensity.

Sharla didn't say anything. It took her a little time to calm her own riotous nerves. Whoever this man was, he was extremely important to Dee or she wouldn't have had such a violent reaction to his presence.

"I apologize," said the stranger. "I didn't know — and I haven't seen Dee for a few months. I thought she might have cut her hair. You look very much alike."

His mention of months triggered a different reaction in Sharla. A little over six months ago, Dee had been on vacation. When she'd returned home she'd suffered weeks of pain and sadness that Carlie and Sharla had sensed, but could do nothing to ease. Dee had refused to discuss the reason for her distress. Sharla bad a feeling she was looking at the cause right now.

She wanted to berate the big man for whatever he'd done to hurt her sister, but she had a feeling he was hurting just as much. He couldn't seem to take his eyes off the picture. He even stroked it with his thumb as if that might bring him closer to Dee.

"How is she?" he finally asked.

"Fine." Sharla couldn't say more without betraying her sister. "You're welcome to keep the snapshot."

Silvery blue gaze locked with hers, sending another wave of strong emotion through her.

"You're sure you don't mind?"

"I have plenty of copies."

"Thank you," he said as he carefully tucked the picture into the pocket, of his shirt. "Will you promise not to think I'm a pervert if I ask a favor?"

Sharla grinned. Whatever this man was, it wasn't perverted. His eyes shone with intelligence, and his actions spoke of sensitivity. He had the bearing of a man who was supremely self-confident and used to getting what he wanted.

"That depends on the favor," she responded lightly. She didn't mind carrying a message back to Dee.

"May I have a kiss?"

The request amazed her at first. Then she realized that he was curious to know if kissing her felt the same as kissing Dee. The sisters had been tested in the same fashion for most of their lives. Sometimes it was annoying and sometimes just amusing. This time, she knew, it was a lot more complicated. It was extremely important to this man.

She surprised herself by stretching on tiptoes and pressing a kiss against his mouth. His arms enfolded her for an instant while he returned the pressure of the kiss. Then he released her with a barely audible sigh.

Sharla's smile for him was sympathetic. She sensed his disappointment. "I'm really not Dee," she told him gently. She and her sisters shared identical physical features, but they were three entirely different people with diverse personalities.

The big cowboy's smile was self-derisive. "I had to find out for myself," he admitted.

"Would you like me to give her a message for you?"

The expression on his rugged features went blank. "No, thanks," he said with a sharp nod of his head. "But I thank you for the picture."

"You're welcome."

With a tip of his hat, he walked away. Sharla watched him until he got lost in the crowd. She wondered what in the world had happened between her sister and the gorgeous cowboy. Whatever it was, it must have been traumatic.

When she finally snapped her attention back to the present, her gaze collided with the glittering gold of Connors' eyes. He was leaning against the opposite wall with his arms crossed over his chest and his legs crossed at the ankles. His stance looked casual enough, but his expression was a mixture of mockery and annoyance.

Sharla instinctively stiffened her spine when he decided to close the distance between them. "Sorry to keep you waiting," she murmured.

"Who was that?" Reed asked the question with a nod in the direction the cowboy had taken.

Warm color invaded Sharla's face. She'd been so surprised by her reaction to the stranger that she'd forgotten to ask his name.

"I don't know," she had to admit.

Reed sighed heavily and raked a hand through his hair. "God, you need a keeper. Why the hell would you kiss a man you don't even know?"

She understood that her actions probably seemed a little strange, but she resented his remark about a keeper.

"He's a good friend of Dee's," she argued in her own defense.

"Then why don't you know his name?" he insisted.

"Because she's never mentioned him to me," she retorted hotly.

Reed's expression and tone grew more grim. "You just took his word for it? A total stranger walks up and says he's a good friend of Dee's, so you start kissing him?"

Maybe her actions didn't seem too rational, but there was no way she could explain the emotional vibrations she'd experienced with the other man. Still, she had to try or let him think she was a complete idiot.

"Carlie, Dee, and I have a highly attuned sensory perception when one of us is experiencing a particularly strong emotional trauma. There's no easy way to explain the phenomenon, it just exists."

Reed studied her expressive features. She was being honest with him, yet her belligerence was evidence that she didn't expect him to understand. He knew little about ESP, but he didn't discount the fact that it existed.

"What does Dee's emotional trauma have to do with the cowboy?"

Sharla sighed. She was relieved that Reed didn't belittle the special bonds she shared with her sisters, but she wasn't sure how to explain her reaction to a stranger.

"I don't know," she admitted. "Nothing like that has ever happened to me, but I was picking up waves of emotion that somehow linked him with Dee. I know it sounds insane, but it happened."

"Maybe he's some kind of con artist or stalker. He might be a real threat to Dee," Reed suggested with a deepening frown.

She vigorously shook her bead and defended the stranger. "I don't know what's going on between him and Dee, but I didn't feel any threatening vibrations, just sadness and pain."

Reed wasn't totally convinced. "What kind of questions did he ask you?"

"He only asked me how she was."

"That's it?"

"That's it."

"Then why the hell were you kissing him?" The last question was asked as he grabbed their bags and headed down the terminal toward the lobby.

She followed at his rapid pace, becoming really aggravated by his attitude.

"I know you'll find this hard to believe," she snapped, "but some men actually like to test us to see if kissing one sister gives them the same thrill as kissing the others. It's a totally barbaric practice, but we've all learned to accept the fact that men don't always think with their heads."

Reed didn't comment. He didn't look at her or slow his pace. Sharla wouldn't have dreamed of asking him to slow down, but she was somewhat pleased to see dark color creeping up the back of his neck. It could have been from anger, or exertion, or even embarrassment.

The idea gave her food for thought. Dee and Carlie had told her Connors' only reason for asking them out was to see if they affected him the same way Sharla did. In his case, she'd thought their suggestion was ludicrous. Could there be some basis to their theory?

No, she thought, it just didn't make sense where Connors was concerned. His heightened color was probably due to extreme annoyance. She'd always found him attractive, but she only seemed to irritate him. Besides, she told herself, he'd never kissed her, so there was nothing to compare. He'd never asked her out, and she'd never rejected an invitation.

If he'd wanted to know what it would be like to spend time with her, he could have asked. She'd never encouraged him, but neither had she discouraged him. At least, not until he'd asked out both her sisters and not her.

Sharla didn't say another word until Reed had taken her to their hotel and deposited her at the door of her room. Then she responded only to his clipped questions.

"Do you have plenty of money?" he asked after unlocking her door and making his usual check of the premises.

"Yes, thank you."

"Are you planning to leave the hotel again?"

"I was planning to find the pool, spend the rest of the afternoon swimming, eat some dinner, and go to bed with a good book," she told him, her tone and expression totally bland.

Reed frowned. "I have some business to take care of, but I'll be spending most of the evening here at the hotel. Charge all your expenses to the room, and let me know if you have a change of plans."

"Yes, sir," she responded in her most obedient tone. She held the door for him to exit her room, noting that he didn't seem pleased with her dismissive attitude.

She hadn't packed a swimsuit, so if he didn't quit ordering her around, she'd buy the most expensive suit in the hotel gift shop and charge it to his account. Let him explain that to his superiors at the agency. Revenge could be sweet.

Reed glared at her with narrowed eyes and fought the temptation to shut her sassy mouth with his own. It wasn't the first time he'd stifled the same urge. He handed her the card key and walked out the door. "I'll call you later."

"Is that a promise or a threat?" Sharla muttered as she closed the door behind him. The man really had a knack for getting under her skin. It was time for some breathing space and to put him out of her mind for a while.

Her afternoon was spent much as she'd told Connors it would be. After eating a late lunch, she bought a modest bathing suit at the hotel, then enjoyed a couple hours at the pool getting some exercise.

Spending as much time as she did in the cockpit of her plane, she had to make time for exercising whenever she could spare a few minutes. Swimming was her favorite form of exercise. They had a pool at home, but she often used hotel pools when she was traveling.

As soon as Reed was settled in his room, he placed a call to Rolf Sanders, his boss. He was assured that their plan was working. Sandy Rudolph was safe, and a reliable informant had ascertained that John Rudolph was ordering his henchmen to follow Reed.

He'd been in charge of protecting Sandy during her husband's trial, and she'd made it clear that she trusted him. Now she had to travel to Nashville to testify against one of Rudolph's partners in crime. Her safety was at risk until the second trial was over. Then she'd be given a new identity and hidden within the protection program.

That's why Reed was playing decoy. The U. S. Marshal Service and the FBI were working together to see who might still be tailing Sandy. They had to flush out anyone who was an immediate threat. The price on her head was staggering.

He left the hotel just to waste time and allow the men following him to get into town. Sanders had said that two of Rudolph's men, Horton and Graves, were tracking him across country. They were a couple of hours behind him, and were unaware that two deputy marshals were following them.

Reed decided he would rather be spending the day with Sharla at the hotel pool. He could envision her shapely body encased in a sleek racing suit or maybe a teeny bikini. The idea held great appeal, but he couldn't chance involving her any more than she already was, even though he didn't think Rudolph's men were likely to bother her. All they could do was wait and hope he'd eventually lead them to Sandy.

It was late afternoon when he returned to his room, and he knew that someone had done a thorough, professional search of his belongings. The only items out of place were the ones he'd deliberately planted to test for a search.

That meant his followers were in town and getting impatient. Rudolph wanted his wife alive, and he wanted her now. Court appeals were expensive, and he needed the money she had access to. He'd hidden all his illegally acquired funds in foreign bank accounts. Sandy had discovered the accounts and shifted the money to new accounts.

Now she was the only person who had the access codes to millions of dollars. Both Rudolph and Uncle Sam wanted the money. Sandy refused to give up the bank account numbers. They were her life insurance policy, but if Rudolph's men got hold of her, they could make her wish she were dead.

Reed was determined to keep the gutsy lady alive and out of harm's way. He'd wanted to continue guarding her himself, but he'd been overruled by Sanders. The decoy plan seemed to be working. He hoped that Horton and Graves were fooled long enough for other agents to get Sandy safely out of Washington.

All he could do was stay alert and hope Rudolph's men kept following him. Two FBI agents would drive Sandy to Newark and a rendezvous with agency pilot Ed Waites. Then Ed would fly her to the agency's safe house in Tennessee.

Reed's ultimate destination was Nashville. That's where they hoped to set a trap for Rudolph's henchmen. If they could be arrested on any charges, it would put them out of commission for a while, and maybe discourage them from taking orders from a boss who was broke and incarcerated.

Reed stripped and headed for the shower, his thoughts drifting to Sharla again. He would send her home as soon as possible after arriving in Nashville. He wanted her out of the way before any real trouble started.

Five

Sharla couldn't believe she'd fallen asleep beside the pool. She rarely slept during the day, yet this was her second consecutive afternoon nap. Maybe her exhaustion could be attributed to the stress of piloting for Reed Connors, she thought.

By the time she returned to her room, it was early evening. Her card key was buried in the bottom of her bag, but she finally found it and inserted it in the lock. Then she grasped the handle and swung open the door.

The next thing she knew, she was being forcefully dragged through the doorway, then shoved aside as a large man lunged past her to get out of the room. She screamed bloody murder, then sagged against the wall as the man raced down the hallway, making no attempt to follow him or get a better look.

Reed was out of his room in less than a heartbeat. He caught a glimpse of a man disappearing through a stairway door, but didn't chase him. Sharla was his main concern. Her scream had taken ten years off his life.

His hair was still damp from the shower. He was only half dressed in baggy cotton slacks and nothing else, but Sharla didn't hesitate to throw herself at him the instant he came through her door.

He locked his arms around her and held her tight. She was trembling and breathing hard. He swore softly, knowing she'd been badly frightened or she never would have launched herself at him. His arms tightened protectively.

"What happened?" he demanded roughly.

Sharla's arms were wrapped tightly around his waist and her face was buried in the softly curling hair on his chest. His hard warmth was reassuring, and once her initial scare was over, she forced herself to breathe deeply.

"There was someone in my room," she managed in a hoarse whisper.

"Someone attacked you when you came in?"

She took another deep breath. "He didn't really attack me, just knocked me out of his way," she explained.

Reed lifted a hand to brush a stray curl off her face. "You're not hurt?"

Her gaze tangled with his. "Not hurt, just startled and a little scared."

"Did you get a look at him?"

She shook her head negatively. "I didn't see his face at all. He was big and tall and wearing a dark jacket. That's about all I had time to notice."

Reed's gaze narrowed in anger, and he pressed her head back to his chest. Her description fit Graves. He continued to hold her and stroke her hair in a comforting fashion until her trembling ceased. Her hair was as soft as satin. Her slim, shapely body was pressed tightly to his, and he liked the way her curves molded to fit his.

She felt good in his arms, just as he'd always known she would. She fit him perfectly — not like Dee or Carlie or any other woman — just Sharla. He had to fight to control his body's natural reaction to the feel of her.

When her racing heart had calmed, Sharla became fiercely aware of Reed's broad, naked chest beneath her face. His waist was hard and narrow, his skin smooth. He was warm, rock solid, and smelled clean and enticingly masculine. She knew she should get herself out of his arms.

A lightweight robe was her only cover for a damp bathing suit, and she belatedly realized that Reed was feeling a very graphic outline of her anatomy. Her nipples grew tighter at the thought, and she forced herself to put a little distance between them.

"You okay?" he asked as she gradually withdrew from his embrace. He was reluctant to let her go.

Sharla managed a smile for him, "I'm fine," she replied, her breathing back to normal. "I wasn't hurt. He just took me by surprise."

When she reached down to retrieve her bag. Reed stepped farther into the room. He flipped on several lights and checked for any signs of damage or theft. None of her belongings *seemed* to have been bothered. The room had been searched, just as his had.

"Do you think it was a hotel thief?" she asked.

"Can you see if anything's missing?" Reed avoided her question with one of his own.

Sharla made a quick check of the room, but didn't find anything out of place. "I had my pocketbook with me, so there wasn't much in here worth stealing," she explained. "It doesn't look like anything was touched."

His expression tightened fractionally. "How about your flight schedule?"

She moved to the table where her clipboard and scheduling information lay. "It's all here," she told him and handed him the board. "Do you think someone was looking for our travel information?"

"Could be," said Reed while checking the forms.

The men following him were one step ahead now. They knew he would be flying to Nashville tomorrow. It didn't matter if they got there first. What mattered was that they'd involved Sharla in their search for information.

"Do you think this has anything to do with the case you're working on?" she asked, trying her best not to dwell on how utterly gorgeous he was. There was something incredibly sexy about a man with a bare torso and bare feet.

"Probably," Reed told her, his tone clipped. "Why don't you pack your stuff, and I'll take it to my room. You'd better spend the night with me."

Sharla wasn't sure that sharing a room was such a good idea, especially after she'd just thrown herself at a man who was doing his best to avoid contact with her. She hadn't planned her actions, but that didn't change the fact that she had really liked being in his arms.

Reed expected her protests and offered some reassurance. "My room has two double beds," he supplied. "And you have my word that I'll behave like a perfect gentleman."

When she continued to hesitate, he added, "You don't really want to stay in here alone, do you?"

If someone had broken in once, they could do it again. It didn't take Sharla long to decide she didn't want to risk another, unwanted visitor, "I'd like to take a shower and change clothes first," she said. "Then I'll pack and move to your room."

He nodded in agreement and headed for the door. "I'm going to order some dinner from room service. Do you want anything, or did you plan to go down to one of the restaurants?"

"I'd rather eat in the room," she said. She didn't feel like getting dressed for a restaurant. "If you don't mind ordering for me, I like any kind of seafood."

"Coffee, wine, or something special to drink?"

"Just some iced tea, please."

"I'll take care of it," he said at the door. "Call me when you're ready, and I can shift the bags for you."

"Thanks, but I can get them. I won't be long."

"Fasten the safety lock," he reminded her as he closed the door between them.

Sharla fastened it, then sagged against the wall and sighed deeply. She felt as if she'd just been sucked into the middle of a cyclone. The man who had broken into her room had given her a major shock, and then Connors had wreaked havoc on her sensory system by holding her in his arms. He'd been surprisingly gentle and patient. It took considerable effort to restore her normal calm.

Connors was an incredibly attractive man and could be very distracting in close quarters. She already knew that from flying with him. Now she was actually planning to spend the night in his room.

Was she tempting fate and asking for trouble? She knew he could be trusted. He'd made it clear that he didn't want anything to do with her on a personal level. He was on assignment, so he would probably be more cautious, but could she trust herself?

Sharla couldn't stop thinking about how much she'd enjoyed the feel of his lean, hard body against her own. She berated herself for her stupidity as she took a very quick shower, washed her hair, and dressed in a powder blue sweat suit. Her intense sensual response to Connors was probably just a nervous reaction, she argued mentally.

She ordered herself to forget the earlier scene as she towel dried her hair, then brushed it so it would finish drying in its usual style of tumbling curls. Within a half hour, she was hauling her belongings to the next room and promising herself to keep everything impersonal between her and her roommate for the night.

Reed opened the door and helped her with her bags. Sharla was almost sorry to see that he'd donned a black cotton T-shirt that matched his slacks. Still, the soft, body-hugging fabric did little to conceal the rippling of muscles in his arms and shoulders.

He went back to her room to double-check for anything she might have forgotten, and Sharla was grateful for the short respite while she settled into his room. Everything was fairly neat and impersonal. Very few of his possessions were visible, so she didn't feel like too much of an intruder.

"You can put your things anywhere," he told her when he returned. "There's plenty of room in the closet and the dresser. Just shove my stuff out of your way."

"Thanks," said Sharla. The only thing she needed to hang in the closet was her jumpsuit for work the next day. Her swimsuit was still damp and needed to be dried, but she didn't want to hang it in the bathroom, so she settled for wrapping it in a dry towel. Everything else was left in her flight bag and stored in the closet.

Reed propped himself in a sitting position near the head of one bed and pretended an interest in the television show he'd been watching. He didn't want to make her uncomfortable about joining him, yet he was fascinated by how soft and huggable she looked in her sweat suit.

Her hair was still a little damp from the shower, but it bounced, healthy and shining, over her shoulders in a cloud of curls. She was efficiently taking care of her things, yet she looked unusually delicate and vulnerable. She smelled sweet, sexy, and feminine.

Her scent was enticing, and Reed couldn't help remembering how she'd felt in his arms, with her face pressed against his chest and her breath hot on his bare flesh. He couldn't help but remember how perfectly she fit against his body, but he knew he had to control any desire for a repeat performance.

She'd come to him for protection because she trusted him. At least, she trusted him more than she trusted the stranger who'd broken into her room. It pleased him that she'd agreed to spend the night with him. It was his fault she'd been frightened, and he promised himself not to do anything that might upset her. He'd pretend she was a witness under his protection. He never let himself be distracted when he was guarding a witness.

Their dinner arrived just as Sharla was wondering what in the world to do or say once she'd taken care of her belongings. She cleared some space at the room's one small table while Reed moved two chairs closer and the bellhop uncovered their trays.

Alone again, they ate in silence, but listened to the evening news while enjoying their dinner. When they reached the dessert stage, she decided to ask some questions.

"Can you tell me anything about the case you're working on?" She knew he'd been concerned about having her pilot for him this trip, but now she was curious as to why he'd worried and why anyone would search her room.

The Rudolph case had made national news, so Reed wasn't divulging any secrets by supplying her with some basic information. "The government has Sandy Rudolph under witness protection because she testified against her husband in his money-laundering trial."

Sharla remembered a few details. "Weren't they both highly respected bankers?" she asked.

He nodded. "That's how John got away with so much of his criminal activity. He had a perfect cover, but he made the mistake of underestimating Sandy. He didn't think she had the courage to thwart him, but once she learned about his illegal activities, she started collecting evidence against him."

"She must be very brave."

Reed smiled and his eyes lit with admiration. Sharla found herself resenting any woman who had that kind of effect on him.

"Sandy is quite a lady," he told her. "She found out where he'd buried his ill-gotten gains. Right before she went to the district attorney with the evidence, she shifted millions of dollars from his foreign bank accounts to hers. Now she's the only one who has access to the laundered money."

Sharla whistled softly. She couldn't remember hearing anything about the hidden money. "I'll bet her husband is one furious man."

"Furious and frustrated," he agreed. "He was found guilty on several counts and is appealing the verdict, but he needs money."

"So he hired men to find his wife?"

"It's my job to see that they never even get close."

"But you're not guarding her."

"On this assignment, I'm acting as a decoy," Reed explained. "Rudolph expected me to guard Sandy, so he's having me followed, hoping I'll lead him to her."

"But you're not going anywhere near her?"

"No."

"That's why you said you weren't sure about having trouble this trip —" It was beginning to make sense to her.

"I didn't expect Rudolph's men to make a move until they thought I was meeting Sandy. Someone obviously got impatient and decided to search our rooms."

"That man searched this room, too?"

Reed nodded again. "This afternoon while I was downtown. Probably right before he moved to your room." He realized now that he could have been the one to walk in on Rudolph's henchman. He wished he had been.

"They didn't leave any listening devices, did they?" Sharla asked, knowing that such things were common in the criminal world.

"No, I already checked. Since I don't have any information for them to find, they left just as frustrated as they came."

"What about my room?"

"They found the flight schedule, but it's no real threat to us or Sandy."

"They know where we're going next," she reminded as she finished off the last of her meal.

"They know, and they're probably already flying to Nashville themselves, but it won't make any difference."

"Because she's not there?"

"She's not there, so I don't expect any more trouble from Rudolph's hired help, but if you'd like to fly home tomorrow, I can take a commercial flight to Nashville."

Sharla gave him a teasing smile, and it did crazy things to Reed's insides.

"Bite your tongue. My mother would have a fit if she knew I left you at the mercy of commercial travel. Besides, if they're hoping you'll lead them to Sandy, they're not likely to do you any harm. As long as there's no immediate danger, I can't see any reason not to follow our original schedule."

He was glad she'd come to the same conclusion he had. He was just sorry that she'd gotten involved enough to be scared by one of Rudolph's men.

"Once you drop me off in Nashville, you can head home," he told her. "One of the agency pilots will fly me back to DC."

Sharla started to stack her dirty dishes on the serving tray. "Why didn't you just have someone with the agency fly you from city to city in the first place?"

"The pilot in question was tied up elsewhere, and we wanted this to look like any other job I might be assigned. We had to see if Rudolph's men could be sidetracked," said Reed as he picked up the tray of dirty dishes and set it outside the room.

"They obviously weren't."

"They took the bait."

"What about Sandy?"

"She's being transferred to another safe house. She's to testify again, then assume her new identity."

Sharla knew he couldn't give her too many details, but she was pleased to be trusted with the basic information. She moved to the extra bed and plumped both pillows near the headboard.

"How can you be sure that Rudolph doesn't have a dozen more men looking for his wife?"

"We can't," Reed supplied in a grim tone. He sat down on his bed and picked up the remote control for the television. "All we can do is try to keep everyone confused until we can guarantee Sandy's safety."

"What about the money?" Sharla wondered. "Who does it really belong to?"

"Legally, it belongs to the government if it's ever confiscated as evidence."

"Doesn't that mean that Sandy is withholding evidence?"

"There's no legal proof that the money exists. The agency has records of the funds Rudolph laundered, but no proof that the money was hidden instead of spent."

Sharla collected a novel from her pocketbook and then made herself comfortable on the bed. "So Sandy Rudolph doesn't have a legal obligation to return the money?"

"Nope."

Sharla tried to imagine what she would do in the other woman's place. If she were assuming a new identity and wanted to live in the comfort she was accustomed to, she'd probably need more money than the government would provide.

"Do you think she'll return the money?"

Reed crossed his arms behind his head. He wasn't sure what Sandy would do. Most people in her situation would take the money and run, but she wasn't like most people. "I don't know," he said.

"Isn't your agency anxious to recover the money? I'd think they'd be putting a lot of pressure on her."

"First, we have to keep her alive. If she turns the money over to the government, her life will be worthless to Rudolph."

Sharla was beginning to understand. "Right now, her husband wants her alive because of the money. If she gives it to the government, will he leave her alone or will he want revenge?"

"He'll want her dead."

The flatness of Reed's tone sent a shiver over Sharla. She didn't envy the other woman, but she respected her courage and sincerely hoped the feds could protect her.

"Do you mind if I watch baseball?"

"No, I have a book to read."

"The TV won't bother you? "

"Not at all."

That marked the end of conversation for the next two hours. Sharla made herself comfortable and became absorbed with the story she was reading while Reed watched baseball. It was much later before either of them spoke again.

The ball game was over and the late news was coming on television when she finished her book. She yawned and stretched, realizing that she'd been sitting in the same position for too long. She was one of those people who got caught up in a good book and forgot everything else.

Reed watched her lazy, catlike movements and swallowed another moan. His whole body was taut with need. The ball game hadn't been nearly as absorbing as her book must have been. He'd spent the last couple hours fighting his acute awareness of her. For a good portion of the night, he'd been openly studying her, and she hadn't even been aware of his intense perusal.

He found himself resenting the fact that he could be so totally ignored. His ego had suffered permanent damage, and his aching body hadn't fared much better. The wide variety of expressions that had crossed Sharla's features had held him captivated for the past hour.

While reading, she'd grinned often, frowned occasionally, and looked moved to tears once. What really drove him crazy was the flush of arousal that had lit her eyes and colored her cheeks a couple times.

"Good book?" he asked when she finally turned her attention to him. His tone was convincingly neutral.

The smile Sharla gave him was bright, but guileless. "Yes, it was really good. It's written by one of my favorite authors. She has a knack for capturing your attention and holding it through the whole book."

His response was a noncommittal grunt. "Is there anything else you need to do tonight?"

"I should call my mother. I've already checked in with Carlie today, but Mother will expect to hear from me."

"Would you like some privacy?" he asked, making no attempt to shift from his sprawled position.

"That's not necessary," Sharla said as she sat on the edge of the bed and reached for the phone. When she connected with Belle, she gave a brief rundown of the day's events, but avoided any mention of her accommodations for the night.

"I'm due into Nashville before noon tomorrow, then I'll be heading home."

Belle asked her if Connors was being a gentleman and if the two of them were getting along all right.

Sharla's gaze darted to the man in question. She found him staring steadily back at her. Their gazes locked. She caught a glimpse of turbulent emotion in his gaze that momentarily stole her breath. The air between them sizzled, and it was suddenly difficult to concentrate on her conversation with Belle.

"Everything's fine," she assured her mother, hoping it was the truth. "Tell everybody hello for me, and I'll see you sometime tomorrow."

Belle said good night and they broke the connection. Sharla leaned over to hang up the phone, simultaneously dragging her gaze from Connors' hypnotic gaze. Her pulse was skipping erratically, and she fought to control any wayward impulses.

"Would you like first turn at the bathroom?"

A small sigh of relief escaped her, and she dared another glance at Connors. His tone was normal, and his attention was focused on the television again. For a minute he'd had her worried. She was battling a strong attraction to him, and if he didn't keep things impersonal between them, they could be in trouble.

"I won't be long," she promised as she left the bed and collected a few things from her flight bag.

"No hurry." Reed managed an indifferent tone, but he was feeling anything but indifferent. His hormones were running rampant. His curiosity was even worse. She was driving him crazy, and she wasn't even trying.

He'd given her a brief, unguarded glimpse at his chaotic emotions, and he'd seen the wariness that leapt into her eyes. She had his promise that he wouldn't bother her. He intended to keep that promise, but he had a feeling it was going to be a long, sleepless night.

Sharla brushed her teeth and then splashed some cool water on her face. Just being in the same room with Connors made her feel warm and flustered. The man was dangerous. Sometimes his golden eyes made her heart race wildly and stirred up desires she didn't want disturbed.

Now she had to decide what to wear to bed. She hated sleeping in her clothes, but she had doubts about the wisdom of wearing only her silk pajama top. The bright red shirt might seem deliberately seductive even though it had long sleeves and reached low on her thighs.

She finally decided on comfort, wearing the pajama top instead of the bulky sweat suit. She didn't normally sleep in her bra and panties, but she made an exception tonight and felt adequately covered.

When she returned to the bedroom she found that Connors had turned off all but one light, the one on the table between their beds. He might have done it to make her feel more comfortable and less exposed, but now the room was seductively shadowed, and she was even more aware of the intimacy of their situation.

"The bathroom's all yours." She strained to keep her tone light as she moved to the closet to repack her sweat suit and toiletries.

Reed watched her move across the room in a flash of red silk and bare legs. The knots in his stomach grew tighter. He headed for the bathroom.

Sharla thought it wise to be tucked in bed by the time he returned, so she climbed beneath the covers and tried to make herself comfortable. Unfortunately, due to her afternoon nap, she wasn't the least bit sleepy.

Reed took his time shaving, brushing his teeth, and preparing for bed. He considered taking a cold shower, but decided against it. All he needed was a little time to regain control of his senses. Once Sharla was settled for the night, she wouldn't be quite so tempting.

He turned off the bathroom light before reentering the bedroom. She was already in bed, so he switched off the remaining light and stripped off his shirt and pants. He didn't want to offend his roommate, but he was going to be uncomfortable enough without trying to sleep in his clothes. He didn't own a pair of pajamas, silk or otherwise.

The imagination could be a brutal thing, Sharla mused as she listened to Reed taking off his clothes. She'd already seen his bare chest, and now she was imagining the rest of him bare. Did he wear boxer shorts, briefs, bikinis, or did he prefer to sleep in the raw?

"'Good night," he said as he climbed into bed. "

"'Night." She hoped he'd attribute her slightly husky tone to sleepiness.

Six

*I*t was a long, restless night for both of them. Neither slept well, and they were up at the crack of dawn. They dressed and prepared for the day with a minimum of conversation. Both of them carefully avoided any physical contact with the other. Despite their combined efforts, sexual tension sizzled between them, and they were too tired to pretend it didn't exist. The best they could do was ignore it.

The hotel restaurant was busy, so their shared breakfast was less strained. The tension subsided somewhat. They were able to relax a little, and even managed some small talk.

By eight o'clock, they were aboard the Saratoga and flying toward Nashville.

The blue skies of Kentucky gradually gave way to increasing clouds. After more than an hour and a half of flying, visibility began to seriously deteriorate. Sharla called the nearest radar tower for an update on the weather.

She learned that rain was expected with a weather system heading north from the gulf, and a cold front was moving in from the west. According to the forecast, they were flying directly toward the area where the two fronts would meet.

"Are we headed for trouble?" Reed asked.

Sharla frowned. She'd flown through high winds, pelting rains, and electrical storms. She could handle almost anything, except ice.

"The cold rain and poor visibility won't be a problem," she explained. "But if we run into sleet or ice, it can be treacherous."

"How far are we from Nashville?"

"Well over an hour."

"Do you want to him back?"

She shook her head. "We've already come more than halfway. The forecast didn't warn about an ice storm, so we'll probably be in Nashville before the weather gets too bad," she explained, then added, "It's up to you, though, if you want to turn back, we can."

Reed wasn't on a tight schedule. It didn't matter what time he got to Nashville, but if they went back, it could be hours or days before the weather cleared again. He didn't want to be delayed too long.

"I'd rather keep heading south," he decided. "Are there any airfields in this area where we could set down if the conditions get too bad?"

"I don't know of any," she said, "but I can request emergency landing instructions from the nearest tower if we run into trouble."

For the next half hour the cockpit was quiet as the weather became their main focus. The wind steadily increased and the skies grew darker. By the time it started to rain, the Saratoga was being rocked by gusts of wind, and the ride grew rougher with each passing minute.

Sharla was pouring all her energy into keeping the plane on course. She'd just decided to call for assistance, when she picked up a warning from the radar tower. The rain was changing to sleet and ice farther south, and there was little chance of flying above the turbulent weather system.

The radio transmission began to break up, and she strained to hear the rest of the message. All small aircraft were being advised to make emergency landings, but she'd lost transmission with the tower, and her radio was nothing but static.

"Can I help?" Reed asked, knowing she had her hands full controlling the plane.

Sharla handed him the radio receiver. "You could try to find another radar station," she told him, showing him how to scan for the nearest tower. "Just keep calling 'Mayday' until you get a response."

"Are we being thrown very far off course?" he asked.

"Not yet, if my instruments are accurate," she said after a glance at her direction panel. "But I don't know how much longer I can risk flying directly into this system."

He knew they couldn't go over or around the system either, so they were basically at the mercy of Mother Nature. He continued his efforts to make contact with a radar tower, but the radio kept shorting out. He occasionally caught the sound of a voice or part of a weather advisory, but no useful information.

"I think we've lost the radio," he announced after a long period of nothing but static. "They may be hearing me, but I can't hear them."

She flipped a few controls and tried the scanner again, but with the same results as Reed. That meant they couldn't depend on local emergency instructions.

"What now?" he asked.

"We ride it out," she responded grimly.

Reed admired her calm tone. He could see the tension in every line of her face and body, but she wasn't the type to succumb to panic. The plane was being bounced around like a helium balloon, yet she was still controlling their course.

He thought about the agency's cabin. It had a small airstrip. He didn't want to lead Rudolph's men to the safe house, but he didn't think there was any way they could track the Saratoga in this storm. It was a risk to take Sharla anywhere near where Sandy would be, yet the risk to keep flying was even greater.

"I know where there's a small airstrip," he told her, capturing her full attention for an instant. "It's short and rough, but you can probably put the Saratoga down on it." He had no doubts about her capabilities.

"Where?" she demanded.

Reed gave her the coordinates. "How close are we?"

Her brows were creased in a frown as she studied the plane's control panels. "It's a few miles west of our original flight path, but a westerly path might protect us from some of the rain," she explained. "Are you absolutely sure about the coordinates?"

"Positive," said Reed. He'd memorized the numbers so that he wouldn't have to carry any written information of the location. "The property belongs to the agency. The airstrip is always in good repair and ready for planes."

Sharla considered the coordinates he'd given her. There wasn't time to debate the pros and cons. She had to get the plane on the ground as soon as possible. The weather conditions would get worse before they got better, and without a radio, they were completely vulnerable in the air.

The gusting wind was blowing east, so she turned the nose of the plane directly west. She'd rather face the wind's ferocity than the ice she knew was southeast of them. She just hoped she could land the plane before the whole region was bombarded with sleet and ice.

The turn westward gradually took them out of the pelting rain and inky black clouds. They moved to lighter skies, light showers, and much better visibility. When they neared their destination, Sharla began to descend through the clouds, and within minutes she could make out the terrain below them. All she could see was woodlands.

"What are we looking for?" she asked.

Reed was straining to see the landscape below them. "The cabin is buried in a grove of trees," he said, then smiled slightly at Sharla's heartfelt groan.

"It's a log cabin with a brown slate roof. The radio tower is behind it, and the airstrip sits to the right of the house. The clearing around the property is fairly large."

"I'll drop as low as I dare," she said. "Let me know as soon as you see something familiar. We're right on the coordinates now."

"And there it is." Reed pointed to a house buried in an ocean of tall pine trees.

Sharla nodded. She didn't get a clear view of the airstrip until she'd flown over it once, so she slowly circled the property and headed back in for a landing.

That's when their luck ran out. As they lost altitude, the rain started sounding louder against the plane, and Sharla swore softly. "Dammit to hell! The rain's freezing." Within seconds the plane was covered with a thin sheet of ice, and their conditions were seriously altered.

"Can you make it down or should we go up again?" he asked, knowing the tremendous strain she was feeling.

"We're going down. Grab a couple cushions from the back and prepare for a crash landing. I should be able to set it down easily enough, but I may not get any traction if I land on a sheet of ice."

Reed grabbed seat cushions from behind them and put one in her lap and one in his. Sharla cut her power as much as she dared on the descent, hoping to alleviate the need for too much braking when they hit the ground.

The touchdown was light, and the plane was perfectly aligned with the airstrip. Reed's eyes lit with awe at her ability to perform an expert landing under so much pressure. Then Sharla reached out and slapped his shoulder.

"Get down and tuck your head!" she cried hoarsely. "We're going to crash!"

She'd cut the power and engaged the brakes as securely as possible, but the wheels weren't getting any traction, and the plane wasn't slowing down enough. They were going to run out of pavement before they came to a stop.

The tall wire fence at the end of the strip was a welcome sight. It might not stop them completely, but Sharla knew it would slow them down and weaken the force of impact with the monstrous tree trunks.

She was soaked with sweat from exertion, and her whole body was taut with brittle tension. Her hands were locked on the controls, but the most she could do was steer the nose of the plane at an angle that would put it between tree trunks. There was no way to protect the whole plane or her passenger.

The force of the wheels hitting the fence jarred the Saratoga and its passengers, but then the left wing slammed into a tree and jolted them to a violent stop. Sharla gasped as her upper body flew forward, her head made contact with something hard, and everything went black.

Reed swiftly shut off the engine, unfastened his seat belt, and gently eased her back in her seat to check for injuries. She had a wide, shallow gash on her forehead, but he couldn't tell if she was hurt anywhere else. He could only hope that her safety belt and the cushion had protected most of her body from the impact

"Sharla." His voice was so gruff that he had to clear his throat and try again. "Sharla, wake up. We need to get out of the plane."

He brushed her hair back from her cheeks and tenderly cupped her face in his hands. Panic shot through him at how frail and still she looked.

"Sharla." His pulse was pounding in his ears at a dangerous level. He was accustomed to wild rushes of adrenaline, but this was different. He hadn't feared the crash nearly as much as he feared she could be seriously injured, and that he wouldn't be able to get help for her. The chances of getting emergency care during an ice storm in this area were slim to none. The only thing he could do was get her into the cabin and take care of her. He preferred that she be conscious.

"Sharla, can you hear me? Talk to me."

Her eyelashes fluttered, she moaned softly, and then looked at him through narrowed eyes. She stirred a little, then went slack again.

Reed swore violently. He laid her head against the back of the seat for support and climbed out his side of the plane. After ducking under the aircraft to get to the pilot's door, he opened it, carefully unfastened her safety belt, and pulled Sharla from her seat into his arms.

Once on the ground with his precious burden, he tightened his grip on her. The fence offered support until he reached a rougher, grassy area that wasn't as slick as the ice-covered concrete of the airstrip.

The house was at least a hundred yards from the plane, and the stinging rain continued to pound them, but Reed made the trip across the open stretch of ground as fast as he could safely move.

They were both covered with a fine sheet of ice by the time they reached the front porch of the cabin. He felt Sharla beginning to stir and eased her into a big wicker chair. Her cheeks were flushed, her hair a wild tumble, and her eyes a little too bright as they gazed at him in mild confusion.

"Reed?" she mumbled, wondering why she was soaking wet, freezing cold, and sitting on a strange porch with Connors kneeling in front of her. Then it all rushed back, and her eyes widened in alarm. "The plane?" she cried hoarsely.

Relief washed through him, so intense that it hurt. "I didn't have time to check it out, but it doesn't look too bad. Just a dent in the left wing," he explained. "Right now I'm worried about getting you inside, dry, and warm. Will you be all right while I check the cabin?"

She nodded, then winced and reached a hand to the swollen bump above her right eye. It felt sticky, so she knew it must be bleeding, but it didn't seem too serious.

Reed retrieved the hidden key, unlocked the door, and made a quick check of the cabin before returning to the porch for her. She muttered a weak complaint when he lifted her into his arms, but didn't offer any real resistance as he cradled her close and carried her into the house. She was shivering badly as he eased her onto a sofa and wrapped her in a wool afghan he found nearby.

"You okay?" be queried softly, his golden eyes filled with genuine concern.

Sharla's teeth were chattering, but the afghan immediately helped combat some of the chill. She gave him a slightly frozen smile. "I'll be fine in a minute," she managed to stutter through stiff lips.

"I'm going to switch on the furnace, start a fire, and find us a change of clothes," he told her, brushing a wet curl off her cheek. "It won't take long."

Sharla nodded and closed her eyes.

"Don't go to sleep." His voice was suddenly sharp.

The rough command held just a touch of panic. The thought made her open her eyes and smile again. "I'll be fine." she insisted.

He was far from convinced, but he had to get some heat in the cabin and get them some dry clothes. He tossed his sopping wet jacket over the back of a chair and lit a fire in the hearth opposite the sofa, thinking it might help warm Sharla faster than the central heat.

Once he had a fire blazing in the fireplace, he reset the temperature on the furnace thermostat and heard it kick into life. Then he headed for the bedrooms where extra clothing was stored. He found a flannel shirt and jeans to fit him and quickly changed out of his wet clothes.

Thanks to some female federal agents. Reed found smaller, feminine clothing in the second bedroom. He deliberately ignored the underwear, except for a pair of heavy socks.

There were two sweat suits in the dresser, one black and one lavender. Thinking the pastel better suited Sharla; he carried it back to the living room. Her eyes were closed, but they opened as soon as he approached.

"You need to change clothes."

Sharla groaned. Her jumpsuit was soaked, but she hated to give up the warmth of the afghan for a second.

"Come on," Reed coaxed gently, half lifting her from the sofa. "I'll hold the blanket while you get changed."

She stood still while he unwound her cocoon of warmth, but moved more swiftly once her wet suit was exposed to cool air again. Despite trembling fingers, she quickly stripped off the jumpsuit and pulled on the sweat suit. She reached for the afghan, but Reed handed her socks instead.

"The afghan is wet," he explained. "Put on some socks while I get you a dry blanket." He tossed the afghan over the sofa with the wet side up so that it would dry, then went to the bedroom and returned with two heavy blankets.

One blanket was spread on the floor in front of the fireplace. Sharla had just managed to get her feet covered when he wrapped the other one around her shoulders and lowered them both to the floor.

It took no effort at all for her to curl herself into the warmth of his body. Reed used his arms and legs to encompass her with his heat. Shivers shook her from head to toe, and she snuggled closer. A few minutes later, she sighed as the heat began to chase away the chills.

He was afraid she might have suffered a concussion in the crash. "Don't go to sleep," he commanded again. This time his mouth was close to her ear, and his tone was softer.

"I won't," Sharla promised huskily. Her face was tucked into the curve of his shoulder; she was mostly concerned about getting warm.

Once her shivering had stopped, Reed took the time to brush her damp hair from her face and neck. He gently combed it with his fingers and spread it over her shoulders to dry.

"I should have gotten a towel for your hair," he murmured as he stroked the mass of thick, silky tresses. He'd imagined it would be soft. Now he knew, and he wasn't in any hurry to stop touching the luxurious strands of gold.

The fire was at Sharla's back, and Connors' heat was pressed firmly against her front side. Within a few minutes, she was growing deliciously warm and drowsy.

"If you don't want me to go to sleep," she mumbled, "you'd better stop rubbing my hair."

Reed grinned. His fingers stopped stroking, but he lifted a handful of hair to his face, unable to control the urge to feel it against his lips.

"You're a pretty nice guy to have around in an emergency," she murmured against his neck.

His smile deepened. "I was thinking the same thing about you when our plane touched down smack in the middle of that airstrip. Most pilots couldn't have made it in good weather conditions."

"You think I'm a nice guy to have around in an emergency?" she muttered. She was toasty warm, and it was hard to ward off sleep.

"I think you're one helluva pilot," he insisted gruffly, his arms tightening around her.

The compliment sent a thrill through her and chased away some of the sleepiness. She allowed herself a few minutes to bask in Connors' praise, then thoughts of her Saratoga surfaced.

"I wrecked my plane."

Her tone was so dejected that Reed found himself smiling again. He couldn't seem to help it, but attributed the uncharacteristic sense of contentment to the fact that he'd just been delivered from death's door. Holding a beautiful woman in his arms wasn't bad, either. Never mind who the woman was.

"I don't think the plane suffered much damage," he offered in a soothing tone. "The left wing is the only section that struck the tree."

"Wings are important, you know," Sharla felt compelled to remind him.

Reed was beginning to feel like an extremely lucky man. He admired Sharla the pilot, but he really liked Sharla the soft, sexy woman with a wry sense of humor.

"When the rain lets up, I promise I'll go outside and check your wing. There's a radio here I can use to call for help if we need it."

"Connors?"

"The name is Reed," he corrected.

Sharla thought about that for a minute. She'd always thought of him as Connors. Reed seemed so personal, even though she usually addressed people by their first names.

"Reed?" she tested his name on her lips.

"What?"

She liked the smile in his voice. "I hate to complain, but my backside is getting scorched."

He chuckled and rolled onto his back, rearranged the blanket, and pulled her on top of him. That shifted her backside from the direct heat of the flames. "Is that better?"

Sharla's murmur was lost somewhere in the curve of his shoulder as she adjusted her body to the shape of his lean, hard frame. Her hands came to rest on the solid wall of his chest, and the steady drum of his heart was soothing.

Reed's arms enveloped her and held her close. For a few minutes he allowed himself the sweet, sensual luxury of having her body pressed close to his.

Growing up on an isolated farm in Iowa, he'd been shy and backward around girls as a teen. Until seventeen, he'd been small for his age and painfully self-conscious. At eighteen his strength and coordination had finally developed to a satisfying extent.

He'd rapidly overcome his shyness as women began to let him know how appealing they found him. He'd been blessed with natural athletic abilities that gave him an edge in sports and seemed to attract more of the opposite sex. There had been no shortage of women throwing themselves at him since those early years, and he'd grown very cynical and hardhearted in his personal life.

Then he'd met Sharla. Something about her flashing eyes and independent spirit had pierced the armor he'd carefully erected and exposed the vulnerable boy again. Reed hadn't liked the feeling one bit.

He'd spent three years fighting the desire to take her in his arms and explore the attraction between them. Now he was greedily absorbing the scent and feel of her. It might not be wise, but it felt damned good.

Their new position alleviated Sharla's problem with the fireplace, but created a heightened sensual contact with his hard body that was even more disturbing. She propped her arms on his chest and looked him directly in the eyes. Her hair curtained them in more intimacy, his eyes gleamed with devilish enjoyment, and she couldn't help but blush.

"I'm all warm now," she felt compelled to confess. Staying locked against his body was playing with fire.

His hands had been resting on her hips, but they tightened at her hint that they no longer needed to be quite so close. He wasn't ready to let her go.

"Shut your eyes," he commanded gently.

Sharla closed her eyes for about 30 seconds, and then opened them again.

"Your pupils are dilating," he declared with satisfaction. "You've got a sizable goose egg on your head, and it'll probably be black and blue, but I don't think you have a concussion."

"That's good to hear, Dr. Connors," she teased.

Her hair was hanging on either side of her face. She reached up with both hands to shove it out of the way, but the action caused the rest of her body to ripple against his. She watched his eyes darken and felt a very male reaction to her squirming.

Reed's whole body felt electrified. The pleasure of having her pressed against him was so intense that his body quaked in response and grew harder. He saw the dawning of concern in her big eyes.

"Don't let it worry you," he whispered gruffly. "It's just the male in me appreciating the feel of the female in you."

"Just a physical, involuntary type of thing?" Her voice had dropped to a husky whisper that matched his.

His response rattled from deep in his throat. "Yeah, just a physical thing."

She might have believed him if his eyes weren't so hot and caressing. They kept focusing on her lips. Her tongue darted out to moisten them.

"There is something very personal that I'd like," said Reed, his eyes hungry as they locked with hers again.

"What might that be?" she managed to ask.

His reply was low and hoarse. "A kiss."

They both knew it was a risk, yet neither of them wanted to halt the growing wonder of discovery.

"Really?" She grew breathless at the thought of sharing a kiss.

"Really." He was already brushing light kisses over her cheeks, nose, and chin. "May I have a kiss?"

Sharla's breathing grew rougher. It made her acutely aware of her breasts crushed against the solid wall of his chest. Her nipples were tingling with sensitivity, and she wasn't sure how the rest of her body would respond if she got lost in his kisses.

"Just one kiss?" she hedged.

Reed slid a hand up her body to cradle the back of her head. He didn't answer her question or ask permission for the long, deep, searching kiss that he stole.

His fingers sank into her hair, his big hand guiding her head so that their mouths could mate more tightly. His tongue plundered the sweetness he found — greedily tasting, stoking, and savoring.

Sharla had wondered, for a long, long time, what it would be like to kiss Reed Connors. Now she was finding that it wasn't like any other kiss she'd ever known. His mouth was hard and hot, his tongue wickedly demanding, his taste unique. His mouth challenged even as it satisfied.

The kiss lit fires throughout her body and made her blood pound heavily in her ears. Reed's other hand began to explore her back from shoulder to hip, growing increasingly urgent in the need to learn the feel of her. Sharla's hands were clutching either side of his head, her fingers sunk in the thickness of his hair.

When their breathing grew too ragged, their mouths separated to drag in air. She immediately buried her face against his neck, effectively putting her mouth out of the reach of his until she'd had time to regain some control. She wasn't accustomed to being so acutely, painfully aroused so quickly. She wasn't sure it was safe.

The air burned Reed's lungs, and his whole body was trembling with need — primitive, riotous, unequaled need. He clutched her tightly to his chest while they fought for control. A kiss. It was only a kiss, he tried to convince himself. Nothing more than a kiss with an attractive woman.

It was a kiss that shook them both to the core. Neither of them was prepared to handle the explosive desire they'd triggered. Neither of them was prepared to cope with the sexual or emotional impact of their first kiss. When their breathing had regulated somewhat, they managed to release the death grip they had on each another. Sharla uncurled her fingers from his hair. Reed's hands relaxed against her head and waist.

"Just one kiss," she murmured, her derision directed at his initial request. She felt his chest heave as he sighed deeply.

"Lady, your kisses pack one helluva wallop." His tone was gruff; his body slow to recover.

Sharla tried to be reasonable. "It just seemed that way because of our unusual situation," she offered hopefully.

He knew better. He'd been battling his desire for her too long. He didn't need to have all his wildest fantasies confirmed. He didn't need to know how good she tasted, how sweet and soft she could be, or how perfectly she fit against his body.

Seven

"If you're warm now, I'd better have another look around the cabin." Reed needed to put some distance between them again.

Sharla rolled toward the fire, taking the blanket with her. She used it as a shield while he rose from the floor. It didn't prevent her from noticing how incredibly sexy he looked in jeans, but it hid her blush. When he'd moved farther away, she sat up and took a look around her.

What she could see of the cabin was one long room. A large desk with chairs and radio equipment was on the wall opposite the fireplace. The front door was in the middle of the room, while a door leading to the rest of the house was directly across from it. A brown plaid sofa, two matching easy chairs, and a coffee table were on her end of the room.

Reed disappeared through the inside door. Sharla rose and straightened her clothes. She folded both blankets and put them on the sofa, then picked up her wet jumpsuit and spread it over the back of a chair near the fire. She was putting their shoes next to the hearth when Reed returned with a first-aid kit.

"Why do I think you're about to play doctor again?" She asked, hoping to dispel the lingering tension between them. Her reward was the sexy curve of his mouth and a teasing gleam in his eyes.

"That's gratitude for you," he grumbled. "I save your life, and you criticize."

"Saved my life?"

"Practically."

"Bull."

Reed was shaking his head and grinning while he looked for antiseptic cream in the box. Then he moved close to her and gently applied the ointment to the scrape on her forehead. He was relieved to see that the swelling had gone down and the abrasion was minor.

"What now?" she asked, holding perfectly still for his ministrations. His touch was light, but his proximity made her pulse race.

The brush of his fingertips over her soft skin set off fireworks in Reed's body again. He quickly finished and concentrated on replacing the cream in the box.

"We have plenty of food in the kitchen and a backup generator if we lose the power. I'll try to make radio contact with someone, but we might have to wait until the storm subsides."

"What about a telephone?"

"It's dead. Probably the first thing that went."

"You think we'll lose the electricity, too?"

"There's a good chance. The clouds are rolling in, and the worst of the storm is reaching this area. It may be hours or days before someone can fly in to check your plane."

Hours or days. Sharla let that information sink in as she moved toward a window and looked at the darkening sky. She didn't want to think about the possible consequences of being isolated with Connors for days.

"Dee will be sick with worry," she murmured as the troubled thought popped into her head. Reed had taken the first-aid kit back to the bathroom, but re-entered the living room in time to catch her softly spoken words.

"We can radio our location to Nashville as soon as the weather improves, but it'll be awhile before they notify your family that you had trouble."

"Dee knew as soon as I knew." The statement was matter-of-fact, but Sharla's tone was firm. "Carlie probably felt some concern, but Dee gets a double whammy. She'll know I made a crash landing."

Reed studied her face as she calmly discussed a subject that was foreign to him: extrasensory perception. Sharla and her sisters might take their uncanny ability for granted, but he found it hard to comprehend.

Over the past few years, he'd heard several members of the Prescott family mention a special bond that existed among the triplets, but he'd never had the phenomenon explained.

"Tell me about it," he demanded as he sat down at the desk and began to check out the radio equipment.

Sharla knew what he meant, but was at a loss to explain. "There's not much I can tell you. There's no scientific data available on the Prescott triplets. My mother refused to let us be tested when we were young, and we've never felt the need as adults. We don't think what we share is particularly special. We all just feel the emotional strain when one of us is under a lot of stress."

"Do you ever experience actual pain?"

Sharla wandered close to the desk. It was easier to talk to Reed's back than have his piercing eyes directed at her. "I only have emotional reactions, but Dee probably felt pressure in her forehead when I hit mine."

That comment brought his head around and made his eyes widen in amazement. If anyone but Sharla had been telling him this, he'd be shaking his head in disbelief, yet he didn't doubt her sincerity. "Sounds painful."

Sharla studied his expression. She rarely discussed her and her sisters' emotional ties and never with someone who was too narrow minded to consider the possibilities. She could understand skepticism from people who didn't understand extrasensory perception, but she couldn't tolerate anyone's blatant refusal to believe the truth.

"It's not too bad for Carlie and me. What we feel is what most people feel if they have a really close bond with a friend or family member. Dee's the one who has the strongest reactions. She says it's because she's the middle child."

"Does she have visions?"

Sharla shook her head negatively. "She explains it as a jolt of alarm that alerts her to a strong emotional trauma. Then if she concentrates, she can pick up specific emotions — such as anger, fear, or pain."

"She experiences the same emotions?"

"To an extent."

"Will she know that you're all right now?"

Sharla imagined that Dee would be worried, but hoped that she would realize there was no immediate need for concern. "I hope so but I'm sure she'll be badgering the officials in Lexington and Nashville. She won't be satisfied until she hears from me and knows all the facts."

"Is she likely to fly to Nashville?"

"I doubt if she'll come right away," said Sharla. "What about your assignment?"

Reed frowned. "This is the safe-house where Sandy is supposed to stay. We hoped Rudolph's men would follow me to Nashville while she got settled here. Now I'm hoping they won't know where we've landed, and that I can warn my boss that the location has been compromised."

Sharla realized he was concerned for her safety. "If we can't leave, then the bad guys can't arrive, can they?"

"Not in this weather," he agreed as they listened to the increasing force of sleet hitting the windows and roof of the cabin. Nothing but static could be heard from the radio. "We're all forced to a standstill for the time being." Reed made the statement as he gave up on the radio and rose from his chair. "How about some lunch? I'm starving."

"Me, too, now that you mention it," said Sharla. "What kind of food do we have?"

Reed gave her a mini-tour of the cabin as they passed through the hallway to the kitchen. "There's a bedroom on either side of the hall. In the past, the men have used the one on the left, and the women use the one on the right. It makes no difference to me. I'll get our bags later, and you can take your pick."

"I'm not particular," said Sharla.

He entered the kitchen and headed for the refrigerator. "There's a small utility room over there," he said, pointing to another inside door. "The room was divided to add the bathroom. It's small, but adequate."

Sharla decided she'd better take a closer look at the bathroom and excused herself. She found a portable washer and dryer in the utility area along with dozens of shelves stocked with canned goods.

After using the bathroom, she caught a glimpse of herself in the mirror over the lavatory and moaned. Her hair was a wild tangle. Her face was wind burned, and the knot on her head was already bruising. Glamorous, she wasn't, but there was little she could do about it.

"I found some frozen submarine sandwiches," Reed told her as she reentered the kitchen. "Will that do for lunch?"

"It sounds fine. What can I do to help?"

"Just sit down. It won't take a minute."

She took a seat without arguing. The table was already set with water glasses, silverware, and condiments. Paper towels were folded in lieu of napkins. A pot of coffee was brewing, and within minutes Reed was serving hot sandwiches.

"The agents who use this cabin pitched in to buy the microwave," he explained as he took a seat opposite her.

"A wise investment."

"An absolute necessity," he corrected. "The freezer is full of meat. All I have to do is thaw something for supper. I can grill steaks, bake potatoes, and heat some canned vegetables."

"Sounds good to me."

Reed took a bite of his sandwich and looked directly into her eyes for the first time since their shared kiss. It was crazy how her gaze could warm him to the bone.

"Are you by any chance laughing at my cooking skills?" he asked.

She shook her head slowly, but her smile widened. "I'm impressed," she teased lightly. "You're so efficient."

His brow cocked. "Complaining?"

"No, sir," came her emphatic reply. "I hate any kind of cooking, even the fast kind."

Reed was shaking his head in disbelief. "I suppose your mother still cooks for you and takes care of all your basic needs,"

Sharla enjoyed a bite of her sandwich, and then responded to his comment. "Mother and Daddy have a housekeeper who takes care of the whole family. The house is subdivided into apartments for each of us girls, but when we're all at home, we usually end up sharing a meal.

"Each apartment is equipped with kitchen appliances and a clothes washer, so I can be self-sufficient when I want," she added. "Although I can't say I like cleaning and laundry any more than I like cooking."

He didn't comment, but his eyes gleamed wickedly as he finished his sandwich.

"I'll bet you think that's terrible, don't you?" she charged. "That I'm so undomesticated."

"To each his own."

"His own being the operative words," she continued in a disgusted tone. "It's been my experience that men are expected to do their own thing, and are praised for it. But women, in general, are only supposed to do their own thing as long as it doesn't interfere with what the men in their lives think is appropriate."

"Whew!" Reed had to control the urge to laugh outright at her indignant tone. He wondered how many men had tried to domesticate her. "What do you do with the men who want to get married and keep you barefoot and pregnant?"

Sharla's gaze narrowed. She couldn't tell if he was mocking her or not. "I avoid them like the plague."

Laughter erupted from deep in his chest. She was dead serious and her tone was threaded with steel. She'd obviously encountered several men who'd wanted to clip her wings. He couldn't help feeling sorry for the poor guys who'd made the mistake of trying to change her, but he was glad none of them had ever succeeded.

Sharla felt a thrill race over her at the sound of his deep, husky laughter. His eyes glittered wickedly, and he was incredibly sexy – even if he was laughing at her.

"Why not share the joke?"

"Sorry." He calmed himself. "I wasn't making fun, only imagining how you'd dealt with anybody who thought they could trap you inside a white picket fence."

Sharla grinned. "It depends on how healthy an ego the guy has," she confessed. "I either tell him to drop dead, or I politely suggest that he find a woman who's more compatible."

"No screaming or temper tantrums?"

"A waste of energy," she scoffed.

"Energy that could be put to better use?"

"Flying, of course," she retorted. "How about you?"

"My work."

They shared an understanding smile, realizing how much alike they were when it came to the subject of altering their lifestyles to fit the accepted norms.

Reed took her by surprise with his next question. "What about all those grandchildren Belle wants?" he asked.

Sharla thought she detected a more serious undertone in his question, but he was drinking coffee, and she couldn't read his expression.

"Dee loves kids. She wants to have about a dozen. That should make Mother happy."

He kept his gaze focused on his cup. "I thought all women wanted babies."

"That's a lie perpetrated by insecure men," she tossed back at him.

"You won't think your life's incomplete if you don't produce two point five children?" he asked as he rose from his chair and poured them both another cup of coffee.

Sharla wondered if there was more than idle curiosity behind his questions. She didn't understand, but she didn't mind answering.

"Mother says I was probably trying to find a way to soar out of her womb while the maternal genes were being divided among my sisters and myself. I didn't inherit any."

For some reason, her explanation earned her an approving smile from

Reed. Most men frowned when she tried to explain that she didn't have any desire to procreate. Maybe he had to regularly fight off women who wanted to tie him down with marriage and children.

"What about you?" She dared since he hadn't hesitated to ask her personal questions. "Do you feel a compelling need to father a child?"

"No." His response was swift and strong. The teasing light left his eyes, and he silently defied her to find fault with his attitude.

Her eyes widened a little in surprise, but she didn't push her luck by asking for an explanation of his abrupt mood swing. They'd both finished their lunch, so she decided to clear the table.

"What do we do now?" she asked, placing their few dishes in the sink and rinsing them.

Reed knew it was time to put a halt to the probing questions and concentrate on their present situation. "I need to check the plane and get our bags."

Sharla glanced toward the window. A steady sheet of icy rain prevented her from seeing anything. . "I don't think it's going to let up for a while."

Reed knew she was right. He opened the doors of a cabinet near the table and displayed a collection of games. "In that case, we have a choice of time-wasting activities," he explained. "Do you prefer board games or cards?"

Sharla wiped the table and glanced over his shoulder for a better look at the selection. She'd never learned to play chess and had no patience for word games. "I think I can handle a couple games of checkers, providing you don't cheat."

He feigned a wounded expression. "I never cheat," he insisted, then qualified, "besides, you can't cheat in checkers unless your opponent falls asleep or leaves the room."

Sharla laughed and sat back down at the table. "Is that what happens at those notorious government stakeouts?" she teased. "Everybody just waits until the other guy gets tired enough to fall asleep?"

"That's about the size of it," he admitted. "Will you be warm enough in here or should we move back to the living room?"

"I'm fine in here."

His gaze went to the knot on her forehead. "Is your head hurting?"

"Just throbbing a little. I found some aspirin in the bathroom and took a couple, so it should ease up in a while."

"Okay, let's play checkers. Lady's choice. Do you want red or black?"

During the next few hours, the weather was ignored while they learned to play together. They played a variety of games and realized that their strong competitive natures were well matched. Reed was an expert on most games and was apt to cheat if Sharla didn't watch him every minute.

He won the majority of their contests, but she always gave him some tough competition and improved her skills with each new challenge. She told him it didn't matter if you won or lost, but how you played the game.

He didn't buy her excuses. He delighted in challenging her and then teasing unmercifully when he beat her. They groaned, argued, and provoked each other, but accepted defeat with good humor.

She insisted that his experience with stakeouts gave him an unfair advantage. She lobbied for a handicap. He refused to give her an edge, proclaiming that it would be a setback for women's rights.

During a game of gin rummy, Reed excused himself to go to the bathroom. When he returned, Sharla won the hand with a king-high, five-card straight, and three aces. He was outraged and accused her of cheating. She adamantly denied it, but couldn't stop laughing long enough to offer a proper defense.

"That does it," he grumbled after adding up their scores. "You're over five hundred, but I'm lodging a formal protest about this one."

"You're in a snit because I've beaten you three games out of five," she insisted haughtily. "That makes me the winner."

"Let's make it the best of seven," he suggested, shuffling the cards.

"Oh, no," she argued. "You said the best of five, and you can't change the rules every time I win. Besides," she tacked on impishly, "I have to go to the bathroom."

His eyes gleamed with the light of revenge, and she went into another fit of laughter. Reed couldn't help laughing with her. She was beautiful, sassy, and a lot of fun. He couldn't remember the last time he'd had so much fun with a woman, if ever.

"I guess we should take a break," he noted. "I'll see if I can get a response on the radio while you go to the bathroom."

She excused herself, and he went to the living room. He added a log to the fire, and then tried the radio. It still wasn't producing anything but static.

When Sharla followed him into the room, she picked up the telephone receiver. "The phone's still dead, too."

Reed opened the front door to check the weather. The sky was still cloudy, but the rain had stopped. Everything in sight was coated with ice.

Sharla joined him and gazed at the glittering world outside the cabin. "It's beautiful, isn't it?"

"As long as you don't have to be out in it," he agreed. "If the sun comes out, it'll be blinding."

Sharla shivered from the cold air seeping in through the door, and

Reed closed it.

"What now?" she asked. "Another game of gin?"

"It's going to take me a little time to get over that defeat," he told her. "I think I'll risk a trip out to the plane while it's still light enough to see."

"Does the bureau supply ice skates?"

"Not that I know of, but I think there's some heavy boots around here someplace. I'll see what I can find. Why don't you rest a while? Your forehead's starting to change colors."

"A little black and blue?" She touched the spot gently with her finger. The swelling had eased, but she imagined it would be colorful.

"Maybe you can cut some bangs or wear a headband for a few days," he suggested.

"Thanks, but I think I'll just leave it for all the world to see and tell everyone I walked into a door."

Reed couldn't imagine her being clumsy, but he'd learned that she really was a good sport. Their situation was far from ideal, yet she hadn't whined or pouted.

"It wouldn't hurt to relax a while. I don't think you have a concussion, but you did crack your head pretty hard." He gently brushed a strand of hair off the injured side of her face. "Dr. Connors should have ordered bed rest this afternoon."

His tone had gone low and seductive. The admiration and genuine concern in his gaze had Sharla mesmerized. He had such beautiful eyes, especially when they went liquid with feeling. How could she have thought him a hard, emotionless man?

Reed didn't seem to have any control over the arm that slipped around her waist and drew her near. Sharla's hands splayed on his chest, gentle and warm, sending a quiver of longing through him. Their stomachs pressed together and he wanted her even closer.

Her gaze remained locked with his. She'd never been so totally fascinated by a man's eyes. The heat in them shimmered over her. She was melting, her body grew languid, her breathing faltered, and she leaned more heavily against him.

"I think I want another kiss," he muttered hoarsely.

Two sets of eyes gazed on two pairs of lips. Then their two heads were coming together in slow motion, the languorous process heightened by fierce anticipation.

Mouths mated, slowly and softly. Reed's right hand sunk into the thickness of her hair. His left arm tightened around her waist. Sharla's hands slid over his shoulders to lock around his neck. She tilted her head to mold her mouth to his.

The kiss was long and deep and sweet. It made them ravenous for more. Tongues tangled, tasting and exploring. Wondering and wanting culminated in a heady feast of mouths. Their bodies strained closer.

Reed slid his hand to Sharla's hips and drew her tightly against the cradle of his body. He was hard and throbbing, and he wanted her to know what she did to him with her kisses.

The feel of his arousal made her knees go weak and her breath catch in her throat. She tilted her head backwards as she broke the kiss and dragged air into her lungs. Reed scattered warm kisses over her face and neck. She moaned softly at the exquisite tension rippling between them.

"Is this just a male, female thing?" she said on a gasp as his hot mouth found the pulse at her throat. He gently sucked the sensitive flesh.

"No." His response was gruff as he strung kisses up her neck and recaptured her lips.

She welcomed his tongue into her mouth with uninhibited pleasure, then sucked gently until his whole body quaked against hers.

His arms tightened, his body grinding against hers in convulsive reaction to her erotic caresses. Blood pulsed through his body in a heated rush, then pooled in his loins.

The grinding pressure of his arousal against her belly created an ache even deeper within her. Her breasts swelled against his chest, her nipples tingling and tightening in need. She rubbed them against him in an effort to appease the sweet ache.

A groan rumbled from Reed's chest. He wanted to feel her skin sliding against his own. He wanted to bare her breasts, lavish them with kisses, and feast on their nipples until they grew diamond hard in his mouth. He wanted to kiss and taste every inch of her, and then he wanted to bury himself so deep inside of her that she'd become a part of him.

The wanting was so intense that it hurt. The need so fierce, that he trembled. The desire so savage that it scared the hell out of him. He was losing control, and that scared him even more.

He dragged his mouth from Sharla's and crushed her face against his shoulder while he fought for breath. Tremors shook him as he battled to rein his rampaging desire. It seemed an impossible task. He'd never been brought to the very edge of release in so short a time with so little provocation. The realization stunned him.

The room was quiet over the next few minutes except for the sound of their ragged breathing. Sharla's gradually regulated. His arms were still crushing her against his hard body, but the air no longer raced through her lungs in a tortured rush. She knew he was having more trouble calming his own breathing. His body was still rigid against hers; making her wonder if it was painful for him.

Reed needed to put some distance between them. He needed relief from the insistent throbbing, yet he found it difficult to let her go. His brain was telling him what he should do, but his body had a mind of its own.

She solved the problem by gently disentangling herself from his grip. She eased enough space between them to relieve some of the tension. When she lifted her gaze to Reed's, her breath caught in her throat. There was such turbulence in his golden gaze that she quivered in reaction.

He closed his eyes. It was time to regain control over his reluctant body. Mind over matter, he mentally commanded.

Sharla grasped his face between her hands. She wasn't quite sure what he was thinking, but she didn't want him to regret what they'd shared. "Don't be upset," she coaxed softly.

He dragged in another rough breath. "Are you telling me this was just a little kiss, and I don't have anything to worry about?"

She understood that things had almost gotten out of hand, but there was no damage done. "What are you worried about? Nothing horrible happened."

She didn't have a clue, he thought grimly. She'd ignited a fire in him that had nearly scorched both of them, but she hadn't done it on purpose. She really didn't know how close he'd come to taking her standing up, fully dressed.

"Let's just say I don't like losing control," he explained, stepping out of her reach.

She let her hands drop to her sides. Her eyes were watching him curiously, wondering why he was so upset with himself. "You didn't. You were the one who stopped."

But it was one of the hardest things he'd ever done in his life. Reed wasn't happy with the knowledge. He rarely lost control, and he didn't like it.

"I think I'd better find those boots and make a trip out to the plane." Maybe the freezing rain would cool his jets.

"Do you want some help? I'd like to see the plane."

"Not this trip," he said. "I'll give it a quick check and then bring our bags when I come back."

Eight

Sharla wandered around the house while Reed went out to the plane. His kisses had made her too restless to sit still, so she paced.

Her experience with wild, passionate embraces was pathetically limited. It wasn't for the lack of a passionate nature, but lack of men who stirred her. If she allowed her passion to surface, they usually got the wrong idea and assumed she wanted to go to bed with them. That's why she didn't normally take chances.

She hadn't planned to take a chance with Reed. He'd caught her by surprise and excited her with little effort. In fact, she couldn't remember ever being so wildly aroused by any man's kisses and caresses. The surge of desire had been so sudden and unexpected that neither of them had time to prepare their usual defenses.

Now what, she wondered? She knew Reed had been badly shaken by his loss of control. She'd been surprised and a little amazed, but not alarmed. Maybe that was naive, yet she trusted him.

She didn't want to admit, even to herself, that she might be falling in love with Reed Connors — that she might have been attracted to him for a very long time. He didn't want it. She didn't want it. Neither of them needed the complication. They had their own separate lives with demanding careers. Falling in love could be a real problem.

She mulled over the idea as she found her way back to the kitchen. Reed had already set meat out of the freezer and found potatoes to bake. Sharla unwrapped the steaks and washed the potatoes, placing everything in a neat row on the countertop. So much for her culinary skills.

Most men laughed when she told them she couldn't cook and didn't have any interest in learning. Then they were horrified when they realized she wasn't joking. Reed hadn't seemed the least bit concerned or disapproving. He understood about her flying.

Other men had said they understood her dedication to a demanding career. One particular man had made her believe he understood, but then he'd expected her to curtail some of her flying to accommodate his busy schedule. She'd told him to go to hell. But it had hurt. She'd given up hope of finding a man who could accept her just the way she was.

It was almost dark when Reed came back to the house. Sharla had been watching for him and quickly opened the door. He was carrying all their belongings plus her pilot's log. She closed the door and helped him with the bags.

"How's the Saratoga?" she asked anxiously.

He dropped his bag to the floor and shed his coat. "I shut the engine off after the crash. When I restarted it just now, it sounded fine. The left wing has a little dent, but it doesn't look serious enough to keep the plane grounded. The landing gear is tangled in the fence. I figure we can take care of that once the ice melts and you get some traction."

"Thank God!" she muttered fervently. "I wasn't looking forward to telling Daddy Bear he had to fly to Tennessee to retrieve my plane."

"Daddy Bear?" he repeated with a grin. He'd sworn he wouldn't let her enchant him again tonight. Two minutes in the house, and he was captivated.

"That was a slip of tongue," she insisted, her eyes sparkling with mischief. "It's an old nickname that Daddy loves, but doesn't want made public knowledge."

"So... I'm finally in the position to do a little bargaining." Reed had kicked off his boots and hung his coat up to dry. He grabbed all the luggage and headed to the bedrooms.

She followed. "What kind of bargaining?"

"A friendly little game of poker would probably keep my tongue from wagging."

Sharla stopped at the door of the room where he put her luggage. She propped her hands on her hips. "I suppose you expect me to let you win."

He dropped her bags on the bed, and then moved past her to put his in the room on the opposite side of the hall. "I don't want any easy wins, just a little handicap."

"Handicap?" she repeated indignantly. "Didn't I ask for a handicap earlier? Did I get any mercy? Oh, no, I got lectured on women's rights. What happened to men's rights and male ego and all that macho stuff?"

"That's for losers," he taunted. "I like to win."

"No kidding?" Sharla spouted, then convulsed into laughter. "Who'd have thought it?"

He loved the sound of her laughter. It was infectious, contagious. He loved the way her nose crinkled and her eyes sparkled when she was amused. He loved her wicked sense of humor and her playful nature. He loved her.

The admission squeezed his heart, knocking the breath out of his lungs. Love. He'd given up on it years ago. He'd never loved a woman. He'd made love to plenty. He'd shared his body, but never his heart. He didn't want to share it now, so he wouldn't think about it.

Sharla saw the turbulent emotion in his eyes and stilled her laughter. Her breath got caught in her throat.

"So, are we on for tonight?" he managed to ask when her curious expression finally snapped him out of his self-induced trance.

She lifted a brow at his phrasing. Reed's eyes took on a wicked gleam, and her pulse fluttered with excitement.

"We're talking poker here, aren't we?"

"Sure," he insisted, regaining his calm. "Strip poker, no handicaps, no extra layers of clothes."

"Don't you wish," she threw back at him. There was no way she'd play strip poker with a card cheat, even though the idea sent a wild little thrill through her.

"Chicken?" he taunted.

"Too smart for that old ploy," she retorted. She propped her hands on her hips and glared at him like her mother glared when someone didn't mind their manners.

Reed threw back his head and roared with laughter.

The deep, husky sound rippled along her nerve endings and brought a happy smile to her eyes. She really enjoyed making Reed Connors laugh. He'd never given her a chance to get to know him before this trip, and she was finding lots of things that she liked about her reluctant roommate.

"All right, all right," he conceded. "You can have one extra layer of clothes."

She just shook her head, not willing to even dignify that suggestion with a response as she turned and headed down the hallway.

"I didn't start dinner, because I wasn't sure when you'd be back," she said. "Now that you're here, you can cook, and I'll watch."

"That's mighty big of you, Ms. Prescott," he teased as he followed her to the kitchen. "Did you forget that I'm the customer and you're supposed to be seeing to my comfort?"

"My duties ended as soon as we climbed out of the plane," she insisted.

"You didn't climb, I carried you."

Sharla ignored the jibe. "I can set the table and make a pot of coffee," she told him. "That should count for something."

"It counts for setting the table and making a pot of coffee."

Such a sweet-talker, she thought, as she watched Reed start dinner with assured, economical movements. He had the steak under the broiler and the potatoes in the microwave before she could get the coffee brewing.

"Were you one of those children who had to fend for themselves? Is that why you're so efficient in the kitchen?"

"No."

She shook her head again, this time in disgust. Getting personal information from the man was a constant challenge. "Did your mother teach you how to cook?"

"Nope."

"Care to elaborate?"

Reed gave her a sharp glance. "Are you prying into my personal life again?"

"I'm trying to," she admitted. "But you're not the chattiest person I've ever tried to drill."

Her candor won her a grin from Reed. "My parents were very old fashioned. There was men's work and women's work. I learned to be self-sufficient after I left home."

He talked about his parents in the past tense. "Both of them are gone now?"

"They died last year, within months of each other. Both of natural causes. They were in their seventies." His mother hadn't wanted to live after his father had died. "I was one of those late-in-life babies."

He sounded as though the loss was still hard for him. "I'm sorry," she offered gently.

Reed's gaze met hers and he saw the compassion. He wondered if she was just being polite or if she could possibly realize how sensitive he still felt about the subject. He wasn't usually so easy to read. "I am, too."

"Did you grow up in DC?"

"Iowa." He didn't want to discuss it. "Are you going to set the table, or do I have to do that, too?"

Sharla figured she'd gotten as much information as she was likely to get for a while. She steered the conversation to more neutral topics while they waited for the food to cook, then ate in a companionable silence.

After the kitchen had been cleaned, Reed picked up a deck of cards and invited her to follow him to the living room.

"I'm ready for that game of strip poker now," he announced, his expression challenging.

"I'll bet you are," she scoffed, following him down the hallway. "But it might get a little boring if you're the only one playing."

"Spoilsport."

"You'd better believe it."

"Okay," he conceded on a heavy sigh as they crossed the room toward the hearth. "We'll have to play pretend strip poker."

Suspicion narrowed her eyes. "Pretend strip poker? Is that pretending to play poker or pretending to strip?"

Reed's grin was wicked. He sat on the floor and pulled the coffee table in front of him. After motioning her to sit opposite him, he explained. "Games of chance aren't any fun unless there's some incentive to win. If you won't agree to strip, we'll have to pretend. You can even keep score. Every time one of us loses, you write down what item of clothes we decide to forfeit."

"And the one who's naked first - strictly on paper - is the loser?" She got the drift, but wasn't too sure she wanted to participate.

"On paper only," he assured her, producing a scrap of paper and an ink pen.

"What are we playing?"

"Five card stud, dealer chooses the wild cards." Reed was already shuffling the cards.

Sharla slid her legs next to his under the table. It was an effort to ignore the surge of heat from the contact, so she shifted until they were no longer touching. Then she lost the first hand and put earring under her name on the paper.

"Earring?" he protested. "That's not clothes!"

"You didn't say anything about clothes," she reminded pleasantly. "You said I have to take something off. I put my earrings on, so I should be allowed to take them back off."

Reed scowled, but didn't argue. Over the next hour, she lost her other earring, her watch and both socks. She wished she'd put her shoes back on after dinner.

He'd only lost his socks, but her luck with the cards started to improve. He was the first to lose a major article of clothing. His expression was wicked as he started to unbutton his shirt.

"That's not necessary," she assured him immediately. "I'll just add shirt to your list of losses." She wished she didn't have such a vivid memory of how good his bare chest looked. She could almost see and feel the mass of golden curls.

Sharla lost her sweat suit in the next two hands. She knew it was ridiculous, but she felt herself blushing as she wrote down each item.

Reed felt the heat of her blush as if it were his own. "Getting chilly?" he taunted. His eyes gleamed devilishly. He slowly ran his gaze over the length of her as if she'd actually stripped to her underwear.

Sharla was anything but chilly. She blamed her heated reaction to his perusal on the nearness of the fireplace.

Silently vowing revenge, she won the next hand, costing Reed his jeans. She couldn't suppress her imagination. Even though they were both still fully clothed, she was visualizing him in nothing but underwear. Would they be briefs or boxers? More heat suffused her.

"Now we're both in our underwear," he mentioned unnecessarily. He liked the imagine the words provoked. "The game is getting really serious. No more Mr. Nice Guy. I'm not giving you another hand."

"Ha!" she countered. "You haven't given me anything. I've won fair and square." He was down to one article of clothing. She had two. It was the first time in her life she'd ever been grateful for a bra. The odds were definitely in her favor.

She won the next hand. Her eyes glittered with triumph. "That should just about make you naked, Mr. Connors," she quipped.

"I'm forfeiting my tee shirt," he said before getting up to put more logs on the fire.

Sharla was frowning when he slid his legs under the table again. She shot a glance at the open neck of his flannel shirt. "You're not wearing a T-shirt!"

Reed arrogantly cocked a brow. "How do you know that? Got any proof?"

Her gaze narrowed. "I can't see it."

"It's one of those kinds that doesn't show."

"And you're cheating," she charged.

"Are you lodging a formal complaint?"

"You'd better believe it."

"Then we're even. We've both contested losses today. Unfortunately, there's no protest committee to hear our complaints, so we'll just have to keep playing."

Sharla fumed, but decided to get even. When she lost the next hand, she forfeited her T-shirt.

Reed protested. "You don't have a tee shirt. I know because I dressed you earlier."

"You didn't dress me! I dressed myself."

"I brought you the clothes."

"And how do you know I didn't find one while you were outside and put it on under my sweatshirt?"

"I can't see it," he charged.

"It's one of those kinds —"

"All right, all right," he growled. The glare being directed at her slowly turned to a roguish grin. "And you accuse me of cheating."

"Turnabout — and all that stuff," she defended, eyes dancing. "And I'm getting stiff sitting like this. There has to be another way."

They pulled their legs from beneath the table and moved it out of their way. Reed leaned his back against the sofa and crossed his legs in front of him. Sharla sat Indian style, with her right side against the sofa, facing him.

"It's my deal," he said, shuffling the cards and using the floor for their flat surface.

"I always seem to lose when you deal."

"Which means you win when you deal. Are you stacking the deck?"

Sharla shook her head in resignation. The man was impossible, and he dealt her the worst hand she'd had all night. She didn't even have a pair.

"Give me four cards."

Reed's grin widened as he passed her four new cards. He didn't take any himself.

"What did you say was wild?" she asked hopefully. The new cards weren't much better than the old ones.

"I didn't. What have you got?"

"A pair of fives," Sharla mumbled.

He laughed as he showed her his full house. "What will it be this time, Ms. Prescott?" His eyes lit with anticipation.

Sharla actually felt as though she were stripping. She'd moved the scorecard to the sofa, and her hand wasn't too steady when she wrote the word "bra" under her list of lost articles.

Reed couldn't help wondering how her bare breasts would look and feel in his hands and his mouth. The thought brought a tightening to his loins. His voice was a little rough as he teased her.

"That should make us even again. Unless you're wearing something else I wouldn't expect."

Sharla witnessed the slight darkening of his eyes when he considered her braless state. She wondered if the idea affected him as strongly as it did her. Her nipples tingled, and she was tempted to cross her arms over her chest.

"We're even," she admitted. "But it's my deal."

She could hardly believe that she dealt them both a pair of sevens, a pair of kings, and a trey. . . "That makes it a tie."

"That means we play one more hand," Reed argued. "My deal."

"Let's call it a draw."

He shook his head. He wasn't ready to quit. Watching Sharla blush and imagining the slow removal of her clothes was driving him crazy but it was the most fascinating card game he'd ever played.

"I'm not playing," she argued, refusing to touch the cards he dealt to her. "We have a tie."

"Ties are for sissies," he insisted. "You have to play to win. Treys are wild."

"Then we can switch to gin rummy."

"More sissy stuff."

Reed picked up five cards and grasped her right hand, intending to make her take hold of them. He realized his mistake instantly. The simple touch was a spark that lit the fuse to dynamite. Lightning struck at the point of contact and quivered over both of them. Their gazes locked in surprise.

Time seemed to go into slow motion as Reed let the cards fall and tightened his grip on Sharla's hand. He turned toward her and wrapped his other arm around her shoulders, pulling her closer. She offered no resistance.

He didn't ease his grip until she was stretched across his lap. Small talk escaped him. "You're beautiful," he managed as he dipped his head to steal a kiss.

Sharla thrilled at his compliment. She knew he didn't give them lightly. The first touch of his mouth made her hungry for more, so she grasped his face between her hands and urged him to deepen the kiss.

His tongue shot into her mouth with barely leashed control. He was starving for the taste of her. He caressed every inch of her mouth with a greedy tongue, seeking all of her honeyed sweetness.

Her senses were already heightened to unbearable levels. Reed felt warm and hard everywhere their bodies touched. He smelled musky and male. Low, hungry moans rumbled from deep in his throat.

When their lips parted briefly, their gazes tangled and reflected a consuming heat. His were alive with need. She quivered in response and recaptured his mouth with hers. Her tongue was bold as it also tangled with his.

Reed tightened his hold on her, pulling her more fully along the length of him. He gently sucked her tongue and felt her body quivering against his. It made his blood race and his chest constrict.

Sharla stretched her arms around his neck and pressed her breasts against the solid wall of his chest. She pulled his head closer and coaxed his tongue into her mouth. Her legs slid between his hard thighs, and both their bodies reacted to the searing contact.

He groaned. She echoed the reaction. Their mouths parted for air and to shower kisses elsewhere, eyes, noses, and cheeks. Then they were kissing again and exploring the sweet sensuality of being so closely entwined.

A few more minutes of Sharla's kisses convinced Reed that he was either the luckiest man in the world or the biggest fool. To continue this sexual torture was insane. He was already too hot and too hard to play games. He had to stop it or take it to a natural conclusion. He didn't know if they could handle that just yet. There was no doubt in his mind that he wanted to make love to Sharla. He wanted her in every sense of the word, but he had no idea what she might want. He knew very little about her personal habits, and nothing about her love life.

When he next dragged his mouth from hers. Reed eased them both to the floor where they laid facing each other. He forced himself to breathe deeply. Then he opened his eyes and stared directly into Sharla's eyes.

"I go a little crazy when you kiss me," he admitted gruffly.

She kept a firm grip on his neck with one hand, but sank the fingers of her other hand into the thickness of his hair. "The feeling's mutual."

"I want to make love to you," he confessed in a broken tone, his eyes dark with emotion. "I want to spend the rest of the night kissing and exploring every inch of you. If you don't feel the same way, then we'd better slow down and keep some space between us."

A shudder coursed through Sharla. Her eyes grew wide and luminous as they searched his. There was no doubting his sincerity. The desire was alive and hot in his unflinching gaze. He wanted her, but he was giving her the chance to stop and consider the consequences. He couldn't know that she'd never made love with a man — that she'd never been irresistibly tempted until tonight.

"I don't sleep around," she told him, her tone shy and honest, "so I'm not prepared for that kind of intimacy."

Reed growled softly as their gazes locked in a deeply searching fashion. She wasn't shocked by his admission, only hesitant. He could easily relieve her concern over-birth control, but first he needed to be sure she really wanted to make love with him.

"I'm not in the habit of sleeping with every woman I meet, either," he assured her, then confessed, "I've wanted you for a very long time, but I don't want to make love unless you're absolutely sure about it."

Sharla's eyes widened at his declaration of wanting her. Had he really been fighting an attraction all the time he'd seemed so indifferent? If *so*, why?

Her palm slid to cup the side of his face. Her thumb stroked his cheek, but her eyes never left his. She asked him why he'd fought the attraction.

It was Reed's turn to hesitate. He wasn't ready to admit his love. The feelings were too complex and too new to him. Neither did he want to risk her disbelief or rejection.

"Nothing will ever be easy and uncomplicated between us. That's why I've kept my distance. I don't usually welcome complications in my life."

Sharla knew what he meant. It had never been easy for her to deal with him, either. She'd always felt the volatile chemistry between them, despite the fact that the relationship had been strictly professional until today.

It was a relief to realize he'd felt it just as strongly. She didn't know if his feelings went deeper than the physical, but hers were much more complex. She wasn't sure that making love with him would be the smartest thing she'd ever done, yet she wanted it anyway.

"I've always found you attractive," she admitted. "But you seemed interested in everybody but me."

"Defensive measures."

Sharla smiled slightly. "It doesn't work."

She was referring to his dating her sisters in hopes that the attraction wasn't anything special. They both knew that the experiment was a failure.

"I had to try," he murmured as his lips lightly brushed across hers.

"Why?"

"Because what I felt for you was too strong and too dangerous."

"How was it dangerous?"

"To my peace of mind."

"Oh." Sharla gave the idea some thought. Was Reed admitting that what he felt for her was more than physical? Could he possibly be as fascinated with her as she was with him?

Her lips parted the instant his mouth settled on hers, and she welcomed the thrust of his tongue with a soft moan. Whatever was happening between them, it was the sweetest, most fierce feeling she'd ever known. She couldn't get enough of him. It was obvious that Reed experienced the same nagging, insatiable hunger.

Sharla arched closer to his hard length, and he pressed her flat against the floor. He eased himself over her without crushing her with his weight. Then he began to scour her face with hot, wet kisses.

"If you don't want this, then tell me to stop right now," he ground out roughly, pinning her with glittering eyes. "I'm one big ache, and the hurting isn't going to stop until I put some distance between us or love you completely."

His husky declaration stole her breath. She wanted him, too. She ached, too, but she was aware of the risks.

He read the concern in her eyes. "You don't have to worry about an unwanted pregnancy. I promise I can protect you."

"How?" she asked in a hoarse whisper. Did he carry protection with him at all times?

Reed closed his eyes. His chest tightened, and he dreaded voicing the facts, but knew she deserved the truth. "I'm sterile," he managed. His tone was rough, almost defensive, as if he expected her to condemn him in some way.

He'd never bothered to explain his condition to other women because he always used artificial protection. He didn't want anything between him and Sharla.

"You're sure?"

"Laboratory tested, proved positive," he rasped, his eyes daring her to disbelieve. "The odds are about one in a million."

Now she understood his intensity earlier in the day when they'd discussed having children. She wondered if his condition really bothered him. His defensive attitude implied that it did.

Was he a loner because he didn't want emotional involvement with a woman who might demand more than he could offer? Did he make love only with women who had no desire for children? Where did she fit in the scheme of things?

Reed saw the questions in her eyes, but was glad she didn't voice them and ask him to explain his emotional needs. He didn't have the words to explain.

"I want you," he whispered against her lips while he gently stroked her hair. "I'm not asking for anything else. I just want to love you."

Sharla wanted it, too. Nothing else seemed to matter right now. Her body was vibrantly alive and singing with anticipation. She wanted him to satisfy the need he'd inflamed.

They shared another long, deep kiss that brought forth matching moans of pleasure.

"Trust me?"

She couldn't seem to find her voice, but she nodded in agreement.

Reed rose to his feet and offered a hand to assist her. When she was standing beside him, he bent and lifted her into his arms. She slid her arms around his neck.

"The fire's nice, but the floor's too hard," he explained, carrying her to his bedroom. Once there, he pulled back the covers, eased her onto the bed, and switched on the bedside lamp. "I want to see you. Do you mind?"

Her throat was too tight for response, so she nodded her head again. Her eyes never left Reed's. The dark intensity of his golden gaze made her feel incredibly special. She hoped he wouldn't find her a disappointment.

With considerable effort, he controlled his desire for quick relief of the explosive pressure in his loins. He was aching, but he wanted their first time to be special. After waiting three years, he didn't want to be rushed.

He didn't know how experienced Sharla was, but he knew she never lacked for male attention. She was beautiful, and he was sure she attracted men everywhere she went. He didn't want to be just one of many. He wanted to love her as no one else ever had or ever would.

Stretching out beside her on the bed, be shifted close, buried his face in the satin tresses splayed on either side of her head, and inhaled deeply. After rubbing his cheek in the sweet-smelling softness, he scattered kisses up her throat and to her lips.

Sharla had been lying perfectly still, but the touch of his mouth on hers reawakened the barely banked fires within her. She clasped her arms around his shoulders and pulled him closer, deepening their kiss by first stroking, then sucking his tongue.

She swallowed Reed's low groan and felt the tension quicken in his body. The hard length of his arousal pressed against her thigh, and his reaction to her caresses excited her more than she would ever have imagined.

Reed dragged his mouth from hers and warned himself to be careful. Her eager responses could easily shatter his control. The feel and scent of her made him dizzy with pleasure, and he drew back.

"Too many clothes," he complained, sliding down the bed to remove her socks. She was startled at first, when he grasped one foot and began to gently knead it.

"Relax," he coaxed, feeling her tension. He rubbed his thumbs over the balls of her foot, and then stroked the arch. "Just relax and let me love you for a while."

Sharla expelled a pent-up breath. She was really tense, but his hands were working magic on her feet. It felt wonderful. She moaned softly and gave him a shy smile.

Reed held her gaze while he slowly removed her sweatpants, baring long, silky legs. He caught his breath as his hands slid over her thighs and calves. Then he treated her legs to the same slow, thorough massage he'd given her feet.

His bands were hard and callused against her bare skin, yet they gave her only pleasure. He brought every nerve and muscle alive with warmth. She was almost sorry when his fingers slipped up her thighs to her hips. She offered no resistance when he grabbed the hem of her sweatshirt, pulled it over her head, and tossed it aside.

As soon as Reed was within her reach, Sharla wrapped her arms around his shoulders and dragged him close for a kiss. She couldn't seem to get enough of his kisses. His mouth was hard and demanding — hers met it with equal demand.

"You keep distracting me," he complained gruffly as he nibbled on her lips. "I'm trying to get you out of your clothes."

"You have all yours on," she countered, reaching for the buttons of his shirt.

He helped unfasten his shirt, tugged it from his jeans, and tossed it to the floor. Then he reached for her again.

She halted him by splaying her hands on his chest. "You're not wearing a tee shirt," she admonished softly, then dipped her head to string kisses across the smooth flesh of his shoulders.

The feel of her warm, wet mouth on his skin set his blood on fire. He clutched at Sharla's head, sinking his fingers into the softness of her hair.

"You'd better stop that," he warned.

She immediately halted her exploration. "You don't like it?" she asked hesitantly.

He clasped her head in both hands and drew her mouth back to his. "I like it too much," he mumbled against her lips. Her relieved sigh whispered against his tongue, and he took his time savoring the sweetness of her mouth.

His hands slid around her body to unclip her bra. It joined the growing pile of discarded clothing. Reed allowed himself an instant to absorb the sight of her long, golden body and full, rounded breasts. He watched her dark nipples tighten as his eyes settled on them, and then he had to know the feel of her.

Sharla felt a rush of heat as his glittering gaze lingered on her breasts. Her nipples tingled and tightened until she couldn't stand it any longer.

She reached for him and pulled his hard chest onto her softer one. The contact ignited an electrical charge that sent shock waves over every inch of her body.

They moaned in unison. Reed closed his eyes and rubbed his chest back and forth across the tight peaks of her breasts. The bold evidence of her arousal was a sweet kind of torment.

Her fingers tightened on his shoulders as she felt the erotic tickle of his chest hair against her nipples. "I like that," she gasped on a broken sigh.

"I like it, too," he said, pressing himself against her breasts and captured her mouth again. "I like everything about you," he insisted, and then plundered her lips with his tongue.

"Your sweet mouth —" he began.

"— your soft breasts." He slid down her body and cupped a breast in each hand, lifting and molding them tenderly.

His tone was hoarse when he continued. "Your beautiful, hard nipples." He used the very tip of his tongue to stroke and tease one tight bud to pebbled hardness.

It was the most exquisite torture imaginable. Sharla's breath broke as he bathed her nipple with his hot, wet tongue. Then he grasped it firmly between a finger and thumb while his mouth shifted to the other nipple and gave it equal attention.

A convulsive shudder ripped through her when he continued to tease her with his tongue, teeth, and lips. Her fingers clenched and unclenched in his hair and her body developed a will of its own.

Reed felt Sharla begin to shift restlessly beneath him and sucked her nipple deeper into his mouth. Her soft whimpers were music to his ears. He wanted her mindless with desire. He wanted her as hard and aching as he was.

Sharla wanted him out of his jeans. She wanted to feel all of him, but his mouth was driving her crazy. She couldn't seem to get anything past her throat that wasn't a moan, so she let her hands slide to the waistband of his jeans.

He didn't need any further invitation to unfasten and kick off his jeans and shorts. He breathed a sigh of relief as his throbbing body was released from confinement. In the next instant, he had Sharla's last barrier of clothing tugged down her legs and tossed aside.

She felt a jolt of alarm as she lay naked and vulnerable beside him. Her gaze flew to Reed's. His were sweeping hotly over the length of her. They were turbulent with admiration and desire as they met hers.

"You are gorgeous," he ground out roughly. He splayed a hand possessively across her abdomen and felt her flesh quiver. He pressed a hot kiss on her lips before returning to his adoration of her breasts.

While his tongue flicked alternately at each nipple, he pressed his hard, aroused flesh against her thigh and let his hand trail to the soft mound of curls between her legs.

Sharla's breath hissed out in an agony of response when she felt him touch her in such an intimate fashion. Her fingers clawed at his shoulders as flames coursed from her breasts to her womb. He was trying to drive her out of her mind.

When she began to writhe against his stroking fingers, he nearly lost control. His erection surged against her, begging for relief. Then he pulled her body completely under his. He gently ground his hips against her abdomen, and felt her body bucking against his in demand.

Stretching, he flattened himself along Sharla's silken length and captured her mouth for a savage, plundering kiss. Their mouths were locked as his straining manhood searched and found the secret haven it sought.

Unable to hold back any longer, he thrust gently, but firmly into her, met a slight resistance, then sank more deeply into her velvet warmth. A scalding release followed his realization that he was the first man who'd ever been sheathed by her smooth, silky body.

He collapsed on top of Sharla. They were both breathing raggedly. Reed's whole body was weak and trembling. After a minute, he managed to support his weight on his forearms so that he could look into her eyes.

"Why didn't you tell me?" he demanded hoarsely.

Sharla's eyes were wide and troubled. She wished she knew what he was thinking and feeling. "Would it have made a difference?" she whispered.

"Hell, yes."

She'd expected as much. "That's why I didn't want to make an issue of it."

He rested his forehead against hers. "Baby, you don't have any idea what it does to a man."

She realized it was difficult for him to express his feelings on the subject. She hoped that meant he was pleased instead of alarmed. "I'm not a naive little girl, Reed. It was my decision and my choice," she reminded softly.

"Why me? Why now?"

"It's what I wanted."

There was little he could say or do to counter that argument. He'd wanted her too desperately — still wanted her. He also wanted to make sure it was an occasion that she'd remember with pleasure the rest of her life.

"You're still tense," he declared huskily while brushing kisses across her lips. "Try to relax again and let me show you all the pleasure you can find."

First his mouth devoured hers, then his lips strung kisses down her neck and fastened on a nipple. His hand slid between their bodies —

searched and found extremely sensitive flesh. Sharla bucked beneath him when he stroked the spot where their bodies were still locked. He felt the joining of flesh and groaned in possessive pleasure.

Her body was going wild again. Reed's mouth on her breasts speared heat against her womb where their bodies were joined. She was drowning in erotic sensations — his swelling flesh buried within her, his loins grinding against hers, and the insistent massaging of his finger and thumb.

She couldn't stand it. "Reed!"

"Don't fight it, baby," he urged as he felt her straining against his hand. "Relax and let go."

"No. I can't," she whimpered, throwing her head from side to side in agitation. She tried to shift her hips, but the twisting and turning only served to heighten the tension.

"Reed!" she screamed as she felt her body exploding with a pleasure so intense it was unbearable. Shudders ripped through her, shocking her with their strength. Reed gathered her in his arms and held her tightly.

The deep, convulsive contractions of her release clutched at his body and stroked him to renewed arousal. His straining flesh was throbbing in demand before the trembling of her body had quieted.

The feel of his throbbing arousal and the rekindling of the fire in her own body stunned her. Her eyes were wide and amazed as they met Reed's.

His husky laughter was purely masculine and filled with triumph. He gently thrust his hips against her and watched her eyes dilate with pleasure. "Want to try again?" he teased devilishly.

"I couldn't," she argued. She was still hot and flushed from her first experience with total satisfaction in the arms of a man.

He smoothed his hands over the damp flesh of her rib cage, then concentrated on her breasts, squeezing and coaxing her nipples to tightness again. He trapped her whimper of surprise with his mouth and slowly began to rock his body against hers.

When she started arching up to meet him, he began to thrust in and out of her softness with increasing vigor. Sharla sobbed and clutched at his shoulders. He grasped her thrashing legs and brought them around his hips.

She was spiraling out of control again. Sharla felt the waves hit her a second time and cried out his name. Her breathing was tortured, her body sated, but he allowed her only a brief instant of pleasure before he started to increase the tension again.

"I can't stand it!" she screamed, raking his shoulders, with her fingers as the tension of each powerful thrust drew her into another whirlwind of sensation.

"You feel so good!" Reed bit out as he felt the tension in his own body coil to a tight, painful knot of excitement. "So hot and tight," he rasped, clutching her hips tighter as he felt her feminine muscles begin to contract again. His own explosive reaction to her climax was the hottest fulfillment he'd ever known.

His trembling arms wouldn't support him this time, so he rolled to his side and dragged Sharla with him. He held her close to his chest as they both fought to drag air into their lungs.

Their ragged breathing was the only sound in the room for a long time after their bodies were replete. When Reed had regained some strength, he lifted a hand to stroke sweat-dampened curls off her face. Her long lashes fluttered, then she lifted her lids and gazed at him with shimmering eyes.

Concern darkened his eyes. "I didn't hurt you, did I?" In the heat of passion, he hadn't given much thought to her inexperience.

Sharla couldn't get words past a throat thick with emotion, but she shook her head negatively. He'd made their loving more special than she'd dreamed possible. The pain she'd expected had been little more than straining pressure. She draped an arm over his waist and gave him a warm, intimate smile.

Reed relaxed and returned her smile as he brushed a kiss across her lips. He ached to tell her how much he loved her, but didn't want her to think his feelings were based solely on the amazing sex they'd shared. His love would have to remain a secret.

When a chill raced over Sharla's body, he hugged her closer. "Ready to take a shower?"

Her eyes widened. "You can't possibly have any energy," she argued.

Reed just grinned and slid out of bed. He lifted her in his arms, loving the feel of her naked flesh pressed against his own.

Sharla sighed and wrapped her arms around his neck. She had a feeling he never ran out of energy. "You're going to break your back if you keep carrying me around."

"'Not this ole farm boy," he countered, taking her down the dark hallway toward the kitchen. "I grew up hefting feed bags and hay bales that weighed more than you."

"You were raised on a farm?" He'd told her he was from Iowa, but she hadn't thought to ask where he'd actually lived.

"Farming's a major industry in Iowa," he explained as he stood her on her feet and turned on the bathroom light.

Sharla blinked and blushed. She wasn't overly modest, but neither was she accustomed to parading around in the nude with a totally immodest and naked man.

Reed chuckled. "You'll get used to it," he declared.

She ignored his teasing, adjusted the faucets, and slipped behind the shower curtain. Within seconds, Reed had joined her. He proceeded to give her a slow, thorough lesson in tandem bathing. By the time they were clean, they were thoroughly aroused again.

They didn't make it back to the bedroom. Reed sat down on a kitchen chair and drew her down on his lap. She didn't need any coaching on how to best lock their bodies together.

He moaned as he felt her heat surrounding him again. Gripping her hips, he guided her erotic movements until they established a rhythm that eventually brought intense release. After another quick visit to the bathroom, he carried her back to bed. This time they found her silk pajama top. He helped her don it and tucked her into bed. Their good night kiss was long and slow and deep.

"You're not going to bed?" She was half asleep already. She hadn't gotten much sleep the previous night, and now she was exhausted.

"I'll be back in a few minutes," he promised, "I just want to try the radio again and turn off the lights.

The radio still crackled with static. Reed assumed the tower was coated with ice and figured it would be going on noon tomorrow before everything thawed. He checked windows and doors, switched off lights and headed back to the bedroom.

Sharla was sound asleep when he crawled into bed with her. She snuggled against him like a trusting child, and his heart swelled with love. He wanted her trust, her loyalty, and her love — even if he knew he had very little to offer in return.

He'd been disappointing the people who loved him all his life. He'd disappointed his parents by not staying on the farm they'd spent their lives building for him. He'd disappointed his ex-wife by not loving her as much as she'd loved him. His inability to father a child had just been another in a long line of disappointments to his family.

Despite Sharla's insistence that she didn't want children, the time would come when she'd change her mind. He couldn't risk a long-term relationship with her. He couldn't stand the thought of ultimately disappointing her, too.

The silk of her pajama top slid seductively against his hands as he stroked her back from shoulders to hips. He drew her tightly against him and felt his body stir in response. He knew she was tired and probably sore, so he mentally commanded his body to relax.

He would never get enough of her. He'd known it before he made love to her the first time. Loving Sharla wasn't something that could be enjoyed and forgotten. She was too special. She was his - an extension of his body- ensconced in his heart and soul. He couldn't promise her a future, but he would offer her his love until she wanted more than he was capable of giving. He refused to think about a time when she'd grow dissatisfied with what they shared.

It was late when Reed finally drifted to sleep, but he slept deeply. The sun shining through the window woke him the next morning. A glance at his watch put the time at nine o'clock.

He yawned, stretched, and then turned more fully toward Sharla. She was sleeping on her back. Her hair was a wild tumble around her face. It created the perfect frame for her lovely features. He reached out and gently touched the edge of the bruise on her forehead, relieved that it wasn't swollen or feverish. Next he traced the full curves of her mouth. Her lips parted slightly, and he felt the warmth of her breath against his finger. The slight puff of warmth inflamed him... and he was suddenly starved for her again.

The muscles in his chest constricted. The rest of his body was already tight with need. Their brief interval of isolation would end today, and he wanted to make her his one more time before the world and duty intruded.

He decided to wake her in a very sensual fashion. The red silk of her pajama top lovingly outlined the firm mounds of her breasts. It was twisted around her waist and hiked up on her bare thighs. His hand dropped to the buttons.

Sharla's tongue darted out to lick her lips. They tickled. She hovered between sleep and waking — not yet ready to give lip the peace of slumber. A chill touched her, and she shifted in search of warmth.

As her hands sought blankets, she felt the delicious thrill of moist warmth on one nipple. Warm, callused fingers engulfed her other breast and that nipple was slowly stroked to warmth. A groan rumbled from low in her throat.

Reed. Her drowsy brain identified the source of so much pleasure. When his hot, open mouth began to suck more demandingly, her fingers knotted into fists. Her legs began to shift restlessly. Heat spiraled from breast to womb.

Sharla opened her heavy eyes and saw his head nestled against her breast. A sob caught in her throat. How she loved this man! She knew now that she'd been in love with him since the first time they'd met and sparks had flown. She'd been so blind, unable to recognize the signs, but now there was no doubt in her mind.

Sinking her fingers in his hair, she clung to him while he continued to adore her with his lips, teeth, and tongue. She was sure he didn't want a pledge of undying love, but she couldn't help feeling it. Keeping the knowledge to herself was going to be a test of her emotional strength.

"Good morning," she whispered in a voice hoarse with sleep and arousal.

Reed gave her a heavy-lidded smile, rose to brush a kiss across her mouth, and then slid back down her body to find more sensitive areas for his kisses.

Her stomach muscles clenched as she felt the soft caress of his lips. Her thighs quivered and her toes curled as his mouth continued its searing downward path. Sharla uttered a small cry as his wet caresses extended to her feet, then started a return journey up her legs.

"Reed!" She managed his name in a husky plea.

He loved the sound of his name on her lips. He loved the way her body trembled for him. He loved the taste, smell, and feel of her. It was sweet agony to treat his senses.

She slid her hands onto his shoulders as his upward progress brought his mouth to her stomach. She kneaded the smooth, firm skin of his neck, shoulders, and arms as his body slowly slid over hers. When his tongue returned to her breasts, her hands clutched him feverishly.

"You're making a total wanton out of me, Connors!" she accused in a jagged breath.

"Good," he mumbled against her breast. He wanted her totally uninhibited.

Sharla wanted to touch and taste him the same way he was exploring her but the desire he generated left her weak. When his eager mouth and hands started teasing both her nipples at the same time, she arched against him and wrapped her legs around his muscled thighs.

Reed didn't need any further invitation. He joined their bodies in one smooth flex of muscles. Sharla's indrawn breath made him go still until he realized that it was a gasp of pleasure. He continued to pleasure them both.

When their bodies were once again sated, he enveloped her in a tight embrace. He wanted to hold her as much in the aftermath of loving as he had at the height of passion.

"I could get addicted to this kind of wake-up call," she told him, nuzzling his neck with her cheek.

His smile was contented. "It's a habit I could learn to live with."

She couldn't help wondering what he wanted, if anything, in the way of a relationship. Once this assignment was over, would he just disappear until he needed another charter? Was she just one of many women he made love to? Would he promise to call and then go his own way?

She'd never allowed a man to stake any kind of claim on her time. Her career had always been all-important. That wasn't likely to change, but Reed represented a whole new aspect in relationships. What she felt for him was unique in her experience. She wanted to spend more time with him. She wanted to stake a claim herself.

"What now?" she asked quietly.

He'd been wondering the same thing. Neither of them were used to compromising. They both had crazy schedules with little personal time to spare. He knew that she'd never had another lover, but he didn't know if there were special men in her life.

He turned to look at her. "Will I have to stand in line to see you on a regular basis?"

She smiled. It was a relief to hear him say he wanted to see her. "There's no line of men," she assured him. "How about you?"

"No special men in my life, either," he teased, then grunted when she yanked at the hair on his chest.

"I'm glad to hear that," she sassed. "How about special women?"

He turned to pull her more fully into his arms. "Just one," Reed insisted. His eyes and tone assured Sharla that she was his one woman.

"Will I get to see you often?" She was already suffering from withdrawal, and they hadn't even been parted.

His eyes darkened. He wasn't going to get tired of seeing her. "As often as you want."

"What about our work?"

"We'll find a way to balance schedules."

"Promise?" she queried in a whisper, cupping his cheek in her palm.

"Promise."

Ten

By the time they'd showered, dressed, and eaten breakfast, the sun was rapidly melting the ice outside the house. The telephone still wasn't working, but they were fortunate not to have lost the electricity.

Sharla volunteered to clean the kitchen while Reed checked the radio equipment. She'd just finished putting the dishes away when she heard him swearing profusely.

"What's wrong?" she asked as she moved into the living room and joined him by the desk. All she heard was static on the radio.

"I got a call through to Nashville." He turned his attention to her. "I was able to tell the officials we're okay and that we had an emergency landing, but then I lost contact again."

"So you couldn't get in touch with your boss and warn them not to bring Sandy here?" she asked, controlling an urge to smooth her fingers over the deep frown line on his forehead.

"No." Reed's tone was grim.

"Do you think the agency pilot will bring her here despite the weather?"

"Probably," he growled in disgust. "Ed's supposed to fly in here sometime this morning, and he won't alter the plans unless he gets a direct order from Sanders or me."

"There's no chance of rerouting them?"

He sighed and raked a hand through his hair in frustration. There was little chance of getting in touch with Ed before he arrived. Not without a radio. Now Sharla was caught in the middle of the battle, and Sandy's safety was at serious risk again.

"There's a chance that our radio transmission will improve before Ed lands. We have an alternate location where Sandy can be taken once they realize this place isn't safe."

"Do you think Rudolph's men know where we are?"

"There's a good chance. The transmission was poor, but they said our flight had been listed as missing. I didn't give them the coordinates, but they picked up our distress signal last night and know approximately where we landed," he explained. "Rudolph's men might have gotten the same information last night."

He'd had serious reservations about the decoy plan from the beginning, and nobody had taken adverse weather conditions into consideration. His boss' well-made plans had been shot to hell. All they'd accomplished was to lead Rudolph's men right to Sandy — endangering Sharla in the process. All he could do now was make the best of a bad situation. It wouldn't be the first time.

"The airport officials will notify your family," he added in an afterthought.

Sharla moved closer and perched on the edge of the desk near him. "That's a relief."

His nerves jangled with awareness as she shifted closer to him. He studied her lovely features. "They've been hearing from Dee every few hours. She told them you'd made an emergency landing."

Their gazes locked, and his tone grew thoughtful. "She didn't know where you'd landed, but she told the authorities that your plane might be crippled and that you might have a head injury."

Sharla smiled and touched a finger to the scrape on her forehead. "I told you she wouldn't be satisfied until she knew where I was and what had happened. Did anyone believe her?"

"Enough to pass on the information," Reed said. "It's hard to comprehend — even with proof of the extrasensory traits — but Dee must be persuasive."

"She never mentions the ESP. She calls it women's intuition. Sometimes it still amazes me," she admitted. "And I've had years to get used to it."

"Do you think she'll try to find us?" Reed didn't welcome any further complications.

"Not as long as my family is assured that we're all right. They'll wait until they hear from me. They know I'll call if the Saratoga is seriously damaged," Sharla explained, frowning at the thought. "I wish the phone worked."

"It's a risk to keep our radio frequency open, but I don't have much choice," he said, giving in to the urge to touch her. Her hands felt small and soft as he took them in his own. "I can only hope that the wrong people won't pick up the signal and determine our exact location."

"I understand." She squeezed his hand, hating the fact that she was an added worry for him. "Maybe the phone service will be returned soon."

"Maybe, it depends on where the line is out of commission. If it's at the point of origination — not here at the cabin — my boss will have the service reestablished as soon as possible."

"How soon do you expect Agent Waites?"

"Anytime. He's a good mechanic, so I'll have him make a quick safety check of your plane. Hopefully we can be headed in different directions before anyone can find a cabin as isolated as this one."

Sharla hated the strain in his tone. She decided to tease him a little. "How about a game of gin while we wait?"

Reed's eyes glinted with admiration and delight. Despite the gravity of their situation, she was being a good sport, and he immediately reacted to the challenge in her voice. He rose from the chair and pulled her into his arms.

"Wouldn't you rather play strip poker?" he asked. She was wearing one of her jumpsuits. He wondered how quickly she could lose it.

"The pretend kind?" she asked in a saucy tone.

"I like the real thing," he said in a deep growl. Then he lowered his head to steal a kiss.

She leaned closer and wrapped her arms around his waist. Her mouth was welcoming — her tongue greeted his with obvious relish. Warmth permeated from one to the other, jolting their nervous systems with ripples of excitement. The kiss escalated until they were both gasping for air.

Reed finally dragged his mouth from hers and pressed his cheek against hers. "Lady, you're a walking, breathing, kissing temptation."

Sharla's response was husky with emotion. "What's wrong with a little temptation?"

"Not a damn thing," he swore, dropping a swift, hard kiss on her lips, "except I have work to do."

"And we'll be having company soon."

"That, too, and we need to be prepared."

She stepped out of his arms with a resigned expression. "I want to check out the Saratoga."

"The ice is melting fast. Ed can supply a little manpower when he gets here. I'd like to get your plane turned around and ready to fly out as soon as possible."

"If the Saratoga is flight-worthy, do you want me to fly to Nashville or back to Lexington?"

"I want you to head for the nearest airport and have the plane thoroughly checked. Then I want you to go home," Reed insisted as he ushered her down the hallway toward the bedrooms.

"What about you?"

"I'll go with Ed."

"And Sandy?" She didn't think that was a good idea. "Won't that make you all a little too vulnerable?"

He hesitated in the doorway of the room they'd shared. "I don't want you any more involved than you already are."

Sharla didn't want him taking extra risks to protect her. "I know, but I am involved. Wouldn't it be more confusing for Rudolph's men if we continued to Nashville, and Ed went a separate way with Sandy?"

He swiftly rejected the idea. "Once Sandy gets here, I'm not letting her out of my sight until she's testified at the second trial and can be processed through our protection program."

Sharla let the subject drop and went into the room where her flight bag was stored. She hadn't used the bed, so there was nothing to straighten. It took only a few minutes to collect her belongings and carry them to the living room.

Reed had his bag. He was strapping a shoulder holster on over his short-sleeved tee shirt. The sight of it momentarily startled her, making her more aware of the constant danger in his line of work.

His gaze met hers. "It's part of my job."

It was a simple reminder. He made no apologies for what he was. She understood, yet couldn't help being concerned. It was something she needed to accept, just like he accepted her devotion to flying. She gave him a smile.

Reed relaxed. He'd tensed when she went still at the sight of his gun, but her smile of acceptance relieved him. He knew she didn't have any great love for the Marshal Service. He'd have to help her understand all the good that they did.

The sound of an approaching aircraft immediately diverted their attention. Reed silently cursed himself for not concentrating on his duties. He picked up the radio receiver, but couldn't reach the incoming plane.

"You stay here while I go make sure that's Ed," he ordered as he pulled on a jacket and headed for the door.

Sharla's expression was derisive as she watched him go. She wasn't used to taking orders, even ones that were issued for her protection. He was obviously used to giving them and having them obeyed.

She moved to a window that faced the airfield. It was too far to actually see the strip, but she caught sight of the small aircraft coming in for a landing.

It seemed a long time later before she saw Reed returning with a tall, thin man and a petite woman. The men supported the woman as they made their way to the house. Sharla met them at the door, throwing it wide as the trio crossed the front porch.

"It looks a little slippery out there," she said, her gaze quickly scanning Reed's two companions.

"It's still slick in spots, but better than it was last night," he told her as he drew Sandy inside and closed the door behind them. Then he made the introductions, his tone assuring the newcomers he trusted her, and they could trust her, too.

Ed Waites flashed Sharla a smile. He was dressed in jeans, a flannel shirt, and a leather bomber jacket. He had short, dark hair and piercing blue eyes that shone with spirited enthusiasm for his current mission and life in general.

Sandy Rudolph was very small and dark-haired. Her eyes were also dark and deeply shadowed. There was wariness in her gaze that implied a difficulty in trusting strangers, and elicited Sharla's sympathy.

The age of both the newcomers appeared to be in the mid thirties, and Ed's hold on Sandy seemed more possessive than protective, but the FBI pilot's eyes filled with masculine appreciation after he'd surveyed Sharla from head to toe.

"Tough luck you two got stranded," he said, throwing the statement out as a question. His curiosity was left unsatisfied.

"It would have been tougher if Sharla's injury had been more serious."

"Reed said you hit your head when you crashed," Sandy offered in a tentative voice.

"It's going to be multicolored for a while," Sharla admitted, giving her a smile. "But it doesn't hurt at all."

"I explained our emergency landing," Reed said. "Ed didn't have as much trouble landing, but he can't take off again with your plane in the way. He needs every inch of the runway and more traction for enough speed to clear the trees. We're going back out to check your plane for damages and then get the Saratoga turned around. I'd rather you and

Sandy stayed inside until we're sure all's clear for takeoff."

His order had come in the form of a request this time, so she supposed they were making progress. Sharla didn't argue, even though she was anxious to get a look at her plane. She knew Reed was concerned about Sandy and with good reason.

"Will it be safe for Sandy to testify in Nashville now that you won't have a chance to trap the men who are chasing her?" Sharla asked.

"I'm going to testify," Sandy insisted. Her tone was threaded with steel and negated any thought that she was too fragile to cope with the unexpected change of plans. "I'm going to make sure all of John's cohorts get put behind bars where they belong."

Ed and Reed exchanged grins, obviously admiring her courage and determination. Then the unexpected ringing of the telephone interrupted their discussion and snapped them all to alertness.

"The phone is obviously working again," said Sharla.

Reed reached for the receiver. "Connors." He listened intently for a minute, then shot a glance at Sharla. His features were grim by the time he hung up the phone.

"That was Rolf," he explained. His gaze locked with Sharla's.

"He just had a call from your sister Dee. She's frantic. She told Rolf she knows you're in serious danger."

Sharla never discounted a warning from Dee. "Did she know what kind of danger? "

"She says there's a circle of evil surrounding you. She's not sure what's happening, but she said the circle's narrowing, and your life is at stake."

"Is your sister a psychic or something?" asked Sandy.

"Not exactly." Sharla hesitated. She knew Dee didn't make mistakes, but she didn't know how much faith Reed would put in her sister's warning or how much he'd want her to explain.

"If they were close, wouldn't they have ambushed us while we were coming in from the plane?" Ed wondered.

"Unless they were right on your tail and had to land a few miles away. They may be moving in on foot."

"Surround the place and take us by surprise," Ed agreed in a grim tone. "What did Rolf suggest?"

"He ordered backup for us as soon as he knew Horton and Graves were in Nashville. They'll be here in less than an hour, but we're on our own until then. I say we barricade and stay prepared. When our helicopter gets here, we can go to the field."

Ed nodded in agreement, and no time was wasted with indecision. The men started moving in a fast, efficient manner before Sharla could catch her next breath. She and Sandy were gently shoved out of the way while the desk was moved in front of the door and furniture was repositioned to provide cover.

Sharla breathed a sigh of relief. She hadn't realized how important it was to her for Reed to understand and take Dee's warning seriously.

"Your sister's never wrong about these things?" Sandy asked hopefully.

Sharla smiled, but shook her head. "I've never known her to be wrong. She doesn't get these impressions often, thank God, but she's always right."

Reed retrieved a key and unlocked a metal gun case where a variety of weapons were stored. He handed automatic weapons and ammunition to Ed.

Turning to Sharla, he said, "This house is fortified, and Ed and I have plenty of firepower. I want you and Sandy to hide and keep out of sight, no matter what."

"But you don't know how many men are out there," she argued. "Why can't we help?"

"No!" His tone was harsh at the thought of her getting caught in a fire fight. "The closet in the women's bedroom has a fake back. I want you to hide in there until I come and get you. Understand?"

"At least give me a gun," she insisted, deciding there was no use arguing. It would only distract Reed if he worried about their safety.

"What can you shoot?"

"Got a thirty-eight?"

"Sandy?" Ed asked. "You want a small caliber?"

The other woman nodded and accepted a gun. Both women checked the guns' safety and ammunition.

"My guess is five of them, at the least," Reed said. "They have a pilot and probably a couple extra goons."

"I'll take the back of the house," said Ed, heading toward the hall. "Ladies first," he added, motioning for them to precede him.

Sharla and Sandy went to the bedroom and opened the closet. There were only a few articles of clothing to push out of the way. The back panel looked solid and it was dark, so they couldn't see any way to get to the hidden cell.

"Reed?" Sharla called loudly.

"There's a nail on the upper right corner of the panel," he supplied. "Push it like a button."

Sharla found the nail and pushed. The panel slid open without making a sound. The interior was totally dark. The women exchanged frowns, then entered the cell and found the nail that closed the panel.

"I wonder if there's a light in here," Sandy whispered.

"Probably, but someone might be able to see it if they glanced in the closet."

"So we wait in the dark."

Sharla admired her calm acceptance of the situation. She couldn't imagine being constantly hunted the way Sandy was. The hiding and running had apparently become second nature to the other woman.

For what seemed an eternity, the only thing that could be heard in the small chamber was the sound of their breathing. They gradually relaxed, but not for long.

"I have movement on the southeast corner!"

They heard Reed's shouted warning to Ed. Then the gunfire seemed to erupt from every corner of the house. Both women tensed as they heard the savage explosion of automatic weapons and repeated sounds of shattering glass.

"It's coming from every direction," Sandy whispered.

Sharla had never doubted they would be surrounded.

They both jumped as one explosion seemed to rock the house, causing the floors and walls to vibrate around them. There was an instant of silence when they held their breath in fear for Reed and Ed. Then the shooting started again.

Sharla's heart raced madly, nearly suffocating her. The sound of the whole scale destruction was muffled, but no less frightening. She didn't like the idea of hiding while Reed tried to fend off hired killers. She didn't like not knowing what was happening.

She wanted to be near him. Whatever he faced, she wanted to face it with him. The intensity of that need was almost overwhelming. She wasn't brave or stupid, but Reed was more important to her than anything else in the world.

The man she loved was dodging bullets. It had taken her twenty-five years to find a man who was perfect for her. Now he was in serious danger. Was this cold, gripping fear a taste of what she had to expect if she and Reed were to have a future? Could she ever get used to having his life at risk on a regular basis?

Her dark thoughts were interrupted when Sandy grabbed her arm. They strained to hear what was happening near them, and realized the bedroom window was being shattered.

Divide and conquer. The phrase instantly popped into Sharla's head. Reed was in the front of the house, and Ed was at the back. If someone slipped into the middle, either or both of them could be taken by surprise.

She moved her lips close to Sandy's ear. "I'm going to see what's happening and warn Reed."

Sandy nodded and touched the nail that tripped the door. Sharla's eyes had grown accustomed to the dark, so she had no trouble moving from the cell to the front of the closet. She opened the door a crack and looked to her left, toward the bedroom's one window.

A small, wiry man was climbing through the opening. His narrowed eyes were trained on the bedroom door, so he didn't see Sharla until he was completely inside the room. By the time her movements caught his attention, she was out of the closet and had her gun leveled at him.

"Don't do anything stupid," she whispered in a low, even tone. She belatedly realized that the house had grown unearthly quiet after so much noise. She could hear the violent pounding of her heart. "I know how to use this," she warned.

The man didn't say a word. He slowly turned toward her. His eyes were hard and cold as he raised his gun.

"Drop it," she hissed, knowing with icy certainty that he wasn't going to obey.

Sandy made a sound behind her, and the man's attention shifted for an instant. Then the door to the hallway flew open and the sound of Reed's gun exploded in the room. The intruder's gun flew from his hand. He swore viciously and lunged toward Sharla.

A second gun sounded. Sandy knocked the man off his feet with a bullet that grazed his leg. He fell heavily to the floor, screaming in pain and outrage.

Reed kicked the extra gun out of his reach. He wasted no time twisting the other man's arms behind his back and slapping handcuffs on his wrists. "Watch your mouth, Horton," he snarled as the man continued to swear and make vile threats. He quickly searched for more weapons and found both a knife and a small gun hidden in Horton's clothes.

Ed came to the door and quickly assessed the situation. He lowered his own gun and looked toward Sandy. She was across the room and locked in his arms before he got her name out of his mouth.

When Reed had Horton completely disarmed, he turned worried eyes to Sharla. She was still holding the gun and was frozen in shock. His lungs constricted.

"You can put the gun down now," he told her quietly, consumed with guilt for subjecting her to such terror.

Her gaze locked with his. "I couldn't do it," she apologized in a hoarse tone. "I knew he could do it. He was going to shoot me, but I couldn't look him in the eyes and pull the trigger."

Reed gently pried her fingers off the weapon and laid it on the dresser. "It's all right," he soothed as he wrapped one arm around her shoulders and held her tight. "You kept him from putting a bullet in my back."

The thought of Horton's cold, emotionless eyes being trained on Reed's back caused a more violent reaction in Sharla. She started trembling uncontrollably, wrapped her arms around his waist, and buried her face against his chest.

Reed glanced at Waites. Ed's nod assured him he would keep an eye on their prisoner. He laid down his rifle and hugged her tightly until the shudders of shock and reaction had subsided.

Sharla realized she was a burden to him and that he still had work to do. They might all still be in danger. She forced herself to withdraw from his embrace and stop thinking about what could have happened.

"I'm sorry," she mumbled, looking, at Sandy and Ed instead of facing him. "I promise not to fall apart again."

Reed didn't like the way she avoided looking directly at him. He hated himself for involving her in the whole ugly situation, but it was too late for regrets. They still had to get everyone safely out of the house. It was his job. One he'd taken an oath to perform.

"How many did you stop?" he asked Ed while sliding the sling of the rifle over his arm again.

"One for sure, another one wounded." Ed moved to Horton and pressed a foot against his injured leg. "How many men with you?" Horton snarled. Ed applied more pressure to the leg. The wounded man hissed the number four at them.

"He's probably lying. We can figure five or six, including him," Reed stated. "I hit two, but I'm not sure how badly either was hurt."

"Want me to go outside and have a look?"

"No," said Reed. "Wait until our backup gets here. They'll radio before they land, and we can cover them while they police the area."

They decided to leave their prisoner in the bedroom while they waited in the living room. Ed put one of his handcuffs on Horton's ankle and fastened the other side to the leg of the bed.

The wounded man complained that he was bleeding to death. Reed got the first-aid kit, then he and Ed quickly taped gauze on each of Horton's gunshot wounds.

"You'll survive," Ed pronounced in a flat tone.

Horton started swearing again when everyone else went to the living room, Sharla's eyes widened at the sight that met them. The furniture and walls were riddled with bullets. Fabric was ripped and wall hangings shattered. Jagged shards of glass were everywhere.

"Be careful," Reed warned as they picked their way through the debris. The sofa was completely destroyed, but Reed and Ed brushed glass from the two chairs so that the women could use them.

Sharla crossed her arms over her chest. The room was cold from air blowing through the broken window.

Reed noticed her shiver and slipped off his jacket. He shook it to make sure mere wasn't any glass clinging to the fabric, then draped it over her shoulders.

"You'll get cold," she protested.

"Not for a while," he said. His adrenaline was still high, and he was sweating from the recent gun battle.

Sharla thanked him. She had a jacket in her flight bag, but she didn't have the strength to get it. She needed to sit still for a minute until her heart stopped racing and her legs stopped trembling. She was still battling to control her reaction to the trauma she'd experienced, but she didn't want him to know it.

"Are you all right?" he asked, cupping her chin in his hands and gently forcing her to look at him.

Sharla managed a tremulous smile. She wanted to insist that she was fine, but she didn't trust her voice. His gaze darkened with concern. He brushed his thumb lightly over her lips, then turned toward the window as if he didn't trust himself to be close to her.

Pulling his jacket tighter around her body. Sharla snuggled into its warmth and inhaled the masculine scent that was a welcome comfort to her senses.

The destruction all around them was a vivid reminder of the violence and danger Reed faced in his line of work. It made her nauseous. It took all her willpower to control her turbulent emotions without falling apart.

Her work was far from risk-free, yet the danger she faced on a daily basis didn't bother her nearly as much as having him face this kind of danger.

Eleven

Sandy was shivering visibly, and her teeth were chattering. She was wearing a coat, but Ed brushed the glass out of the afghan and wrapped if around her, too.

"Any chance of hot coffee?" she asked.

Reed left his post at the window. "I'll check."

The two men exchanged glances. Sharla and Sandy shared a similar exchange. The kitchen probably looked as bad as the living room. Even if Reed found the coffeepot intact, he wasn't likely to find four unbroken cups.

"How have you managed to cope with it?" Sharla asked the other woman.

The question didn't need to be clarified. "I don't have any choice except to die," Sandy explained with a weary sigh.

Her quiet words put a whole new perspective on the situation. Sharla was gaining a better understanding of the constant battle that some people had to wage against injustice and crime. Sandy had literally risked her life to stop her husband's criminal activities.

Reed, Ed, and thousands of other law enforcement officers were devoted to helping people like Sandy — good, decent people who found themselves tangled in a web of danger and deceit. Sharla felt guilty for criticizing the federal officers before having any real understanding of their work.

She wasn't ignorant about the nation's increasing instances of violent crime. She read the papers and listened to news broadcasts. The escalating level of crime in the U.S. concerned her, yet her own life had been a very sheltered one in many ways.

Being raised on Air Force bases had given her a wide view of the country and world, but she'd never encountered the violence at a personal level. Loving Reed and knowing he was dedicated to law enforcement would doubtlessly broaden her experiences in many diverse and unexpected ways.

Before long, the smell of coffee brewing wafted into the living room. Nothing seemed to daunt Reed. She wondered how he would manage to bring them some.

The answer came a few minutes later in the form of Styrofoam cups. Reed brought the women a cup each, then returned to the kitchen for two more.

It was black, strong, and hot. Sharla sipped hers and gradually felt the heat chase away some of her chills. The room was quiet as everyone took the time to enjoy their coffee.

The sound of an approaching helicopter eventually broke the silence, and all eyes turned toward the window facing the airstrip. A voice came over the radio, alerting them to the helicopter's intention to land.

Reed went to the radio and explained their situation. He warned the incoming team that wounded, armed, and possibly dangerous men were scattered around the cabin.

Sharla listened to his deep, commanding tone and was amazed yet again at his confidence and control. This sort of thing was obviously routine for him. The thought boggled her mind. She had a lot to learn about the man she'd fallen hopelessly in love with.

"It'll be over soon and you can get to your Saratoga," he told her when he'd finished on the radio.

Sharla's gaze met his as he approached her chair. She slowly stood and stepped close to him, her eyes never leaving his.

"Could you spare a kiss?" she asked, almost humbly.

His eyes widened in surprise, then mirrored a heated response. He splayed a hand on the back of her head and brought her mouth to his for a hard, possessive kiss that only hinted at the pent-up emotion he was feeling.

There was so much he wanted to say to her, but there wasn't time or privacy. He needed to apologize for putting her life in danger. He'd never forget the look of stunned disbelief in her eyes as she'd recognized Horton's cold-blooded intent to kill her.

He wanted her to respect the work he did, but he hadn't wanted to subject her to the violence in his world. It was his job to protect her from the evil he encountered almost daily. He hadn't succeeded.

Sharla eased away from him and gave him a smile. "Thank you," she said. She'd needed some reassurance that she hadn't completely alienated him with her lack of courage and inability to function when lives were at stake.

Reed's hand dropped to his side. Letting her put distance between them ripped him apart. He was tempted to tell his co-workers to go to hell while he straightened out his private life and took care of the woman he loved.

The sound of shouting outside the cabin snapped his attention back to the problem at hand. Despite his personal wants, he couldn't ignore the demands of his job. He dragged his gazes from Sharla and looked toward Ed.

"The 'copter's down and the men are fanning out to search the area," Waites told him.

"I'll cover them from here."

Ed nodded his head and went to the kitchen to provide any necessary cover at the back of the cabin.

Within an hour, the federal officers found all the men they believed had attacked the house. They were loaded into the helicopter to be transported back to Nashville.

When the area was safe again. Reed and Ed had one of the men guard Sharla and Sandy while they checked both of the small aircraft and made sure they were safe to fly. All their luggage was loaded and then the backup team departed.

Sharla and Sandy stood at the window of the cabin and watched the helicopter rise and circle the area before heading south. The sun was shining brightly, and it bathed their faces with warmth, dispelling any remaining chill.

"I don't suppose there's any chance that you and I will be able to keep in touch," Sharla said. Despite their short period of acquaintance, she admired the other woman and would like to get to know her better.

"I doubt if it will be possible," Sandy returned in a sad but resigned tone. "Sandy Rudolph ceases to exist as soon as I testify. It will be a blessing."

"I wish you all the happiness in the world," Sharla responded with heartfelt sincerity.

Sandy smiled in appreciation. "I wish the same for you. I get the impression that you're very special to Reed, and I hope you'll have a long, happy future together."

Sharla hoped so, too, but she didn't mention her doubts. "What about you and Ed? The two of you seem really close. Will you be able to see each other again?"

"We're working on it," Sandy admitted. "We're trying to arrange something that won't compromise my new identity."

"Good luck."

Reed and Ed started boarding up the windows of the cabin until crews could be sent to do the major repairs. The women's offer of assistance was declined again, but they busied themselves by cleaning up some of the debris.

Sharla was getting increasingly restless. She was anxious to get to her plane, yet she dreaded the time when she and Reed would go their separate ways. She didn't want to leave him, but she needed to get home and assure her family she was safe and unharmed.

Her emotions were so chaotic that it was a relief when the men finished and were ready to go to the airstrip. Sharla was still wearing Reed's jacket. When they were on the front porch, and he was locking the cabin door behind them, she slipped it off.

She folded it over her arm and brushed some dirt from the sleeve. Then her fingers stilled when she found a rip in the shoulder pad. Her heart stopped. She forgot to breathe. The rip had been caused by a bullet — a bullet that had passed perilously close to Reed's body.

Reed turned to Sharla and was alarmed by her sudden pallor. Her normal, glowing complexion was deathly white. The expression of shock he'd witnessed earlier had returned to her eyes. He felt the impact deep in his heart.

"What's wrong?" he demanded, his tone terse to disguise his panic.

Her mouth was too dry for speech. She pointed to the bullet hole, unable to lift her gaze to his face. She didn't want him to see the terror she knew was reflected on her features. He would think her the worst kind of coward.

Reed grabbed her hand. It was ice cold. Fear clawed at his insides. He wasn't afraid that she was falling apart on him but that she was realizing she could never learn to cope with the hazards of his job.

He didn't know what to say. There was a knot of fear clutching his throat. His jaw clenched in frustration as he took the jacket from her and slid his arms into it.

Sharla's gaze lifted to his right shoulder where the bullet hole proclaimed his narrow escape of injury, or death. A shudder wracked her body and nausea churned in her stomach. Fearing she would really shame herself, she abruptly turned and followed Ed and Sandy.

Reed took a deep breath and forced himself to relax. He wanted to hold her and comfort her, but his emotions were too raw. He thought it best to give her time.

The sight of the Saratoga, ready for flight, lifted Sharla's spirits a little. From the right side, she couldn't see any obvious damage. She hurried to the pilot's side of the aircraft and closely examined the left wing. The dent wasn't too deep and didn't look too serious.

"It's hard to believe anybody has the courage to fly these things all over the country," Sandy said as the other three joined her beside the Saratoga.

"I don't just fly it — I love it," Sharla insisted. She'd regained her composure and managed to encompass them all with a smile. "I'm anxious to get it in the sky."

Ed grinned. "I taxied it out here, and it handles real well. You shouldn't have any problem."

"Thanks," said Sharla, offering her hand to him. "I appreciate your help, and I'm really glad we met."

"Ditto," he said with a grin.

She turned to Sandy next and gave her a fierce hug. They squeezed each other tightly, then shared a smile.

"Take care of yourself," Sharla insisted, fighting another wave of emotion.

"You, too," Sandy returned softly.

Ed wrapped an arm around the other woman's shoulders and guided her to the second airplane. Sharla watched them go before risking a glance at Reed.

His expression was indecipherable. She searched his face for some hint of what he was feeling, but couldn't find a clue.

"Are you sure you want to fly by yourself?" he asked. "We could radio Dee or Carlie to come for you."

She was shaking her head: "I have no fear of flying," she assured him. "It gives me strength."

Reed nodded in understanding. He knew she'd be fine once she was allowed to return to her private world. What he doubted was her ability to adapt to a lifestyle completely beyond the realms of her family and career.

His gaze held hers for a long, poignant minute. "Do you think you could spare me a kiss?" he asked, repeating the request she'd made earlier.

Sharla launched herself into his aims. She clasped his head between her hands while their mouths met in a rush of feverish need. The thrust of his tongue was greedily welcomed into the depths of her mouth where she lavished it with adoring attention.

Reed's whole body reacted to the erotic stimulus. His pulse accelerated. Blood raced from his heart to groin. He dragged Sharla closer. With one arm around her back and one hand on her hips, he spread his legs and urged her to nestle between his thighs.

She shifted as close as she could get, thrusting her hips against him and grinding herself against the hard evidence of his desire. Heat rocketed through her as she swallowed his groan of arousal. She was tempted to beg him not to leave her.

She'd never known such emotional turmoil. She'd never felt so insecure, so vulnerable, or so dependent on someone else for her emotional well-being. Loving Reed was both a promise of paradise and a threat to her sanity.

He dragged his mouth from hers, drew in a ragged breath, and then shifted his lips to the base of her throat where her pulse pounded. He sucked the tender flesh and felt a shudder wrack her slender body. A responding tremor surged through him.

Sharla was gasping for breath. Reed's hot mouth and hard body were making her dizzy with desire. She desperately wanted another chance to show him her love because she was so afraid to speak of it.

Reed wanted, too — he wanted weeks to teach her all the ways of loving. Months. Years. He didn't even have an hour. Their time was running out for the first time in his career, he resented having to finish an assignment.

Sandy's life was dependent on his professionalism. He couldn't let his personal needs interfere with the way he handled a case. He knew he had to get control of the situation.

He eased his death grip on Sharla. The last kiss he gave her was gentle. He licked her lips, and then slid his tongue into her mouth to tenderly demonstrate his reluctance to let her go.

The tension in Sharla's body gradually lessened. She relaxed against him and returned his kiss with the same sweet reluctance. By the time their mouths finally parted, they had their desire under control again.

He rested his forehead against hers for just a minute while they drew air into their deprived lungs. "I'll see you in a few days," he promised huskily.

"I'll miss you," Sharla swore softly.

Reed sighed deeply and let go of her. They stepped apart, but didn't lose eye contact. Both felt their parting was more than a temporary setback in their relationship. They hadn't had nearly enough time to develop a sense of security about a long-term commitment.

"You'll be careful?" she asked.

"I'll be careful. You, too?"

She smiled and nodded. Then she turned her back on him and climbed into the cockpit of the Saratoga. It was a wrench to force her attention to the task at hand, but the familiar feel of the pilot's seat helped ease the transition.

Within minutes she was revving her engine in preparation for takeoff. She allowed herself one last glance at Reed, began to taxi, and then increased her ground speed until she had the power to clear the airstrip.

Once airborne, she radioed the nearest tower and set her course for Lexington. She would stop there to refuel and call her family. She had a night license, so she wouldn't stop again until she was home.

Thoughts of Reed accompanied her all the way back to Virginia. Sharla had never relied on her experience as much as she did on the long flight home. Most of the time her thoughts were scattered. She'd never been so distracted while flying, and she wasn't pleased that she depended on training and instinct rather than concentration.

It was early evening, and the sun was down when she finally saw the welcoming lights of the Prescott runway. Mentally and physically exhausted, a ragged sigh escaped her when the wheels of the Saratoga made contact with the ground, and she could finally bring the plane to a stop. She summoned more energy to face the coming reunion with her family and pretend that she was perfectly all right.

They were all waiting. As soon as the engine was shut off, she saw four figures running toward the plane. Her heart swelled with love, and she felt precariously close to tears as she jumped from the plane into Bear's big, strong arms. She hugged him fiercely and then hugged Belle, Dee, and Carlie with equal enthusiasm.

"We were so worried," Belle attested while stroking Sharla's hair and patting her own eyes with a handkerchief.

"Lord protect us from ice storms!" exclaimed Carlie.

"Amen," said Sharla.

"And all the other unknowns you faced out there," added Dee.

"Another Amen," said Sharla. She didn't say more because she didn't want to go into details.

She turned to Bear. "I wrecked my plane!"

He gave her another quick hug. "Don't you worry about the Saratoga, baby girl. It got you home just fine, so there can't be much wrong with it. I'll have a look first thing in the morning."

"It's time to close the office," Belle insisted. "Why don't you girls go on home while your dad and I lock things up here. We can have dinner and hear all about your trip when we get there."

The sisters' ancestral home was within a half mile of the air service, and they often walked the distance to get some exercise after a long flight. By mutual agreement, they linked arms at the elbow and started walking.

Sharla felt secure again with a sister on each side of her. She was home and drawing strength from the silent support given by her siblings. For a few minutes, she simply enjoyed the soft spring breeze and the sounds and smells of the plantation.

"Do Mother and Daddy know about the warning you sent through Reed's boss?" she finally asked Dee.

"No. They were worried enough about the emergency landing. But I did tell them I thought you'd crashed and hit your head pretty hard."

"Is it all right?" Carlie asked with concern.

"Just a scrape," said Sharla. "There's an ugly bruise, but no real damage."

"What about the other?" Dee wanted to know.

"I can't tell you everything because it's privileged information, but we were in serious danger. Your warning came just in time to give us the edge in an armed attack. You saved my life and three others."

Dee sighed. "Thank God that Marshal felt like humoring me. Can you tell us who the other three were?"

"Reed, an agent named Ed Waites, and a woman named Sandy who's in a government witness-protection program."

"Whew!" exclaimed Carlie. "I can't believe Reed let you get mixed up in that kind of a situation."

"He wasn't very happy about it, either. I was supposed to be on my way home before the trouble broke out. The ice storm caused a major change of plans."

"You weren't hurt at all?" Dee wanted to know.

Sharla glanced her way. "What did you feel after you sent the warning?"

"Chaos and destruction, then you were hurting, but I couldn't tell if it was physical or emotional."

The statement sent a shudder over Sharla. "You weren't far off the mark. We were in a cabin that got riddled with bullets. It was a scene straight from a gangster movie, but none of us were hurt."

It took a minute for her sisters to absorb the shock her description caused. Then Carlie said, "If I had to be in a situation that dangerous, I think I'd be happy to have Reed Connors on my side. I'm glad he was with you."

The thought of Reed brought on a rush of longing that Sharla couldn't hide from her sisters. Anything she felt so strongly made an impact on them as well. She had never been able to disguise her feelings where they were concerned, but then her emotions had never been so chaotic.

"I always thought you and Reed would fall hard if you decided to risk the involvement." Carlie's statement came as no surprise.

"At least he feels as strongly about you," Dee said.

"Impossible." Sharla trusted Dee's instincts where she was concerned, but not where Reed was concerned.

They were all quiet as they crossed the last few yards to the house. When they reached the patio, they stepped into brighter light, and Sharla turned to Dee.

"I wanted to tell you that I met a friend of yours when we stopped over in Lexington."

"A friend of mine?"

"An admirer, I'd say."

"A man?"

"Very definitely male," Sharla teased, her memory presenting a clear picture of the tall, handsome cowboy who'd mistaken her for Dee.

"Who was it?"

"I don't know."

"Then what makes you think he was an admirer of mine?" Dee challenged.

"He mistook me for you and nearly swept me off my feet. Then he demanded a kiss."

Dee and Carlie laughed. "You're sure you aren't talking about Michael?" asked Carlie. "He's the one who likes to pick people up and sweep them off their feet."

Sharla shook her head. She'd told Carlie on the telephone about the evening with her ex-brother-in-law. "This was the next day. I didn't get a chance to tell you about this guy."

"Okay, my curiosity is thoroughly aroused," Dee admitted. "If you don't know his name, then describe him."

"In a word — gorgeous."

"Mmm... my kind of guy," said Carlie. "Are you sure he wasn't one of my admirers?"

"Positive," Sharla insisted, "I had the strangest reaction to him. I was actually feeling the same kind of strong emotional vibrations I get from you guys. It was as if something about him actually linked him with Dee."

Her sisters dropped their teasing attitudes. They'd never encountered this sort of perception before. Now that they were close to the house, they stopped and studied each other with identical expressions of interest.

"What did you feel about this guy?" Dee asked a bit hesitantly.

Sharla wished she'd waited to explain to Dee when she wasn't so tired. She hoped she wasn't going to cause her sister unnecessary heartache.

"Sharla?" Carlie coaxed when she didn't reply.

"I felt pain," she told them. "Waves of pain, loneliness, and troubled emotions. The same type of feeling I was getting from you after your vacation last year."

Dee caught her breath and paled as their attention shifted to her. Sharla and Carlie felt a resurgence of pain.

"I'm sorry, Dee. I really am," she apologized. "I didn't mean to upset you. I'm not thinking too clearly."

"There's a man responsible for all the emotional upheaval you experienced last year?" Carlie wanted to know. She was always protective. After suffering through a bad marriage and a worse divorce, she was particularly defensive where men were concerned.

Dee didn't answer the question, but her lack of denial was a sufficient response.

"What did he look like?"

"He was big, tall and muscular. He was wearing a cowboy hat, so I didn't get a good look at his hair, but his eyes were the most incredible silvery shade of blue."

Dee closed her eyes, and it was obvious that she recognized the man from Sharla's sketchy description. It was just as obvious that the memory made her unhappy.

"He demanded a kiss?"

"Not really. I was teasing about that, but he did ask very nicely."

"Why?"

"The old try one and see if she's just like the others trick," Sharla explained. "At first he thought you'd gotten your hair cut and were giving him a hard time. When I explained that I wasn't you, he asked if he could kiss me."

"How unique," Dee snapped, surprising her sisters with the uncharacteristic irritability.

"He wasn't being fresh," Sharla quickly explained. "We were in a crowded airport lobby and ran into each other by accident. He didn't know you were one of triplets, and I guess we look so much alike that he wanted to see if I taste as good as you do."

Carlie chuckled and Dee gasped. "He said that?" she demanded angrily.

"No." Sharla's attempt at teasing had backfired. "I got the impression he missed you and was almost desperate for anything that might offer a link between the two of you. He was definitely disappointed with me."

Dee's harsh laughter was as uncharacteristic as her snappish attitude. "Believe me, you don't need to waste your sympathy on Logan Bradford. He's perfectly capable of taking care of himself, and I know for a fact that he isn't the least bit interested in me. He was probably just making a play for you." With that, she entered the house, leaving her sisters staring after her in surprise.

"Logan Bradford," murmured Carlie. "Lock that name in your memory, and if you ever see the man again, punch his lights out."

Sharla laughed and opened the door for Carlie. They entered the house without any further discussion on the subject, but Sharla wasn't sure Dee's friend could be so easily dismissed. Dee obviously had strong feelings for the man, and he'd done something to hurt her.

If her suspicions were correct, she'd be willing to bet that whatever Logan Bradford had done to Dee, he was sorry for it now. Of course, they were both adults, and he'd had plenty of time to set things straight, providing Dee hadn't refused to talk to him at all.

The subject wasn't mentioned again. Dee didn't ask Sharla for any more details about her encounter with the mysterious cowboy, and Sharla didn't broach the subject. She had too many other things on her mind.

The evening was spent assuring her parents that she hadn't suffered any ill effects from her plane crash and her forced confinement with Reed Connors. She explained that he'd warmed her when she was cold, doctored her when she was hurt, entertained her when she was bored, and protected her when she was in danger.

She didn't tell them that he had also loved her when she needed loving. The only thing she could fault him for was not falling as hopelessly in love as she had. Now she realized that she'd loved him from a distance for a long time — but up close, she'd fallen hard.

Twelve

On Saturday morning, a little over a week after Sharla's return to Virginia, Reed came to the air service to pick up his car. It was early morning, so Belle and her daughters were going over the day's schedule. They were all seated in the office when he came through the door.

He was wearing faded jeans and a loose-fitting navy jacket over a pale blue knit shirt. As soon as he came through the door, he took off his sunglasses and found Sharla with his dark eyes.

All the breath left her body at the sight of him. The room grew warmer, and her every nerve ending sizzled with excitement. She'd missed him more than she'd ever known it was possible to miss someone, but there was nothing in his expression that revealed whether or not he'd missed her.

"Good morning, Mr. Connors," Belle greeted him. "I thought you might be needing your car soon."

"Morning, Mrs. Prescott, ladies," he said with a nod that encompassed them all. His gaze came back to Sharla as he moved farther into the room.

She rose from her seat when he approached the reception desk, but didn't know what to say to him. Mentioning his assignment might make her mother too curious. She would have liked to throw herself into his arms, but there was no invitation or intimate warmth in his expression.

"Did you get Sandy settled?"

"Safe and sound. She asked me to say hello." Reed's tone remained impersonal.

Sharla acknowledged the comment with a smile. She hadn't heard a plane land, so she guessed he'd come by car. "Did you have to bum a ride out here?"

"Ed brought me. He's out talking airplanes with your dad. He's thinking about starting his own air service."

"Really?" Sharla studied him carefully, wondering if he was trying to tell her something important without being too specific. "He's planning to quit the bureau?"

"He's thinking about it as soon as he can get his own business started."

The comment puzzled her until she remembered that Sandy had said she and Ed were looking for a way to be together. They obviously couldn't do it until Ed resigned from the FBI.

"Tell me," she asked with dawning comprehension, "did Sandy return all that money she had access to?"

Reed's smile was slow and incredibly sexy. "She turned over the principal, but decided to keep the interest for all the trouble she's had. The interest is enough to take care of her for a lifetime."

"Probably enough to launch a little air charter service, too," Sharla suggested, her heart going wild at his sexy grin. She wondered if he would share more information with her. "Where is Ed planning to go into business?"

His eyes gleamed with satisfaction. "He's thinking about leasing some land in Iowa from a friend."

Sandy and Ed were going to live on Reed's family arm in Iowa. Sharla was really happy for them. She was even more thrilled that Reed trusted her enough to share the secret.

Could Sandy be traced through Reed, she wondered, and asked, "Is Iowa a nice, safe place to live?"

He'd promised Sandy to let Sharla know where she was. There was nothing in his personal file that could be traced to his family's property. He'd made sure of that to protect his parents while they were alive.

"A person could get lost forever in the wide-open spaces," he assured her.

"Is there much of a demand for plane charters in Iowa?" Belle asked, unaware of the double meaning behind the conversation they were having.

"Not much," he explained, turning his attention to Belle, "but there's a lot of demand for crop dusting and some for flying lessons. Ed's considering several options."

"Ed is the FBI agent who checked Sharla's plane before she flew home?"

Reed shot a quick glance at Sharla. Her eyes flashed a warning not to discuss details of the episode in Tennessee. "Ed's a good aircraft mechanic," he replied. "He's one of the agency's pilots."

"Well, we're certainly grateful for the assistance he gave Sharla. I'd like to thank him personally," said Belle. "And we want to thank you for taking such good care of her under unpleasant circumstances."

"Bear has already done that," Reed assured her, but his eyes were on Sharla again, and were no longer smiling.

She wondered what he was thinking. Was he blaming himself for getting her involved in the first place, or was he remembering just how good his care had been?

Reed wondered what brought the blush to her cheeks. Being close to her and not touching her was torture. He stepped up to the reception desk. "My keys?"

"Here they are," she responded, handing him a key chain. "I imagine your car will be a little stuffy. If I'd known you were coming today, I could have aired it a little."

"Don't worry about it." He took the keys and turned to the door as his friend entered the office.

When Ed's eyes adjusted to the inside lighting, they shifted from Sharla, to Dee, to Carlie, and then back to. Sharla. "Well, I'll be... there's three of you."

Dee and Carlie, who'd been quietly working on their flight plans, but listening intently, were quick to correct him. "There's only one Sharla," Dee explained patiently. "My name's Dee, and this is Carlie

"We really aren't interchangeable," Carlie admonished mildly. Her eyes challenged him to argue.

"Why do I feel like I just put my foot in my mouth?" Ed asked good-naturedly.

"Probably because you did." Reed was unsympathetic.

Sharla let him off the hook. "We do understand that seeing us together can be a little disconcerting."

"And no, we don't all smell, feel, and taste exactly the same," Dee mumbled irritably.

"Darla JoAnn Prescott," Belle scolded, aghast. "Please excuse my daughters, Mr. Waites — sometimes they get a little testy. Mr. Connors told me that my husband thanked you for helping Sharla, but I'd like to add my thanks."

"You're more than welcome, ma'am, but I didn't do much of anything. The plane was in good condition." To Reed he said, "I've got to be on my way." Then he nodded to the women. "It's been a real pleasure."

"I have to go, too," said Reed. He turned to Sharla. "Can you spare a minute?"

"Sure," she agreed, laying her flight log on the desk. Good-byes were exchanged as they left the office. Ed said he'd be in touch and climbed into his car. Sharla wished him luck and asked him to keep in touch. Then she and Reed walked to the private parking lot behind the building.

It was a beautiful spring day with brilliant sunshine and a soft breeze that gently tossed Sharla's hair. Her golden curls looked soft, silky, and touchable. Reed had to ball his hands into fists to keep from reaching out to her.

She'd been on his mind constantly. During the daytime hours, he'd tormented himself with memories of making love with her — her sweet passion and uninhibited responses. His dreams were troubled with visions of her facing a hired killer and the terror in her eyes when she'd found the bullet hole in his jacket.

There was no way he could rationalize having an affair with her. It would only bring pain and heartache. He couldn't offer her a future with a family, and he couldn't live with himself if he gave her less.

No matter how much she might protest, she deserved a man who could give her all the best things life had to offer. He had to make her see that they were all wrong for each other. It would be the hardest thing he'd ever asked of himself, but he knew it was for the best.

"Did you just get back this morning?" Sharla asked to break the tense silence that stretched between them.

"Yesterday," he told her. His shiny red Corvette was parked in the shade of an ancient willow tree. He leaned against the front fender, crossed his arms over his chest, and gave Sharla his full attention.

She was hurt that he hadn't called her as soon as he returned, but she tried not to reveal any emotion in her expression. He hadn't touched her, not even a hand to her arm as they walked. It made her wary.

"Your head looks like it's healed."

"It went through the usual stages of color, but it didn't bother me."

"Good." Everything about her was good, he admitted to himself. While Sharla reached out and played with a branch of the willow, he let his eyes feast on each beloved feature. Just looking at her made him hurt.

The silence lengthened, and Sharla's nerves grew tight with tension. Reed wasn't going to take her in his arms. If he wanted her, he wouldn't be shy about it. He hadn't asked her out here so that he could hold her or kiss her or tell her how much he'd missed her.

He wanted to tell her that what they'd shared in Tennessee was a mistake — or at best, a one-night stand. How many times had she faced a situation like this, but from the opposite point of view? How many times had she searched for the words to tell a man she just didn't care enough about him to make a commitment?

Her heart pounded painfully in her chest. Her stomach rolled. She had to find the courage to hear him out without giving in to tears. Pride was about all she had if he didn't want her. She braced herself and faced him.

"If you're struggling for the kindest words to offer me, then I'll save you the trouble. This may be my first experience with the losing end of a brush-off, but the situation is familiar enough. I take it you've changed your mind about wanting to see me on a regular basis."

Reed's jaw clenched, and his whole body stiffened. Her words ripped him apart. Her voice was steady, but her beautiful eyes were filled with pain. He forced the breath out of his lungs and agreed.

"I think becoming any more involved would be a mistake for both of us."

You promised! She wanted to scream the words at him. He'd promised that he would try to see her as often as possible. He'd promised, and he'd lied.

It took every ounce of her control to continue in a reasonably calm tone. "I think you're wrong, but I'm not in the habit of throwing myself at men who don't want me, so I guess I don't have any choice but to accept your decision."

Reed's eyes darkened with emotion. His mouth was set in a grim line, and Sharla could see the tension in every angle of his body, yet he didn't refute her words. He just stared at her with unflinching intensity.

"I would appreciate an honest answer to a question I have," she said. A glance beyond him to the rolling green hills of her home helped her remain in control.

"What do you want to know?" he asked warily, then fervently hoped she wouldn't ask him if he loved her.

"Is it something I did, or didn't do, or did wrong?"

Her voice was barely audible, but pain sliced through him when he recognized her insecurity and vulnerability. He grabbed her by the shoulders and forced her to look directly at him.

"This has nothing to do with the loving we shared!" he rasped harshly. Then his tone gentled. "That was good, really good, the best."

Sharla's body threatened to disgrace her when the heat from his touch singed her nerves. She bit her lip to keep it from trembling, and then mustered the courage to ask another question. "Is it because I couldn't shoot Horton?"

Reed shook her gently. "Hell, no!" he bit out.

"I don't know what I would do if I was faced with the same situation again," she argued, sure that he was put off by her cowardice. "I've never had to handle something like that before and I froze, but that doesn't mean I'm a complete coward. Surely you and everybody else has a few doubts the first time they come face to face with death!"

"Dammit, Sharla," he said on a groan of frustration. She was making him crazy. His grip on her tightened, but the action brought her close enough to feel her heat and smell her sweetness. He swiftly set her away from him.

"I didn't expect you to shoot Horton," he snarled. "I don't ever want you in a situation like that again!"

"Is that why you're dumping me?" she managed. "Because you don't want me involved in your work?"

"I'm not dumping you!" he snapped, then raked a hand through his hair in agitation. "My job is only part of the problem."

Sharla dragged in a deep breath. His frustration threatened her control. If it wasn't the sex and it wasn't her cowardly behavior, then he must realize that he could never love her as much as she needed to be loved. She wasn't sure she wanted her suspicions confirmed, but she had to know what had changed his mind.

She stiffened her spine and lifted her chin. "Could you please tell me exactly why you don't think we should see each other again?"

Reed thought she was the most beautiful, courageous woman he'd ever known. He wanted her with a desperation that threatened his sanity, but he wouldn't ruin her life.

"We're all wrong for each other," he declared. "We've known it since the first time we met. That's why neither of us did anything about the attraction until we were thrown together by accident. We live in two different worlds, and that's not going to change."

She started to argue, but realized anything else she said would sound like begging. Her pleas had already made this more difficult than it had to be.

"I can't offer you a future," Reed said softly. He wanted to reach out and touch her, but didn't. "You have a family that cares and a career you love. I want you to stay happy, secure, and safe."

Sharla looked him squarely in the eyes, almost drowning in their liquid warmth. Her next words were barely audible. "Why can't you be like other men and take what you can get with no strings attached?"

The soft, challenging question made a direct hit on his defenses. He dragged his eyes from hers. "You're not cut out for a casual affair, and we both know it."

Casual. The word nearly shattered what was left of Sharla's control. All he was denying himself was a casual fling while she was struggling to deal with gut-wrenching, unrequited love. Without another word, she turned and walked away. She would have said goodbye or take care, but she knew her voice would crack on any final parting words.

She didn't glance back when she heard the powerful engine roar to life. She looked straight ahead until she rounded the office building and nearly collided with Dee and Carlie. They felt her pain, and she felt their sympathy and understanding.

"Men," hissed Carlie, "they're all bastards."

Dee handed Sharla her flight schedule. "Would you rather cancel for today?"

"No," was all she could manage.

"I can't promise the pain will go away, but working does help you cope with the loss," Dee told her gently, speaking from very recent, painful experience.

Carlie had been falling in and out of love since grade school. Dee was more cautious and had allowed only a select few men to get close. Sharla had always been totally immune to any kind of masculine appeal. She'd always been the most independent and emotionally secure of the sisters. Her unhappiness hit them all hard.

*F*or the following week, Sharla pushed herself harder than she ever had in her life. She flew as many hours as was safe and then worked in the office, in the hangar, or at her apartment until she was so exhausted that she fell into bed each night.

When thoughts of Reed or the time they'd spent together tried to surface, she determinedly forced them out of her mind. When she caught herself wondering if he'd call or if he missed her, she berated herself for stupidity. He'd made himself perfectly clear. He didn't want her.

April passed into May, and Sharla spent the next two weeks accepting dates from the men who regularly asked her to go out with them. She went to dinner and dancing, to the movies, and to the theater. When she wasn't working, she was trying hard to play.

She needed to fill every waking hour, because every time she went to sleep, her dreams were filled with Reed. Her subconscious replayed their time together like an unending reel of film. The memories of his rejection were just as haunting. Sometimes she woke up crying — sometimes calling his name — always alone and hurting.

After two weeks of frenzied partying, she stopped dating. Trying to erase the memories was futile, and she finally admitted that she was on her own. No other man was going to replace Reed in her heart or her life.

The weekends were the worst, especially Sundays. Now that the business was financially secure, Belle insisted they take a day of rest, and it gave Sharla too much time to think.

During the middle of May, the weather turned really hot. The Prescotts spent one lazy Sunday lounging around their Olympic-sized pool — a favorite addition to the property Belle had inherited from her Virginia ancestors.

They cooked their meals on the grill, played water games, and worked on their tans. Even though the triplets were blondes, they could tolerate a reasonable amount of sun.

At dusk, they all said good night and headed for their own living quarters. The apartments had been created within the ante-bellum mansion, but with outside access doors that offered more independent living. Each unit had a sitting room, bedroom, bath, and kitchenette.

Sharla lit one lamp in her sitting room, turned on the radio, and headed for the bathroom. She had finished her shower, used the blow dryer on her hair, and donned a yellow satin nightgown when she heard someone knocking at her door.

Thinking it must be a family member, she threw open the door without asking who was there. She froze in shock at the sight of Reed Connors.

He was wearing faded jean cutoffs that hugged his body like a second skin. The red sweatshirt was equally faded with ragged edges where sleeves and a neckline had once been. His body was lean, hard, and deeply tan. All the breath rushed from her body.

While she was drinking in the sight of him, Reed was busy studying her from her damp curls to her bare toes. The nightgown she was wearing fit her like a slip. It was cut deep in the front and cut high on the thighs.

The light was behind her, and he could see the enticing silhouette of her shapely body. Firm, high breasts with dusky nipples taunted him through the transparent fabric. He ground his teeth together as desire slammed into him, hard and fast.

"Reed?" Sharla managed to speak his name.

After a slight hesitation, he found his voice. "Can I come in?"

His deep tone rippled over her body like a caress. Her heart threatened to slam right through her rib cage. Her gown was clinging to her damp skin, and her nipples tightened at the touch of his gaze. She felt naked and incredibly vulnerable, but she had nothing to fear from him. She stepped aside and allowed him to enter.

He was carrying a flight bag, and he set it down inside the door.

It was the exact color and size of the one she'd taken on their trip. "I bought a bag to replace the one that was destroyed at the cabin. Sorry I didn't get it to you sooner."

Her bag and some of the contents had been riddled with bullets. She'd trashed it in Lexington so that her parents wouldn't see it and start asking questions.

"You didn't have to replace it."

"I wanted to. If you'll give me a list of anything else that was destroyed, I'll see that you get reimbursed."

"That's not necessary," she insisted.

For another long minute they just stared at each other. Neither of them was concerned about words or reasons or intentions. Being close again was the most important thing they had to worry about.

"I've missed you," she finally dared to admit.

Reed's body tightened, and his eyes flared with desire. "I need to hold you," he confessed in a raw tone.

She searched his features, but didn't learn anything he hadn't already admitted. He wanted her. He wasn't confessing love, making promises or excuses, just stating a need.

She had a need that was greater. She could have refused him — ranting, raving, and demanding more — but she didn't. What she did was open her arms and moan with pleasure as he dragged her against the warm, solid wall of his chest.

Their mouths locked in a fevered rush — his tongue thrusting deeply and being wetly welcomed by hers. She twined her arms around his neck, and his strong arms locked behind her back. They spent several long minutes just absorbing and enjoying the taste and feel of each other.

When they broke for breath, Reed lifted a hand and speared his fingers through her silky tresses, cupping her head while gazing into her eyes.

The slow, sensuous rhythm of a popular love song was playing on the radio. "Dance with me," he coaxed, his golden eyes holding hers.

Sharla slipped one hand in his and kept the other around his neck while they swayed to the music. Their eyes stayed locked as the satin of her gown brushed against the rougher texture of his clothes, and her soft curves rubbed against his hard angles.

She wanted him to talk to her. She wanted him to admit that he was suffering as much as she was — that he'd been wrong about them not having a future. She wanted him to tell her he loved her, but the words didn't come.

Reed hadn't planned to touch her. He'd just wanted to bring her bag and see her again. He hadn't planned to invite himself into her apartment, but seeing her had only increased his need to touch her. Everything inside him was dying without her.

Nothing had changed. He still couldn't offer her a future, but he could give her a night of loving that came straight from his heart. Another man might be able to give her babies, but no other man could love her more than he did.

They circled the room slowly as one song ran into another and another. They savored the closeness — the sight, scent, and feel of each other. They were making memories to cherish.

Reed drew both of Sharla's arms around his neck again, then slid his hands down her arms to her waist. He pulled her closer as his lips fell to the curve of her neck. He kissed and tasted her sweetness.

She threw back her head and offered him free rein as he covered her neck and shoulders with tender kisses. His caressing mouth made her tremble, and her legs grew weak. Their dancing had slowed to the gentle swaying of bodies, but even that became too much for her dissolving strength.

When she grew languid, Reed swept her into his arms and carried her toward the bedroom. Once inside the door, he stood her beside the bed and began a renewed assault of kisses. His mouth slid up her neck and throat, over her chin and lips, then locked with her mouth.

Sharla moaned softly, needfully. Her hands locked in his hair and she sucked his tongue deeply into her mouth. His groan mingled with hers as they strained to get closer.

His hands tightened on her waist, then moved up to her bare shoulders. They glided over her soft flesh to the straps of her gown and slowly slipped the fabric down her arms. When the satin clung to the curves of her breasts, he dropped his mouth to gently nudge it out of his way.

She felt the gown slide to the floor, then felt the heat of Reed's gaze as he leaned back to look at her naked, quivering flesh. Her breasts were throbbing, her nipples tight. She clutched at his head and pulled it down to relieve the ache — moaning when his hot mouth sucked first one nipple and then the other.

Her hands found the hem of his shirt and tugged until the offending fabric was discarded. She stroked his hard, muscled arms and then searched the tight curls on his chest until she found nipples to lavish with attention.

A groan rumbled from deep within him. The breath hissed out of his lungs, and a shudder wracked his body when her wet mouth replaced the teasing fingers on his chest. He sank his fingers into her hair as her hot tongue teased his nipples. When his legs began to tremble, he eased her to the softness of the bed.

They spent the next few hours adoring each other with slow, seductive caresses — then primitive, raging passion. They learned the taste and texture of every inch of the other's body. Later in the night, exhausted and sated, they resisted sleep and shared an intimate conversation.

"You promised," Sharla charged softly, reminding him of their promise to see each other often.

She was cradled against his body, and his arms tightened around her. "I know," he admitted huskily. "I wanted to honor my promise."

"What changed your mind?"

It wasn't easy for Reed to bare his heart, but he owed her an explanation. "I couldn't stand to lose you." It was already too late, and he knew it — but he was still trying to save them both more pain.

"Why are you so sure you would eventually lose me? You have to know how much I love you."

He moaned softly and pressed a hard kiss against her brow. Then he forced himself to tell her how he always disappointed the people who loved him, and that his parents had never forgiven him for his decision to leave the farm and join the U.S. Marshal Service.

"Sometimes love isn't enough," he stated gruffly.

"Do you think my parents love me any less because I chose to be a pilot?" Sharla asked.

Reed sighed and rested his chin on her head. "Bear and Belle adore you, and they couldn't be more proud."

"That's my point," she insisted. "Belle spent years trying to mold me into a sophisticated socialite. She dreamed about elite colleges, proper marriages, and my becoming a doting wife and mother."

"I shattered those dreams, and she was disappointed — but that doesn't mean she stopped loving me, or that she isn't proud of me."

"Belle's one in a million," Reed murmured, but he tried to consider his parents in a different light.

"I'm willing to bet your parents were pretty special, too," Sharla whispered, rubbing her face against his chest. "I'll bet every neighbor within a hundred miles of them knew that their son was a U.S. Marshal. I'm sure they missed you and worried about you. They probably nagged you about settling down, but they had to be so proud."

Reed frowned, wondering if he'd been blind where his parents were concerned. Had he wasted years misunderstanding them? "I can't be what everybody wants me to be," he clipped.

"I just want you to be yourself."

"Right now," he challenged. "But someday you'll get tired of my job. You'll want me to do something safe behind a desk. Someday you'll want children, and I can't give them to you. I know my limitations."

"If you're willing to accept me as a career woman dedicated to flying, why can't you trust me to accept you just the way you are?"

Reed pulled the covers over their cooling bodies. He didn't respond to her question, but he gave it a lot of thought. Trust. Mutual trust. Could he trust her with his heart and soul? Did he have enough faith in their love to risk his sanity?

Thirteen

The alarm clock startled Sharla awake on Monday morning, and she quickly hit the snooze button until she could drag herself out of a deep sleep. Stretching, she became aware of her nudity, and memories of the night surfaced with a surge of heat. She reached for Reed, but he wasn't in her bed. He was gone.

A slow, sleepy smile curved her lips. He might still be running, but after the night they'd just spent, she was filled with joy and optimism. Reed hadn't wanted to succumb to the love they shared. He'd never spoken the words she most wanted to hear, but he loved her.

She no longer doubted the depths of his love. She might not be very experienced with making love — but what they'd shared last night went far beyond the boundaries of a casual affair.

Once during the night, just to tease him, she'd asked him to show her all the things a man liked so that she would be more exciting for her next lover. Reed had gone wild. He couldn't stand thinking about her with other men any more than she could stand the thought of him loving another woman.

Sharla's smile grew as she climbed from bed. He'd mentioned babies several times during the night. If his inability to reproduce was all that stood between them, then she would convince him that it didn't matter. Nothing mattered as much as having his love.

She'd give him a few days. If he didn't come to her again, she'd go to him. Belle's files would provide his home address. The coming weekend was her turn for three days off work. That should be long enough to convince a reluctant lover that he wanted to be a husband.

Her confident, happy mood lasted all week. No one mentioned the abrupt change in her attitude, but her sisters knew it had a lot to do with a certain red Corvette being parked outside her apartment Sunday night. They worried, but didn't interfere.

By Friday evening, Sharla was exhausted and fell into bed as soon as she'd had her shower. She decided to wait until Saturday before confronting Reed on his own territory. Sleep claimed her while she was unrepentantly planning his seduction.

Near midnight, she woke abruptly and sat straight up in bed, listening intently for any sound that would explain her sudden alarm. Her pulse was pounding as she strained to hear anything out of the ordinary. After a few tense minutes, she heard Dee softly call her name.

Sharla blinked and watched as her sister entered the room through the inside door. Dee joined her on the bed. She was dressed in pajamas, her hair was tangled around her shoulders, and she looked like she'd been asleep, too.

"What's wrong?" Sharla asked groggily, wondering why Dee was wandering around in the middle of the night. Then she thought of her parents. "Daddy?" she gasped in alarm.

"No, no, nothing's wrong with Daddy or Mother," Dee assured her. "Everybody's asleep, but I had a dream that woke me."

Sharla didn't like the anxiety in her tone. She didn't like having her troubled emotions compounded by Dee's. "What kind of dream?" she asked.

Dee relaxed a little and propped herself against the headboard of the bed beside Sharla. "It's the same way I felt when you were in Tennessee. I get this feeling of being surrounded by evil — as if danger is all around and closing in on you."

"Do you think someone's outside now?"

Dee shook her head vigorously. The plantation and airfield were protected by a dependable security system.

"I've checked the security. The cameras aren't picking up anything — not even a strange car within miles."

Sharla's frown deepened. They both knew Dee's fears couldn't be discounted. "Have you noticed any change in the powers you have?" she asked. "Are you starting to pick up images from other people? Maybe even strangers?"

Dee was shaking her head. "It's never been this strong for anyone but family."

"Are you sure Carlie's okay?" Sharla asked. Her question was answered by a knock at the door.

Carlie let herself in and joined them on the bed. She was wearing a robe, and her eyes were as sleepy as the others. "I couldn't sleep," she explained. "I kept getting these nagging feelings of unease, and I assumed you two were at the root of them."

"That settles it," said Dee. "Something is definitely wrong here."

"If we're all okay, then why don't I feel any better?" Carlie wondered aloud. "Are we starting to pick up vibrations from other people?"

"That's what I asked Dee," Sharla told her. "She says it happens just with us." Then she remembered the man in Kentucky. Her eyes widened. "Dee, I felt something altogether different with that cowboy friend of yours. I'd never felt so much emotion from anyone but family. You don't suppose you're doing the same thing?"

Dee paled a little. "You think Logan might be in serious danger?"

Sharla was shaking her head. "No, not Logan — but what about Reed? He was with me the last time you had these feelings, and he's in a dangerous line of work. What if he's the one who's surrounded by evil?"

They all stared at one another for a brief instant. It was a shock to think their powers of perception could reach beyond their immediate family. If so, it would be unprecedented.

"Maybe the feelings are so strong because Sharla loves Reed," Carlie suggested thoughtfully. "Maybe her love or their love is strong enough to create an emotional bond that triggers your protective instincts."

Dee and Sharla stared at her for a minute. What she was suggesting seemed impossible. "It never happened when you were married to Bill," Dee reminded.

Carlie's laugh was brittle. "We never had a strong emotional bond."

Sharla turned to Dee and hesitantly asked, "How much do you care about Logan Bradford?" When Dee's eyes grew dark and angry, she rephrased her question. "Would you at least say there was a strong bond between the two of you?"

Dee didn't reply, but nodded her head in grudging agreement.

"Damn!" Carlie whispered. "What if it is possible?"

"What if Reed's in danger?" Sharla asked fearfully. "What if Rudolph has decided to go after Reed to get to Sandy?"

"I don't know who Rudolph is, but we have to warn Reed somehow," Dee insisted. "The feelings aren't going away. If anything, they're stronger. Somebody is in trouble."

Sharla bounced across the bed and grabbed her telephone. She'd gotten his unlisted number from Belle's files, and she rapidly punched the digits.

"Busy signal," she exclaimed in disgust. "At least he's awake and alert."

"Or the phone's off the hook," Dee suggested slowly.

Sharla's whole body went rigid. "Dee! Can you give me anything more specific? Please! I have to find a way to reach him!"

"I have a feeling he's totally isolated," she whispered reluctantly.

"No!" Sharla screamed, jumping from the bed. She stripped off her gown and started pulling clothes out of her dresser. "I have to get to him!"

"Do you want me to get a plane ready?" Carlie asked.

"It'll take too long," Dee injected. "At this time of night we can make better time in a car."

There was never a doubt that Carlie and Dee would accompany Sharla. "Grab something from my closet so we don't have to waste any more time," she told them.

As they all tugged off nightwear and quickly pulled on jeans, Dee had another thought. "We can call Reed's boss. I called him after your wreck," she explained. "There's someone in their office all the time. Maybe they can get some men over to Reed's apartment."

Sharla was reaching for the phone. Dee gave her the number, and she waited impatiently for an answer.

"May I speak with Marshal Sanders?" she asked the man who identified himself as Deputy Marshal Powers. She was told that both Sanders and Reed were gone. Powers explained that Reed had left for home a couple hours earlier.

"I have reason to believe that Marshal Connors is in serious danger," she told Powers. "I don't have time to explain, but I think it has to do with the Rudolph case. Can you possibly get some men to his apartment?"

"I'll try to reach him," Powers promised patiently.

"There's no time!" Sharla insisted, panic entering her tone for the first time. "Connors is in danger right now! All you'll get on the phone is a busy signal!"

The urgency in her tone finally got through to the man. "Who are you and exactly why do you think Connors is in danger?" he asked suspiciously.

Sharla explained that she was the pilot who'd flown Reed to Tennessee. That brought an abrupt end to his questions. "I'll send some men over there pronto," he assured her.

As soon as she hung up the phone, she tried Reed's number again, but with the same response. "Let's go!"

They took Carlie's Firebird, and she kept the accelerator floored most of the way. The car was equipped with a radar detector, but they didn't encounter any patrolmen.

Sharla would have welcomed assistance from the highway patrol, the DC police, or anyone else who might be able to reach Reed before she could. The closer they got to the city, the more agitated she became.

She allowed herself a flicker of doubt about what he would say if they barged in on him while he was trying to sleep, or if he was just on the phone with a friend. She thought about charging his apartment and finding him with a woman, but swiftly put that thought from her mind.

The strength of Dee's concern didn't lessen, and all three of them grew more apprehensive about what they might find at Reed's apartment. Fear gripped Sharla as she remembered the deadly intent in Horton's eyes as he'd faced her with a gun.

They wouldn't kill Reed, she reminded herself. They wanted information that he wouldn't supply. But they could hurt him badly. They could try to beat or torture the information out of him. She couldn't bear the thought.

"Are you sure you want to love a man whose job is a constant threat?" Carlie asked.

"Wanting has little to do with it," Sharla replied flatly. "I don't want him risking his life, but I don't have a choice. He's a crime fighter — one of the guys with the white hats. It's what he is, and it's his life."

"Couldn't you ask him to limit his fieldwork?" Dee suggested.

"I could, but I wouldn't," Sharla explained. "And he'd never ask me to stop flying."

At Reed's apartment, the man in question was rubbing his hands and arms to stimulate the circulation after being released from rope that had bound him to a chair.

Four of his fellow officers had taken his two assailants by surprise and subdued them without a fight. The two were being handcuffed.

"How did you know?" he asked Powers.

"We had a tip from that pilot who was involved with the other incident."

"Sharla?" Reed said in surprise. Then, as if the mention of her name had conjured her, the lady in question came racing through his front door.

"Reed!" she cried at the sight of him. "Are you all right?"

"I'm fine," he assured her as she launched herself into his arms. He hugged her close.

After one fierce hug, Sharla drew back and took a good look at him. She'd been right in thinking that he'd be tied and beaten. His arms had rope burns, one of his eyes was slightly swollen, and there was a drop of blood at the corner of his mouth.

The sight of his blood made her blood boil. Frustration at not reaching him sooner kept the adrenaline pumping through her with a shocking force. The thought of his being beaten consumed her with a fury unlike anything she'd ever known.

She turned to one of the men who'd assaulted him. Two officers were holding him. Without a word, she curled her fingers into a ball, drew back her arm, and slammed her fist against his face with all the strength she could muster.

The blow knocked his head sideways. A stunned silence fell over the room as she turned to the second assailant and slammed her left hand into his stomach. The whoosh of the breath leaving his body gave her some satisfaction.

"How do you like being pounded on while you're defenseless and unable to retaliate?" she snarled at the man. "You probably kick dogs and beat children, too, don't you, you disgusting bully?"

His vulgar response made Sharla swing her leg backward in preparation for a kick to his shin.

Reed grabbed her before she could inflict any more pain on the handcuffed man. He was laughing so hard, he could barely control his bundle of fury.

When the other officers roared with laughter, the criminals started swearing and were hustled from the apartment.

"I'll lock these guys up," Powers told Reed with a chuckle. "You can take care of the paperwork in the morning."

Reed nodded his agreement and fought to control his laughter. Sharla's arms were clinging to his waist while she rested against his chest. When they were alone, he cupped his hands around her head and lifted her face toward his.

"God! I love you!" he whispered gruffly, adoring her with his eyes.

Sharla sagged against him. Her eyes went liquid with pleasure. "I know," she returned softly, "but it's nice to hear the words."

"Say them to me," he commanded gruffly.

"I love you."

He moaned and hugged her tightly. "I love you, but I can't have you fighting my battles," he teased.

"I don't want to fight," she argued, then locked gazes with him again. "But I do want the legal right to be by your side no matter what you're doing."

Legal right. Marriage. The thought of marriage to Sharla had been on his mind constantly. He couldn't bear the thought of letting any other man near the woman he loved. Neither could he bear the thought of life without her. He'd thought he could let her go, but he was badly mistaken.

"Maybe—"

Sharla put her fingers against his lips. "No maybes, ifs, or buts," she insisted. "I know beyond a shadow of a doubt that I want to spend the rest of my life with you. Whatever the future has in store for us, we can handle it together."

The truth was in her eyes. She loved him just as much as he loved her. Reed couldn't doubt the sincerity of the emotion that bound them together. He pulled her into his arms and held her tightly.

"I suppose we'll have to have a formal wedding," he whispered against her ear.

"Carlie eloped, and Mother cried for two weeks," she informed him.

Reed moaned, and she compromised. "It can be a very small, informal wedding. Just the family. I only need two bridesmaids."

The two would-be bridesmaids had bombarded Agent Powers with questions, then entered Reed's apartment to find their sister locked in his embrace. They stepped into the room and closed the door.

He gave them a smile. "Who do I have to thank for my timely rescue tonight?"

Sharla eased herself from his arms, smiled at her sisters, and explained. "We've just realized that our extrasensory perception might be extended to someone that one of us loves very much."

Reed lifted a brow. "No kidding?"

"Providing that someone's love is just as strong," Carlie qualified.

"In my line of work, that could be a real bonus for me, but a real detriment for the rest of you," Reed said, pulling Sharla against his side with an arm around her shoulders.

"The solution is for us to be together as much as possible," she declared, giving him a squeeze. "Then Dee and Carlie can just send a telepathic message when we need to be alarmed."

"Better yet," added Dee, "don't get yourself in any more dangerous situations."

Reed couldn't make any promises, but he relieved one worry. "This should be the end of the Rudolph problem. I told Graves that the money has been returned. Now his boss is broke without hope of regaining his lost millions. No self-respecting criminal is willing to do somebody else's dirty work for nothing."

"Graves?" Sharla questioned. "I thought you captured him in Tennessee."

"He was wounded, but he escaped before our backup got on the scene. We've been waiting for him to recuperate and resurface. That's why we didn't publicize the fact that Rudolph's money has become confiscated evidence."

"It's all over?"

"It's all over," repeated Reed before dropping a kiss on her lips.

"Until the next time," she countered derisively. His eyes met hers.

"Think you can stand being married to a fed?"

"Married!" Dee cried.

"Married!" exclaimed Carlie.

Sharla ignored her sisters' shocked chorus as she gazed into Reed's eyes. "I'm improving already. This time I wasn't so scared, just furious."

He laughed. Then he grasped her hands and inspected them. "You'll probably have more bruises."

"Why?" demanded Carlie.

"What happened?" Dee wanted to know.

Reed filled them in while watching Sharla blush. Her sisters looked at her in amazement, unable to imagine her losing control so completely.

"Don't you dare tell Mother and Daddy," she warned them fiercely.

"Or what?" Carlie chided. "You'll punch us out?"

Dee started laughing. Then Carlie joined her, and soon they were all laughing until tears ran down their faces. Sharla knew she'd never hear the end of the teasing about her burst of temper, but she didn't really care. If anybody dared to hurt Reed, she would always be ready to come to his defense.

Sometime later, Carlie and Dee said good night and headed back to Virginia. Sharla chose to spend the rest of the night with Reed. Tomorrow would be soon enough to share their news with her parents, and she didn't want to be parted from her new fiancé tonight.

When they were alone, Reed locked the door and turned out the lights. He carried her to his bedroom and kissed her breathless. His hands roamed hungrily over her body until he realized she wasn't wearing a bra. A groan escaped him as his hands found soft, bare breasts.

"I dressed in a hurry," she offered as an excuse.

Reed pulled her shirt over her head and tossed it to the floor. "Did I thank you for coming to my rescue?" he mumbled as he lifted her off her feet and captured a nipple with his mouth.

Sharla's fingers speared through his hair. Her hips arched against him as pleasure swept from her breasts to her womb. "You have the rest of our lives to say thanks," she promised huskily.

Logan's Lady

One

Logan sunk both his hands in the heavy thickness of Dee's hair and drew her closer. The honey blond tresses tumbled over his face and chest in a sensual caress. Her hair felt like silk against his skin and smelled honeysuckle sweet. He inhaled deeply, knowing that the scent of her was indelibly printed on his mind and in his heart.

She was all woman in his arms: strong, supple, sexy. He'd never known anyone more passionate, more responsive, or more giving. A tremor shook him at the feel of her lush curves sliding over the masculine angles of his hard form. Warm feminine flesh melded with hot male flesh, bringing forth a shared moan of satisfaction.

Since meeting Dee, he'd started thinking about things like promises, permanency, and serious commitments. The feelings were new, exciting, and exhilarating.

He slid his hands over her bare shoulders as her lips nibbled at his. He sipped at the sweetness of her mouth while his hands stroked the smooth, bare curves of her waist and hips. Kissing Dee had introduced him to a whole new realm of sensuality, had taught him that kissing could create an aching need that was so much deeper than the physical. As she sucked gently on his tongue, his arms engulfed her, and he dragged her closer.

"I love you." His voice was hoarse with arousal. He'd never said those words to another woman in all his thirty-five years, but there was no hesitancy. He loved her. He'd fallen swiftly and completely. It was scary, but the lightness of it seared his soul.

"I love you more."

Her husky whisper sent a shudder over his big body and made his muscles tighten with tension. Blood throbbed heavily through his veins. This time his mouth devoured hers. Their tongues slid against each other in a deep rhythm, twisting and tangling in pleasure.

When it was necessary to draw a breath, Logan gently lifted Dee until he could bury his face between her breasts. He nuzzled their softness, then slid his lips to one plump nipple and greedily suckled until it beaded in his mouth. He wasn't satisfied until he'd done the same to its mate. The soft, sexy sounds she made had him shivering with desire. Even more so when she writhed against him in demand.

He couldn't get enough of her. He never seemed to get close enough to her. His need for her was insatiable. He'd worried that his relentless desire might frighten her, but she didn't complain. She wanted him just as much.

Her soft hands on his body nearly drove him insane. His every nerve ending was tight with tension. His stomach muscles coiled and his blood ran hot. He wanted to sheathe himself in her softness. Nothing else could satisfy the savage hunger. Nothing short of total possession could sate his primitive need to make her a part of him.

Lifting his hips, he searched for the secret part of her where he could lock them together and feel whole again. He strained towards Dee's softness; seeking, seeking, but not finding.

His body didn't find the warm counterpart it sought, and a strident ringing in his ears pierced his sensual haze.

"Noooo!" An agonized groan erupted from deep in his chest. "No! Dammit! No!"

Logan's voice was thick with anger and frustration as his alarm clock shattered the sweetness of his dream and forced him into consciousness. He slammed a hand against the clock to halt the jarring noise and allowed himself a shuddering moan.

It was just another erotic dream to threaten his sanity. His body was tight with tension, aching and soaked in sweat. He shifted his legs restlessly and groaned in an agony of need.

The recurring dreams were driving him crazy. It had been months since he'd held Dee in his arms. She'd made it clear that she didn't want anything to do with him, yet the dreams were still vivid enough to make him ache with unfulfilled longing.

Last night he'd tried to satisfy the need with another woman. He hadn't succeeded, and the dream taunted him for the useless attempt to wipe her from his mind. He didn't want anyone else. No other woman excited him the way she did. The dreams were his only link with the woman he loved, but had deliberately alienated.

Leaping from bed, he strode to the bathroom, and then suffered another brief, brutally cold shower. The icy barrage didn't cool his temper. The anger he directed at himself never seemed to abate.

Dee had confessed her love to him, and he'd shared her desire for commitment. Then he'd learned she was a professional pilot. When she'd described her dedication to her career and her devotion to her family's business, his confidence had crumbled. He'd panicked, and had been paying every since.

Pride had been his downfall. He'd been scared and had reacted without thinking. He'd behaved like a total jerk and demanded that she choose between him and flying. He'd let his own fears and insecurities destroy their fragile relationship. He was a fool. She'd never forgive him.

He lived with the agony of not knowing whether she gave her sweetness and passion to other men because of his cruel rejection. It had been months since he'd seen or talked to her. It seemed like years, an eternity.

Logan shaved and dressed in his usual boots, soft jeans, and cotton shirt. It was barely dawn, but he left the house and headed for the barns. Within an hour of waking, he was astride Brutus, his big gelding, and was galloping across fields toward the construction site. Brutus loved to run, so his master gave him his head, and they raced across rich Kentucky bluegrass in an effort to burn off pent-up energy.

When Logan finally reined his horse, they were perched atop a rolling hill overlooking a long, flat plateau. Below them was the nearly completed construction site of an asphalt runway and metal hangar.

The thought of having planes landing and taking off from his property created a turbulent mixture of emotions. Sometimes the idea chilled him to the bone. His aversion to flying was deep-seeded and intense, but he was committed to the expansion plans.

Jake agreed with him. His foreman said it was high time the Circle B's had its own air transportation. They raised saddle horses, and the business had prospered over the past few years. They sold horses to all areas of the country, but it was becoming too expensive and time-consuming to transport their stock by truck and trailer.

So he'd invested in an airplane. The Bradford Bluegrass emblem of interlocking B's within a circle would appear on the plane just as it appeared on every other vehicle and product of the ranch.

Construction was scheduled to be completed within two weeks. The plane would be delivered soon. He, Jake Travis, and their youngest trainer, Butch Troyer, were going to take flying lessons so that they could share the piloting.

A shudder ripped through him at the thought, and his hands tightened on the reins. Sensing his tension, Brutus shifted restlessly beneath him. Logan relaxed his grip and soothed the horse with gentle words and a kinder hand.

The flying lessons would start as soon as Jake found a qualified instructor willing to live at the Circle B's for four to six weeks. That was the average length of time needed for all aspects of the training and to clock both dual and solo flying hours. Logan was familiar with the routine and was trying to mentally prepare himself for the ordeal.

They couldn't spare the time to travel any distance for lessons, so Jake was looking for someone who was willing to come to Kentucky. Logan didn't want any part of the hiring. He'd left all the details to his foreman, avoiding all aspects of the project until it was absolutely necessary to become involved.

He'd offered the training to all his employees, but Jake and Butch were the only takers. They'd gotten a lot of ribbing from the rest of the men, but it was good-natured, and they were looking forward to the training.

He was not.

He could only hope that his pride was a strong enough motivator to force him inside a cockpit. He'd planned carefully so that there was no coward's way out. He'd have to conquer his fear of flying or he'd never be able to hold his head high again.

He wasn't looking forward to the battle, but then he hadn't looked forward to much of anything lately. Even the height of the foaling season hadn't stirred much interest. He loved to work with horses, but his usual enthusiasm just wasn't there.

If fear was the best motivator, he was going to find out which was stronger, his fear or his pride. He hoped the flying instructor Jake hired would have lots of patience and nerves of steel.

Thinking of pilots always turned his thoughts to Dee. He still couldn't reconcile himself to the fact that his sexy, ultra-feminine lover was a pilot. Reaching into the back pocket of his jeans, he withdrew his wallet and found the picture of three women with lovely, identical features.

Three sets of beguiling green eyes smiled at him and created an ache in his heart. Dee hadn't told him about her sisters, but he'd accidentally run into one of them in Lexington. She'd given him the photograph.

Triplets. They were wearing matching khaki uniforms with the name Prescott Air Service in blue over their hearts. Logan tried to picture Dee in the cockpit of a plane, but the image caused a shudder to course over him. He had to find a way to squelch the sick fear he experienced at the thought of her risking her life each day. Battling his fear was the only way he could hope to set things straight with her.

So he was attempting to combine her world and his. He was having an airstrip constructed on his property. It was a start, but just barely. He had a great deal more to accomplish before he considered himself worthy of Dee's love.

Darla "Dee" Prescott had five years of experience in flight instruction. She'd started teaching at the age of twenty. That's when her family had launched an air charter service on the Virginia plantation that had belonged to her mother's family for generations.

Dee had a wealth of patience. She loved people, she loved flying and training other people to pilot a small plane. Sometimes she was asked, and agreed, to spend a few weeks instructing students on their own private airstrips.

Raised as an Air Force brat, she was used to traveling around the country. She didn't mind the occasional assignment that sent her to interesting locations. Sometimes the assignments offered her a pleasant change from living and working closely with her family.

"Mr. Travis has asked that you come to his horse farm in Kentucky for at least a month," explained Belle, Dee's mother, and the charter service's receptionist and schedule manager. "You'll have the opportunity to extend the lessons if you think it's necessary."

"The farm's owner is presently constructing a hangar and runway. He's purchased a small transport plane and wants to train three men to fly it. I got the impression that the farm is more like a big ranch operation, and the business is thriving."

"Why do they need an airstrip?" Dee asked. She and her sisters, Sharla and Carlie, were getting their usual Monday morning briefing from their mother.

"They raise and sell horses," Belle explained. "I believe he said both saddle horses and some thoroughbreds. They want to be able to transport the horses by air instead of trucking them all over the country."

"What's the name of the farm?" asked Dee.

"The Circle B's."

"Did Mr. Travis say what the B's stand for?"

"Something to do with bluegrass, I believe," Belle told her.

"Are all the prospective pilots men?" asked Sharla, Dee's older sister by two minutes.

Her sisters also piloted for Prescott Air Service. The three of them were triplets and nearly identical in looks. They stood five and a half feet tall, had brilliant turquoise eyes and sun-streaked, honey blond hair. Today, as most days, they were dressed in matching khaki uniforms bearing the Prescott Air Service emblem.

Their hair was the only feature that distinguished their differences. Dee's fell heavily to her waist, Carlie's was cut in a smooth pageboy with wispy bangs, and Sharla's curly, layered style fell over her shoulders like a cloak.

"I believe all three are men, but they've assured me that Dee will be adequately chaperoned. She'll be treated as a guest in the owner's home, and his household staff lives on the property. He's willing to furnish you with a car while you're there and take care of your expenses," she told Dee.

Belle epitomized the socially and morally correct southern belle. Despite a few age lines on her face and the silver in her hair, she was as beautiful as her daughters and very concerned about proper behavior.

The pilots and their mother were sharing a rare slow morning at the service. Since the office was within walking distance of the family home where they each had apartments, they spent a great deal of time together. Today, they'd arrived at work early and were discussing upcoming projects as they lingered over coffee.

"Anyone care for more?" Sharla asked, as she refilled her cup and then moved around the homey reception room to refill the others.

"Sounds like a cushy job," Carlie teased, eyes dancing. "Of course you'll be stuck in Kentucky for a month, but then your social life isn't exactly thrilling here, either."

"My social life suits me just fine," Dee retorted. She didn't date much, but it was by choice, not for the lack of interested men.

"Mr. Travis did warn me that your students would still have their usual work load and that you might have to keep odd hours, but he agreed to be as helpful as possible."

"The summertime is probably the busiest season on a horse farm," said Sharla.

Carlie added, "It's also the best time to learn to fly, since the weather is more settled. They probably want to squeeze their lessons in between their other chores."

"Is Travis the owner of this operation?" Dee wanted to know.

"I believe he's the manager or foreman or someone in authority whom the owner trusts to make major decisions," said her mother.

"While you're there, you might look over their stock and pick out some horses for us," Carlie suggested. "We've been promising ourselves we'd buy riding horses for five years."

The Prescott family lived in the sprawling mansion on the plantation, but until their business was established, had little time for recreation. Now that the air service was thriving, they had plans to hire an extra pilot, and they were looking forward to some free time again.

"That's a good idea," chimed Belle. "It's been years since we had riding horses on the property. Your dad had the barn restored, but never has gotten around to buying stock."

"I don't know much more about horses than how to ride them, but if Mr. Travis raises them, he should be able to offer some advice. How many do you think we should buy?"

"I don't know," Belle said. "We'll have to ask your Papa Bear." His daughters had dubbed Harold "Bear" Prescott Papa Bear while they were still toddlers.

Now a retired Air Force Sergeant, he'd been nicknamed Bear while in the service. The name was more of a physical description than a characterization, yet only his family dared to add Papa to the nickname.

Bear's specialty is airplane mechanics. Most of his time is spent keeping Prescott Air Service aircraft in mint condition, but his second love is the restoration of the family plantation.

"If we get too many, we'll have to hire extra help," said Sharla. They employed a married couple as housekeeper and caretaker, but the grounds were extensive. "Horses need daily attention, and none of us can spare the time."

"Besides, Sharla's going to get married and leave home," Carlie reminded. "If Dee keeps going off for months at a time, I'll be the only one here to exercise a horse."

Sharla had recently become engaged to U.S. Marshal Reed Connors, and the family was still trying to come to terms with the idea of her leaving home. The sisters were especially close and had never suffered lengthy separations.

"I'm not going to live on the moon," Sharla chided. "I'm just moving to D.C., and I'll be here every day for work. Reed and I will be coming for visits, you know."

Belle sniffed and reached for a handkerchief, as she did every time Sharla's marriage was mentioned. She was thrilled about the engagement, but she still got emotional about having one of her babies leave home.

All three sisters grinned. Dee and Carlie knew that Sharla and Reed were deeply in love. They were happy for the couple, but they also realized that life as they'd known it for twenty-five years was changing.

Except for Carlie's brief, disastrous marriage at the age of eighteen, the triplets had made their home with their parents, and had been devoted to their work and family.

"Have you two settled on a date yet?" Dee asked.

"We want to wait until we both have some time for a honeymoon," Sharla explained. "Reed will have a month's vacation coming in September. By then Dee should be back from Kentucky, and Daddy should have another pilot hired."

Bear had been advertising for an experienced pilot to join the service on a full-time basis. The triplets had worked unselfishly to get the business established, but they wanted and had earned more time for their personal lives.

"So you'll be spending most of July and maybe some of August in Kentucky?" Sharla asked Dee.

"I think so," she replied. "It'll be a challenge to train three men at one time. I taught those three teenagers in Texas, but they weren't on a limited schedule It should be interesting."

"When will you be leaving?" asked Carlie.

Dee glanced at her mother.

"Mr. Travis says they'll be ready after the holiday on the fourth. I'll schedule your arrival for the Monday after," she said.

Belle's organizational skills were legendary, but until the air service had been launched, the skills had been utilized for social activities, her daughters' education, and taking care of her family. She'd surprised them all when she'd decided to put her skills to use in the business. She argued that if she ever wanted to see her loved ones, then she had to be near the airfield.

Dee trusted her mother to take care of all the arrangements for her stay in Kentucky. Belle was a stickler about insuring the safety of her daughters, so Dee didn't worry about what she would find at her temporary home.

"I've done some checking on this farm you'll be visiting," Belle said, causing the grins on her daughters' faces to widen. "The property has been in the same family for generations and the present owner is highly respected. I've been assured that he's a gentleman and will be a considerate host."

"Is he tall, dark, handsome, and disgustingly rich?" Sharla wanted to know.

"Is he married?" asked Carlie.

Belle frowned a little. "He's a confirmed bachelor. One of those horsy types, I imagine, but his sister lives with him and so does his housekeeper."

"Just so Dee is properly chaperoned," Carlie teased, tongue in cheek.

Their childhood had been spent moving from one Air Force base to another, and the triplets had learned early in life to adjust to new surroundings. Bear had insisted that they all be trained in self-defense, so none of them was especially concerned about chaperons, but they liked to humor their mother.

"If you aren't satisfied with the arrangements," Belle told Dee, "then you can come right back home. I made it clear to Mr. Travis that you're to have the right of refusal if you don't like their operation."

"Does Mr. Travis have a first name?" Dee wanted to know.

"His name is Jacob, but I believe he told me he prefers to have it shortened to Jake. He and his boss will be students along with one other member of their staff. He'll be the one coordinating the training, so I imagine he'll give you all the details. I told him you would stop on a brief visit this week to finalize your plans."

"When am I doing that?"

"We have a charter for Louisville tomorrow. I thought you could stop over in Lexington on the way back."

Dee nodded in agreement. "What ages are we talking? Are all three men about the same age?" Having been with a student when her mother made arrangements with Jake Travis, she hadn't met him personally and didn't have a clue about his identity.

"Mr. Travis is in his early thirties. He said one of the students is just out of high school, and his employer is older. He didn't mention his boss's age. I assume he's middle-aged."

"Variety is the spice of life, they say," Dee teased as she finished her coffee and disposed of her cup. "I'll feel like an old-fashioned schoolmarm with students in every age group."

"I can actually picture you with your hair in a bun and a yardstick in your hand," Sharla told her. "The image suits you. You've always been the most old-fashioned romantic in the family."

"Me?" Dee challenged. "You're the one who's had stars in her eyes since flying into the sunset with an incredibly sexy Marshal."

Sharla put both hands on her hips and glared at her sister. "You shouldn't be noticing how sexy my man is!" she insisted.

Dee and Carlie laughed outright, while their mother smothered a smile. They were all very pleased by Sharla's first and only experience with true love. They delighted in teasing her.

"Girls," admonished Belle, "it's not proper for young ladies to be thinking about or discussing a man's sex appeal."

"I wonder if Dee's new crop of students will be a sexy bunch," Carlie said, totally ignoring her mother's rebuke.

"You shouldn't concern yourself with such things," Belle insisted demurely. "However, Mr. Travis is quite handsome, and he has lovely manners."

"Handsome and sexy, Mother?" Dee taunted with a mischievous smile.

"If I hadn't sworn off men altogether," chimed Carlie, eyes glinting wickedly, "I'd come to Kentucky and help you teach those cowboys how to really fly."

"Carla Denise!" Belle admonished in a scandalized tone.

"Uh, oh," said Sharla, "It's time to get to work if Mother's going to start tossing out middle names."

"Right you are, Sharla Louise." Dee leveled her taunt as she headed for the door and held it open for her sisters.

"Can it, Darla Joann."

Belle clucked her tongue at her squabbling offspring. She'd been making the same motherly noises for more than twenty-five years. They ignored her, as usual.

She'd given birth to and raised three beautiful, intelligent daughters, but they did tend to be a little spirited and headstrong. They loved to tease one another, but despite their diverse personalities, they were devoted sisters. She and Bear were extremely proud of them.

Over the years, there had always been something to worry about when raising their daughters. Right now, she was worried about Darla.

Dee was technically her middle child, and the most gentle, sensitive person she'd ever known. She had a sixth sense, a special ability to feel things that most people couldn't. Belle's maternal grandmother, Ida Batiste, had been the same.

People called it extrasensory perception these days, but in her grandmother's time, people had just accepted the fact that Ida could feel and see things that were beyond the normal person's vision.

In recent years, Dee's abilities had grown stronger. It was both a gift and a curse. Last month her unusual perception had saved Sharla and Reed's lives. That was truly a blessing.

But Dee was also plagued by the ability to know exactly how people felt about her; whether they liked her or were just pretending to like her. She knew if they were jealous, envious, or downright vicious.

Dee's unique sensitivity had caused her to become rather isolated in recent years. She was open and loving with her family, and always friendly, but she remained a very private and self-contained woman.

Last winter, she'd gone on vacation after Christmas and come home with deep emotional wounds. Belle knew that Dee had finally trusted someone with her heart, and that she'd been hurt in the process, but she'd adamantly refused to discuss the matter with her family.

Bear had wanted to find the man who'd hurt his baby and tear him limb from limb. Sharla and Carlie had tried to comfort their sister, but Dee had been inconsolable. She was just beginning to recover her normal, sunny disposition.

A frown marred Belle's features as she wondered if sending Dee to Kentucky was a good idea. She hadn't discussed the decision with Bear. He didn't approve of her meddling, but a mother had to do what was best for her babies.

Anyway, Dee would go there tomorrow and learn the truth. It was up to her to make a final decision about accepting the assignment.

Two

The late June sunshine was bright and warm as Dee flew her Cessna through the blue skies over Kentucky. She'd taken a charter to Louisville at noon and then headed back east toward Lexington. Now she was nearing the property where she'd land just long enough to meet her prospective students.

As she neared the coordinates she'd been given for the horse farm, she gradually decreased elevation and flew closer to the ground to search for Circle B's airfield. Once she caught sight of the paved strip, she circled the property and radioed her approach to their base operator.

Touchdown was smooth and easy. The winds were calm and the strip was paved, either new or recently resurfaced. Its excellent condition would be a real benefit to student fliers; easing their takeoffs and landings.

The two men at the edge of the tarmac waited for the plane's engine to die before approaching the aircraft. They watched intently as a slender, shapely, uniform-clad body stepped from the cockpit.

Then their eyes widened with admiration and pleasure. They'd known Prescott's flight instructor was single and female, but they hadn't known or expected that she would be young, blond and gorgeous.

As Dee climbed from the cool cockpit of the plane, she was engulfed by sunshine. A soft, sweetly scented breeze filled her lungs and brushed her skin, refreshing her after hours spent in the confines of the Cessna.

She was a true sensualist who loved to feel the sun's warmth on her face and the wind against her flesh. She had keen instincts and a unique ability to judge the physical and spiritual hospitality of most places she visited.

Dee always trusted her instincts, and so far, this little chunk of Kentucky was very pleasing to her senses. A serene smile was extended to the men who met her halfway to the hangar.

"Miss Prescott?" queried the older of the two. The tall, solidly built man reached her in a few strides and offered a hand in greeting. "I'm Jake Travis. Welcome to the Circle B's."

Dee liked the feel of the strong, work-roughened hand that dwarfed her own. Her first impression of Travis was favorable. His hazel eyes were honest and welcoming without being flirtatious. She made steady eye contact for several seconds, making certain there was no sign of the chauvinism or an underlying resentment of her gender.

"This is Butch Troyer, one of our trainers and one of our wannabe pilots," said Jake.

Dee turned to the sandy-haired youth and extended her hand. The younger man's grasp was brief, but his grip was firm. He was a head shorter than Travis, with a lanky build and a too-thin face. His eyes were blue and endearingly shy, but he didn't hesitate to enthuse over her landing.

"It's a pleasure to meet you, Ms. Prescott. You sure did set that plane down nice and gentle. It was a pure pleasure to watch."

His praise was sincere, but the teacher in Dee didn't want him to think it was always mat easy. "That's because you have some nice, smooth asphalt," she countered. "It makes a lot of difference in the landing."

"Everything's new," Jake explained. "The strip was just finished last week. Our plane won't be delivered until Friday. I hope you didn't need to see it today."

Dee shook her head, tossing her long, heavy braid from side to side. "We won't be flying it for a while. There's a lot of classroom work to do first, and I usually do most of the dual time in my Cessna. It's equipped with an extra set of controls for training."

"We'll get to fly that plane?" Butch asked in an awed tone as he gazed at her aircraft.

"It's a lot more streamlined than a cargo plane," Dee explained. "We'll train on it and then adjust for your carrier when everyone's comfortable with the controls."

Butch couldn't seem to take his eyes off the plane, and Dee smiled with gentle understanding. "You're welcome to check it out, if you like," she told him. "Climb all over it if you want."

Butch's eyes lit with excitement. He shot another glance at Dee and then to Jake.

"Go ahead and look it over," the foreman told him. "I'm going to take Ms. Prescott up to the house to meet the boss."

"You're sure you don't mind?"

"I'm sure," she said. "If you're going to learn to fly, you need to get familiar with every inch of it."

"Right!" said Butch, her reasoning putting wings on his feet as he flew toward the plane.

Dee watched him, appreciating his enthusiasm. Students who were genuinely thrilled with planes were by far the easiest ones to teach.

"Butch's been impatient ever since we mentioned the idea of taking flying lessons. He's a first-rate horse trainer, but I'm beginning to think his real passion is airplanes," said Jake as Dee turned her gaze back to him.

"He seems genuinely interested," she teased.

Jake shared a grin with her, admiring the way her eyes sparkled with amusement. They were beautiful eyes, their color just a shade greener than the turquoise in his belt buckle. She also had a sense of humor. That was a must for functioning with his crew.

"I'll take you up to the house. It's a pretty long walk across the fields, so we'll go by truck."

They fell into step and headed for a dusty pickup parked near the hangar. Jake opened the passenger door for her and offered a hand of assistance. Then he closed the door and moved to the driver's side. Dee made a mental note to mention his good manners to her mother.

"Are you on a tight schedule today?" he asked as he put the truck in gear and headed down a narrow dirt road.

"No," she said, brushing a wispy curl off her face. "I had a charter this morning, but I don't have anything else scheduled until evening."

"Have you had lunch?"

"Yes, thanks. I ate in Louisville."

"How long can you stay? Would you like a complete tour of the property?"

"Not this time," she told him, turning her face to catch the breeze through the window. "I only stopped to meet everyone, then I have to be on my way. I want to be back in Virginia by late afternoon."

Jake nodded. "Well, you've already met Butch and me. The boss'll be your third student. He's supposed to be at the house. He can answer any questions you have about your contract and show you the guest suite you'll be using."

"He and his sister are in residence now?"

"Yeah. Patti just graduated from college, and she's spending the summer at home trying to decide if she wants to get a job or go back to school for her master's degree." His tone was a mix of affection and exasperation, implying that the woman in question didn't know what she wanted to do.

Dee was surprised. She'd thought the owner's sister would be much older. She'd imagined a career woman, a widow, a spinster, or a divorcee. She hadn't considered other reasons a woman might be living at home with her brother.

"Mattie Walters is the cook and housekeeper. She lives here, too, in an apartment on the top floor of the house. She's been with the family since Patti was a little girl. She's a real nice lady, and I'm sure the two of you will get along just fine."

"Do most of the employees live on the properly?" she asked.

"I have a small house down by the river," Jake explained. "It comes with the job. A few years ago, we converted an old smoke house into two efficiency apartments. Butch and our other trainer, Grif Myers, bunk there, but most of the help lives off the property."

The staff sounded like a tightly knit family, and Dee wondered how well they worked together. She was extremely sensitive to high levels of tension amongst the people she worked with, so she avoided situations where there was constant emotional turmoil. That's why she never agreed to long-term training schedules until she'd gotten a feel for the overall atmosphere of a prospective training center.

"This certainly is some beautiful country," she commented. From the air she had seen miles and miles of white board fences that framed patchwork fields. The truck was moving down a narrow road that wove between grazing pastures. In the distance, she could see rolling hills and dense woodlands. A wide, winding stream seemed to meander across the entire property.

"We've been lucky so far this summer," said Jake. "We've had plenty of rain, but no flooding. It's been good weather for crops and livestock."

"Mother said you raise saddle horses. Do you raise a lot of crops, too?"

"Mostly alfalfa and oats for the livestock," he explained. "In years past, a lot of tobacco was raised in this area, but not so much anymore. We run a few head of cattle, but just to supply beef for the local area."

"How far are we from Lexington?"

"We can be there in a half-hour or so, depending on how fast you drive," he said, throwing her a teasing glance.

Dee matched his smile, and then turned her attention to the huge white house that came into view for the first time. As they rounded a corner and passed through an ornate iron gateway, she got a full view of a sprawling, two-storied house that matched her own mansion home in size and grandeur. It was another plantation home like the many that dotted the old South.

The house didn't have stately pillars like her Virginia home, but a wide verandah circled the entire building, and was adorned with an inviting collection of wicker swings, gliders, and rocking chairs. Heavy willow trees guarded the homestead, and an abundance of flowerbeds provided a riot of color to the picturesque scene.

"What a gorgeous place," she enthused, feeling a deep, unexpected affinity for the gracious old home.

"It is that."

Jake swung the truck around the circular drive and parked near the front porch. Dee opened her door and was immediately assaulted by the sweet, heady scent of honeysuckle. A profusion of flowering vines wove through the latticed rails surrounding the verandah.

She inhaled deeply as she stepped from the truck. "I love the smell of honeysuckle."

Jake grinned. "Then you're going be right at home here." He lightly grasped her elbow and ushered her up the porch steps to the front door.

When she stepped through the door into a large foyer, Dee was bombarded with sensation. The big old home seemed to open its arms and envelop her with welcoming warmth. The feelings of belonging, of coming home, were so strong that she was temporarily disconcerted.

She'd been in plenty of houses that she found warm and aesthetically pleasing, but she'd never experienced such a dramatic sense of affinity with someone else's home.

Jake led her through a wide archway and into a huge, brightly lit living room with several long windows and an incredibly high ceiling. The windows were framed by sheer, lacy Priscilla curtains that allowed the sun to bathe the room and sparkle with prismatic beauty on the crystal of an old-fashioned chandelier.

The room's carpeting was a shade between blue and gray. The furnishings were a high-back, early American sofa, a loveseat, and easy chairs in a pleasing blend of dusty blue and pale green. The overall effect was bright and pleasing to the senses.

"What a wonderful room!" she exclaimed in delight.

A soft, feminine voice responded. "Thank you."

Dee and Jake turned toward another doorway as the owner of the voice moved closer. Dressed in cut-off jeans and an oversized T-shirt, the young woman looked like a teenager, but her eyes shone with the wisdom and intelligence of added years.

"I just had the room redone this spring," she said, joining them. "My brother thinks it's too pretty and feminine, but I think it's perfect."

Dee returned her smile. "I think you're right."

"Patti," said Jake. "This is Ms. Prescott. She's a flight instructor; here to decide if she wants to tackle the job of teaching us men to fly."

The younger woman's hair was pale blond and just touched her shoulders. An abundance of soft curls bounced as she nodded her head in greeting. Blue eyes were brimming with curiosity, but her manners were above reproach.

"Welcome to the Circle B's. I heard your plane land. I don't know why anyone would take-on the awesome task of teaching three hardheaded men to fly, but I sure wouldn't mind having another female on the property. After four years of college dorm life, this place seems awfully quiet."

"Quiet?" Jake argued, giving Dee the impression that he made a habit of disagreeing with the boss' sister. "How could anybody call this place quiet?"

Patti ignored his question and gave Dee a grin that made her elfin features radiate mischief. "Notice that he didn't attempt to correct my remark about hardheaded men."

Dee's smile widened as she glanced from Patti to Jake. There seemed to be a very strong attraction between the two of them, yet she had a feeling neither was willing to accept the fact. Still, the vibrations were strong.

While Patti's gaze challenged, Jake was shaking his head in resignation.

"My father was a career Air Force sergeant," Dee offered. "So I'm more used to hardheaded men than any other kind."

"That's good," Patti replied, "because my brother —"

Jake interrupted her. "Where is your brother?"

"He's in the office, snarling at someone on the telephone."

"Probably Ross Parker. He wants us to board that mean-spirited stallion of his until his trainer gets back from vacation."

"The horse that nearly killed two of his men?"

"The very same," said Jake, frowning.

Conversation halted and all three of them turned to the inside doorway as they heard the heavy sound of boots moving toward them across hardwood floors. A shiver of unexpected anticipation hit Dee, unsettling her with its intensity.

She tensed, eyes widening and heart racing, as a tall, broad-shouldered man strode into the room and closed the distance between them. Her breath hissed out in shock as silvery blue eyes immediately locked on her.

"Dee!"

The sound of her name on his lips was incredibly intimate, and stunned everyone in the room — especially her.

She didn't want to hear his husky voice brimming with pleasure. She didn't want his gaze locked on her in amazed delight. She never wanted to be anywhere within miles of Logan Bradford.

She hated him. She'd never hated anything or anyone in her life until she'd met Logan Bradford. She'd learned how to hate at the same time she'd learned how to love with all her heart. She'd given him her love, and he'd thrown it back at her. She hated him with a passion intensified by the depth of emotion he'd introduced her to.

Her eyes frosted with displeasure, then shot from Logan back to Jake. If Logan was the boss of this operation, she didn't want anything to do with it. "I think there's been a serious mistake here."

Logan flinched at her tone. Normally a very private man, he'd been caught off guard by the sight of the woman who made passionate love to him nightly, but only in his dreams. He fought to contain the heady rush of pleasure that left him raw and vulnerable.

She didn't share his elation at seeing each other after months of separation, and that knowledge reinforced his defenses. His expression grew tight and guarded, his posture stiff and eyes challenging as he took the offensive.

"What's wrong, Dee? You couldn't have been here more than a few minutes. Are you finding the backwoods of Kentucky so unappealing already?"

Dee's eyes flashed, displaying a depth of fiery spirit that would have seemed unlikely a minute earlier. She rarely lost her temper, but when she did, people took notice.

She knew Logan was referring to her rejection of his marriage proposal six months ago. He was suggesting, that she'd refused him because of where he lived, and that had little to do with her decision.

"I'm a professional flight instructor," she informed him stiffly. "I don't have to love a location before I can train people to fly."

Logan went pale beneath his tan. For a stunned second all he could do was stare at her. He'd been so damned pleased to see her that he hadn't considered why she was here. Now he took in her attire and shuddered. The jumpsuit she was wearing matched the one he'd seen her sister wearing at the Lexington airport, and bore the emblem of Prescott Air Service.

He'd deliberately let Jake handle the hiring of an instructor, avoiding the project for as long as possible. He'd known Dee was a pilot, but not an instructor. Never in his worst nightmare had he imagined his foreman would hire the one woman in the world he didn't want to know about his aversion to planes.

If Dee's emotions hadn't been in such a turmoil, she'd have realized that he was more shocked than she was. Nobody could fake so violent a reaction.

Patti immediately realized the depth of her brother's response. "Logan?" she injected in confusion and concern.

"Leave us." He couldn't find the strength to soften his command. His gaze never left Dee, but his order was directed at his sister and foreman.

Patti started to protest, but Jake nudged her toward the door. "I could use something cold to drink," he said, following close behind her until they were out of the living room and headed for the kitchen.

"Did you hear his voice when he said her name? Did you see him close up when she gave him the cold shoulder?" Patti's whispered questions came in a fierce rush after they left the room. "You know the only woman who could affect him that way is the one who nearly destroyed him last winter. How could you bring her here?"

"Her name is Darla," Jake growled. "I've only heard Logan mutter the name Dee. How the hell was I supposed to know?"

"You should have done more checking."

"Do you have any idea how hard it is to find a pilot willing to travel to a training site? I was lucky to find someone with her qualifications and reputation. I didn't demand a personal history of her love life."

"Maybe you should have." Patti snatched a pitcher from the refrigerator and poured them glasses of iced tea.

In the living room, Logan and Dee continued to stare at each other. Both of them were breathing hard, having sustained an emotional blow that was more debilitating than an unexpected physical attack.

Dee was trembling violently. Coming face to face with the only man she'd ever loved and lost would be upsetting under normal circumstances. In her situation it was unbearably painful. Anger seemed the safest outlet for emotion.

"Is this some kind of sick joke?"

Logan struggled with the need to touch her; to reach out to her in some fashion. He tightened his hands into fists and stood stock-still. He didn't want to antagonize her, but he was on the defensive.

"I was as surprised to see you as you were to see me," he responded without emotion. "Did you actually come here without knowing that I own this place?"

His question triggered immediate resentment. Was he egotistical enough to believe she'd have come if she'd known the truth? Dee trembled with the effort to control emotions she'd kept in tight check for six months.

"If I'd had any idea you owned this place, I'll guarantee you I wouldn't have come within an inch of it."

She'd just recently begun to feel good about herself, to regain some self-respect and enthusiasm for the future. A place that had seemed so welcoming was rapidly becoming an emotional booby trap.

Logan's gaze devoured her, taking in every tiny detail of her appearance; the honey gold satin of her hair; the flashing brilliance of her eyes, the womanly body that could drive him wild with need. His dreams didn't begin to compare with the reality.

He knew she didn't want to hear how much he'd missed her, so he decided engaging her in an argument would at least make her open up and keep her near while his senses feasted.

"Are you in the habit of accepting jobs without doing a background check?"

Dee bristled. "I was told that Jake Travis was in charge of hiring a pilot. Since my mother always does a thorough background check, I had no reason for concern. All she told me was that the owner's family had lived here for generations, and the name of the place had something to do with bluegrass."

"Bradford Bluegrass," Logan supplied, fighting a savage urge to drag her into his arms and plunder her mouth with his own.

"Believe me," she snapped. "If I'd heard the name Bradford, I would have run screaming!"

Logan had assumed that she was a charter pilot for a small firm, but he knew very little about her career. He hadn't known that she could be hired for extended periods. He hadn't thought about her working so much with men, and he didn't like the idea at all.

"You have no problem moving in with a complete stranger and working strictly with men?" The thought made him insanely jealous, even though he hadn't thought anything of hiring her himself. He wondered how often she was at the mercy of strangers.

His censorious tone infuriated Dee. He had absolutely no right to pass judgment on her. "I was assured I would be properly chaperoned," she snapped, "not that it's any of your business who I live or work with!"

"It's my business if you work for me."

"Well, rest assured, I have no intention of working for you," he insisted fiercely. "You can consider our association at an end from this minute forward. There's no way in hell I'd work for you."

Her scathing dismissal fueled Logan's anger. He knew she had every right to despise him, but the loathing in her eyes and tone were still a grim shock. They'd parted in anger, yet he hadn't realized just how much she hated him.

He'd nurtured the hope that someday she'd understand and forgive him for his callous actions. That had obviously been another mistake. Her present attitude didn't leave much room for understanding and forgiveness.

Frustration heightened his self-disgust and triggered defensive anger. He had only a few seconds to decide if he wanted to send her out of his life again or find a way to keep her close while he battled his other demons.

The internal struggle was brief. There was really nothing to decide. He wanted her near him. He ached for her in a way no other woman could satisfy, so he changed tactics.

"I thought your work was all-important to you. I thought you prided yourself on your professionalism," he reminded grimly. "Your professional manner sure won't win any awards today. I'm a prospective client, and you're being as nasty as hell."

The blood pounded in Dee's temples at an alarming rate. Her eyes glazed with fury. She felt as though she might explode. "How dare you!" she gasped, enraged.

She'd loved him to distraction, given him everything she had to give, but all he'd given her in return was a macho demand that she abandon her career to become his full-time playmate.

"How dare you criticize my professionalism? What makes you think you have a right to judge me? The only thing you ever really wanted from me was sex. No woman in her right mind would exchange a respectable career for a shaky future with the worst kind of chauvinist!"

The muscles of Logan's jaws worked furiously. His chest was tight, his breathing constricted. He wasn't a chauvinist. He'd spent months trying to correct his mistake. He hurt, too, and he wanted a chance to make it up to her. Taking a deep breath, he mustered the courage to tell her the truth, but pride kept the words lodged in his throat.

"I'm leaving," Dee exclaimed, shaking with the effort to control her temper and her emotional upheaval. "You can tell Mr. Travis that I'm not interested in a contract. He can start looking for another instructor."

She turned to leave the room, and Logan reached out a hand to halt her. The instant his fingers made contact with her arm, electricity leapt between them. She swiftly jerked out of his reach.

"Don't touch me!"

The rejection hit him hard. He was having a rough time dealing with his own rioting emotions, but he didn't want to let her go. Reaching out a hand again, he grasped her arm more firmly and whirled her closer to him.

Dee didn't even think, she just reacted from sheer protective instinct and the sudden terror of being too close to him. She drew back her hand and slammed it against the side of his face.

The sound of flesh slapping flesh, and the uncharacteristic violence of Dee's attack, stunned them both for an instant. The room went deadly still, the only sound was the harshness of their breathing. They glared at each other like sworn enemies.

Dee's control was near shattering. Her pride and self-respect were taking a beating. She'd never struck another human being in her life. She couldn't even bring herself to smash a bug, yet she'd slapped Logan with enough force to numb her hand and leave a welt on his face.

She knew she was dangerously close to losing all control. Her legs were shaking, and she was in danger of collapsing in a quivering heap on the floor. Instead, she turned on her heel and marched toward the front door without another word or glance at his angry, flushed features.

The violent slamming of the front door brought Jake and Patti from the kitchen. Logan was staring after their departed guest, his fingers brushing the red, hand-shaped mark on his face.

"Go after her," he told Jake, his tone deep and rough as he fought the need to follow Dee. He couldn't risk alienating her even more. It would take a lot of time and patience to win her trust again, and he needed Jake to secure that time for him.

"Do whatever it takes. Triple her pay, promise her anything, but get her signature on that contract."

"Logan!" Patti protested. She was one of the few people who understood her brother's intense fear of planes. She knew how hard it was for him to face his fears, and she didn't want his pain intensified by a woman who'd already caused him so much heartache.

Jake's brows met in a frown. "Are you sure?"

"I'm sure," Logan snapped. "Whatever it takes."

Three

Dee was fighting hard for control as she walked down the road Jake had used to bring her from the airstrip. She was trembling violently and tears welled in her eyes, but she fought back any visible sign of her shattered emotions. She concentrated on getting back to her plane and getting home as fast as she could manage.

A low, wounded moan escaped when she heard the approach of the pickup truck behind her. She fervently prayed that Logan wasn't following her. She didn't think she could bear another confrontation with him right now.

The truck drew near and a horn tooted softly. Dee ignored the summons and dredged up reserves of control. She heard the vehicle being shifted into park and realized the driver had stopped to follow her on foot.

"Ms. Prescott." It was Jake's voice. "Please let me drive you back to your plane."

He laid a tentative hand on Dee's arm, and she came to a halt. Her throat was too tight to allow a response. Glancing over her shoulder, she made sure Logan was nowhere in sight, then she nodded her head in acceptance of the lift.

When they were both in the cab of the truck, Jake immediately put it in gear. He offered her an apology as he drove, but kept his gaze averted from her sad, shimmering eyes.

"I'm really sorry about the mix-up. I had no idea you and Logan knew each other."

"And that we couldn't stand each other?" she managed in a shaky, strained voice.

"That either," he added, grimacing. Jake thought Logan's opinion differed, but he didn't argue. "I want to assure you that nobody deliberately deceived you or brought you here under false pretenses. You have to know that Logan was as surprised as you were."

Dee didn't doubt that he'd been surprised, but she was just too shaken to consider anyone else's reactions and motives.

When she didn't respond, Jake continued, "He usually takes care of all the hiring himself, but other than writing the checks, he hasn't wanted much to do with this project. We tried to hire someone from Kentucky first, but with no luck, so we started looking out of state for an instructor. He was pleased when I told him I'd found someone willing to come here, but he didn't ask for details."

Dee recalled the argument with Logan that had destroyed their brief, passionate relationship. He'd been very blunt about his opinion of pilots. He'd wanted her to give up her career. He hadn't wanted her involved with flying in any fashion, and he'd behaved like a totally irrational jerk.

Since that time, Dee had gradually accepted the fact that his irrational behavior was simply a means to an end. Logan had wanted to put an end to their affair, so he'd chosen a method that was so unreasonable he knew she couldn't accept it.

Not many women these days were willing to give up hard-won careers to become a rich man's possession. She'd actually considered it, she'd loved him that much, but she also loved her family. They would have been so hurt.

The realization that he'd wanted an excuse to dump her was what had ultimately caused the most pain. It would have been kinder to tell her the truth; that he'd enjoyed their time together, but not enough to make a long-term commitment and compromises. Instead, he'd left her feeling used and discarded.

"Logan still wants you to work for us," Jake offered when the silence in the truck got too heavy. He didn't think his passenger wanted to talk, but he was running out of time.

Dee snorted at the thought of working for Logan Bradford. If he wanted anything, she doubted it was flight instruction.

"I'm dead serious, Ms. Prescott."

"Dee," she automatically insisted, well past the stage of formalities.

"Dee," Jake corrected, his tone growing heavy. "Please don't let your personal differences with Logan interfere here. I know you had a shock today, but don't write us off in haste. We're in desperate need of an instructor. You must know how hard it is to find someone who'll travel, and we've already got a quarter of a million dollars tied up in this project. If we don't get our training before winter, it could cost us another year."

Dee tried to harden herself against his persuasive arguments. She didn't want to concern herself with his problems. She was having a hard enough time coping with her own.

They pulled to a stop near the hangar and Jake turned to give her his full attention. "Give it a little time," he coaxed. "It's really important that we start lessons this soon, and I can guarantee that you won't have to spend as much time with Logan as you will with Butch and me."

Dee didn't like being reminded of Butch and his youthful enthusiasm. She'd always been too much of a softy, but this time she couldn't allow herself to be swayed.

Jake knew he wasn't making any headway. She didn't look very receptive to his pleas. "I don't need your signature on a contract until you've had time to consider the job, and you can alter the contract to suit yourself."

"You need to be looking for someone else," was her only comment as she climbed from the truck.

Jake jumped from the driver's side and followed her across the pavement. "I promise I'll keep searching, but you know there's not much chance that I'll find anybody."

It wasn't her problem. She wasn't committed to anything, Dee argued to herself. She'd have her mother do some looking, too, but she wouldn't let it worry her. The Bradford crew wasn't her responsibility.

"We're having a big community barbecue for the Fourth of July. Why don't you come and bring some friends," Jake suggested on impulse. "Give yourself a chance to get to know everybody. Maybe you'll realize that working here wouldn't be so bad. You might even get to like us."

Dee slowed her progress as she reached her Cessna. She turned and looked him directly in the eyes. "I don't have anything against you or your crew, Mr. Travis."

"Jake."

"Jake," she repeated. "But I have to be honest with you. No matter how much I like you, Butch, the staff, or this property, I have no intention of working with Logan."

"We'll double the fee you were offered."

Dee's eyes widened. She was already being offered a generous salary. Did Jake have the authority to offer anything he wanted, or had Logan believed money would sway her decision?

"Money isn't the issue," she insisted.

"We'll triple it."

Her eyes narrowed and renewed anger washed over her. "I'm not for sale, at any price, and you can tell your boss that there are still some things money can't buy!"

When she started to turn away, Jake gently touched her arm. "I'm sorry," he said with quiet sincerity. "I didn't mean to offend you or show any disrespect. I'm a desperate man, and we need your help. Losing a whole year will cost us more in the long run."

Dee wanted to tell him that it wouldn't do any good to lay a guilt trip on her. She couldn't and wouldn't work with Logan Bradford.

"I'll ask my mother to do some checking for you. Maybe she'll find an instructor who can take my place."

"What will you tell her?" he asked. "If anyone learns that you rejected the position, then they're going to be curious as to why."

Dee closed her eyes and stifled a moan. She hadn't thought about that. How was she going to explain this to her mother? Her parents didn't know anything about Logan, and her sisters knew very little.

She did a thorough check of the plane. It was automatic for her to explain the process as she moved around the Cessna, and Jake's attention was diverted as he followed her, asking questions.

The subject of employment was dropped, but Dee had to think about it again when she was alone in the cockpit. How could she explain her rejection of the contract without telling the whole truth, or flat-out lying?

The question plagued her all the way home. The trip didn't take long enough for her to formulate a reasonable excuse for not taking the assignment, and she really didn't want to discuss her personal feelings on the subject.

Belle had assumed that her stop in Kentucky would be a simple matter of introductions. What would she think when Dee rejected the assignment? She was still too shaken to discuss the subject rationally, so she decided to tell her mother that she had some reservations.

No. That wouldn't work. If Belle was going to be asked to find a replacement, then she'd have to know the truth. Dee hated being put in such a difficult position. She was damned if she did, and damned if she didn't. It was a no-win situation.

And of course, both her sisters would have to be in the office when she arrived home. She entered the reception area and gave her eyes a few seconds to adjust to the change from sunlight to interior lighting.

Then she glanced from Sharla to Carlie. She could tell by their expressions that they immediately picked up on the emotional distress radiating from her. Sometimes she felt like a walking radar station.

"What's up?" Carlie asked, not even bothering with a hello.

"Where's Mother?" asked Dee.

"She and Daddy are going out to dinner, so she left early. We're minding the store."

"Did you run into trouble in Kentucky?" asked Sharla.

"What I ran into in Kentucky was Logan Bradford," Dee explained in a curt tone. She slapped her flight pad down on the reception desk and busied herself with work, but she could feel the waves of concern emanating from her sisters.

Sharla and Carlie exchanged frowns. They knew very little about the man in question, only that he'd hurt Dee. Sharla had met him briefly, and personally thought he was hurting, too, but Dee had refused to discuss him with her.

"Where did you run into him?" asked Carlie.

"He's one of the B's that goes with the Circle B's," Dee explained. "I didn't realize it until Jake Travis took me to meet his boss."

"Did he know you were the pilot his foreman had hired?"

"Apparently not. Jake said he didn't want anything to do with the hiring, so I was a big surprise for him, too."

Dee still hadn't turned from the desk to look at them. It was a bad sign, and meant that she wasn't coping with the shock too well. She couldn't hide her reaction completely, but her sisters knew she was trying to minimize the affect it had on her.

Carlie moved close and laid a comforting hand on her sister's back. Feeling Dee's stiffness, she began to rub her shoulders. They all knew how sensitive Dee was, and how much she hated confrontational scenes.

"Was it really unpleasant?"

Dee sighed deeply and tried to relax. Until Carlie had touched her, she hadn't realized that her muscles were still knotted with tension.

"It was the pits."

"How did Logan react?"

Dee had only to close her eyes to bring a vivid picture of him to mind. She didn't want to remember the way his eyes had flared with pleasure or the sound of her name on his lips.

She didn't want to think about how utterly gorgeous he was or how her heart had raced at the sight of him. He was poison, and she couldn't allow herself to forget past mistakes. She wouldn't survive another such mistake.

"You'd have thought we were old friends, and that we'd parted on friendly terms, that miserable rat." For all she knew he might have a love 'em and leave 'em attitude toward all the women he met.

"He had the nerve to berate me for being willing to live and work with strangers," Dee added in disgust. "And then he suggested I was being unprofessional by refusing to work for him!"

She turned and looked at her sisters. "I might have behaved in an unprofessional manner, but not without provocation. Just being near Logan Bradford is enough to provoke violence!"

Sharla and Carlie's eyes widened in surprise. Dee rarely raised her voice in anger. She had plenty of spirit, but it took a gross injustice to rile her.

Sharla's tone was tentative. "You weren't provoked to violence, were you?"

Dee blushed and glanced at her right hand. She could still feel the stinging heat of her flesh against Logan's.

"You didn't actually punch him, did you?" Carlie asked in amazement. The idea was inconceivable.

Dee's expression was a mixture of satisfaction and guilt. "I guess that was a little unprofessional, but he had it coming." Maybe he hadn't deserved it today, but he'd touched her, and that had triggered her desire to strike out against him. It was a need she'd harbored too long.

Sharla needed the words. "You actually hit him?"

"Yes, I hit him," snapped Dee.

Her sisters exchanged stunned glances. It was nearly impossible to imagine Dee physically assaulting someone, especially a man who had to be twice her size.

Carlie decided they all needed a stiff jolt of caffeine. The office was comfortably furnished and had a small bar stocked with beverages for the family and customers. She went to the refrigerator and got colas for she and her sisters.

"It sounds to me like you still have some strong feelings for the man," she declared.

"You're absolutely right," said Dee. "I hate him."

Her sisters got their second big shock of the afternoon and nearly choked on their drinks. Hate was a word that Belle had always forbid in their home. Her daughters were allowed to despise bullies or have an intense dislike of spinach, but the word hate had never been tolerated.

"You hate him as in wishing he were dead?" asked Sharla.

That was the criteria their mother always used for the black emotion called hate.

Dee frowned and dropped her gaze to her drink. She'd never wished anyone dead. Even though she couldn't stand Logan, she couldn't honestly say she wanted him dead. What she wanted was to see him suffer the way she had.

"Will you tell us what happened between the two of you?" Carlie asked as she sat down in an easy chair.

Sharla stretched out on a matching sofa. "Maybe if we know the whole story, we can understand how you feel."

A wave of depression swept over Dee as she allowed herself to think about the time she'd spent with Logan. There was no way she could tell her sisters the whole story, she was too ashamed, but she needed to talk about her relationship with Logan.

"We met during the Christmas holiday, when I went to Florida for a week," she said, pacing the room.

"And you fell head over heels in love,'" Sharla suggested softly.

Dee's expression was pained, but she nodded in agreement. "We were so wrapped up in each other that we didn't bother to discuss the more mundane aspects of our lives." Warmth radiated through her at the memory of such long days and nights of loving. She'd never known a time so filled with sensual exploration and pleasure.

"When our vacations were over, Logan asked me to marry him. He said he couldn't bear the thought of being parted for any length of time, and he thought I should just fly back to Kentucky with him."

"He must have been serious if he wanted to marry you and take you home with him."

"I don't think he really wanted to marry me, he just wanted me to live with him a while. He changed his tune when he learned I was a pilot.

You'd have thought I confessed to being a hooker. He was stunned, and insisted that I would have to give up flying. No wife of his was going to be risking her life day in and day out," Dee mimicked Logan's exact words. They were forever engraved in her mind.

"He refused to accept the fact that I had obligations to my family, and that I wasn't willing to give up my career for him. He was totally irrational, saying he had plenty of money to 'take care of me.' I was furious."

"That's understandable," said Sharla, "but it sounds like the two of you parted ways without resolving anything."

"What's to resolve?" growled Dee. "He was just using my career as an excuse to dump me. I provided entertainment for his vacation, and if I didn't want to continue to entertain him on his own terms, then he wasn't interested."

Carlie and Sharla exchanged glances again, their eyes filled with questions. Dee seemed to be describing two different men. They knew she wouldn't have fallen hopelessly in love with the man she was trying to dismiss as a worthless cad. She was much too good a judge of character.

"Maybe he's never been in love before," Sharla suggested, thinking of how hard Reed had fought falling in love. "Maybe he was afraid of losing you and reacted badly. You didn't really have enough time to work out a compromise."

"Are you suggesting that I don't know what I'm talking about? That he might have really wanted me for a wife, not just a playmate? You're wrong, so don't try to defend his actions."

"You know Sharla always has to play the devil's advocate," reminded Carlie, trying to calm her. She didn't like to see Dee so agitated.

"Nobody's defending Bradford. He hurt you, and that's enough reason to want him tarred and feathered, but you might be doing yourself an injustice by believing that you loved him more than he loved you."

"I did," Dee could be very stubborn.

"Maybe he has some macho hang-up about a woman having to prove her love by following her man anywhere," suggested Sharla. "Or maybe he's one of those men who thinks he has to be the sole supporter."

"Bullshit."

Sharla and Carlie gasped in feigned shock and then grinned.

"That's what you call a combination four-letter word," Carlie teased. "And you've already used one other bad word this afternoon. I hope Mama Belle doesn't have this office bugged."

The teasing brought a smile to Dee's face, but her eyes remained sad. "I don't know how I'm going to explain this all to her. I promised Jake

I'd have Mother help him find another instructor, but I don't really want to discuss it with her."

"Did you rip the contract to shreds, or anything?" Carlie asked.

"No. I never actually saw a contract, but it doesn't matter. I don't intend to work with Logan."

"What did you think of his house and his staff?"

Dee sighed heavily. "I really liked Jake and Butch. They're the other two men who want the training. They were friendly and enthusiastic. I also met Logan's sister, Patti. I didn't even know he had a sister."

"What about the Circle B's?"

Another sigh escaped Dee. "It was absolutely gorgeous. It smelled of honeysuckle, and it felt so good."

The wistfulness in her voice didn't surprise her sisters, nor did her description of feeling the property. Dee always reacted to locations and situations with all her senses. She felt things as much as she saw them.

"It's a shame you have to give up," said Sharla. "Is there any way you can resolve your differences with Logan?"

Dee's eyes flared. "I don't even want to try!"

The next question was more hesitant. "Are you still in love with him?"

"No!" Dee knew her protest was too swift and too defensive, but she couldn't help her gut reaction. Any leftover feelings she had for the man were negative.

Sharla had her doubts, but she made a suggestion. "Maybe you should take the assignment. If the two of you have to work together, you'll get a chance to put the past behind you. Then you can put him out of your life."

"Sharla may be right," injected Carlie. "You need to put Bradford out of your life. The best way to do that is to meet him on his own turf and see how the two of you get along on a normal basis."

Dee was shaking her head in vigorous rejection of their theories. She didn't want to admit just how much seeing Logan had shaken her, and she didn't think the two of them could work in harmony. Old lovers might make the best of friends in some cases, but not this one.

"I have no desire to work things out with Logan. I don't want to be anywhere near him."

"If you really don't love him anymore, then why aren't you willing to forgive him?" asked Carlie. She couldn't remember Dee ever carrying a grudge.

"It seems like that kind of hate can only do you harm," she added. "Remember what you told me when I divorced Bill? You told me to vent my anger and then put the negative feelings behind me. You were right, and it worked for me."

"If you're not sure how you feel about him, wouldn't it be better to find out?" Sharla suggested tentatively. "You can't hide from yourself, Dee. You loved Bradford, and he hurt you. You won't be happy until you've confronted the conflicting emotions and resolved them. One way or the other."

Dee was shaking her head again. They didn't understand, and she couldn't explain without telling them the secret she'd promised herself not to tell. Being near Logan could only cause more heartache. She might not love him, but she still had strong feelings about the way their relationship had ended.

"It just wouldn't work. If you'd been there today, you'd understand. The two of us can't be in the same room without tempers flaring. It's asking for trouble."

Sharla and Carlie were quiet for a while as they considered Dee's response. "Maybe you're right," Carlie conceded. "Maybe it's better to just forget the man, his home, and his need for a flight instructor."

Sharla nodded in agreement. "Some things are better forgotten, I guess. Especially if you've seen him, and you know that you're completely over him."

The ringing of the telephone prevented Dee from responding. She was closest to the desk, but she ignored the summons. Sharla finally rose from the sofa and answered.

"Prescott Air Service."

"Mrs. Prescott?" asked a deep male voice.

"I'm sorry, she's gone for the day. This is Sharla. How may I help you?"

"This is Logan Bradford."

"Yes, Mr. Bradford?" Sharla spoke his name aloud so that her sisters would know to whom she was speaking. They both turned their attention to the conversation.

"Dee was upset when she left my house today. I wanted to make sure she got home all right."

"She's fine, Mr. Bradford. Dee's a professional pilot. She's trained to fly well even when she's having a bad day."

There was a heavy sigh on the other end of the line.

"When she left," he finally continued, "she said she wouldn't work for me, but the offer's still open. I hope she'll take some time before making a final decision. Did she mention our Fourth of July barbecue?"

Sharla's gaze shot to Dee. The fourth was only a few days away. "No, she didn't."

"I'd like her to come. It wouldn't commit her to anything, just give her a chance to get better acquainted."

Sharla didn't think it was likely, not in Dee's present state of mind. "I'll mention it to her."

Her tone wasn't encouraging, and Logan's voice deepened. "I wanted to come after her today, but I knew she'd had a shock and needed time. If she doesn't come to Kentucky on the fourth, I'll be there on the fifth."

Sharla made a face, but her tone remained professionally polite. "That sounds like a threat, Mr. Bradford."

"It's a promise, Ms. Prescott."

She didn't doubt that he would keep his promise. "I'll pass along your message. Thank you for calling."

Sharla hung up the phone and looked at Dee. "Bradford said you were invited to a barbecue on the fourth. He says if you don't come to Kentucky, he's coming here."

Dee visibly paled. "Why?"

"He didn't explain. Unfinished business, I guess."

"Damn! Damn! Damn!" exclaimed Dee with unusual ferocity. "I don't want him anywhere near here."

"If he was so interested in seeing you again, why did he wait until now?" asked Carlie.

Dee knew she owed her sisters an explanation. Their concern was genuine. They were always supportive and ready to defend her. "I didn't tell him where I lived when I left Florida. He eventually had me traced and called, but I told him I was seeing another man, and that he'd be in the way."

"Whoa! Major ego buster," said Sharla.

"It was either that or a restraining order, and I didn't want to involve the police."

"He didn't hurt you, did he?" asked Carlie, obviously shaken by the thought.

Dee's face softened with compassion. Carlie's husband had been a bastard, and he hadn't been above hitting his wife. "Logan never resorted to physical violence. He was furious, but I'm not afraid of him."

"Only of the way you feel about him," Sharla surmised.

Dee's expression was tight. She honestly didn't know how she felt about Logan, except for the ongoing anger and resentment. She'd thought she'd put him out of her heart and mind forever. After today's confrontation, she knew she hadn't been totally successful.

"Do you and Reed have plans for the holiday?" Carlie asked Sharla.

"He has to be out of state."

"Then why don't the three of us go to a barbecue? I'll admit I'm curious about this guy. We can check him out, lend Dee some moral support, and help her shake off any lingering confusion over Logan Bradford."

Her suggestion hung heavily in the room for a few minutes. Then Sharla spoke. "Dee?"

She looked from sister to sister. They were the best; always her champions, always fiercely protective. Sharla was older by mere minutes, but she loved playing the role of big sister. Carlie thought she was tough and was always ready to fight her sisters' battles.

Dee normally depended on her own serenity to keep them in balance, but not where Logan was concerned. This time she welcomed their interference, yet she had some serious doubts about the wisdom of the decision she made with an affirmative nod of her head.

Four

*T*hey flew to Kentucky on July fourth. The barbecue was scheduled to begin at four, so they were circling the Circle B's airstrip at half past that hour. They planned to arrive after most of the guests were assembled, so that their host would be occupied with hosting duties.

Sharla was flying her Saratoga. Like many experienced car drivers, she couldn't stand to sit in the passenger seat and allow someone else to handle the controls. She always piloted when the sisters traveled together. Dee and Carlie didn't mind humoring her. She was the best.

"Ooohhh . . ." Sharla enthused as she brought the plane in for an incredibly soft landing. "Brand new asphalt."

"Everything's new," said Dee.

"They didn't even buy a used plane?"

"Ordered it special."

"Dam, I wish I had instructor certification."

"I wish you did, too," said Dee. She couldn't help feeling guilty about leaving Jake and Butch in a spot. It wasn't her responsibility to train them. She had every right to refuse the assignment, yet she'd agonized over the decision for days. She didn't want the job, but she wished she knew someone who did.

There was one helicopter and another small plane at the end of the runway near the hangar, so they knew more of Bradford's guests had arrived by air. That meant it was a pretty big party. The base operator had informed them that they'd be met and driven to the house.

Butch Troyer was helping transport guests, so he was close at hand when the unfamiliar plane landed. The boss hadn't been expecting anyone else by air unless the Prescott pilot decided to come. When the plane came to a stop, he saw the Prescott Air Service logo and grinned widely.

Within a few minutes, his eyes had widened and his mouth dropped open in disbelief. Not one, not two, but three beautiful women stepped from the plane. And they all looked just alike; breathtaking, confident, and chic.

They had to be sisters, maybe triplets. They were so much alike he couldn't tell which one he'd already met. None of them had her long braid. Their hair was all twisted in little knots on top of their heads, and they were dressed the same.

"We're going to roast in these jeans," Carlie grumbled as she and her sisters left the air-conditioned comfort of the cockpit for the shimmering afternoon heat.

"These jeans were the best we could do without a special shopping trip," put in Sharla. They'd decided to wear matching white jeans that hugged their hips and tapered down long, shapely legs to end just above their ankles.

When they'd been younger, their mother had delighted in dressing them in matching outfits. The sisters rarely dressed alike these days unless they deliberately set out to cause a sensation, as they had today.

They'd paired the jeans with short-sleeved silk blouses in the same button-front, tailored style, but in different colors. Carlie wore red because it was her favorite color. Sharla wore dark purple, and Dee wore a deep turquoise that enhanced the brilliance of her eyes. Their blouses were a sharp contrast to the spotless white of their pants, and white huarache sandals completed the outfits.

Butch's eyes were still rounded and his mouth was hanging open as they approached him. It had been a long time since the Prescott triplets had attempted to stun people with their looks, so his expression was evidence of their success.

"I guess we haven't lost our touch," Carlie murmured.

"We'll knock 'em dead," Sharla assured. "And if we don't take an immediate liking to anyone, we won't even bother to tell them who's who."

Dee appreciated the thought, but knew it wasn't likely. As far as she could tell, everyone who lived and worked at Bradford Bluegrass was likable and friendly. Since Carlie and Sharla didn't have a snobbish bone in their bodies, they'd probably feel right at home in no time.

She wasn't feeling quite so confident, despite their support. She'd agree to come because she'd really wanted another chance to visit, but she'd hoped that having her sisters with her would make her feel less vulnerable. Now she wasn't so sure the old method would work.

"Ms. Prescott?" Butch attempted when he'd regained his composure and approached the women.

All three of them nodded in response to the appellation, and he turned a dull red. Dee instantly took pity on him, attempting to put him at ease.

"These are my sisters. Butch," she said, identifying herself to him. "This is Sharla." She motioned to her left, and then to her right. "And this is Carlie." It was her habit to stand in the middle.

"Butch is a trainer here, and he wants to become a pilot," she explained.

Both her sisters offered their hands, and Butch shook them briefly. He was sure the one in purple had been in the pilot's seat. "But that means Sharla was flying the plane," he said, still confused.

"We're all pilots," explained Carlie. "We just have different specialties and different planes."

"Carlie actually does the kind of cargo hauling you want to do," Sharla told him, "but she isn't certified as an instructor. Dee does the training, and I usually handle the charters, but we can all pilot a variety of planes."

Now the young man really was in awe. "Wow!" was the only response he could manage.

"Feel free to check out Sharla's Saratoga if you want," Dee said, knowing how much he'd enjoyed looking at her plane. "It's a lot different from the Cessna."

Butch shot an admiring glance at the airplane. "You're sure you wouldn't mind?" He sounded as though they'd offered him a special treat, and his enthusiasm brought smiles to their faces. Sharla and Carlie realized why Dee had taken an immediate liking to him.

"Sharla treats that plane like a baby," Carlie told him. "But she doesn't mind someone else admiring it."

"I'll be real careful," he promised.

"We trust you," said Dee.

"Are you our escort to the party?" Sharla gently reminded him that they were waiting for a ride to the barbecue.

Butch blushed again, stammered an apology for keeping them waiting in the sun, then lead them to the car he was driving. He'd thoughtfully left it running with the air conditioner cooling the luxurious interior.

"This is the boss's car," he explained. "We didn't want to pick up guests in a truck, and Patti's car is too small, so we're using this one. It's three years old, but it's like new 'cause it mostly sits in the garage. The boss drives his truck most of the time."

Dee sat in the front with Butch. The car's interior was leather, and the scent enveloped her as she sank into the plush bucket seat. She didn't want to enjoy anything that belonged to Logan, but it was difficult not to like his car.

"Doesn't your boss have a special lady in his life?" Carlie asked with poorly disguised curiosity. "I'd think he'd use his car for dates."

Butch shot a glance at Dee, and the slight action told her that her relationship with Logan wasn't a secret anymore. She wondered just what he'd told his family and staff. Details of their disastrous affair had probably created a wealth of gossip here in his domain.

"Logan doesn't date much," Butch finally responded. He didn't elaborate, and his hesitancy spoke of his loyalty to his boss.

"Are there a lot of guests today?" Sharla asked. "I noticed a couple other aircraft."

"Nearly a hundred," he told them. "They're mostly neighbors and friends of the family, but a few customers flew in for the weekend. It's a good time to look at this year's crop of foals.

"We've been thinking about buying some riding horses for our place in Virginia," said Carlie.

She didn't add that the idea had been put on hold since Dee's last visit, but the comment put Butch at ease. He described some of the livestock they might want to look at. The short trip to the house was made without any farther discussion of Logan, which pleased Dee.

She was feeling more nervous by the minute. Her palms were sweating and her stomach was rolling. Her pulse hadn't regulated since landing on his property, and the closer they got to the house, the worse she felt.

She'd hoped that facing him again would be easier, especially since Sharla and Carlie had accompanied her. Now she wasn't so sure. Any meeting had to be better than their disastrous accidental meeting, she supposed, but she was still sick with apprehension.

The pain, anger, and guilt had to be put behind her. She'd learned that she wasn't the type of person who could live with that kind of emotional baggage, yet now she was wondering at the wisdom of confronting Logan on his own territory. If it hadn't been for her parents, she'd have made him come to her if he wanted to talk.

"I see what you mean about this place," Sharla commented as they traveled the tree-lined road that lead to the house. "It's really lovely."

"Now I understand your original assessment," Carlie added.

The Bradford Bluegrass farm had the kind of tranquil beauty that Dee normally found soothing. Under different circumstances, she'd have loved to spend time exploring the property. Regardless of her qualms about being here, the place touched her in a strangely appealing fashion. She allowed herself a pang of remorse for what could never be.

Logan was standing on the front porch as his car came into view. He'd received a call that three women had landed a small plane, and he'd known that Dee had come. His elation was tempered with dread. He'd promised himself to be totally civilized. What he felt was impatient and primitive.

He wanted Dee desperately, wanted her near him, regardless of the private doubts and fears he still needed to conquer. He had to find a way to regain her respect, and he couldn't do that if she refused to spend time with him.

Despite the fact that Logan had a photograph of the triplets, and he knew how much alike they looked, it was still disconcerting to see them climb from his car. He descended the porch steps as they approached; presenting a united front that was easily recognizable as a defense against him.

Even though Sharla had run into Logan on one occasion, seeing him in his own environment was different. Carlie was no less impressed, and Dee felt her sisters' immediate reaction to his sheer male magnetism. No woman could be totally immune to the man.

He was half a foot taller than the triplets with a breadth of shoulders that would nearly double their width. Heavily muscled arms were dusted with golden hair and left bare by his short-sleeved navy dress shirt. He had thick, pale blond hair that was cut military short. His blue-gray eyes were sharply piercing, but carefully guarded, giving the appearance of a man suppressing incredible power and energy.

His gaze quickly shifted from one of them to the other, then focused on Dee. The green of her blouse deepened the color of her eyes. She was easily identifiable by the sparkle of animosity in her gaze. Still, the sight of her made his blood run hot. Heat rocked through him, but he fought down his natural responses.

"I'm glad you came," he said, his voice sandpaper rough, yet incredibly seductive.

"Your invitation was too delightful to refuse," she challenged lightly.

Logan's full lips thinned. He doubted that his threat was her only reason for coming, but he didn't care. After another minute of intently scouring Dee's features, he glanced at her companions.

"Sharla." She introduced herself and held out a hand to him. "We met briefly at the Lexington airport."

Logan's lips curved rakishly at the reminder. He'd forced himself to go to the airport in an effort to get used to the idea of being around planes again. When he'd run into Sharla, he'd mistaken her for Dee, and demanded a kiss. She'd accepted his demand without thinking him a pervert.

"I remember," he said. His eyes glittered, and his grin was potent. "You took pity on me."

"Excuse me if I don't think you're the least bit pathetic," she teased, trying to lighten the heavy tension that seemed to have paralyzed Dee.

When her sister didn't make any attempt at introductions, she added, "This is Carlie. She's the baby of the family."

Logan released Sharla's hand and reached for Carlie's. Her eyes weren't nearly as friendly as Sharla's, and he knew she was prepared to dislike him. He had a gut feeling that this sister wasn't too fond of men in general or him in particular.

"Carlie," he greeted. His gaze locked with hers in honest, open appraisal. He didn't try to impress her with flattery or social graces.

"I'm only the baby by a few unfortunate minutes," she explained, responding more to his commanding presence than she would have to flowery compliments. "But my sisters never let me forget those minutes."

The disgust in her tone won another of Logan's brief grins, and Dee's heart did a little somersault in her chest. There was no doubt he was a charmer. It wasn't an overt, practiced charm, but rather an inherent masculine appeal that flattered any woman he chose to honor with his attention.

She felt almost envious until he turned his gaze back to her. Something flickered in his silvery eyes that made her heart pound in alarm. She warned herself not to relax her guard.

Logan resented the fact that he had to take his new guests to join the rest of the party. He wanted time to get to know Dee's sisters, and he wanted time alone with her. But he knew he had to be on his best behavior, even if it killed him.

Jake and Patti were in the living room when he ushered the triplets into the house. They both stared in amazement, but their reaction wasn't unusual or offensive.

"Damn!" said Jake.

Patti recovered first. "Watch your language, Travis," she scolded good-naturedly.

"You'll have our guests thinking we're a bunch of heathens."

"Sorry." He apologized, but didn't sound the least bit repentant. "Which one of you is Dee?"

Sharla and Carlie each pointed a finger at her, and Dee gave him a brief smile. Jake had been kind on her last visit. She didn't have any reason to be rude or defensive with him. She actually felt like they were old friends.

"Hi, Jake. Any luck finding a new instructor?" she asked, deliberately bringing up the sensitive subject.

"Nope," he replied. Logan had ordered him not to even try. "Is there any chance you'll reconsider?"

"Nope."

"Damn," he said again, earning himself a silent reprimand from Patti.

Logan interrupted the exchange to introduce everyone, and then shepherded them all toward the backyard where dinner was being served, picnic style. The late arrivals caused quite a stir, and more introductions were necessary, but the furor soon settled and everyone filled plates to eat.

Sharla and Carlie stayed close to Dee, and she was thankful for their support. Logan was kept busy with the duties of host, but she could feel his gaze following her everywhere. Although she filled her plate with delicious-smelling food, she couldn't eat. Her nerves were raw, and she was being bombarded with a variety of sensual reactions from everyone in attendance.

As usual, whenever she found herself in a crowd, she was nearly overwhelmed by the avalanche of sensations. She felt waves of curiosity from Logan's quests. There was open admiration, a lot of speculation, a little envy, and a lot of curiosity, but no real hostility. Still the sensations were unnerving in such abundance.

She knew a few people were dissecting her and her sisters, wondering if their hair was naturally blond and if they were on the prowl for men. A few men, young and old, single and married, were wondering if they slept around. That didn't bother her, either.

Those were normal responses, and they weren't alarming. After a while, she began to relax a little and was able to ignore the jumble of perceived sensations. Overall, the Prescotts' reception at the barbecue was congenial.

The next few hours passed without incident. It was only Logan's continued attention that bothered Dee. No matter where he was or what he was doing, she could feel the strong vibrations from his presence. His gaze found her wherever she moved.

He might be biding his time, but she knew he was determined to confront her about their failed relationship. Dee sensed it, accepted it, but dreaded it. She wasn't anxious to dredge up all the hurt and humiliation, yet she needed to air her grievances and put the whole affair behind her. Then maybe she could get on with her life.

As the afternoon slipped into evening, everyone finished eating. Logan and his staff moved tables and cleared a space on the patio for dancing. Japanese lanterns were lit and a three-piece band set up equipment. The air was quickly filled with popular selections of country and western music.

Sharla and Carlie were immediately tapping their toes, but Dee panicked at the thought of Logan asking her to dance. She didn't want to be in his arms. Neither did she want to make a scene, so she decided to go indoors and search for the ladies' room.

The sound of laughter and music was muted as she entered the house. The sun was fading, and Dee welcomed the cool shadows of the big house. She was happy that the bathroom was unoccupied, and that no one saw her as she continued to move from room to room, acquainting herself with the welcoming feel of the Bradford family home.

The kitchen was as big and open as the living room. There was a formal dining room that didn't appear to get much use. She guessed that the next room she entered was a family room because it had a more lived-in appearance with a wide-screen television and an enormous entertainment center.

The last room she entered was opposite the living room and on the left side of the front entry hall. As soon as she stepped through the doorway, she knew it was Logan's room; a combination office and library that held his scent. The light was dim, but she could see a large desk piled with papers. Bookcases lined one wall and an open fireplace took up most of another. Despite the tingling awareness of being in his private office, Dee was compelled to step further into the room.

Pale moonlight was filtering through floor-length curtains behind the desk, and she moved closer. Behind the curtains were French doors that led to the side yard and a small pool. She slid one of the doors open and music from the backyard poured into the room along with the scent of honeysuckle on a cool breeze.

She breathed deeply, feeling strangely comfortable for the first time since their plane had touched down on Bradford property. She didn't care to analyze the sudden contentment that settled over her, she simply relaxed and enjoyed the solitude.

The soft strains of one slow, sultry ballad after another lulled Dee's senses as she gazed at the stars collecting around the moon in a velvet sky. A heavy sigh escaped her.

Crowds unnerved her more these days than they had when she was younger. Her extrasensory perception was growing stronger with each passing year, and sometimes the strain of it was nearly suffocating. There was little she could do but seek the solace of solitude.

Her family was understanding and supportive. She was lucky in that respect, but sometimes she yearned for someone special to share her problems; her ups and downs, her hopes and dreams. She envied the love Sharla had found with Reed.

She wanted the same type of commitment, yet Logan had destroyed her hopes of finding a mate she could trust without reservation. He'd captured, and then crushed her heart, and she no longer had faith in a happily-ever-after for herself.

For the last six months, she'd been in an emotional vacuum, a highly charged state of limbo. Memories of him had haunted her, preventing her from looking forward to the future.

Accompanying her thoughts of Logan, Dee felt a chill run up her spine. The fine hairs on the back of her neck tingled and she knew he was close. She turned and saw him silhouetted in the doorway opposite her.

He didn't say anything in the way of greeting. He shut the door behind him and slowly walked to his desk, his gaze never leaving her. Then he snapped on a small lamp that rearranged the shadows of the room.

Dee fought off the panic that threatened to overwhelm her. It seemed an eternity since they'd been together. During their brief, but passionate affair, they'd never been alone without wanting to touch each other in some fashion.

He was a virile, sensual man with a seemingly insatiable appetite for tasting, touching, and loving. He'd spent hours stroking her hair, caressing every inch of her skin, and making love to her until she'd been mindless with pleasure. They hadn't been able to touch enough, get close enough, or sate the desire that raged between them.

Scalding, achingly familiar heat raced through her veins, making her limbs heavy and her pulse pound in her ears. There was no denying that he was still devastating to her senses, but she was determined to resist what she knew was nothing more than carnal magnetism.

Small talk seemed ridiculous, so Dee didn't attempt to break the heavy silence that pulsed between them. Being alone with him was enough of a strain on her frayed nerves.

Logan was remembering the same long hours of sensual exploration, of sweet, slow loving and fast, frenzied mating. He ached, unbearably and continuously, with needs that were too long unfulfilled and that no other woman could satisfy.

His body was swiftly, painfully aroused at the sight of Dee. Just being alone with her brought him to an urgent, throbbing state of arousal, yet he knew she wasn't interested in his needs. She hated him. He wasn't sure how to overcome past mistakes, but he knew he had to try. He couldn't let her walk out of his life again. He didn't think he would survive.

His only hope for salvaging their relationship was that she seemed to hate as passionately as she had loved. If he could still spark such violent emotion, then maybe there was a chance to rectify the mistakes he'd made. Long, tension-filled seconds passed in silence. Then another few minutes passed as they stared at each other. Silvery blue eyes were locked with glittering green ones. Neither pair seemed capable of breaking the contact. Logan gradually moved closer until he was within inches of her, and she forced herself to face him without flinching.

"I've missed you," he finally confessed in a barely audible tone.

The gruff admission shivered over Dee like a caress. If her back hadn't already been pressed tightly against the door, she'd have retreated more.

She wished she could tell him that she hadn't missed him, but it wouldn't be completely true. She'd missed the closeness they'd shared, the immediate, soul-satisfying rapport they'd developed, and the incredible loving. She also missed the dreams he'd shattered. She found herself pining for the joy of life he'd stolen from her, that she hadn't found a way to reclaim.

"You're the one who put an end to what we had," she reminded him in a carefully measured tone.

"I was a fool."

Dee's heart stopped, then raced madly. She didn't appreciate her body's violent response to his growled statement. She didn't want to believe him, didn't dare trust him. She couldn't even trust her own instincts where he was concerned. For all she knew, he might be playing her for a fool so that he could seduce her again. She refused to be a plaything that he accepted or rejected on a whim.

"You were a fool," she agreed after a few more seconds of strained silence.

She wasn't going to make it easy for him. Logan's gaze roved over her lovely features. Her expression was tight and filled with simmering anger. He knew she had every right to an apology and explanation, but the words were still hard for him. He'd never been good at begging.

"Can you forgive me?"

"Never."

The retort was swift and as sharp as a dagger to his heart. He forgot his pride and struggled to understand why she was still so furious and unforgiving. He'd never physically abused her, and he was sorry for hurting her feelings with his callous demand that she choose between her career and marriage. He was more than willing to make it up to her if she'd give him half a chance.

"How can you be so quick to deny what's between us?" he demanded in frustration. "You might tell me you hate me until hell freezes over, but the attraction is still so strong that I'm shaking with it."

Dee wanted to put her hands over her ears and shut out his evocative declaration, but she didn't want him to realize how vulnerable she was. When she found her voice, it was high and sharp.

"That's your problem, not mine."

Logan's eyes flared with anger, then determination. He took a half-step closer and slid a hand inside the collar of her blouse to the soft curve of her neck. "Is it just my problem, Dee?" he taunted. "Is that why your pulse is so frantic? I know you're not afraid of me. You can keep stoking your anger forever, but you can't deny wanting me as much as I want you. That much hasn't changed."

She forced herself to remain stiff and unresponsive to his touch, even though her insides were quivering like jelly. The feel of his warm, callused hand and caressing fingers ignited smoldering embers of fire in her. She didn't welcome the heady rush of desire.

"I can't deny the body chemistry," she whispered through still lips. "But I can guarantee you that my heart and soul are a lot less forgiving."

Logan's body clenched with anger. The muscles knotted in his arms, but his touch was gentle as he used his thumb to tilt her face to his. He seared her with molten eyes. His voice was low and gruff.

"Then I guess I'll have to be satisfied with just the body," he whispered as his mouth descended to hers, capturing her quick rush of shocked breath.

Five

Dee was so stunned by the feel of his hard, hot lips that she momentarily froze. A furious protest rose in her throat. She lifted both hands to his chest to shove him away, but Logan wasn't an easy man to push. The hard muscles under her hands flexed, but didn't give. Then he stepped closer, crushing her hands between their bodies.

He was an inferno of heat that threatened to engulf her. Dee shuddered, digging her fingernails into the soft cotton of his shirt. She tried to shift her head, but he moved a hand to her nape. He held her still with a gentle, but firm grip. Then his other arm slipped around her waist, pulling her so tightly against him that she could feel every hard angle of his big body.

She gasped at the blanketing contact, and Logan's tongue moved into her mouth in a deep, searching foray that stole what was left of her breath. Her chest heaved in protest, but she was sinking in a quicksand of emotion.

She'd forgotten how big and hard and hot he was. She'd forced herself to forget how incredible it felt to be pressed against his solid length. She'd tried not to remember the delicious taste of him, of how ravenous his mouth always was and how his hot, searching tongue always reduced her to a quivering mass of need.

Dee was so brittle with tension that she feared she'd shatter into a million pieces. She remained unresponsive, but she gradually stopped fighting him. It had been so long, and his unmistakable hunger was an insidious threat to her control. His heart thudded riotously against her palms. His muscles were coiled with tension, his arousal turgid.

He was holding her firmly, but as though she was utterly precious to him. His mouth was alternately urgent, then coaxing. His tongue was warm and wet and seeking. She was melting, inch by trembling inch.

Logan could hear the blood pounding in his head. His whole body was clenched with desire. He was hot and aching and needy. Months of celibacy and erotic, torturous dreams had made him nearly insane with hunger for this woman. The taste and feel of her inflamed him beyond reason. He wanted her desperately, but he wanted her to want him just as much.

He knew the instant she stopped fighting him. He knew she wasn't frightened of him, and he pressed his advantage by muttering his need against her lips while sucking in a ragged breath.

"Kiss me, Dee. Put your arms around me and hold me."

His voice shook with the force of his desire, and Dee quivered in his arms. She couldn't fight him anymore, but she was waging a savage battle with herself. He was offering heaven and hell. She'd be the worst kind of fool to subject herself to either.

Logan wrapped both his arms around her and crushed her close to his body. She threw her head back, and his lips fastened on the pulse throbbing erratically at her throat. A tiny moan escaped her. His blood boiled, then rushed like molten lava to pool in his loins.

He pulled her hips closer and ground himself against the feminine cradle of her body. His mouth clamped on hers, growing more urgent and demanding in a frenzied effort to demolish her defenses.

Dee's head was reeling, her body pulsing with an excitement she could no longer deny. His raw need shattered what was left of her resistance, making her go soft and pliable in his arms. When his tongue thrust into her mouth, her tongue met it in a feverish demand.

A groan rumbled from his chest, and he kissed her as if she were the best and only reason for living. His hands slid between them to guide her arms over his shoulders. Then he dragged her as close as humanly possible.

He felt her nipples pebble against his chest, and his desire raged out of control. He clutched her hips, lifting her to grind his throbbing arousal into the softness of her abdomen. His kisses grew feverish; his hunger insatiable. He pressed her against the wall to lock her closer while freeing his hands to explore the soft curves of her hips, waist, and breasts. They shared strangled moans of pleasure as his palms cupped her tightly budded nipples.

"So sweet," he murmured in a husky, heavy tone. He made love to her with his mouth. His kisses grew longer and deeper, his tongue filled her mouth in thrusting, seductive rhythm while his hands adored her.

He had to have her, had to be a part of her again, had to bury himself in her heat and softness. He knew how tightly she would sheathe him and how perfectly they fit together. He knew she could satisfy longings that were beyond the physical. They were made for each other, and he was going out of his mind.

Logan slid his hands down her rib cage to her hips. His fingers clenched the rounded fullness as he slipped a knee between her legs and slowly lifted it until her feet were off the floor, and she was riding his thigh. Her arms tightened around his neck. Her nipples stabbed at his chest and the tiny cry of arousal she uttered made his head spin.

He wanted her. Right here. Right now. Standing up, on the desk, or on the floor. Anywhere. Any way. He wanted her with a desperation that threatened his control and scared the hell out of him.

His mouth eased off hers long enough to drag in a scorching breath. He opened his eyes and gazed at Dee. Her eyes were closed, her long lashes resting on flushed cheeks. Her lovely features were bathed in moonlight, and he could see that she was just as aroused as he was.

A moan tore from his throat as he peppered her face with kisses while murmuring incoherent compliments and sweet words of longing. One of his hands found the waistband of her jeans, and he deftly flipped the snap, then parted the zipper.

The feel of his hand splayed on her stomach jolted Dee out of the sensual haze she'd been drowning in. A shudder racked her body as sanity returned, and she struggled to resist the temptation that was Logan.

"No!" The hoarse cry of denial wasn't nearly as firm as she intended it to be. The pathetically weak sound was nearly lost as Logan's mouth fastened on hers again.

Dee jerked her arms from his neck and flattened her hands on his shoulders to force some space between them. At the same time, she twisted her mouth free and squirmed to escape the muscled thigh that had her pinned between the wall and his hard body.

"No!" Her second refusal was louder and much more forceful.

Logan's hands circled her waist to steady her as she tried to force more space between them. "You can't mean that," he insisted in a raw tone.

Dee was fighting for breath and control. She didn't look him in the eyes, but she felt his shocked gaze burning over her face.

"I mean it," she assured him.

"I'm on fire!" he growled hoarsely.

He didn't need to tell her that. They were both inflamed beyond reason, and that's why she had panicked.

"You started it," she accused, managing to shift her body from intimate contact with his.

"You were with me all the way," he reminded fiercely. He kept one hand locked on her waist. He used the other to force her chin up so that she couldn't avoid looking directly at him. "Don't pretend that you don't want me just as much as I want you!"

His blistering gaze seared her, but Dee didn't blink or shift her gaze. "My body might want the sex, but I don't want you," she declared baldly.

He might have ignored her protests if her eyes hadn't been glittering with so much blatant disgust. He ground his teeth together and fought to rein his desire. His muscles were tight with tension, his body hard and heavy with need.

"Why?" he forced himself to ask as he dragged air into his heaving chest.

Dee took advantage of his confusion to squirm out of his reach, but she was still pinned between him and the door.

"How can you ask why?" she argued angrily. Her fingers trembled uncontrollably as she concentrated on smoothing her blouse and refastening her jeans.

Logan grasped her head between his hands and forced her to give him her full attention. He allowed a small amount of space between them, but only because he needed to protect himself from more brutal enticement.

"I'm asking because I don't know why the hell you're denying us something we're both aching for."

"Because it's wrong!" she snapped. "Because I don't even like you. Because you have a hundred guests outside. Because somebody has to consider the serious consequences of irresponsible, unprotected sex!"

Anger surged through Logan, replacing some of the sexual tension. Her passionate insistence that she didn't like him pierced his heart. Her suggestion that he was irresponsible stung his pride.

"I can protect you," he snarled. "I was always willing to protect you."

"Sometimes," she argued, shifting so that no part of their bodies was even brushing.

"All of the time," he shot back.

"Not all of the time!" she accused fiercely. "Not one hundred percent of the time. And you weren't too concerned about the times we forgot!"

"Because I loved you!"

"Well, you have a hell of a way of showing it," she snapped, eyes flashing fire. "You wanted everything your way and damn the consequences."

Consequences? The only consequences of unprotected sex between them would have been an unplanned pregnancy. Logan stiffened in shock as everything suddenly fell into place. Understanding dawned; the reason she hated him so fiercely,

the reason she rejected him while wanting him, the reason she panicked at the thought of making love.

"You're pregnant?" he whispered hoarsely. He shook his head as if to clear it. His gaze swiftly roamed her body, and then locked on her face. "No, you couldn't be. You'd be showing, even with your first."

He watched all the color drain from Dee's face. Her eyes became guarded, her expression distraught. He knew she hadn't intended to expose so much.

"What happened?" he demanded, grasping her by the forearms and keeping her from dodging past him to the door. "Were you pregnant? Why didn't you get in touch with me?"

Her expression grew mutinous, and Logan's frustration intensified. When he'd traced her after their separation, she'd told him there was another man. Had she been pregnant and unsure who the father was? The idea enraged him, and he shook her in agitation.

"Were there other lovers?" he demanded tightly.

"No!" Dee was startled into an honest retaliation, then instantly wanted to recall the damning truth.

"Then the consequences must have been a pregnancy. You were carrying my baby and you didn't let me know?" he demanded, outraged.

Tears welled in her eyes, and she went as white as a sheet. Her legs would have folded, and she'd have crumpled to the floor without his support.

"Dee!" His voice quivered in a combination of fear and rage. "What did you do?"

For an instant the bleakness and misery in her eyes were so intense that it hurt him. She shook her head from side to side in denial, but Logan wasn't sure whether she was too ashamed, too afraid, or just too upset to tell him.

"Did you harm our baby?" he finally managed in a strangled whisper.

A sob tore at Dee's throat. Had she hurt their baby? Could she have done anything to save him? Would he have lived if she'd cut back on work and gotten more rest? If she'd taken her vitamins and eaten better? If she hadn't been so emotionally distraught? The doctors had told her she wasn't responsible for the miscarriage, but their assurances hadn't appeased her incredible guilt.

"Dee!" Logan barked, tightening his grip on her arms and giving her a rough shake to snap her out of her numbed state. His voice was raw with leashed fury. "Have you had an abortion?"

A sob caught in her throat. She blinked back tears and stared at him, stunned out of her pained stupor. He thought she'd deliberately destroyed their baby? Didn't he know her at all? Could he have given her any more proof that his vows of eternal love had been nothing more than lies?

An unwelcome flash of insight helped her realize that she'd needed to unburden herself about the baby. She'd been desperate to mourn their son with his father, but she'd never dreamed he would accuse her of harming the life they'd created.

Logan watched her eyes harden into a mutinous glare. Her mouth thinned into a tight line. When she didn't answer him, he took her silence as a confession of guilt. Her refusal to deny his charge came across as a defiant admission that she'd aborted their baby and knew there was nothing he could do about it.

"Damn you," he ground out roughly. "Damn you to hell!" Pain and rage warred within him. His blood boiled, shooting a fiery path through his body, glazing his eyes, and exploding in his skull. His body quaked in an effort to control the need for violence. His fingers bit into Dee's arms, and it took all his considerable strength to loosen his grip enough to shove her out of his reach.

She watched him rake both hands through his hair as he deliberately turned his back on her and put some distance between them. She knew he was devastated and fighting for control. She'd faced the same emotional devastation — alone.

Any impulse she had to comfort him died a quick death. Where had he been when she'd needed comfort? She'd learned she was pregnant after he'd brutally rejected her. She'd been so hurt and humiliated that she'd refused to see him, and had lead him to believe there was another man in her life. That's when she'd discovered she was pregnant.

She'd tortured herself for weeks about whether or not to contact him. She'd been sick and frightened and so alone; too ashamed to share her secret with her family. She'd felt used and cheap. Then she'd lost the baby, and nothing or no one could have consoled her. He didn't have to condemn her to hell. She'd been living in it for months. She'd only begun to pull out of the quagmire of depression when she'd come to Kentucky and run into him.

He might be comforted by the fact that their baby hadn't been deliberately aborted. Dee considered trying to explain, but she couldn't find the courage or strength. In his present state of mind, she doubted he'd even believe the truth. Regardless of what he believed, nothing was going to bring their baby back.

For a long time, only the sounds of their ragged breathing could be heard in the room. It was minutes later before they were both in control of their ravaged emotions, but it would be still longer before either could forgive.

Once Logan had a grip on the rage that threatened to consume him, he was hit by a wave of crushing guilt. If he'd swallowed his pride and told her the truth in the beginning, they wouldn't have separated in anger. She wouldn't have been alone and pregnant.

He had only himself to blame for the unplanned pregnancy. She'd been innocent and admittedly unprotected while his passion had raged out of control. He'd promised to protect her, but he'd been careless, and she'd had to face the consequences. The knowledge didn't lessen his pain or his rage at her decision.

"When?" he was finally calm enough to ask.

Dee had dropped into the chair behind his desk. She turned to look at him when he spoke, but his question didn't immediately register in the confused jumble of her thoughts.

"When what?"

"When would the baby have been born? When did it die?"

She answered without thinking. "He would have been born in October. He died on March 30th."

"He?" His dangerously low tone alerted Dee to the mistake of telling him any of the details. She clamped her lips shut and promised herself not to tell him another thing about the baby he thought she'd killed. . .

"You knew it was a boy?" Logan demanded. "Did you have tests run, or do they tell you that kind of thing at abortion clinics?"

Dee glared at him in icy silence. Her strength was returning, and she rose from the chair. She didn't have to respond to any more of his insults. She wanted nothing more than to escape Logan Bradford's presence and his home.

"Sharla and Carlie will be getting worried about me." She managed a calm tone, ignoring the glacial look in his eyes.

They were already looking for her. Once Dee's emotional upheaval had subsided a little, she'd begun to feel her sisters' concern. They'd be scouring the house soon, and she didn't want them to find her with Logan,

"Your personal bodyguards won't like losing sight of you for so long, will they?"

"No, they won't."

"Did they know about the baby?" he asked. His question was intended to wring more information out of her, but it caused a surprising flash of alarm in her eyes.

"They don't, do they?" he demanded. "You would have been too ashamed to tell your family since you hadn't even told them about me," he guessed accurately.

Dee clenched her teeth in anger. She was a fool. She wasn't good at hiding her emotions, and he was very good at reading them.

She'd inadvertently handed him a weapon to use against her, and she hated the way his eyes gleamed with the knowledge. Her family was more important to her than anything else in the world. They'd be shattered by the fact that she hadn't confided in them. She didn't want them hurt by her mistakes.

The sound of Sharla's voice carried into the room from the direction of the kitchen, and Dee stiffened She wanted him to swear he wouldn't divulge her secret, but she had no way of obtaining his silence.

"What's it worth to keep me quiet?" he taunted, knowing exactly what she was thinking and deciding to take advantage.

Her temper flared. "I won't make any bargains with my body, if that's what you're hoping," she snapped. "I don't want to upset my family, but I won't prostitute myself to keep you quiet."

Logan's mouth twisted in distaste. His eyes were as hard as flint when they locked with hers. "You don't have to worry on that account," he mocked. "I've suddenly lost all interest in your sweet little body."

His mocking dismissal stung, but Dee tried not to let him see how much. "Since that's all you ever wanted in the first place," she accused, "then I guess there's no use discussing blackmail."

She knew the accusation struck a nerve by the narrowing of his gaze.

Despite the fact that Logan was outraged by her actions, he wasn't ready to let her walk out of his life. He wanted more time. "I still need a flight instructor."

"You can forget that, too. There's no way I'd sentence myself to spend hours in a classroom with you."

"That suits me fine," he countered. "I've lost the desire to take lessons. But I have a whole lot of money wrapped up in this project, and I have two men who need the training. You agree to cooperate, and I won't share your secret with your sisters."

Dee could hear Sharla and Carlie's voices coming closer. She had crossed the room and grasped the door handle when Logan's hand settled over hers. She didn't look at him, but she could feel the heat of his body and the warmth of his breath as he whispered near her ear.

"What's it going to be, Dee? Should I invite them in for a chat or are you going to come work for me?"

Both suggestions were abhorrent to her. He knew it and was delighting in baiting her. She wasn't sure whether or not he'd follow through on his threats, but she didn't want to take a chance.

"I'll call and let you know," she hedged.

His low, wicked laughter was completely devoid of humor. "I don't think so. I want your promise. Here and now, or I'm going to do my best to make your life a living hell."

"What makes you think you haven't already accomplished that?" she snapped, turning her eyes up to his with a look of loathing. They glared at each other for a few tension-filled seconds. Then footsteps approached the door from the hallway.

"What's it going to be?" he prodded, his eyes cold and challenging.

Dee knew Sharla would be feeling some of her chaotic emotions. Anger and frustration warred, but concern for her family finally overrode all else.

"All right. You have my promise. I'll teach Jake and Butch, but I want you to promise to stay away from me."

Logan's grin wasn't pleasant. "I live here, remember? You'll be a guest in my house, and I'm the one with the blackmail material. I don't have to promise you anything."

Dee angrily slapped his hand off hers and twisted the knob. She jerked the door open, and came face to face with her sisters.

Sharla and Carlie were bombarded with visual and sensual evidence of Dee's turmoil. Their eyes sharpened, and they tensed, ready to defend her if necessary,

"We were getting worried," said Sharla.

"I'm sorry, I should have stayed close to you." Dee attempted a reassuring smile, but it wasn't the least bit convincing.

"Are you all right?" Carlie demanded. The light in the hallway was dim, but she could still see how disheveled and upset Dee was.

"I'm fine, but I'm ready to go home. If you two want to stay a while, I'll wait for you in the plane."

"We're ready if you are," Sharla insisted.

Logan didn't try to delay their departure. He wanted a few hundred miles between him and Dee until he'd had time to cool down and come to terms with what he'd learned tonight.

"I'll have Butch bring the car around to the front door," he said, as he brushed past all three women and strode toward the back of the house.

"Whew!" said Carlie when he'd disappeared from sight and out of hearing range. "I was ready to tear into him, but I think he's even angrier than you are."

Dee didn't comment. She didn't think it was possible for anyone to be more furious man she was at the moment. She wanted to rant and rave and curse the day she'd met Logan Bradford. What she didn't want was to explain herself to her sisters, so she was forced to contain her rage.

"I hope Logan will make our excuses," Sharla commented as the three of them moved toward the front door. "Except for our host's somewhat abrupt farewell," she added, "everyone has been really nice and friendly."

"We'll send them a thank you note," said Carlie as they stepped onto the porch to wait for their transportation. She'd had a good time, but she wanted to get Dee away from here.

"I'll have Butch say something to Jake and Patti," Sharla decided as the man in question pulled Logan's car to a stop by the steps.

Much later that night, Logan paced the darkness of his bedroom like a caged tiger. His emotions were still churning, and his body was still strung as taut as a bow. Worst of all, he still wanted Dee.

The burning ache had intensified rather than diminished. He'd had her in his arms, stroked her soft, sexy body, and felt her catch fire for him. The taste and feel of her was too vivid. No other woman inflamed him the way she did. The memory of her kept him hard and aching.

He'd tried drowning his sorrows with alcohol for a few hours, but when he'd been on the verge of crying in his beer, he'd sobered up fast. He'd also been tempted to slake his sexual hunger with any available, willing woman. There'd been a few at the party, but none who deserved to be treated so badly. It wasn't their fault Dee had left him feeling raw and needy.

She'd promised to return. Had she lied? Would she keep a promise that had been coerced from her? If she didn't, he'd make a trip to Virginia and raise some hell. He wasn't letting her get away with jerking him around like this. He was going insane.

He wanted what she'd stolen from him. His masculinity and his child. He wanted to sate himself with her beautiful body, and give her another baby. Once he'd had his fill of her, he didn't care if she stayed or not, but he wanted a child.

A son. He'd fathered a son, and he hadn't even known until it was too late to protect him. The thought tore an anguished moan from him. He and Dee had made a baby together. He'd planted his seed in the heat of passion, and she'd destroyed the fruit of their love. How could she have done such a thing?

He wasn't getting any younger, and he wanted a family. Dee was going to bear a child for him. If she didn't want to marry him and help him raise a child, then he'd fight for custody and raise him or her himself.

When she returned — not if, but when — he was going to give her a few days to settle in and get comfortable, and then he would be relentless. The fierce desire that flared between them wasn't likely to die until it was thoroughly quenched. He'd wear down her defenses until they were lovers again.

The thought sent another hot rush of blood to his loins. There was no doubt that his body was willing and able to follow through with a plan of seduction. He wouldn't be satisfied until she was begging and helpless.

Six

By Friday of the week following the fourth, Dee was in a state of total exhaustion. She'd made every effort to banish Logan from her mind, but she hadn't succeeded. She wasn't sleeping, she had no appetite, and she couldn't seem to shake off the depression that had settled over her since leaving Kentucky.

Her family had been patient and considerate. They hadn't bombarded her with questions. They respected her privacy, but they'd made it clear they were willing to listen if she wanted to talk. She just couldn't talk about Logan.

She'd cleared her training schedule in preparation for the assignment in Kentucky, so she didn't have any students right now. She'd been helping Sharla with charters and Carlie with cargo, trying to keep herself too busy to think. By the end of the week, she was dragging.

"You look exhausted, Darla Jo," Belle admonished when Dee entered the company office on Friday afternoon. "You've been taking on too much work this week."

"You might be right, Mother," Dee admitted as she turned her flight log over to Belle. "A cool shower and bed sound pretty inviting."

"Well, I hope you're going to make time to eat. If you don't feel like cooking, you can have dinner with your dad and I."

"Thanks, I might take you up on the offer after I get clean and change into something cooler."

"Sharla's going out with Reed, but Carlie said she'll have dinner with us," explained Belle. "Would you rather wait until later to discuss the new contract from the Circle B's?"

Dee stilled. "New contract?" she asked in a wary tone.

"It came this morning. Most of the details are the same; the training time, working conditions, and salary. The only change is that you'd have two students instead of three. Mr. Bradford has obviously decided not to take the training."

Dee nodded. She hadn't told her mother much about their visit to Kentucky, only that there had been some indecision and that everything had been put on hold. She'd secretly hoped that Logan would find someone else to train his men and leave her alone. The new contract confirmed the fact that he intended to follow through with his threats.

"Mr. Bradford won't be taking the training from me," she explained.

"Are you still planning to go there and train the other two?"

Dee clenched her teeth, furious with Logan for putting her in so difficult a position. She didn't want to go to Kentucky, but she had a feeling he would come after her if she refused. He couldn't force her to do anything, yet he could cause a lot of heartache. Either way, she and her family would come out losers.

For days she'd mentally reviewed their arguments. It had been a relief to unburden herself to Logan; sharing the guilt she'd carried so long. It had also been a mistake to give him information he knew she didn't want told. She'd considered telling her parents and sisters the whole truth so that his threat would be useless, but she just couldn't bring herself to hurt and disappoint her family.

"I'm still considering it," she told her mother. "Logan Bradford is an old acquaintance I don't want to renew." That was as much as she cared to admit. "But everyone else at the Circle B's was kind, and it's a beautiful place."

"They want you to move in this weekend and start work Monday," Belle informed her. "I don't want you to go unless you're absolutely sure."

Dee swallowed a moan. He wasn't allowing her any more time. The new contract was a reminder that he wasn't going to let her off the hook.

"I'm too tired to think about it right now. I'll read the contract and decide later," she said, accepting the bundle of papers from her mother. "Sunday will be soon enough to go to Kentucky if I don't start lessons until Monday."

Belle watched her leave the office, wondering if any contact with Logan Bradford would prove a disaster for Dee. Apparently, the two hadn't worked out their differences.

Later, after reading the contract several times and doing more soul-searching, Dee joined Carlie and her parents for dinner. She told them she'd decided to go to Kentucky. Not wanting them to worry, she made it sound as though she welcomed a chance for a change of scenery.

Carlie wasn't convinced, but she didn't say anything during dinner. After the sisters said good night to their parents, they took a brief walk outdoors while heading for their individual apartments. It was another sultry evening filled with the sounds and scents of summer. Twilight enveloped them, and Carlie took the opportunity to question Dee about her trip.

"What made you decide to go to Kentucky?"

Dee sighed. "A combination of things," she admitted. She'd come to the conclusion that she had to take the assignment and prove to herself that she had the strength and courage to deal with Logan Bradford. She wanted him out of her system forever.

"Are you sure it's a wise decision?"

"No."

"If you have serious doubts, then why don't you tell them to find someone else?"

"I tried, without success. At this point, Logan isn't going to settle for anyone else."

"What kind of hold does he have on you?" Carlie asked softly. "Surely it's nothing so terrible that you're afraid to fight him on this."

"It's complicated," was all she admitted. "I could refuse to go train Jake and Butch, but that's not really in anyone's best interest. I loved Logan, and I thought he loved me. I was wrong. I need to put it behind me and get on with my life. I won't be able to do that until I can immunize myself against him. I want to be near him and not feel anything. This is a chance to do that."

"You haven't really known him that long, and only while both of you were on vacation," Carlie commented. "Maybe you'll find out he's a jerk in real life. He could be spoiled, opinionated, pompous..."

Dee agreed. "Arrogant, overbearing, obnoxious..."

"Bossy, spiteful..."

"Domineering, judgmental..."

"Malicious..."

"Selfish..."

"Ill mannered..."

"He probably has tons of bad habits," Dee injected, looping her arm through Carlie's as they strolled around the house. "Probably chews tobacco and spits on the floor."

"Probably guzzles beer and belches like a pig," Carlie added, enjoying their game.

"Probably kicks his dog..."

"Probably hates cats..."

"Probably swears like a sailor..."

"Probably tracks mud on clean floors..."

"Throws his dirty clothes all over the house..."

"A real slob..."

"Leaves the toilet seat up," Carlie concluded with a grimace, and they were both chuckling as they reached Dee's apartment door.

"Dr. Carlie Prescott predicts that you'll be cured of any adolescent crush on Mr. Logan Bradford within two weeks of living with the man," Carlie teased. "I may not be the most clairvoyant person in this family, but I'm considering fortune-telling. What do you think?"

Dee felt like laughing for the first time in days. She gave Carlie a parting hug. "I think I like your prediction. You may be right about Logan. When I get to Kentucky, I'm going to keep a running list of his imperfections. I should be cured in no time."

She tried to find comfort in that thought for the rest of the night and all day Saturday. By the time she was flying to her temporary home on Sunday afternoon, she'd almost convinced herself that she could live in

Logan's house and remain unaffected.

Arriving at the Circle B's, she learned from Jake that his boss was gone on a buying trip to New Mexico. The knowledge brought a rush of conflicting emotions. Dee realized that she wasn't as brave as she'd pretended, and she was glad for the reprieve. It was important for her to concentrate on setting up her training program. It was much easier to do without worrying that he might show up at any moment.

Jake loaded her cases into his truck and took her to the house where she was warmly greeted by Mattie Walters. The housekeeper was a small, middle-aged woman with short, curly silver hair, twinkling brown eyes and an abundance of energy. The two women had met at the barbecue, but hadn't had a chance to really get acquainted.

"Patti decided to go with Logan, so I'm the official welcoming committee," she said. "You and Jake just follow me, and I'll show you where you can put your things. Then we'll have a chance to visit a bit."

Mattie led the way to the room at the back of the house that had been readied for Dee. The housekeeper threw open the door and stepped aside to let them enter.

It was a huge room with a king-sized, solid oak bed and matching furniture. The style was old-fashioned, but the room was done in delicate shades of mauve and blue. Dee could see Patti's hand in the decorating.

As soon as Jake set down the luggage, Mattie told him to get lost while she helped their guest get unpacked. She mentioned that men were handy to help, but they shouldn't dally in a young lady's bedroom.

"Gee, Mattie, I can take a hint, you don't have to be so blunt with your dismissal," he teased. "I don't want to invade anyone's privacy."

It was obvious that he and the housekeeper had an amiable relationship. Dee could sense genuine respect and affection in their teasing.

"I always say it's more practical to be blunt. That way nobody misunderstands," Mattie clarified.

Dee laughed and Jake threw his hands up in mock surrender. "I'm outta here. Dee, when Mattie dismisses you, we'd be happy to have you check out the room we've set up for lessons. You can let us know what changes need to be made."

"Carlie's an hour or so behind me," she explained. "I couldn't bring all the equipment on the Cessna, so she's bringing the ground simulator and some other supplies."

"If you have work to do, just go along with Jake," Mattie insisted. "I can unpack for you. When Logan and Patti are gone, I don't have enough to do around here anyway."

"I'm not in a hurry," Dee assured her. "I can't do much until Carlie comes, so I have time to get organized in here first."

"Patti says you're to use her car for running back and forth to the airfield. Jake can bring it from the garage and leave it in the drive. That way you won't have to wait for one of the men every time you want transportation," said Mattie.

"I'll do that now and head back to the field," Jake told them as he stepped into the hallway.

"I'll be out shortly," Dee called to his retreating figure. Then she turned her attention to Mattie.

"This room was the master bedroom when John and Martha, the senior Bradfords, were alive. It's the only bedroom downstairs. You have your own bath," she explained, waving her hand toward the inside door, then moving to the French doors to pull back the drapes.

"I keep heavy drapes in here. They keep out the cold in winter and sun in summer. There are sheers underneath, so you can adjust them any way you like. The doors have a safety lock so you can secure it twice if you feel the need."

Dee didn't try to interrupt, just nodded her head and started opening her suitcases.

"You're on the outside corner of the house and have a small patio. The sidewalk from the right leads around to the big patio where we held the barbecue the other night. From there it leads to the barns. The sidewalk to the left leads to the pool. It's too small for a crowd, but it'll cool you off if you want to use it anytime."

"The kitchen's in the middle of the house. You've seen the family and living rooms, I imagine. The only other downstairs rooms are the formal dining room, another bathroom, and Logan's office. It's kind of a big, sprawling place, but not the least bit hard to get used to."

"I'm sure I'll be fine," Dee managed before the housekeeper continued her dialogue.

"Since this isn't a complete apartment, you'll be taking meals with the family. Anytime you feel the need for a snack, just go to the kitchen and help yourself. I'm not one of those fussy people who throws a fit when someone enters my kitchen. I always say a person should eat when they want to eat. If our schedule doesn't suit you, then make your own."

"I'm not hard to please," Dee injected as Mattie stopped to catch her breath.

"I have breakfast ready at seven o'clock," the older woman continued while throwing open closet doors and dresser drawers. "You can situate your clothes anyway you like. There's plenty of space, and I always say it's best for a person to do their own arranging."

In half a second she continued. "Lunch is at noon, supper's at six. Patti says it's supposed to be called dinner after six, so I tell her we'll eat at five minutes before the hour. It's just a little joke we've always shared. We eat early 'cause the men are hungry by then, and I like to get the kitchen cleaned by a reasonable time. I'm not as young as I used to be."

The older woman talked as fast as she moved, and she moved with the speed of a hummingbird. Dee stopped trying to watch her, but listened carefully as she busied herself arranging her clothes in the dresser and closet.

She hadn't brought a lot of extra clothing. She normally dressed more casually when training at a private residence, but she'd wanted to appear very professional while in Logan's territory.

"The laundry room is between this room and the kitchen, but you have to go down the hall. There's no door from this room," Mattie explained. "You don't have to worry about doing any laundry unless you want to. I have little enough to do, so I don't mind taking care of that. Just drop your dirty clothes in the bathroom hamper, and I'll collect them every morning. I'll be more than happy to tidy your room, too."

"I don't mind straightening the room," Dee said. "I'm used to keeping my own apartment, so making the bed and picking up after myself are habit."

Mattie nodded in an approving fashion. "I change all the linens every Monday morning, so you can strip the bed or leave it. I'll remake it for you that day."

"Sounds good to me," said Dee. "I'm happiest when I can be outdoors or giving lessons."

"And I'm happiest when I'm busy," Mattie added, closing Dee's cases and storing them in the top of the closet. "Patti and Logan spend most of the day outdoors, too, so I have plenty of uninterrupted time to keep things organized inside the house."

She propped her hands on her hips and quickly surveyed the room, satisfying herself that all was well. "If you're hungry, help yourself to anything that appeals to you. I'll fix something light for supper since it's just you and me. Or you're welcome to invite your sister to join us when she comes."

"I imagine Carlie will want to fly right back to Virginia," said Dee. "And I had a big lunch, so something light sounds fine. I'll take care of everything at the airfield and join you again at five minutes until six."

Mattie chuckled and reached for the door. "We'll get along just fine. If any of those boys gives you any trouble, you just let me know. They're a pretty good bunch, but boys will be boys, and Logan wouldn't want you to put up with any shenanigans. He's always been the chivalrous sort, though he'd deny it to his last breath."

"I don't usually have trouble dealing with men," Dee told her with a smile. She appreciated the older woman's offer of support, but ignored the comment concerning Logan's character. "But thank you for the offer."

"You're welcome," said Mattie. She was still talking as she left the room and pulled the door closed behind her. "Just make yourself at home. Jake will have Patti's car out front. I'll see you in a little while."

Dee sighed softly as the door closed. Now that she'd arrived and found Logan gone, she could allow herself to relax and enjoy her surroundings. The room she'd been given was lovely. The carpet was mauve, textured and plush. The artfully draped windows faced west and provided plenty of late afternoon sunlight to brighten the room, while the air conditioner kept the temperature at a comfortable level.

She couldn't have felt more welcome. Everything about Logan's home was warm and inviting. Everything but the man himself. She hoped he stayed away for the whole time she was in residence. Dee enjoyed new challenges, and she was looking forward to teaching Jake and Butch to fly.

She was anxious to see the area they'd furnished for a classroom. Once Carlie brought her supplies, they'd be ready for training. It would be a pleasure to get on with her job. Then she'd have a lot less time to worry about Logan.

Her bathroom was decorated in the same shade of mauve used in the bedroom, but coupled with rich cream-colored walls and tiled floor. It wasn't very large, but it had a big bathtub and shower stall. Dee took the time to glance in the mirror, smooth her hair, and splash a little water on her face. Then she headed out of the room and out of the house.

A sporty blue, late-model Corvette was parked near the front porch steps. Dee whistled in admiration as she caught sight of it. Patti must be a generous person to allow guests to drive this car, she thought as she eased herself into the low bucket seat.

It took her a couple minutes to familiarize herself with the controls, but then the powerful engine was purring, and she was following the road she knew led to the airfield.

The hangar was another pleasant surprise. Half of the long building was used as a garage and storage area for planes. The other half was partitioned into the two smaller work areas, one for a radio room and the other for a classroom.

As teacher, Dee had been given a big desk and a blackboard, which she would definitely use. Despite the austere style of the building, the walls were freshly painted, a serviceable carpet covered the concrete floor and there was air-conditioning. Several more comfortable chairs accompanied straight-back chairs.

When Carlie arrived, Butch and Jake helped to unload more supplies. The ground flight simulator was transported to the classroom and readied for use. Dee hung several graphs and charts around the room and made sure she had everything she would need before seeing her sister off again.

Shortly after Carlie was in the air, the men headed for the barns to do their evening chores. Dee made her way back to the house to join Mattie for supper.

While they ate, the housekeeper continued to describe the normal routine of the Circle B's, providing her with more information than she normally would have obtained in several weeks. The two women shared the duties of cleaning the kitchen and then carried their coffee to the patio.

The temperature had hovered in the nineties all day, but a gentle breeze helped make the heat more bearable. They carried aluminum lawn chairs to the shade of an old oak tree and made themselves comfortable.

As soon as they sat down, a big, aging Labrador retriever rose from his resting spot near the trunk of the tree and ambled over to put his head on Dee's lap, begging for attention.

"Well, I'll be," Mattie said. "That's the first time I ever saw old Ace get up and move for anybody but Logan. He's paying you quite a compliment. He used to raise a fuss every time a stranger came near the house, but he doesn't worry himself over much anymore."

"Hi, there, old man," Dee crooned in a low tone as she patted the broad, black head of the Lab. The inky fur was liberally sprinkled with gray. "You must be getting up there in years."

"He's seventeen years old this summer. Logan's had him since he was just a pup, and the two of 'em are real pals. Ace moped around here something terrible when Logan was in the service. Then he came home, and that dog refused to leave his side. Everywhere Logan went, Ace went."

"The service?" Dee repeated in surprise. Logan had never mentioned being in the military.

Mattie shifted her gaze, looking uncomfortable for a minute. "The Navy," she explained, then quickly changed the subject back to the dog. "Patti thought Logan should have old Ace put to sleep this summer. She's afraid he's going blind and suffering in his old age."

"Oh, no," Dee countered, scratching Ace's ear and feeling the contentment of the old dog. She had an unusual affinity with animals and usually knew if one was in pain.

"Ace might have had a rough start in life, and he might have a lot of old scars, but I'll bet he's had a cushy life," she declared.

Mattie's eyes were sharp as they rested on Dee's lovely features. "How did you know that?" she asked in surprise.

Dee glanced at her. "Know what?"

"That he had a rough start and has collected lots of scars over the years," Mattie clarified. "Has Logan told you about Ace?"

Dee shifted her gaze back to the dog. She hadn't meant to hint at her uncanny knowledge of animals. Few people could understand her extrasensory perception. It was hard to describe the feelings she experienced when it came to human beings. Explaining about animals was nearly impossible. She didn't discuss it, especially with people who didn't know her well. She'd never even mentioned it to Logan.

"He didn't tell me where he got Ace." She managed to sidestep the question without lying.

"It was an accident," Mattie explained. "Ace was one of a litter of pups the neighbors owned. He was about eight weeks old, all clumsy and long-legged. Logan happened to be riding near the road and saw the pup get hit by a truck. The driver didn't even stop to see if the dog was dead or alive."

Dee nodded and kept petting Ace.

"Anyway, Logan got the dog to the vet. It was touch and go for a few days. John, Logan's dad, thought maybe they shouldn't try to save him because he had several broken bones and an injured lung. But Logan insisted. He refused to let the dog die. Sat up with him most nights and carried him around until his legs healed. They've been firm friends ever since."

Dee nodded. Something about Ace had made her think of old scars. That's why she'd made the unusual slip of the tongue that Mattie had been quick to notice. The dog didn't seem to be suffering in the least. He was healthy, yet she had a feeling that he was growing tired; the kind of tired that couldn't be remedied with sleep.

"I always say old Ace is part cat, because he's had more than nine lives. He's been shot a few times, run over by a truck, kicked by a horse, and tangled in barbed wire, but he's a survivor. At one time, he was the local Romeo, and serviced all the female dogs within ten miles of here. Now he's content to lay under this old shade tree."

"It's funny how people say, 'It's a dog's life,' and mean that life is rough," Dee commented, "because some dogs have a better life than people, and without the stress of coping with a lot of emotional problems."

Mattie agreed. "You can say that again. I've got a friend who treats her dog like one of the family. Let's it eat at the table and sleep with her."

"We never had pets when I was growing up," Dee mentioned. "My mother has allergies and we moved too often to make it practical."

"Old Ace and a few of his offspring are the only dogs we've had around here. He's outlived them all, but he doesn't roam like he used to. Like I said, Logan's about the only one he thumps that heavy tail for anymore."

Ace had flopped beside Dee's chair. His head was hot and heavy where it rested on her foot, but she didn't make any attempt to move him. Mattie continued to make small talk as they drank their coffee. Once their cups were empty, they put them on a nearby table and two tawny cats jumped into Dee's lap.

"Well, I'll be," Mattie declared in amazement. "Every critter on the farm must have decided to say hello. Those cats hardly ever leave the barn. They don't usually make up to people. Just shoo 'em away if you want."

Dee stroked both cats and gave Mattie a smile. "Animals just naturally gravitate to me," she admitted. "I guess they know I'm an easy target. I have a real soft spot for little creatures. Maybe it's because I had to settle for goldfish as pets."

Mattie laughed at the idea of petting a goldfish. "You'll have plenty of opportunity to fuss over animals around here. There's always a new litter or baby. Dolly, there on your right knee, has a litter of kittens in the barn. They're about three weeks old and getting frisky. The one on your left knee is Tom. He's probably the father, but it's hard to tell about these things unless you actually witness the conception."

Dee smiled and stroked the cats. Dolly was a calico and Tom was tiger-striped. Their fur was silky smooth, and she imagined they had some pretty offspring.

"I'd like to see the kittens."

"They're in the main horse barn. That's the one closest to the house. Jake will probably show you all around the property tomorrow, but feel free to explore. You probably won't be stuck in the hangar all day, will you?"

"We've decided to start with a couple hours in the morning and a couple in the evening."

Mattie approved. "That sounds reasonable. Jake's a little pressed for time with Logan gone, but he should be back early in the week."

The thought wasn't reassuring to Dee. She was rapidly learning to like everything about his home and staff, but she wasn't anxious to put herself to the test of living under the same roof with him.

She needed a little more time, and hoped he'd stay away longer than expected. Mattie's earlier question about Ace led her to believe that the family knew she and Logan had been acquainted before she was hired for the training. She just didn't know how much they knew.

Her sisters were the only people who'd witnessed the aftershocks of their argument on the fourth, but Patti and Jake were aware of the tension between them. Jake hadn't said or done anything that suggested he was taking sides.

Patti might have a different attitude. She seemed close to her brother, and maybe a little protective. The whole situation could become difficult if Logan involved the family and staff in their personal problems. Dee had always thought he was too private to openly express his emotions, but then she'd realized that she really didn't know him at all.

Despite her conflicting emotions, Dee settled down to bed that night feeling totally at peace. She gave some thought to sleeping in his parents' bedroom, yet felt no disquiet. She couldn't help but wonder where Logan's bedroom was located, but she didn't investigate the second story. She was a guest and, despite Mattie's suggestion that she explore, she didn't want to invade anyone's privacy.

Seven

For the next couple of days, Dee settled into a slow-paced routine that included early-morning training sessions, explorations of the Bradford property, and getting to know all of Logan's staff.

Everyone she met was friendly and anxious to please her. Before long, she realized that Logan's employees knew he was interested in her on a personal level rather than a professional one.

She was being privately labeled Logan's woman, whether she wanted to be or not. No one actually said anything that she could refute; yet everyone treated her with cautious respect. They thought their boss was trying to win her affection, so they went out of their way to tell her what a great guy he was.

On one occasion, Jake mentioned that Logan was a hard worker and never asked his men to do anything he wasn't willing to do himself. On several different occasions, he praised Logan's talents in handling the horses, saying that he was the best in the business.

Butch mentioned that Logan was an honest and fair man to work for. The young trainer admitted to idolizing his boss, and praised him for being a strong, dependable man with a wonderful reputation in the community.

Mattie explained, several times and in great detail, that he was a concerned employer who cared about his staff and was generous with those who worked for him. She also mentioned that he'd raised Patti since their parents' death when she was still a youngster, and that he was a loyal, devoted family man.

Grif Myers, the senior horse trainer, even managed to get in a word about what a fine specimen of manhood Logan was, and that single, hard-working young men were hard to find these days.

Everyone seemed to be in agreement about their boss's strengths and attributes. According to the Circle B's staff, their boss was a prince among men.

Dee wondered if Logan realized how much his employees cared for him. She knew they wouldn't be trying to impress her by outlining his more admirable traits unless they were genuinely fond of him and concerned about his happiness.

As far as she was concerned, his employees were the loyal, dependable ones. They easily won her respect and affection. Still, she was far from persuaded that he deserved their high marks in character.

By the time Butch and Jake had finished their classroom training on Wednesday evening, Dee was certain they were the most cooperative students she'd ever taught. Despite the fact that they had to fit classes into their long work days, they were still attentive. Both were intelligent and learned quickly, making them easy to teach.

In a short three days, Dee and Mattie became firm friends. The two of them shared the house, meals, and lots of interesting conversation. When Dee wasn't working in her classroom or accompanying Jake around the property, she helped the housekeeper weed the garden, pick vegetables, and preserve some of the produce.

The weather remained hot, but not unlike the weather Dee was accustomed to in Virginia. The house was cool and always offered a pleasant relief from the heat. At night, Dee showered and slid into bed feeling tired, but with the satisfaction of having accomplished something worthwhile.

Not long past midnight on Wednesday, after being asleep in bed for just a short time, she dreamt of Logan. It was the first time he'd invaded her dreams in several weeks, and it was an incredibly erotic dream that left her trembling and shaken.

Her mouth was dry, her breathing rough, as she dragged herself to consciousness, kicking the sheet off while fighting the effects of a dream that seemed so real it left her heart racing. Despite the air-conditioned comfort of the room, she was hot and sweating, restless and frustrated.

She slid her legs over the side of the bed and sat up to rake the hair off her face and neck. She always left it loose when sleeping. Right now it felt like a woolen blanket clinging to her neck and shoulders.

Dee pushed herself off the bed and realized her legs were shaking, then damned the vivid memories of Logan that left her weak and wanting. She hated herself for recalling every nuance of his voice and every tiny way he knew to drive her mad with desire.

Her skin tingled, her breasts felt tight and achy, and her body throbbed with a need that no amount of wishful thinking could will away. She paced to the French doors, drew back the drapes, and stared into the moonlit night, but this time her restlessness couldn't be soothed by the quiet beauty of the night.

The crescent moon warded off complete darkness. The sky was dappled with stars and fireflies twinkled in abundance. A distant security light kept the area around the back of the house dimly lit.

She found herself wishing she'd brought a bathing suit with her. It was tempting to make use of the pool, but she wasn't bold enough to skinny dip. Sliding open the door, she decided to at least escape the bedroom until she could regain control of her senses.

Her pajamas were hot pink and very skimpy, little more than silk boxer shorts with a matching tank top. They hugged her body and left a lot of bare skin, but she didn't expect to encounter anyone at this time of night.

It was a short walk to the pool, and she made it in silence. The night air was warmer than that of the bedroom, but not uncomfortably so. Dee inhaled deeply, enjoying the heavily scented sweetness of the air, and trying to calm her riotous emotions.

How could her subconscious torment her with memories of Logan's loving, she wondered in irritation. Was she a glutton for punishment? Some kind of masochist? Why couldn't she completely banish the man from her memories? If she had to dream about him, why did the dreams have to be so real, leaving her so weak and wanting?

Why couldn't she just stop wanting him? He'd betrayed her trust m the worst sort of way, yet she still yearned for everything he'd offered her. She didn't want to be his plaything, nor did she want to be a helpless victim of her own desires.

She had to let go of the memories. She knew that, but how was she supposed to do it? No other man interested her. No other man sparked a fraction of the passion Logan could stimulate with just his hungry eyes. Was she doomed to be forever held in the grip of an unrequited love?

The pool was small, kidney-shaped, and darkly shadowed. Dee didn't mind. She didn't intend to swim; just to dip her feet into the water and hope it would help her relax a little. Mattie had told her there were underwater lights, but she didn't want to use them. She felt less vulnerable in the darkness.

The thin barrier of her silk shorts wasn't much protection as she sat down on the edge of the pool. The concrete deck was cool and damp, the water even cooler as she slid both feet into the shallow end by the steps.

As soon as she was seated, she flipped her hair over her shoulders and gazed around her. It wasn't until then that she noted the dark shape in the pool. Her heart lurched in her chest as she recognized Logan's form gliding toward her beneath the water.

He surfaced close to the steps where her feet were resting. His naked body glistened with pagan beauty, muscled, sleek, and all male. The sight of him made her breath catch, her pulse accelerate, and her limbs quiver. She cursed herself for ever leaving the bedroom.

"Dee."

His voice was deep and throaty. The way he said her name made her pulse pound with a mixture of apprehension and anticipation. He was thigh-deep in the pool; his masculine form boldly exposed. Water swirled through the dark golden curls on his chest and ran in rivulets down his powerfully masculine body.

Seeing him while she was still emotionally and physically disturbed by her dreams was an unwelcome shock that she desperately wanted to conceal.

"Logan," she returned in a quiet tone that belied the emotions running rampant within her. "I didn't realize you were home." She didn't have to add that she wouldn't have risked a late-night stroll if she'd known he was back.

Despite all that had transpired between them, including the anger and resentment that were still strong, neither of them had the energy or inclination to argue.

"We got back half an hour ago. I've been driving since six this morning. I needed some exercise." In a few succinct sentences he explained his presence at the pool.

Dee could feel his weariness, and that shocked her. Logan was the one person who had always confused her senses, leaving them in chaos. She'd never been able to read him like she did other people. Now she studied his facial features with wary eyes. He looked tired and strained, but his eyes gleamed brightly in the shadows. His scrutiny was intense, and she quickly averted her gaze.

Deciding to make a hasty retreat. Dee started to pull her feet from the water, but he moved swiftly to stop her. One of his wide, cool hands settled on her hot thigh, and her nerves sizzled. She felt a jolt of sensation from the tip of her toes to the top of her head. It was more than a little alarming.

"I need to get back inside," she insisted huskily.

"No," he countered in a rough growl, "you can't run and hide forever. It's a waste of time to try."

"It's my time," she challenged, but as he stepped closer, her heart leapt with excitement. She continued to fight him mentally, but her body had a mind of its own. There wasn't an inch of it that didn't respond to the memory of how incredible he could make her feel.

Their gazes eyes clashed; hers wary, his determined. Dee caught her breath at the sensual intent she read in his heated gaze. He might hate her, but there was no doubting that he wanted her. Desire radiated from his big body, enveloping her in a cocoon of heated sensuality.

One of Logan's hands slid around her waist and the other under her hips. He shifted her until he could step between her legs and pull her close. Then he lifted a hand to sink it into the heavy thickness of her hair.

The feel of his hard, naked body between her thighs triggered a gasp from Dee. Her hands automatically splayed against his chest to ward him off, but Logan pulled her head closer until he could trap her mouth with his own.

No! Dee's mental cry was anguished. She couldn't bare the incredible tension. She wanted him too much. Still aroused by her own erotic dreams, she didn't have the strength to deny him, but knew it would be a stupid mistake to let Logan make love to her.

His mouth was cool, wet, and demanding. He wasn't rough, but the hungry little bites he took of her lips were more effective than any force he might have used. He shifted closer until he was firmly nestled against the cradle of her body with only thin silk to separate them. Then he sunk both hands in her hair and held her head captive while he continued the gentle, persistent assault on her mouth.

Dee's fingers flexed against his chest, and she gradually relaxed the pressure she was exerting to keep him at bay. He felt so good, so very good. His skin was cool and damp; his chest corded with muscle. His heart was pounding wildly against her palm.

It had been this way since the first time they met; she touched him and he responded. That had always been Dee's undoing — his swift, honest reaction to her lightest touch. He had a deeply sensual nature that perfectly matched her own. The knowledge was a potent aphrodisiac.

He shuddered when she finally opened her lips to allow the hot penetration of his tongue. Dee moaned at the evidence of his tightly leashed control, and a tremor shook her to the soles of her feet.

One of Logan's arms enveloped her to draw her closer while his other hand cupped the back of her head. She flattened her hands against his chest, but stopped trying to push him away from her. His nipples harden against her palms, and her own nipples puckered painfully in response.

His mouth devoured hers, his tongue plundering the heated sweetness he found. Dee's tongue welcomed him in a ritual of mating until they were both gasping for breath.

Then Logan's head dipped and his strong arm arched her upward so that he could nuzzle her breasts with his face. His lips found a thrusting nipple beneath the silk. He sucked it into his mouth and lathed it with his tongue.

Dee cried out softly at the exquisite sensations racing from her breasts to her womb. She began to writhe in his arms, and her hips involuntarily thrust against the hardness of his arousal.

"Logan, stop!" she cried in a last-minute attempt to halt the avalanche of passion. "You have to stop it!"

His voice was thick and hoarse with arousal. "I can't stop it," he growled in a mixture of raw desire and self-disgust. "It's eating me alive! I wish to hell I could stop wanting you, but I can't."

Her hands slid up his body until her fingers were locked tightly in his hair. His mouth searched until finding the bare skin where her shorts and top parted. He shoved the flimsy material out of his way and began to suck deeply on her nipples again. She uttered a soft cry at the exquisite pleasure.

Her fingers clenched in his hair as fire raged through her. The involuntary arching of her hips brought the softness of her body into searing contact with the hardness of his.

"Dee!" Logan's cry was hoarse with urgency. His mouth sought hers while he pressed her flat on her back and stretched himself along her length.

"It's not right!" she found the strength to insist before his mouth took hers again. Then she was drowning. Her heart and mind knew all the reasons she shouldn't make love with him, but she wanted him, body and soul.

Logan was burning, on fire with need. The blood pounded in his head and surged with violence through his veins to his loins. Everywhere their bodies touched, his flesh was scorched and straining.

Dee's mouth offered the hottest sweetness possible. His fingers clung to the silk of her hair while the silk of her pajamas and skin enticed him beyond reason. Her budded nipples in the plump cushion of her breasts were stabbing him to relentless excitement. A sheer layer of silk was all that kept the straining strength of his arousal from the sheathe he so desperately sought.

"Dee?" His tone asked and coaxed at the same time. His body thrust against hers in persistent demand.

Her arms were locked over his shoulders and around his neck. She gasped for breath as his mouth left hers just long enough to issue a plea. When she didn't respond, his lips captured hers again. The kiss was deep, and hot, and needy.

Another low moan escaped her throat and was lost within their mouths. Logan moaned, too. His hands glided from her hair to the bare flesh beneath her top, then lower. He caught the elastic band on her shorts and peeled the offending fabric off her hips.

As his turgidly aroused flesh surged between her legs, she arched against it, giving him all the response he needed. He wanted to take her, to bury himself in her fast and hard, without thinking, just feeling. But he forced himself to be as slow and gentle as possible. He knew Dee wasn't sexually active, and despite the driving force of his need, he didn't hurt women.

She gasped as he filled her. Her eyes flew open and slammed into the silvery brilliance of Logan's gaze. The savage hunger startled her because he was keeping his body under such tight control. She felt an intense need to shatter that control, and she dragged his head down to hers as she arched wildly beneath him.

Logan lost it. Every ounce of control was destroyed by her surrender and impatient demand. He dragged her closer and gave in to the need to lose himself in the hot, wet softness of her body.

Strangled cries of release were forced from both of them as they swiftly reached completion. Their arms tightened as they clutched each other closer. Then they clung as they fought the aftermath of such violent loving.

When Logan had regained some strength, he pulled Dee's top over her head and tossed it aside. Then he eased her in the water to cool and cleanse their overheated bodies.

She twisted her hair and pulled it over her shoulder so that it wouldn't get soaked. Other than that, she had very little energy and was content to relax against him. He supported them both at the shallow end of the pool until his strength returned.

The feel of her soft, pliant body in his arms soon had renewed desire coursing over Logan's body. He'd been without her too long, was too hungry, to be sated with one quick coupling. He wanted more, right now, before Dee had time to reconstruct barriers.

Taking his time, he began to scatter kisses over her neck and shoulders. She trembled against him, and his kisses became more feverish. Within minutes, his body was hard and throbbing again. He leaned his back against the side of the pool, grasped Dee's hips, and eased her onto his straining flesh.

Satisfaction was longer coming this time, and they were both gasping for breath, their lungs tortured, before they were temporarily sated. Dee didn't have enough strength left to lift her arms, but Logan supported her as they sunk low enough in the shallow water to cool themselves.

The next time strength returned, he lifted her from the pool and carried her to her bedroom. He intended to put her to bed and leave, but the sight of her beautiful, naked body spread on tangled sheets set his body on fire again. He rested a knee on the bed beside her, and leaned over to steal another kiss.

One kiss wasn't enough. He wanted to take more time to caress her breasts with his hands and mouth. He wanted to feel her nipples tighten to rigid hardness under the stroke of his tongue. He wanted to feel the slide of her soft thighs around his own. He wanted to stay buried inside the pulsing heat of her body.

He wanted to hear her cry his name in passion. He wanted her begging and writhing beneath him. He needed to know that she was as much a victim of the passion as he was. He wanted hours, days or weeks, whatever it took.

The taste of her was like a drug in his veins. He couldn't resist. Didn't even want to try. Tomorrow, he promised himself; tomorrow he'd regain some control and try to sort out his tangled emotions. But tonight, he was a man in need. Tonight he was blind and deaf to everything but the wanting.

Dee's needs matched Logan's. She didn't want to think, or worry, or question what they were doing. She just wanted to share the passion and feel whole again. Logan was like a missing part of her soul, she only felt whole when she was in his arms.

She wanted to wallow in the sensual and emotional satisfaction he supplied. Tomorrow she'd worry about the rightness or wrongness of their loving. Tomorrow would be soon enough for self-loathing and considering consequences.

Eight

A knock at the door woke Dee the next morning. She struggled to prop herself on her elbows and drowsily realized she was naked. While pulling the sheet up to cover herself, she glanced at the clock. A groan escaped as she noted that it was after ten o'clock, and she'd overslept for the first time in years. Breakfast was long past, and so was the normal starting time for her morning training session.

Another knock had her calling, "Who's there?"

"Just Mattie," responded the housekeeper as she opened the door a few inches and poked in her head. "This is the first time you've missed breakfast, and I just wanted to make sure you're all right."

Dee managed a sleepy smile for her. "I'm fine, thanks. I must have forgotten to set the alarm." She didn't think so, but it was possible.

"No problem," said Mattie. "Logan and Patti got back late last night, so she's sleeping in, too. I'll fix you both something to eat when you're ready. Logan said not to worry about the lessons, because he's gonna need Jake and Butch for most of the day"

The thought of Logan brought warmth creeping up Dee's chest, neck, and face. She dipped her head to hide the rush of color. "Was there anything else?" she asked.

"I was just gonna collect your dirty laundry, but I don't need to unless you want something cleaned today."

"No, there's nothing to worry about, but thanks," said Dee. Her hair was a tangled mess, so she used one hand to drag it off of her face, being careful not to let the sheet slip from her other hand.

"Then I'll see you later. Just come on out to the kitchen when you're ready to eat," the housekeeper added as she closed the door.

Dee collapsed backward on the bed and stared at the ceiling in numbed shock. Memories of the previous night made her go hot all over, then totally cold. She and Logan had made love for hours. How could she have done it? How could she have been so stupid? So totally irresponsible?

Logan had caught her unaware and vulnerable. She hadn't had time to erect her usual defenses against his potent virility. It had been too long, she'd missed him too much, and they'd both been too needy.

Dee wanted to lay all the blame on him, but she knew she was equally guilty. She'd wanted him just as badly as he'd wanted her, and they'd both succumbed to the desire. What in the world was she supposed to do now? How was a woman supposed to react in such a situation?

They'd made love for hours last night — repeated, unprotected sex. Was she a complete fool? What in God's name would she do if she was pregnant? How could she bear to carry another child so soon after losing her first?

She'd taken the same risk the first time she and Logan had been together because everything had seemed so right, so utterly perfect. She hadn't felt any uneasiness or shame about sharing his bed then, but this was different.

Back then, she'd been relatively innocent and hopelessly in love. She couldn't claim either now. She felt like the last six months had aged her beyond her years, yet her behavior last night had been immature and negligent. Was she becoming one of those people who allowed sex to control every aspect of their lives?

Kicking the sheets aside in agitation, she climbed from bed. Her body was stiff and sore from hours of Logan's intense loving. After months of abstinence, his passionate, unselfish attentions had left her exhausted and had taken a toll.

As soon as she entered the bathroom, Dee saw her pink pajamas on top of the hamper. Logan had obviously brought them from the pool. She didn't know if he could be credited for thoughtfulness on her account or a selfish desire to keep everyone in the household from knowing how intimate their relationship was.

It didn't really matter, Dee thought as she stood under the pounding spray of the shower. What was done was done. She couldn't change it, but she could make sure it didn't happen again.

She shampooed the chlorine from her hair and scrubbed every trace of Logan's loving from her body. When she was finished, she' felt refreshed and in better control of herself. She decided to forget last night and make sure there was no repeat performance.

Since arriving at the Circle B's, she'd dressed in her Prescott uniform each day, always aware that Logan could arrive home at any moment. She was serious about proving her professionalism, but today she was too tired and irritable to consider the uniform. She'd already missed her morning lessons, so she donned a pair of tan shorts and a sleeveless blouse in a tan and green floral print.

Dee knew it would take quite a while for her hair to dry, even after a few minutes with the blow dryer. She was tempted to leave it loose, but decided to braid it. Logan hated for her to restrain it in any fashion, but she wasn't going to pander him. It was bad enough that she remembered every sweet word he'd ever whispered while stroking her hair.

When she started to make her bed, Dee noticed that it had already been straightened a little. She and Logan had completely destroyed it, so she assumed, he'd made some reparation before leaving her.

When had he gone? Had he left her as soon as she'd fallen to sleep, or had he awakened early and slipped from the room without waking her? Was he sharing the same doubts right now or was he feeling smug? Was he as drained as she was? Or was he used to long hours of strenuous sex?

Dee left her bedroom and headed for the kitchen. She sincerely hoped he didn't think her moment of weakness would set a precedent for her remaining stay in his home. She couldn't correct last night's mistake, but as she began her day, she vowed that it wouldn't happen again.

Logan's train of thought followed just the opposite pattern all morning. After having Dee in his arms for most of the night, his appetite was more than whetted. He ached. One night wasn't nearly enough. He wanted her with him all the time.

With the need came a new determination. He'd taken her by surprise last night, but she'd be quick to build up the defenses again. Despite the fact that she was a sensual, sexy lady, she was also stubborn.

He was the only man in her life. He was her first and only lover, and he intended to keep it that way. He would never forgive her for destroying their baby, but he could damned well enjoy her body.

Tension coiled low in his loins at the thought. He'd awakened with her in his arms and had wanted her again, but had forced himself to leave her bed. She was too addictive, and he didn't like the way she threatened his control.

As the morning hours passed, he couldn't help but wonder if she'd conceived another child during the night. The thought brought a thrill of satisfaction, even though he was still furious with her. Their loving had been totally unplanned. They hadn't done anything to prevent a pregnancy unless she'd gone on the pill after the first one.

So it was a possibility. Too often in the past week he'd found himself thinking of babies. He'd never been one to fantasize, but he wanted a family, and lately he'd been visualizing a son who shared his and Dee's characteristics. Sometimes his mind would conjure images of baby girls, three of them with heads full of blond curls.

"Hey, boss!" Jake's shout drew him out of his introspection. Even though they were working together, they had to yell over the sound of machinery. They'd been baling and loading hay most of the morning, but they were finishing their last load

"Yeah?"

"You want me to take this one in?"

Butch was driving the tractor pulling the baler while Jake and Logan stacked the hay on the wagon. The two older men had been taking turns pulling wagons back to the barn, where more hired hands were doing the unloading.

"I'll drive," Logan replied, jumping from the wagon to change the hitch from the baler to the second tractor. Jake would ride the wagon, and Butch would follow with the rest of the equipment.

They were all hot, tired, and dirty. Their shirts had been stripped off hours ago. Dust and hay clung to their bared torsos, and as soon as the last load was stored in one of the smaller barns, Logan sent the men on lunch break while he headed for the washroom in the big barn.

He paused just inside the door to let his eyes adjust to the dim lighting, but when he started to turn toward the water pump, he halted in his tracks at the sound of light, feminine laughter. It wasn't just any feminine laughter; it was Dee's, and the sound slammed into him like a fist.

Her laughter was so soft and sexy, it mesmerized him. He'd heard it often when they'd been lovers, and the sound was burned into his memory. His body reacted immediately to the reminder.

He strained to pinpoint her exact location, and the next sound he heard was a husky chuckle of sensual delight. His muscles clenched.

A small noise above him had Logan lifting his gaze to the hayloft. It sounded as though Dee was squirming in the hay, giggling as someone teased or tickled her. The idea brought a swift surge of black, raging jealousy.

Who the hell was she playing with in the hayloft? Every man on the farm had been helping him work the hay. None of the men could have gotten to the barn before he did, so who was with Dee? Had she met someone at his barbecue? Someone who could have enticed her to come back?

He'd kill him, whoever he was. He'd use his bare hands to strangle the life out of any man who touched her. With that thought, Logan took the few steps up the wooden ladder to the loft. His eyes were as hot as molten steel as his head topped the last rung, and he saw Dee.

She was sprawled in loose hay with her legs spread in front of her and her back propped against more bales of hay. Her eyes were shining with delight, and she continued to giggle while halfheartedly fighting-off an attack by six frisky kittens.

Logan's fury was swiftly replaced by a rush of hot desire. Her husky laughter did strange things to his insides. She looked sexily disheveled and so completely irresistible that he envied the kittens crawling all over her.

Long tendrils of hair had escaped her braid to curl around her flushed face. The top few buttons of her blouse were undone, exposing creamy skin and the curve of her breasts. Her eyes sparkled with unadulterated delight as the kittens vied for her attention.

"Easy there, you little monster," she gently scolded one who was using her breast as a stepping stone. "Sheathe your claws."

She grabbed the offending kitten and gently pried his claws from the fabric of her blouse. Then she held him close to her face and cooed to him as she rubbed her cheek against the softness of his fluffy coat.

Logan felt like someone had kicked him in the gut. Every muscle in his body knotted as he watched her cuddle each of the kittens. Dee's inherent sensuality had always excited him more than other women's blatant sexuality.

"I wonder if anyone would mind if I named you Trouble," she murmured to the squirming calico who'd become her favorite of the litter. He had a penchant for mischief. He was the runt, but made up for size with spirit, energy, and unending curiosity. As soon as she let go of him, he tried to dive inside the collar of her blouse to explore.

"Little heathen!" she chided, grabbing him before he could sink his claws into her flesh. At the same time, she sensed Logan's presence, and her gaze flew to his. There was no mistaking the dark glitter of desire she saw there.

Her body's response to him was instant and intense. The light was dim in the loft, and all she could see of him was his head and shoulders, but that was enough to set her pulse racing. She fought to conceal the fierce excitement he generated.

Logan watched the sparkle in her eyes die, and something inside of him died a little with it. She couldn't have made her opinion of him any more clear. All the joy and innocence left her expression to be replaced by wariness.

Her reaction and his response to it dampened his desire and renewed his anger. The woman was a menace to his peace of mind, but he wasn't going to let her play havoc on his emotions. What he wanted from Dee was strictly physical.

"If I'd known you wanted to romp in the hay, I'd have been happy to oblige you," he taunted in a deliberate attempt to annoy her.

He succeeded. Dee clenched her teeth in annoyance and quickly straightened her blouse. Was this the type of treatment she could expect for the next few weeks? Was Logan hoping to enjoy her body whenever he wanted, then use demeaning sexual innuendo to get even with her for all the wrong he thought she'd done him?

She decided to ignore his statement and returned her attention to the kittens. Five of them were settling down for a nap. She laid the runt down beside them, and stroked his back while he settled down, too.

Her deliberate snub inflamed Logan. He wanted to climb into the loft and demand her full attention, but he didn't dare. If he touched her now, he wouldn't be content with anything less than hard, pounding sex. The memories of last night were still too potent, and he'd been in a state of semi-arousal all morning.

"Are you going to stay up here all day?" he asked in a less offensive tone.

Dee shot a wary glance at him. "Just 'til they're settled. They're still babies, and they need their sleep."

The mention of babies was a mistake. Dee realized it as soon as she saw Logan's features harden. She felt a pang for having reminded them both of the child they'd lost.

"Too bad you didn't feel so protective of ours," he ground out roughly.

Dee lowered her lashes to hide the pain his words inflicted. She could correct his impression that she'd aborted their baby, but she didn't have the heart to try. She selfishly wanted him to realize that she wasn't capable of doing such a thing. All the explanations in the world were useless unless he could give her the faith and respect that came with true love.

Whatever she felt about his harsh comment would remain a mystery to Logan because Dee was effectively shutting him out again. Her defensive barriers were firmly in place, but he could only blame himself. He'd never known how to handle her or her incredible sensitivity.

Sometimes she was fierce, and he could deal with that aspect of her character. But when she withdrew inside herself, he didn't know how to reach her. He ended up making them both furious.

"It's lunch time," he finally declared in a neutral tone.

"I just ate," she said, rising to her knees and brushing the hay off her clothing. She was ready to leave, but didn't want to move toward the ladder while he was still on it.

After another minute of watching her tidy her clothes, Logan realized that she was stalling. He wanted to make sure she got down the ladder, and she wanted him out of her way.

"Come on," he said. "You might have eaten, but I'm starved, and I have hay all over me. I'll help you down and then I can wash off."

She could see bits and pieces of hay clinging to the sweat-dampened expanse of his shoulders and chest. Hours of work in the hot sun had turned his flesh to bronze, and his arm muscles rippled when he gripped the top of the ladder.

She didn't want his help. She didn't want him touching her, even impersonally. He was too much of a temptation, and her body was highly attuned to his presence. Still, she knew they could spend the rest of the day in a stubborn standoff if she refused.

"I'm coming if you'll get out of my way," she finally said, moving closer.

Logan gave her a mocking glance and started down the ladder. His gaze never left her as she turned her backside to him to follow. His body tightened at the sight of her long, bare legs and supple thighs exposed by the cut of her shorts.

Once his feet touched the floor, he stepped away from the ladder, but moved forward again as soon as Dee's feet touched the last rung. Even as he cursed himself for stupidity, his arms went around her, trapping her in their circle as he grasped hold of either side of the ladder. He was too dirty and sweaty to press himself against her, but he held her captive in his arms.

Her breath caught as she felt the heat of him against her back. "Logan," she warned.

"I know," he whispered as he buried his face in the curve of her shoulder. "I know I shouldn't touch you," he growled near her ear. His lips sought the pulse at the back of her neck and he sucked her tender flesh. "I know we drive each other crazy," he added, feeling her shudder.

"You're poison," he accused roughly, "but you're in my blood, and I can't get enough of you. You might as well stop fighting it."

"No!" she managed in a gruff whisper as goose bumps shivered over her body. "Last night was a mistake — a stupid, irresponsible mistake."

Her words sent a little thrill over Logan. He was willing to bet she wasn't on the pill, and that meant she could already have conceived. "Because we needed each other so much, or because we didn't use any protection?"

"Both!" Dee declared huskily. "It's insane to want each other when we don't even like each other. And it's even more insane to take that kind of risk."

Logan wasn't taking any risks. He knew exactly what he wanted; her pregnant with his child. "What's insane is trying to ignore something that's stronger than both of us."

His decisive tone sent a wave of desperation over Dee. If he wasn't interested in keeping some distance between them, that meant she was on her own. He wouldn't help her fight the attraction, and she wasn't sure she could fight it by herself.

"Turn around and kiss me," Logan commanded, his voice low and thick with arousal. Just being close to Dee and smelling her sweetness was more enticement than he could ignore.

"No!" she argued, holding herself rigid within the circle of his arms.

"I'm filthy," he countered while gently thrusting his hips against her buttocks, "but if you don't make the first move, I'm going to turn you around and drag you as close to me as possible."

Dee felt his hardness and her knees grew weak. She was holding herself as rigid as possible, but she started to tremble when he issued his gruff threat. It was too easy to imagine herself crushed against his naked, sun-baked chest. Her breasts swelled at the thought, but she forced herself to breathe deeply and control her wanton desires.

"Dee," he challenged with increased warning. "I want your mouth. Either give it to me, or I'll take it."

Frustration had her turning in his arms, but she planted her hands on his chest and kept a careful distance between their bodies. Her eyes flared with irritation as they locked with his, but the open hunger she found caught at her breath.

"You're a fool for wanting to further this relationship," she charged.

He ignored the warning. "Kiss me."

Didn't the man ever hear anything he didn't want to hear? "Logan! No!"

"I want your mouth," he insisted. "I want a whole helluva lot more, but I want your mouth first."

Didn't he know the meaning of the word no? "It's not that easy," she argued, trying to make him see sense.

"If it's too hard for you to handle," he growled, "then I'll take care of it."

His mouth swooped down on hers. His lips were hot and his tongue swiftly probed her lips for access to deeper targets. Dee decided to let him have his kiss, but to remain completely detached. Maybe then he'd learn that she wasn't interested in playing games with him.

Logan got wise to her quickly. "If you don't kiss me back," he warned while he nipped her lips. "Then I'm going to have to get really serious and use more than my mouth to convince you."

"You're dirty and you smell bad."

He chuckled at her attempt to discourage him. "I know, and you're going to be just as bad if you don't cooperate."

Finally, in aggravation, Dee grasped his hard head between her hands and slammed her mouth against his. For an instant they warred, tight lips against tighter lips. But she couldn't fight him for very long. His tongue plunged through her teeth to caress her tongue. His kisses were deep, delving, and addicting. She always forgot all her complaints when he kissed her.

As the kiss lengthened, she slowly relaxed, and her body gravitated closer to his. He shifted his hands from the rungs of the ladder and grasped her forearms, not wanting her any closer while his control was so fragile or he'd want to completely lose himself in her softness.

They kissed long and deep until they heard someone shouting for Logan. It was lunchtime, and he dimly realized Jake was calling him to eat.

They broke off their kiss and each took a step backward, breathing roughly. Neither could believe how quickly the other made them lose control or how hard it was to resist each other.

Logan wanted Dee all to himself for about a month. A night or two, a week or two, wouldn't be nearly enough. He wanted unlimited time to sate himself with her.

Dee wanted distance between them. She didn't like being reminded of how little control she had where he was concerned. She didn't like being reminded of her weakness for his loving, and she wasn't a risk-taker.

"This has to stop," she insisted huskily.

"Why?" he challenged.

"Why?" she repeated in amazement. "You know all the reasons why!"

Logan turned toward the pump and washbasin. "We're both consenting adults," he reminded.

Dee clenched her teeth and locked her hands into fists. She watched him sluice water over his face, chest, and arms, then roughly rub himself dry. She struggled for a reasonable response to his offhand declaration.

"Whatever hopes we had for a future were destroyed," she finally managed. "I don't want a casual affair, and I don't want to risk another pregnancy."

"I wouldn't call what we have casual," he replied in a low drawl. He turned back to Dee and pinned her with his gaze. "And it's a little late to worry about conception. You could already be pregnant."

Dee went pale at the thought. She searched his face, but couldn't decide how he felt about the possibility. He didn't seem overly concerned.

"Doesn't that worry you?" she asked in a suspicious tone.

Logan didn't hesitate. "I don't care if you get pregnant. I want a child."

She sucked in a harsh breath. "You can't mean that."

"I mean it."

"And you think I'm willing to have a baby just because you'd like one?" Her tone and expression were shocked, her eyes wide with disbelief.

His features hardened. "I'm damned sure you wouldn't abort another baby of mine."

Dee couldn't believe what she was hearing. He didn't pretend to love her, want to marry her, or have a family. He wasn't implying that their relationship had any future. He just wanted her to give him a child.

Had he deliberately seduced her with the hope that she'd get pregnant? "What makes you think I'm not on birth control pills?" she snapped.

"You aren't, are you?"

She refused to verify his arrogant assumption. Neither would she lie.

Logan smiled at her stubborn refusal to respond. Her silence was all the answer he needed. They both knew that she could already be pregnant.

"I don't guess there's anything more to say on the subject," he declared, heading for the door.

Dee followed and grabbed his arm to stop him. "Logan!" she snapped. She blinked as they stepped into the sunlight and quickly pulled her hand from his arm.

"Dee?" he queried maddeningly.

"Don't you walk away from me," she snapped. "I'm not about to accept this attitude of yours."

One of his brows rose in arrogant response. "What do you plan to do about it?" he taunted.

Her eyes narrowed and her temper flared. "If I were a man, I might consider beating the hell out of you!"

Logan roared with laughter. He had to give her credit for spunk. He was glad that all her fiery passion wasn't limited to sex. It increased the chances that their child would be strong-spirited.

His laughter didn't do anything to lessen her outrage. "You're pretty damned sure of yourself, aren't you?" she challenged. But her temper was rapidly dissolving into pain. "Well I've got news for you, I intend to fulfill my contract and then I'm leaving, whether or not I'm pregnant. And there's absolutely nothing you can do to stop me."

The threat had Logan's eyes narrowing again. "You'll never keep me from claiming another child," he warned. "If you try, I'll have you in court so fast it'll make your head spin."

Dee didn't attempt a response. The two of them just glared at each other for long, tension-filled minutes. Each was convinced they'd been wronged by the other, and neither was prepared to compromise.

Then Jake was calling for Logan again. Mattie had fixed lunch for all the hands, and they were waiting for him. He turned abruptly and left her standing alone in the barnyard.

She watched him stride toward the house, her emotions in total chaos.

Nine

*D*ays passed with Logan and Dee carefully avoiding each other. They shared meals, but made a point not to be alone at any time. They maintained an attitude of polite indifference when in the company of other members of the household, or when they accidentally ran into each other on the farm property.

Logan didn't stop wanting Dee, but he needed to prove to himself that he could master the desire. He didn't like the power she had over him, nor his own lack of control when he was with her.

Thoughts of her accompanied him everywhere, day and night. He couldn't stop thinking about the baby she'd aborted. It was like an open wound that festered, yet he couldn't reconcile his image of Dee with the cold-hearted woman he'd labeled her.

He watched as she gradually charmed every man, woman, and animal on his property. He saw the genuine pleasure in her eyes when she cuddled a kitten, stroked a horse's neck, or fussed over his aging dog. If she was faking her caring attitude, it was the best performance he'd ever seen. She really seemed to thrive in his world.

And he was making some progress in her world, but slowly and painfully. He couldn't sleep, so he forced himself to spend more time at the hangar and review all her training information. He still broke out in a cold sweat when he took the controls of the simulator in his hands, but the sick fear wasn't as bad as it once had been. It would still be a long time before he was comfortable with piloting again.

Dee was relieved that he didn't challenge her decision to keep a safe distance between them. She found it difficult enough being exposed to him on a daily basis. Instead of learning things about him that she didn't like, she found too many things she liked too much.

He was courteous, thoughtful, and hard working. He wasn't a particularly demonstrative man, but his love for his sister was obvious, as was his respect and affection for Mattie. He was an opinionated boss, but he listened to complaints and suggestions from his employees.

He was gentle with and knowledgeable about his livestock. Whenever Dee saw him working with the horses, she was amazed by his endless patience. The more she saw of him, the more confused she became. He wasn't living up to her opinion that he was a callous jerk.

They never discussed her work. Jake and Butch ate a lot of meals with the family, and they often enthused about their training, sharing their progress. Logan listened, but made no comments.

Discussions of the flight training seemed to make Patti and Mattie uncomfortable. Dee could sense their unease whenever the subject arose, but she couldn't understand what prompted their tension.

She couldn't gauge Logan's reactions at all. He seemed to block out all emotion when everyone else talked about flying. She couldn't help but wonder if his attitude had anything to do with his original demand that she give up her career.

If he hated the idea of piloting, then why had he decided to buy a plane and pay to have his men trained to fly it? She wondered if he had decided against learning himself, or if he intended to take instruction elsewhere.

Logan never came to the hangar when she was working with Butch and Jake, yet she sensed that he spent time in her makeshift classroom when she wasn't there. She even suspected that he used the flight simulator, but she didn't have any evidence.

For all she knew, Butch or Jake could be acting as a go-between and repeating her instructions to Logan. It wouldn't do him much good in accumulating ground or flight hours, but he could still learn that way.

Since he'd come home from his buying trip, Dee had become more reserved. She wasn't quite as comfortable with Mattie, Butch, or Jake. They seemed to accept the fact without being offended. She still tried to be as helpful as possible, yet she couldn't totally relax with so much tension between herself and Logan.

One thing that didn't change was her affinity with the various farm animals. She was rarely outdoors without a parade of cats and kittens following in her footsteps. The horses weren't any less devoted, just restricted by gates and fences. When she was near, they gave her their undivided attention. Old Ace even made an effort to spend time with her when he wasn't tagging after Logan or sleeping under his favorite tree.

Dee always managed to give Ace special attention. She liked the old dog and had learned how much he meant to Logan. She tried to convince herself that Logan's affection for the pet had nothing to do with her concern for the aging dog, but she couldn't be sure.

Whenever she was near the Lab, she sensed that he didn't have much time left, and her heart went out to him. His life had been full, but it was waning. She feared the end was near, yet she didn't sense that he was sick or suffering in any way.

On the second Friday of her stay in Kentucky, shortly after her morning training session, Dee found Ace lying on the sidewalk near the kitchen door. Since he preferred the comfort of the shade during the daytime, she was surprised to see him lying in the fall sun.

"What are you doing here?" she asked as she knelt down to pet him. As soon as she touched his head, she knew what was wrong. He barely found the strength to open his big brown eyes, and she realized he was dying.

"Mattie!" Dee couldn't quite contain the note of panic in her voice. "Mattie!"

Patti came to the back door in response to Dee's call. "She's upstairs. What's wrong?"

"It's Ace," Dee said, glancing at the other woman with pained eyes, then returning her attention to the dog.

Patti didn't hesitate. "I'll call the vet."

"No!" Dee's tone was unusually insistent. All she wanted was to move Ace out of the sun, and he was too heavy for her to lift. "Just get Logan."

"But —"

"Please!"

Patti conceded. "He's on the phone. I'll get him."

Dee continued to stroke the dog's head while crooning to him in a soothing tone. He heaved a sigh and closed his eyes, but perked up a little at the sound of Logan's voice.

He and Patti came outside. "What's wrong?"

Dee lifted her gaze and there was a wealth of sympathy in their turquoise depths as they locked with his. "He's dying." She responded as gently as possible.

Logan studied the concern etched on her features. He crouched down beside her and placed a hand on the Lab's head.

"What's wrong, old buddy?"

Ace managed to thump his tail for his master, but he didn't open his eyes.

"Why didn't you want Patti to call the vet?"

"He doesn't have that much time." She wasn't sure how she knew that, but she was sure.

"I don't want him to suffer," Logan's voice was a little hoarse.

"He's not suffering, I promise," Dee insisted.

Logan looked her directly in the eyes. They were closer than they'd been for days, and his gaze was probing. "How do you know?" he demanded.

How could she help him understand? This was beyond her experience, so how could she console Logan? "I can't explain it, but I know he's not in any pain. He's just very weak and tired. He needs you and his favorite spot under the oak tree."

Her voice quavered a little and tears welled in her eyes. Logan wasn't sure why he trusted her, but he didn't argue or question her instinctive knowledge.

"Thanks," he said softly. "I'll take care of him." He carefully scooped the big dog into his arms, speaking quietly to his old friend.

Patti and Dee patted Ace's head and said their good-byes, then watched as Logan carried him to the backyard. Dee's heart was in her eyes, but she didn't follow. When Logan disappeared from sight, she glanced at Patti.

Both of them had to look through a veil of tears. The obvious tension between Dee and Logan had kept the two women from becoming close friends, but they'd grown fond of each other. Neither of them felt the need to apologize for the outpouring of emotion.

"How did you know?" asked Patti, sniffing.

Dee could only shrug her shoulders and swipe at the tears that streamed down her cheeks. "Just intuition, I guess. It's not something I can explain."

"I've watched you with the other animals. I've never seen anything quite like it," said Patti as she scrutinized Dee. "Logan is the best handler I've ever watched and the animals respect him, but it's different with you. You have a special gift, don't you?"

Dee's eyes widened in alarm. She was never really comfortable discussing her ESP, and she'd never mentioned it to Logan. She didn't want anyone to start asking questions.

When she failed to respond, Patti apologized. "I'm sorry. I have no right to pry into your personal affairs. I'm just one of those nosy psychology majors who likes prying into peoples' psyches. Logan tells me to leave his psyche alone, so you're welcome to tell do the same."

Dee actually flinched at learning that Patti was a student of psychology. Belle had expended a great deal of effort over the years to keep her away from people who wanted to delve deeper into her psychological makeup.

She didn't want to alienate Patti, but she didn't know how to answer her question. "Maybe it would help if you'd define gift," she said.

"I was curious to know if your sensitivity applies to humans as well as animals."

That's what Dee had dreaded most. "I'm sometimes very sensitive to what my sisters are feeling," she admitted.

"I guess that's not too surprising, considering you're triplets."

"I think it's fairly common," she said. "My sisters and I have varying degrees of sensitivity to varying degrees of emotion. I know that's hard to categorize," she added with a smile, "but it's something we've accepted as normal for most our lives."

"Could I ask one more little question?" Patti teased, aware of Dee's disinclination to discuss her sensory perception.

Dee managed to return her smile. "It depends on the question."

Patti pulled her bottom lip between her teeth, then said, "It's about you and Logan."

Dee was shaking her head before the question was verbalized.

"Okay, I'll mind my own business. I hate to do it, but I guess I'll manage," Patti said on a sigh, then contradicted herself. "I just wondered if you can read his emotions, too."

Dee kept shaking her head. "I don't mind answering that one. The answer's no. Something about his chemistry reacts negatively with mine. I've decided we're totally incompatible."

That made Patti chuckle and shake her head. "You and Logan might have some major problems, but I'd bet my last dollar that chemistry isn't involved. I've never seen two people with such strong vibrations bouncing between them."

Dee frowned and let the subject drop. It was apparent that she didn't want to discuss the topic. By mutual agreement the two women headed into the house. They found Mattie in the kitchen, explained what was happening with Ace, and men helped prepare lunch.

Dee couldn't get Patti's statement out of her mind. She wondered if everyone on the Circle B's was speculating about her and Logan. If so, were they wondering what was the matter with her? They all seemed to think Logan was a saint, so what did that make her? A sinner? A woman scorned?

What would they think if they knew the whole truth? What if they were to learn Logan's version of the truth? Would they all hate her and label her a monster if they believed she'd aborted his child?

Dee was surprised at how much she cared what the others thought.

She was learning to care for them all, and she'd didn't want them to think as badly of her as Logan did.

She found herself speculating on how the Circle B's family would perceive her if they learned about her ESP. Would they think her a freak? A weirdo? Would they shy away from her, or would they be able to understand? Would Logan hate her even more for not telling him in the very beginning?

Until now, she'd been getting mixed, but favorable reactions from his family and staff. She knew Butch had a crush on her, so she was careful not to encourage him on a personal level. Jake found her attractive, but wasn't interested in pursuing the attraction.

Patti liked her, when she wasn't feeling possessive or protective about her brother. The younger woman was very much in love with Jake and a little jealous of the time he spent with Dee.

Those were all normal reactions, and didn't alarm Dee. Mattie and the rest of the employees had accepted her without qualms, which pleased her enormously. She just didn't want to risk that acceptance.

Her main concern was to keep the truth from Logan. Dee was relieved that he didn't question her about her sensitivity to Ace's situation, especially since the old dog died within a few minutes of Logan placing him under his favorite shade tree. She thought Logan might be too upset to broach the subject, and she didn't offer any explanations.

The next day was Saturday, but Dee continued her classes through the weekend and there was nothing special to mark the end of the workweek. She preferred it that way because she was happier when she was busy.

Patti coaxed Jake into taking her to see a movie Saturday evening and Mattie retired to her apartment early. So Dee did the same. She wasn't really sleepy, but she went to bed early so that she wouldn't risk an accidental meeting with Logan.

She didn't know how long she'd been sleeping when she awakened in alarm. At first, she couldn't pinpoint a problem, but she forced herself to relax and concentrate. After a few minutes, she realized that her acute feelings of anxiety were stemming from one of her sisters.

Sharla came to mind first, because she'd been in grave danger once when she'd piloted for Reed. But this was different. Dee dragged her hands through her hair and jumped out of bed in agitation. She paced the room until the full extent of the sensations had time to register.

Then she knew it was Carlie.

Carlie was in trouble, trapped and frightened. Dee didn't like the waves of negative emotion pouring over her. She hoped it was just a bad dream, but she knew she had to reach her sister or she'd never be able to calm her own rioting nerves. Grabbing a short, satin robe, she wrapped it around herself and left the bedroom in search of a phone.

She was a few feet from the kitchen door when she heard someone in the kitchen. She didn't want to explain herself, so she quickly turned and headed for Logan's office. It was late, and no one was likely to bother her there.

The front of the house was dark except for the light shining from the porch, but Dee made her way without switching on any other source of light. The office was in darkness, but she could see well enough as she headed straight for the phone on his desk.

She called Carlie's number first, but wasn't really surprised when she didn't get an answer. She didn't want to alarm her parents if it wasn't necessary, so she dialed Sharla's number next.

"Come on, Sharla, please be home," she whispered as the third and then fourth ring sounded in her ear.

"Hello," Sharla's drowsy voice came over the line.

Sharla was never too alert when she woke from a deep sleep, but Dee hoped she would wake up fast. "Sharla, it's Dee. Wake up and pay attention."

"You're in Kentucky," her sister informed her.

Dee moaned. "Sharla, are you alone?"

"Huh uh."

"Is Reed there?"

"Uh huh."

"Give him the phone."

Dee heard mumbling. The next voice she heard was that of her future brother-in-law. Reed's tone wasn't the least bit drowsy. "What's up?"

"It's Carlie," Dee said in a rush of relief. "I was hoping she was home, but I couldn't reach her by phone."

"She went out earlier and probably hasn't gotten back."

"Damn," Dee whispered. "I was afraid of that."

Reed's tone grew deeper. "What's wrong?"

"I'm not sure, but I think she's in trouble — serious trouble." Dee's tone grew more urgent as increasing waves of emotion washed over her. "I think she's somewhere she doesn't want to be and that somebody's trying to hurt her."

Reed swore and Sharla wrenched the phone from him. She'd heard Dee and was wide-awake now and demanding details. "Can you tell us where she is?"

"I was hoping you could tell me."

"She had a call earlier, then said she was going to meet a friend downtown. She's been gone a few hours."

"You don't know who the friend was?"

"No."

"Or where she was going?"

"No," Sharla repeated again. "What are you feeling?"

Dee closed her eyes and concentrated harder. After a short time, she responded. "It feels like she's surrounded by people, but nobody can hear her. She's getting really scared!" The last words grew more anxious. "You've got to find her!"

"Help us!" Sharla insisted in increasing alarm. She had more faith in Dee's perception than even Dee herself. "Tell me where to look."

"I can't see anything!" Dee argued. "I can only feel. She's closed in a small part of a bigger building. Someone's with her, but the people all around her aren't aware that she's in trouble."

"Maybe she's at a party at someone's house," Sharla suggested.

"It's bigger than that."

"How about a hotel?" Reed suggested. Both he and Sharla were listening to her every word.

"Yes!" Dee agreed with enthusiasm. "That must be it. It feels right. But it must be a really big one."

"There's a few dozen of them in D.C.," Sharla reminded, her tone rough with worry. "How are we going to find the right one?"

"Could you check Carlie's room? Maybe she wrote down the name of the hotel or the person she got the call from."

Dee heard noises and the sound of a door closing.

"Reed went to check," Sharla told her. "Try to concentrate. Maybe you can get more details."

Dee clutched the telephone receiver in one hand and dragged her other hand through her hair in agitation. "I don't want to concentrate," she grumbled. "Every time I concentrate, I feel Carlie growing more agitated." Tears filled her eyes and the quaver in her voice expressed how badly she was reacting to her sister's distress.

"Please, Dee," Sharla continued in an effort to calm her. "I know it must be hard on you, but the more we know, the faster we can get help to Carlie. Do you think her life is in danger? Has she been mugged or kidnapped?"

Dee slowly allowed herself to slip to the floor. She leaned her back against Logan's desk and rested her head on her knees while shifting her total concentration to Carlie. She felt anger, humiliation and increasing fear. There were waves of desperation, and a feeling of being trapped. Then there was pain. Familiar pain.

Dee flinched. "Familiar pain," she mumbled into the receiver.

"Familiar?" Sharla gasped. "You mean something that's happened to her before?"

"Familiar," was all Dee could manage.

"Bill!" Sharla yelled into the phone. "Bill's the only one who ever deliberately hurt Carlie. He's never accepted the fact that she left him, and we know he's capable of hurting her."

The instant Dee heard her ex-brother-in-law's name, all her impressions of an attacker solidified, and she was certain. "Yes. She's with Bill, and he's scaring her."

There, were more muffled sounds from Sharla's end, then she came back on the line. "Reed found me word Hilton written on a notepad by Carlie's phone," she said, "but no name or address."

"How many Hiltons in D.C.?" Dee fretted.

"Too many if Carlie's in trouble."

Reed's voice came back over the line. "We're going to hang up now and call Bill's airline. Maybe somebody there will know where he's staying while he's in town."

"Okay, but you'll call me right back?" Dee insisted. Then she realized that the ringing of the phone might disturb everyone in the Bradford household. "No, wait, I'd better call you." She was too upset to make explanations.

In the next instant, Logan's hand reached to take the receiver from Dee. She was so startled that she didn't even struggle.

"This is Bradford. Call as soon as you know anything or if we can help."

"We will," Sharla promised. "Take care of Dee."

The connection was broken and Logan replaced the receiver. He reached down and pulled Dee to her feet. She was trembling, so he lifted her in his arms and moved to the chair behind his desk. He sat down and propped his bare feet on the desk, cradling her in his lap.

She wrapped her arms around his torso and clung to him with all her strength. He was big and warm and solid. She couldn't stop the tremors that shook her body, and she was too upset to reject the comfort he offered.

She'd been sick with worry last month when Sharla's life was in danger, but she'd known Reed was with her and would protect her with his life. This was much worse. The sensual alarm was more intense. She knew Carlie was alone and growing more frightened every minute.

Logan tightened his grip on Dee every time he felt another tremor pass over her. She seemed so fragile and helpless. Her distress roused all his protective instincts. He didn't want to care so much, but there wasn't really any choice. She badly needed support.

A half an hour passed without a word between them. Dee pressed her face against his chest and continued to shudder at intervals. Her breathing grew rough and an occasional sob rose from her chest. Logan could feel her anguish, but didn't know what else to do.

He held her close and stroked her hair while trying to reassure her. The words he whispered to her were more like the soft, crooning words of a lover, but he didn't know what else to say.

He wanted to understand what was happening. He'd been sitting in his office dreading another sleepless night, when she'd appeared and made her frantic call home. Despite hearing every word of her conversation, he still couldn't comprehend it all.

He'd heard of twins and triplets who instinctively knew when a sibling was in trouble, but he'd never met anyone with that kind of sensitivity. Dee wasn't just aware of Carlie's distress, she was experiencing it.

He thought about the way she'd handled the situation with Ace. He'd thought of little else since he'd buried his old pet. Dee had understood. She'd felt his grief and shared it. She'd known what was best.

Was she even more sensitive about people? Or was it just with her sisters? Did they share a sort of mental telepathy? Was Dee psychic? Did she have visions? Could she predict the future? Did she read minds? The thought boggled his mind. He had no experience with the phenomenon of extrasensory perception.

Another half hour passed, and Dee's breathing began to quiet. She gradually relaxed. Her grip on him eased, and Logan felt the tension draining from her body.

Ten

"Is it over?" Logan asked softly.

Dee took a deep breath. She felt drained, but relieved. "She's safe now."

It was a good while later before the phone rang. He stretched to pick up the receiver and then placed it where they could both hear. "Bradford."

"This is Sharla. Can I please talk to Dee?"

"She can hear you. Are you with Carlie?"

"I'm calling from the hospital emergency room. Carlie's okay. She didn't think it was necessary to come here, but Reed insisted."

"You're sure she's all right?" Dee asked gruffly.

"She's going to have some bruises and a swollen mouth, but thanks to you, we got to her before he could break any bones or do any serious damage."

Logan felt Dee cringe, and changed the subject. "How'd you find her?"

"We called Bill's airline. They told us where several of their pilots and hostesses were staying. Reed got hold of some friends in law enforcement and they found them. Bill's been arrested and taken to jail. He probably won't stay there long, but at least he knows he's not going to get away with this again. Carlie's going to file formal charges as soon as we leave here."

"Does he have a history of violence?" Logan asked.

Sharla hesitated, not knowing how much personal information she should impart. She didn't know how Dee felt about involving Bradford in family matters.

Dee chose to explain, although her voice still wasn't too steady. "That's why they divorced in the first place. Bill's a bully and a manipulator. I can't believe Carlie went to meet him alone."

"She didn't know the message was from Bill," explained Sharla. "He tricked her into thinking she was going to meet Michael."

That was easier to understand. Their whole family adored Michael. "Michael is Bill's brother," Dee injected for Logan's sake. "He's a real sweetheart, but Bill's a first-class bastard."

"If Carlie wants to get away for a while, tell her she's welcome to come here," he said into the phone.

Dee stirred in his arms. The offer was very thoughtful, and she knew he was sincere, but she wasn't sure she wanted him embroiled in her family's problems. She definitely didn't want any in-depth discussions about her powers of perception. This incident was beyond anything she'd ever experienced, and she wasn't comfortable with it herself.

Logan sensed her objection, and took it as a personal rejection. "You don't want her here?"

"Don't worry about it," Sharla declared before the matter could be resolved. "I thought Carlie might want to keep this a secret from Mother and Daddy, but she doesn't. She's bruised, but she's not going to run and hide."

Dee sighed. "She's right. She doesn't have anything to feel guilty about. She's the victim. I just hope this doesn't force her into another post-divorce depression."

"Her attitude is more furious than wounded," Sharla said. "It's not like the last time. I really think she's going to be all right."

"I hope so," Dee said.

"I've got to go now," added Sharla. "I'll have Carlie call you the first thing tomorrow."

They said a collective good night after she promised to call if there were any new developments. Logan replaced the receiver, then leaned back in the chair and put both arms around Dee.

For a short time, he was content to hold her in his arms. She was so soft and smelled so sweet. She'd always felt right in his arms. Now that the crisis was over, his desire for her wasn't so easily ignored. He knew he couldn't hold her much longer without her feeling the evidence of that desire. She wasn't in any shape to make love.

"Ready for bed?" he asked quietly.

Now that she'd begun to relax, Dee was rapidly succumbing to the exhaustion that came in the wake of such a traumatic experience. She didn't speak, but nodded her head in affirmation.

He rose and carried her down the hall to her bedroom. Once there, he leaned over to lay her on the bed, but she didn't loosen her hold on him.

She'd never had a sensory experience as violent as the one tonight, and she was badly shaken. When Carlie had been married to Bill, she'd often felt uneasy, but the emotions had never been so powerful. It was more than a little frightening, and she needed the reassurance of human contact. She also needed to know that Logan didn't think her some kind of freak.

"Stay, please, for a little while," she coaxed.

Her plea slammed into him with brutal force. He didn't know if he could hold her and control his desire. She'd suffered a bad scare, and he knew she was exhausted, but that didn't stop him from wanting her.

Nevertheless, Logan found himself climbing into bed and stretching out beside Dee. Holding her was slow, sweet torture at most times, and tonight was no different. He doubted he could sleep, but he found enormous pleasure in being close to her. After what he'd witnessed tonight, he needed a little comfort, too.

She relaxed as soon as she was tucked close to his side. He stroked her hair and studied her lovely features in the dim light of the room. Her face looked pale, her lashes dark against the creamy smoothness of her skin. Her lips were full, sensuously curved, and kissably soft. She was a beautiful woman.

A myriad of images ran through his mind as he reached out a hand to gently caress her cheek. He saw Dee running on the beach, laughing, and her eyes shining with love. He saw her expression of disbelief when he'd given her that stupid ultimatum, and remembered every harsh word they'd exchanged. He saw her playing with kittens and comforting a dying pet.

His thoughts were troubled as he listened to the soft sound of her breathing. It gradually slowed as she drifted to sleep, and he continued to stroke her hair, enjoying the simple pleasure of touching her.

He'd thought he knew her so well, but he was realizing how wrong he'd been. When they'd been together last winter, they'd spent hours discussing everything from sports to politics, yet neither of them had shared information about their families or private lives. He wondered if the dodge of personal questions had been a subconscious defense mechanism on her part.

For him, it had been an effort to block out the world and keep her all to himself. It had been a selfish mistake. After she'd given him the well-deserved brush-off, he'd figured that she'd kept her secrets because she hadn't loved him as much as he'd loved her. Now he knew that she had to be careful about letting anyone close to her.

Dee wasn't shallow and self-centered, as he'd tried to convince himself. She was just the opposite, with an emotional depth that was exceptional. She was devoted to her family, and totally loyal to those she loved. Besides that, her incredible sensitivity made her the most vulnerable person he'd ever met. And he'd preyed on that vulnerability.

Enveloping her with both arms, Logan drew her close to his chest so that he could feel her heart beating against his own. Then he buried his face in her hair and inhaled deeply. God! How he loved this woman.

He'd been fighting the truth because the intensity of his feelings was beyond his control. What could he do about it?

Had he destroyed any love she'd felt for him? Was desire all she felt now, or had that been extinguished, too? There were too many questions that had been left unanswered for too long. He didn't have the answers, but vowed to do something about it.

Dee's softness and warmth blanketed him and brought a contentment that he hadn't felt in months. Having her close had a healing effect, satisfying a need that was soul-deep. That, combined with her gentle breathing and his exhaustion, finally lulled him to sleep.

Hours later, he woke, surprised at how soundly he'd slept. Dee was still sprawled on top of him, and the feel of her brought his body to swift, aching arousal. For a few minutes he fought the temptation to wake her with slow, leisurely loving, but he resisted.

There was too much that needed to be resolved between them before they could make love again. He ached with a need he had no intention of satisfying, so he decided he'd better get out of her bed. She mumbled sleepily as he shifted away and withdrew his arms.

After tucking a sheet around her, he brushed a light kiss across her lips and got out of bed. It was about an hour before dawn, so he went to his own room, showered, and dressed for the day's work.

Dee's alarm rang at six o'clock, and she blindly reached out a hand to shut off the buzzer. The room was dimly lit by the rising sun, and she blinked sleepily until her eyes could focus.

Much to her surprise, she found Logan sitting in a chair he'd pulled close to the bed. His hair was damp from the shower, he was fully dressed, and his eyes were troubled as they rested on her.

She felt an instant of panic as memories of the previous night washed over her. She shivered at the memory of Carlie's scare and the way she'd gone to pieces on Logan; even begging him to stay with her. Had she shocked him beyond belief? Did he think she was demented? Or worse, did he think she was a psychic freak to be avoided at all costs?

"Logan," she began, licking her lips.

"Morning," he greeted, his gaze scouring her sleepy features.

She struggled into a sitting position and realized that she was still wearing her robe. Logan had put her to bed and held her until she fell asleep. That much she knew. He'd been patient, but she didn't have any idea how he felt about what had transpired between them.

"We have to talk."

Dee tensed. She didn't like the gravity of his tone or the determination in his eyes. Was he going to demand explanations? Would he berate her for not telling him the whole truth about herself? Was he going to tell her he wanted her off his property? She wasn't sure she was ready to cope with his questions this morning.

"Can't it wait?"

"No."

"I don't think too clearly in the morning," she groused.

"I've got all day."

A heavy sigh escaped her. He wasn't going to give her any slack. She tossed her hair behind her shoulders, and rested her back against the headboard.

"Okay," she replied, mentally preparing herself. She dreaded his interrogation, but she knew she'd already tried his patience enough.

"You never had an abortion, did you?"

Dee stopped breathing, and her eyes widened in shock. Nothing could have prepared her for that particular question or brought her more abruptly awake. The only response that came to mind was the absolute truth, yet she stalled, wanting to know how much he'd guessed.

"You sound awfully certain after being just as certain that I did.

"It's not the first mistake I ever made," he commented. A brief flash of pain crossed his eyes. "It might be one of the worst, but not the first."

Dee didn't know how to respond. When she was silent, he offered an explanation for his change of mind.

"It took me a while, but I finally decided that you aren't capable of having an abortion," he declared with certainty. "You can't even bring yourself to smash a bug. You just shoo 'em away.

"Jake says you even begged him not to kill a mouse the other day. You just wanted it tossed out of your classroom. I guess you can't stand to end the life of any living thing."

Dee had dropped her gaze. She couldn't look at him. She was relieved that he'd come to know her better, but still unsure and confused about what she wanted from him. On one hand, she wanted him to have faith in her and understand her sensitivity. On the other hand, she didn't want him to be too alarmed by or wary of that sensitivity.

She didn't like reliving those bleak months after they'd gone their separate ways. When she finally found her voice, it trembled with emotion. "The pregnancy was an unwelcome shock. I was ashamed, but I never considered terminating it. I barely survived the miscarriage. I don't have the emotional stamina for an abortion."

Logan closed his eyes. A groan rumbled in his chest, but he locked his jaws to keep it from escaping. Her answer was what he'd expected, what he'd concluded himself after witnessing the pain she'd suffered through Carlie. But it still hit him hard. She'd been alone and carrying his child, while he'd been nursing his ego.

How must she have suffered? His pride had kept them apart, leaving her alone to bare the pain. He'd never forgive himself. When he opened his eyes, they were raw with agony. "Can you talk about it?"

Dee couldn't stand to see him suffering, but she didn't know how to console him. "There's not much to tell," she explained, plucking nervously at the sheet. "I was sick the whole three months, and then I miscarried. The doctors said that something was probably wrong with the fetus, and that the miscarriage was unavoidable."

"Were you in a lot of pain?" Logan forced the question past a dry throat.

Dee shrugged and dropped her eyes. She knew he meant physical pain, but it was hard for her to separate the physical and emotional pain. The guilt was the worst, and she couldn't seem to come to terms with it.

"I should have been more careful," she fretted. "I should have taken better care of myself."

"No!" His tone was harsh as he came out of the chair. He clenched his hands into fists and fought the urge to take her in his arms. "Don't do that to yourself. If anyone's to blame, it's me. If I hadn't walked out on you, you wouldn't have been under so much stress."

"You didn't exactly leave me," Dee reminded, "you tried to reach me, but I deliberately discouraged you."

"Why?" The question had been eating at him.

It was hard to formulate a response, but she tried. "Because I was hurt and angry. I didn't like the idea that you could take me or leave me without a qualm." She saw his eyes flare with anger, but he didn't interrupt.

"I didn't know I was pregnant when I lied about having a new man in my life. When I found out, I wanted to call you, but I was afraid of how you might react. Then I lost the baby."

Her voice quavered on the last word, and Logan's muscles knotted. He fought the urge to comfort her; knowing he had no right. He'd let her down when she most needed him, and that was a heavy burden.

"Why did you let me believe the worst?"

Dee studied his tight expression and tried to explain without baring her heart. "I guess I was just so furious that you believed it in the first place. It was an unwanted reminder that we really don't know each other at all."

"Only in the carnal sense?" Logan suggested with a grim expression as he began to pace the room. "Not in all the other important ways?"

She felt heat invading her cheeks. "That's about the size of it, I guess."

He dragged a hand through his hair. For the first time in years he was unsure of himself and his future. All the dreams he'd been building around Dee were crumbling. In his way of thinking, his inability to protect her when she most needed him was unforgivable. He'd let her down badly and had forfeited her respect. Then he'd compounded the sin by ridiculing her and endangering her with more unprotected sex.

Despite everything, he still wanted her to have his child. That hadn't changed. It was a deeply ingrained wanting that he couldn't deny. For both their sakes, he hoped she hadn't conceived since moving into his home. She might never forgive him.

When next he spoke, his voice was devoid of emotion and his expression tightly controlled. "Has there been enough time to know whether or not you're pregnant now?"

Dee's blush deepened. It was ridiculous to feel embarrassed since the two of them had been intimate on more than one occasion, but she did. She might not have been so uncomfortable if he'd been holding her m his arms, but his distance and reserved attitude were disquieting.

She had no idea how he felt about the possibility of a pregnancy. The status of their relationship had undoubtedly changed, but she wasn't sure where they stood now. That was even more troubling.

"I won't know for a few more days," she finally told him. Then she found the courage to ask: "Have you decided that a baby wouldn't be such a good idea after all?"

Logan clenched his teeth to keep from answering with the truth. She would hate another pregnancy so soon after her miscarriage. He didn't want her to think he was a heartless bastard for wanting something he had no right to want, yet he couldn't have her believing he'd resent a baby he'd fathered. It was a no-win situation.

"Whatever happens, you have my promise that I'll stand by you this time. You won't be alone. We'll get married if you want, and I'll take full responsibility for the child."

Dee heard his stiff declaration and studied his tightly drawn features. For once in her life, she hated not being able to understand what someone was feeling. She didn't doubt that Logan meant what he said, but she didn't know how he felt. The proposal of marriage might have cheered her if it hadn't been offered with terse reluctance.

"There's no sense worrying about it now," she said.

Logan nodded. He turned toward her and studied her upturned face. Dee felt the heat of his gaze, but he was keeping his emotions tightly in check. She had no idea what to expect.

Looking directly at him, she found the courage to ask: "Do you want me to leave?"

His eyes narrowed, and his chest constricted. He wouldn't keep her here against her will. "Do you want to leave?"

She didn't hesitate. "No."

Relief flashed briefly in his eyes, and Dee was relieved to see it. She didn't want to go home, but she didn't want to stay unless he was comfortable with the decision. She couldn't stay if he considered her some kind of freak.

"Does it bother you that I have some strong psychic powers?" she forced herself to ask, unable to hold his gaze any longer. His rejection would hurt too much.

"It bothers me," he declared in a low tone.

Dee's heart sank, and she gripped the sheet tighter to still the trembling of her hands.

Logan cupped her chin in his hand and turned her face up to his. He saw the vulnerability and then her guarded expression.

"It bothers me," he repeated, "but only because you thought you had to hide it from me. Why did you want to deny something so special?"

Dee forgot to breathe. She hadn't realized how badly she wanted his acceptance until he actually verbalized his feelings on the subject. She couldn't have tolerated any criticism about something that was an inherent part of her.

"ESP isn't widely understood," she reminded. She'd learned at an early age that people were sometimes wary, fearful, or uncomfortable around someone who was different. "People tend to be suspicious of things they can't understand."

"You thought I was a redneck farmer with no sensitivity?" Logan concluded. He pulled his hand from her face and turned away, his eyes hard. His tone was even harder. "I might not have a lot of experience with the phenomenon, but I'm not too set in my ways that I can't be educated on the subject."

Dee bit her lip to keep it from trembling. She'd hurt him and that hurt her. "It's an automatic defense," she explained. "I'm too aware of most peoples' reaction to anyone who's different, so I'm careful."

"And you couldn't trust me with the truth?" he stated baldly. He walked to the window and kept his back to her.

"Our relationship was too fragile," she said, silently adding, too new, too unexpected, too wonderful to risk. "I didn't deliberately lie to you about my abilities. There just wasn't an occasion to bring up the subject."

Logan turned slightly toward her. He needed to see her eyes. "Do your abilities apply to everyone? Every living person or thing? Or is it mostly your sisters?"

He wanted to know if she could read him the same way she read her sisters. The only way she could reassure him was to explain how her abilities had progressed over the years. There was no sense delaying a full discussion.

"It's changing as I grow older. I don't know why, but it is. The feelings concerning my sisters grow stronger all the time. I've always been able to tell how people reacted to me; if they liked me, resented me, pretended to feel something that wasn't honest. I really don't know what the future holds. My reactions are growing stronger, too, and sometimes crowds bother me."

"Because you're getting too much feedback from too many people?" he asked in a genuine effort to understand.

Dee nodded and continued. "I don't run into much hostility, so it doesn't cause a lot of problems. Sometimes I can block out all the emotions. I really have to concentrate if I want to know what one particular person is feeling."

"Like you did last night with Carlie?"

"Yes."

Logan wondered what it must have been like for her to be so sensitive as a child and teenager. He could understand why she'd needed to erect protective barriers. He thought he understood why the animals were so drawn to her and why she was extra-sensitive to her sisters. What he didn't know was how she felt about him.

"Am I as easy to read as most other people?"

Dee shook her head vigorously, tossing her hair from side to side. "You completely confuse me," she admitted with candor. "Sometimes I run into people who are so reserved or so private that I don't pick up any emotion. It's like that with you."

Logan felt a rush of relief. It wasn't that he feared or resented any reaction she might have to him, but he didn't like the idea of his emotions being so exposed. He was feeling raw, and didn't want Dee knowing how he felt until he was sure of her feelings for him.

He moved to the side of the bed again. His gaze never left her's, but he didn't touch her. "I'm sorry I let you down," he bit out gruffly. "If there's any way I can make it up to you, I'm willing to try."

Tears immediately blurred her eyes. She didn't want him to feel any obligation toward her. She didn't want him to feel indebted in any way. They couldn't change the past. It was stupid to try.

"All I want is to be accepted for just who I am," she whispered. "I'm one of triplets, an individual, yet an integral part of a close family. I love my family, and I'm always going to be very emotional where they're concerned."

Logan nodded. He understood how important her family was and didn't want to diminish that in any way.

"I'm also a flight instructor. I love teaching and flying. That's not going to change, either."

A frown creased his brow. He was learning to deal with her career. He was fighting his own demons, but he wasn't ready to consider the battle won.

"I won't interfere with your work. Everybody's happy with the progress Jake and Butch are making."

"They're great students," said Dee, inordinately pleased by the praise. "If you're still interested in lessons, I can rearrange the schedule. It wouldn't take too long for you to catch up with them."

He seemed to stiffen at the suggestion, and Dee wondered if he'd completely changed his mind about learning to fly or if he just didn't want her for a teacher.

"Thanks," he clipped. The idea made him tense, his tone terse. "But I have other plans."

He hated the wounded look in her eyes, but he wasn't ready to discuss his problems. "It's nothing against you," he swore, cupping her cheek in his hand as their gaze met and locked.

His touch sent warmth spiraling through Dee. She reached up to clasp his hand with hers, and they stared at one another for a long, tension-filled minute.

"I've been doing all the explaining this morning," she said. "Why don't you tell me what it is you have against pilots? Did you just use my career as an excuse to get rid of me?"

"No!" Logan's eyes flared and his tone was vehement. "I didn't want to get rid of you."

"You sure had a poor way of showing it," she replied, the physical contact and his closeness making her breathy.

"I know," he almost growled. His expression was pained and self-derisive. "I overreacted and acted like an ass, but it was my problem, not yours."

"Tell me about it?" she coaxed.

Logan was tempted. He'd never discussed his problem with anyone, but he'd never known anyone with a bigger heart or more beguiling eyes. A man could lose his soul and never regret it. But pride was hard to humble, and he still had a long way to go before he felt worthy of her.

He ignored her question, but posed one of his own. "Can I have a kiss?"

Dee couldn't get a word past the tightness of her throat, but she nodded her head.

Logan brought his mouth to hers and kissed her gently, then fiercely, then gently again before releasing her and stepping to the door.

"I'd better get out of here and let you get dressed," he declared. "Mattie will have breakfast ready soon."

Dee didn't respond as he opened the door, and then closed it behind him. It was several minutes before she could drag herself from bed and get on with her morning routine.

Eleven

Dee tried to go about her normal routine for the rest of the morning, but she couldn't help being distracted by thoughts of her conversation with Logan. They'd cleared the air on several important issues, yet she really didn't have any better understanding of how he felt about her.

His realization that she couldn't have aborted their child had lifted a heavy burden from her heart. His acceptance of her psychic abilities seemed like a dream come true, but she couldn't allow herself to get too hopeful. It was one thing to say you accepted something, and an altogether different proposition when you had to deal with it on a regular basis.

Too often people were intolerant of anything they didn't fully understand. Basically good, intelligent people were sometimes unnerved by repeated contact with someone who was different.

Dee had no way of knowing what the future held in relation to her ESP. Her abilities had intensified since her pregnancy. She didn't know why, only that they had. Her reactions to her sisters' emotions were stronger, as were her reactions to other people and even animals.

If her sensitivity continually increased, could Logan learn to cope with the effects? Wouldn't he or any other man get tired of the constant strain? She was having trouble coping with the changes herself. Last night's episode with Carlie had been frightening. Could she stand the added pressure of emotional involvement right now?

The question was unimportant. She didn't really have a choice in the matter. She was emotionally involved with Logan whether she liked it or not. While he'd treated her like a criminal, she'd been able to nurse a grudge. Now she was finding it hard to maintain her anger, even for their initial separation. She was more confused than angry.

She was beginning to realize that there had to be more behind his unreasonable actions back then than his wanting her to give up her career. She couldn't read his emotions, but she sensed that there was a deeper reason for his resentment of pilots.

Could he have known other women pilots? Maybe been in love with one? It wasn't impossible, but highly unlikely. That would explain why Patti and Mattie were uncomfortable every time the subject of flying arose. But if that was the case, why was Logan so reluctant to tell her about it?

Commercial pilots often had the reputation of being promiscuous, of having a lover in every corner of the world. Dee had assured him that she wasn't like that, and he'd believed her. He'd insisted that he didn't think her chosen line of work didn't diminish her femininity or appeal. So what was his real objection?

Whatever it was, the fact that he couldn't discuss his innermost concerns meant that he didn't trust her enough or have enough faith in their relationship. She'd bared her heart to him, but he couldn't do the same. Could you love someone without trusting them? Was there any hope of salvaging their love? Did she really want to?

Letting herself love Logan meant taking a tremendous risk. There were too many complications, and she didn't know if she could survive losing him again. Dee didn't want to admit, even to herself, that she' didn't have a choice in the matter. She preferred to tell herself that her feelings were still ambivalent where he was concerned.

At least her work was going well, thought Dee as she finished her morning class. Jake and Butch were progressing rapidly in their training. They'd completed their classroom instruction and clocked the required hours on the ground simulator.

Starting tomorrow, she would be flying with Butch in the mornings and Jake in the evenings, until she was satisfied that they could handle the plane by themselves. Then they'd start clocking solo hours.

When the two men left the hangar. Dee took a few minutes to tidy the classroom. She wasn't in any hurry to leave her little sanctuary and risk running into Logan. She'd been late for breakfast, and he'd already left the kitchen before she'd gotten there. She had no way of knowing how he'd treat her for the rest of her stay in Kentucky, and she wasn't ready to face him just yet.

A short time after her students' departure, Dee heard the approach of a familiar plane. Within a few minutes, the sound of Sharla's voice came over the base radio, and Dee gave her the clearance to land.

She left the hangar and walked to the end of the runway, then watched as the Saratoga touched down and taxied to stop beside the Cessna. The sight of both her sisters embarking from the plane put wings on her feet. She started running toward them and threw her arms around Carlie as soon as her feet touched ground.

Carlie moaned, expressing some tenderness in her ribs, but she wouldn't let Dee ease her grip. They hugged each other tightly, both needing the contact and reassurance.

"Thanks," Carlie whispered. Her voice nearly deserted her in an effort to express how deeply she appreciated the way Dee had precipitated her rescue the previous night.

"Are you all right?" Dee asked as she stepped back and studied her. Anger flared in her eyes. It was hard to contain the fury that surged through her at the sight of her sister's bruised and swollen face. Even though Bill had been cruel in the past, it was the first time Carlie had allowed her family to see the ravages of his temper.

"I'm fine, really"

"How did it happen?"

"Bill took me by surprise," Carlie explained, giving her another brief hug, then adding, "It's not as bad as it looks."

The remark was an attempt to appease her worry and totally wasted since Dee had experienced the pain right along with her, but she didn't contradict.

"Why were you alone with him?"

"He told me he and Michael were sharing a room. He said Michael was seriously ill and refused to see a doctor, then asked me to try and talk some sense into him. He sounded so damned sincere." Carlie berated herself for being fooled. "And I was stupid enough to trust him."

"That's how he got you to his room?"

"I really thought he'd gotten over his obsession to control me. It's been nearly two years since we talked to each other. I had no reason to suspect his motives, and he sounded really concerned about Michael."

"Reed figures Bill got rejected by some other woman recently and decided to turn his attention back to Carlie," said Sharla.

"He doesn't accept rejection well," Carlie agreed. "He never thinks he's at fault. He still thinks I should be his devoted slave, even though we've been legally divorced for four years."

Dee shook her head in disbelief. Bill was a handsome, charming man. She doubted that very many women ever said no to him, and he was spoiled beyond belief. He was one of those commercial pilots who'd actually earned the reputation of having a bevy of lovers, but Carlie hadn't known that until after she'd married him.

Her sisters were wearing comfortable cotton shorts and shirts, as was she, but it was still very warm in the sun. "Come into my classroom where it's cooler. Can you stay a little while? We could go somewhere for lunch."

"Just a few minutes," Sharla replied as they headed for the hangar. "Mother and Daddy don't want to let Carlie out of their sight for long."

"They've been fussing over me all morning," Carlie told her. "I really hated to upset them, but I'm not going to let Bill disrupt my whole life again. I won't hide until all evidence of his abuse is faded. We're finished, and I'm going to get a permanent restraining order against him this time."

"I thought he agreed to get counseling after your divorce," said Dee as she ushered them into the building.

"He went to a couple group meetings and decided all the other people in the group were beneath his station in life," Carlie explained, making a face at such arrogance. "I hope he gets a court order for therapy."

"Ditto," said Sharla.

"I'll get some colas. There's a small refrigerator in the radio room." Dee continued to talk to them as she entered the second half of the building and then returned with cold drinks. "We don't have a full-time base operator, but there's a man who works when he's needed, and Butch and Jake are learning to handle the equipment."

"It's good that they want to learn," said Carlie.

"This has really been fixed up nice," Sharla noted as she wandered around the room. "It beats every classroom or hangar I've ever seen."

"I told you it was decorated in style," Carlie added, having seen the building when she'd delivered equipment.

"It's certainly the nicest work area I've ever used. As soon as I get home, I'm going to bend Papa Bear's ear with suggestions to improve our classroom," Dee teased as they all found chairs and relaxed. "You two can prepare him with a few comments on how much you like this one."

"You should be about done with the classroom work, shouldn't you?" asked Sharla.

"We finished this morning." Dee smiled with satisfaction. "Butch loves that simulator; so he might get in a few more hours on it tonight, but tomorrow he takes the controls in the Cessna."

"Have they been good students?" asked Carlie.

"They've been great, I'm really pleased with their progress. . I don't think they'll have any trouble getting their licenses, provided they don't panic once we're airborne."

"Is Logan taking the training elsewhere?"

Dee shook her head. "I think he spends some time in here, but as far as I know, he isn't taking lessons. I asked him if he wanted me to fit him into the schedule, but he said no."

Sharla and Carlie were watching her so closely that Dee could feel their curiosity. She knew they had a lot of concerns about her relationship with Logan. "Go ahead, spit it out," she teased.

Sharla grinned. "Now, how could you possibly know that we're dying of curiosity?"

"Just intuition, I guess," Dee quipped, tongue in cheek.

"We were wondering what was happening between the two of you," Carlie admitted. "Sharla said he was with you last night when you called her. I don't know how you feel about it, but I'm glad you weren't alone."

Dee's gaze dropped to her can of soda. She wasn't quite sure how to begin. "He was wonderful last night. He offered his unconditional support without really understanding anything."

"Had he known about your abilities, or did you have to explain all of it?" asked Sharla.

"I explained as much as I could. It's changing all the time, and *I* really don't understand it myself."

"Was it bad last night?" Carlie asked, her expression turbulent with emotion.

Dee looked directly at her and knew she was worried about any suffering she'd caused, even indirectly. She debated about sugarcoating the truth, but decided against it. They needed total honesty between them.

"It was a nightmare. I felt your fear, anger and pain," she admitted candidly, but without dramatics. "I've never experienced anything like it, and I hope I never have to again. I don't know how you coped."

Tears welled in Carlie's eyes. "I'm so sorry, Dee. I hope you never have to feel it again, either."

"It's not your fault. None of it is your fault," Sharla insisted. "Don't even think it for a minute."

"You aren't responsible for my sensitivity," Dee declared fervently. "I don't know why it's growing stronger all the time, but nobody is responsible for my reactions. It's just something I'll have to learn to live with."

"It still doesn't seem fair," Carlie argued, swiping the tears from her cheeks.

"It may not be fair," Sharla tacked on, "but I'm sure glad Dee was sensitive to your situation. I'm glad she saved my hide last month, too, even if I don't wish her any extra worry and pain."

"I guess you're right," said Carlie. "I don't have any reason to complain. It's not everybody who's blessed with a guardian angel."

"That makes us pretty special, doesn't it?" Sharla added with a grin. "Even though 'angel' is a bit of a stretch." Her teasing brought a return of grins.

They were quiet for a few minutes, and then Carlie broke the silence. "So what's happening with Logan? Have the two of you discussed your personal problems?"

"We discussed some things."

"Have you resolved anything?"

"We resolved a couple major problems," Dee admitted, "but there are still a lot of unanswered questions."

"Like why Logan threw a fit because you're a pilot, then built an airstrip, hired you to teach him to fly, and then changed his mind about learning?" asked Carlie.

Dee could understand how confusing it all seemed. She was still confused. "Well, he didn't know I was being hired. That part is clear. The rest of it makes no sense to me at all, and he wouldn't talk about it."

Sharla cleared her throat and then spoke with uncharacteristic diffidence. "A . . . I . . . have a bit of information that might supply some answers."

Dee's expression immediately lit with interest. "What kind of information?"

"Well," Sharla hedged, actually blushing. "You know how I hate bureaucratic practices that allow federal agents to butt into people's private business."

"But you had Reed check into Logan's past?" Carlie surmised correctly.

Sharla nodded, looking guilty, but straining with excitement. Still, she was reluctant.

"So? What's in Logan's past that has any effect on the present?" Dee wanted to know.

"Reed found out that he joined the Navy right out of high school."

"Mattie mentioned that he'd been in the Navy, but she didn't elaborate," said Dee.

"Not just the Navy," Sharla emphasized. "The Naval Flight Corps."

"So he's more than a little familiar with planes?" Dee said in surprise. Maybe that accounted for the time he spent on the simulator.

"Not just working on planes," Sharla added, carefully gauging her sister's reaction. "He was a Navy pilot. A fighter pilot, and one of the best in his unit. He had an excellent record and a reputation to go with it. He planned to make a career of flying."

Nothing she could have said would have shocked Dee more than learning that Logan had trained as a fighter pilot. She visualized cocky, confident young men in leather bomber jackets. They had nerves of steel and daredevil smiles. Despite the contrast to the man she knew, she could imagine Logan that way. He would have been devastating.

"Are you sure Reed checked out the right Logan Bradford?" she queried.

Sharla took offense. "Reed is an excellent sleuth. He wouldn't make that kind of stupid mistake," she insisted on her fiancé's behalf.

"But what in the world made him leave the Navy?" Dee wondered. "And why does he have such a poor opinion of pilots?"

"Because he was a poor pilot!" The harsh edict came straight from the man in question as he appeared in the doorway of the hangar.

Three identical sets of eyes turned to the big man silhouetted in the door. Their expressions registered surprise, curiosity, and concern.

Logan had the sun behind him and his Stetson shaded his face, so Dee couldn't see his features. But the deep, low timbre of his voice sent a shiver over her. How much of their conversation had he overheard?

Sharla recovered first. She wasn't the least bit shy about querying him further. "I find that hard to believe. Reed says you were one of the best. You were moving rapidly through the ranks and your record was exemplary."

"Records don't always tell the whole story."

"I don't suppose you'd volunteer the whole story?" Sharla asked, intrigued. She'd grown up idolizing fighter pilots.

Logan didn't move from his position in the door, but Dee was gradually able to see his features. His gaze was fastened on her. Then it shifted to Sharla, giving her a negative nod of his head in response to her question.

Next he studied Carlie's battered face. "Are you okay?" he asked.

It took Carlie a second to adjust to the abrupt change of subject. "I'm fine, thanks. And thanks for your help."

"I didn't do anything, but I wouldn't have minded getting my hands on your ex-husband."

Carlie gave him a warm smile, and Sharla commented, "Reed had the same reaction. Fortunately, or unfortunately, Bill was already handcuffed and being led to a police car by the time we arrived."

Logan nodded, satisfied that some sort of justice would be invoked. His gaze sought Dee's again. She was watching him intently. He wondered what she saw when she looked at him and what she felt. Did she hate him for not leveling with her in the very beginning? Would she be able to understand what he'd done without losing respect for him?

"Why did you leave the Navy?" she asked.

Everyone seemed to hold their breath, waiting to see if he'd ignore her question or explain his ambiguous remark about being a poor pilot.

Logan's jaws clenched and his hands were knotted into fists at his side. He'd never discussed his motives for leaving the service to anyone, but Dee deserved an explanation.

"There was a fatal crash. It went into the records as an error of experimental equipment, but I was piloting. I never took the controls again."

Dee sucked in her breath. He'd survived a fatal crash? Her chest constricted at the thought. She searched his face for some clue to the emotion behind the statement, but his feelings were closely guarded.

"How did you survive?" Sharla asked after recovering from the initial shock of his declaration.

"We were coming in for landing, and the explosion triggered the pilot ejection system. I was ejected at a survivable altitude."

He'd survived, but how badly had he been hurt? Dee knew he couldn't have escaped injury in an explosion and crash. She remembered one bad scar on his right leg. Had there been other physical wounds, or were his most debilitating scars the emotional kind? Had he been so badly hurt that he couldn't face flying again? The thought brought her pain, and her eyes went wide with concern.

It explained so much; his initial vehement objections to her career and his subsequent agreement to drop himself from her training course. Just the thought of her teaching him anything about flying was ridiculous. He'd probably forgotten more than she'd ever known.

But why had he gone to the trouble and expense of building his own airfield if he didn't want anything to do with planes? Had he changed his mind? Was he trying to ease back into piloting?

Logan didn't know how long he could withstand her scrutiny. He knew Dee had a lot of questions, and she had a right to the answers. He'd planned to tell her the whole truth. He'd almost confided in her this morning, but he'd never put his deepest fears to words, and he didn't know where to start. Now he wasn't sure he could handle a full confession.

"After the crash, you finished your time and were discharged?" Sharla asked.

"I got out," was Logan's only comment. His gaze finally left Dee and turned to Sharla. "Will you be staying a while, or do you need some help getting the Saratoga back in the air?"

"We have to leave," said Carlie, rising from her chair. "We promised the folks we wouldn't be gone long."

"I have plenty of fuel, and I'll do my own flight check," Sharla said as she rose to her feet. "But thanks for the offer."

Logan's gaze glanced off Dee's face again, and then he turned and left the building. Sharla and Carlie's gazes flew to their sister.

"Go after him," Sharla insisted. "Get some details. I'm dying to know the whole story, and I know you must be worse than me."

"What makes you think he'll discuss the subject with me?" asked Dee. "He's kept it a well-guarded secret so far, and believe me, there's been ample opportunity." Now she knew why Patti and Mattie always got so uncomfortable about piloting discussions.

"I'm sure he wants to tell you about it," Carlie said. "Now that you know the basics, it might be easier for him to explain. If you care about him at all, you need to find out what's still bothering him after all these years."

"We have to go anyway," Sharla added.

Dee didn't need much persuading. She was on her feet and heading to the door. "Give my love to Mother and Daddy, and have a safe flight home. I'll call you later."

Outside the building, she quickly searched for Logan. All she saw was the back of him as he rode through the woods on horseback. There was no way she could follow him in Patti's sports car.

Instead, she drove to the barn, found Jake, and asked him to saddle a horse for her. She rode as often as possible, so he didn't find anything strange about the request. He saddled Molly, her usual mount.

"You sure you don't want to change clothes before you ride?" he asked. "Those shorts and sandals won't be much protection for your legs."

"I'm chasing Logan," she admitted, grinning when his eyes widened. "I'm not planning to ride for very long."

Except for his surprise at her bold announcement, Jake took the situation in stride. "We heard a plane, and he rode out to check for visitors."

"That was my sisters, Logan already talked to them, and they're leaving again." The sound of the Saratoga's revving engines accented her statement.

Jake gave her a foot up to the stirrups. "Sometimes Logan goes to the hill above the airfield. He can see the whole strip from that vantage."

"Thanks. I'll check there first."

"I'll tell Mattie not to worry about waiting lunch for you," he teased.

Dee grinned and glanced at her watch. It was almost noon. She and Logan definitely wouldn't make lunch if they had an in-depth discussion.

"Thanks," she repeated as she took the reins and turned Molly from the barn. Jake wished her luck.

She wasn't sure she could find Logan, but she rode back to the hangar and then headed in the direction she'd seen him take. Molly easily followed the beaten path through the woods, then the trees gave way to rolling pasture, and Logan came into sight.

He was standing beside his horse on the ridge overlooking the airstrip. Dee slowed Molly's pace when she got a clear view of him. He turned at the sound of her approach, but she couldn't see his eyes or judge his reaction to her pursuit.

Dee eased Molly to a walk until she was close enough for Logan to reach out and grasp the horse's halter. He held Molly still and offered a hand to help her dismount, then grounded the reins so the horse could graze with his.

"We need to talk," she declared softly, repeating the same words he'd used on her earlier in the morning.

Logan's silvery gaze met hers without flinching. He grasped both her forearms, pulling her close to him. "I'd rather make love in the grass."

His touch, the heat of his body, and the gleam in his eyes made her blood sizzle, but she wasn't going to be distracted. "You'd rather put off my questions for a while longer," she countered, yielding the urge to slide her hands up his rock-hard chest.

"I'd rather kiss than talk," he mumbled as he lowered his head and covered her mouth with his.

It started as an attempt to delay his confession, but as soon as Logan felt the softness of her lips, he forgot everything but her sweetness and how badly he needed her. He moaned and deepened the kiss, thrusting his tongue into her mouth to plumb the honeyed depths. Dee involuntarily shifted closer, tilting her head and welcoming the hungry invasion of his tongue. Her fingers flexed against his chest, and a tiny moan found its way up her throat.

He wrapped his arms around her and drew her tightly against him. In a matter of seconds, she inflamed him with her responsive mouth and sexy whimper of hunger. He couldn't get enough of her.

Dee returned his kisses with fervor and molded her body along the hard length of his. Her breasts swelled and pressed against his chest. Logan's hand slid to her hips and urged her still closer to his hardness, but when she felt the rigid evidence of his arousal, she knew she had to find the strength to resist him.

They couldn't make love with so much unresolved conflict between them. She'd been honest and trusting when she'd answered his questions. She deserved no less from him.

Dragging her mouth from his, she dropped her chin until his mouth rested on her forehead. They were both breathing roughly, but she managed to find the breath to explain her withdrawal.

"I want explanations, Logan." Her whisper was husky, but firm.

She felt his chest rise with a deep inhalation of breath, then heard his long, slow exhalation. She knew how he felt. She was just as needy, but this time she wanted a whole lot more than physical gratification.

He drew back and locked gazes with her. Dee's legs went weak at the heated intensity of his eyes.

"You're sure you wouldn't like to love me first and talk later?" he ground out hoarsely. He was desperately afraid that his confession might destroy her desire for him. He wanted the empowering strength of their physical bond to cement their relationship before he threatened it again.

Dee stepped away from him and the temptation he represented. She'd have to be dead to remain unaffected by the passionate intensity of his eyes and voice. She was tempted to let him have his way with her, but she resisted.

"Talk first," she said softly, adding a promise. "Then we can make love all you want."

Logan groaned and turned his back to her. "I'm going to hold you to that promise," he swore roughly.

He headed across the ridge toward a sprawling willow tree. Dee followed slowly, allowing him time to get control of his desire. When he ducked under the heavy foliage of the willow's branches, so did she. The tree became an umbrella that offered sun-dappled shade and provided a measure of privacy.

She moved to the trunk of the tree and sat down, using it as a backrest. The grass was thick, soft, and cool against her bare legs.

Logan began to pace, so she patted a spot beside her. His gaze met hers, and then shifted to her hand. He eased his long length to the ground, stretching out to lie on his back. Tipping off his hat, he locked his hands behind his neck, and stared at the canopy of leaves above them.

Twelve

Dee didn't prompt Logan with questions. She just tried to relax and enjoy the quiet beauty of the morning. Her emotions were in chaos, but she didn't want to push him. She wanted him to explain his past in his own words. After several long minutes, he began.

"I met a guy named Harvey Harris my first year at the academy," he explained in a low, even tone. "Harvey was from West Virginia, and he got a lot of ribbing from our preppy classmates about his 'hillbilly' upbringing. They nicknamed him 'Hick,' but he didn't mind." A half-smile touched his lips. "He preferred it to his given name.

"The insults didn't bother him, either. When he responded, it was always in his slow, laid-back fashion. Nobody ever got under his skin, because most people just weren't important to him."

"Except for you?" Dee asked a minute later when he appeared to get lost in his memories.

"Yeah," Logan admitted. "We came from different backgrounds, but we were both country boys at heart. We liked the simple life and shared a fascination with airplanes. For me, it was a dream to fly. For Hick, to create a fighter plane that was superior to all others.

"His poor-boy manner disguised sheer brilliance. His IQ was double the average, and he got a real kick out of the dumb-hillbilly routine. People mostly amused him. The only thing that really challenged him was an unsolved puzzle. If he didn't know the reason for something, he was like a madman until he found the answer. He was a mathematics and electronics genius."

Dee noticed that Logan spoke of his friend in the past tense. She didn't know if he was referring to a time long past or the man, but she guessed that Harvey had been lost somewhere along the way.

"The two of you were together all four years of academy?"

"Yeah, and then we requested assignments to the same base. I learned to fly a fighter, and Hick got to dissect the plane's computer systems."

Logan envisioned his old friend. Hick had been tall and lanky and always looked underfed. His appetite was voracious, when he remembered to eat. Sometimes, if he was involved in a project, whole days would go by before he realized he was starving.

A few minutes of silence passed. Dee studied Logan's face. She loved every curve and plane of it. He was the only man she'd ever loved, and despite everything that had happened to them, she still loved him.

Like most of her emotional reactions, it wasn't something she could control, it just came naturally. There was no use denying it. However terrible his secrets about the past were, she knew they wouldn't change the way she felt about him.

"Hick was the best friend I ever had," Logan eventually continued, his tone gruff. "We were more than friends: it was like having a soul mate."

It was difficult for him to share his deepest feelings. Dee doubted he'd ever shared them with anyone, but she was glad he was willing to do so for her. He was an intensely private man, and it was hard for a man to admit his love for another man. Women tended to discuss their love more freely, but men often considered it emasculating. She thought it was a measure of strength and character.

"We worked together for almost four years after the academy," Logan continued. "I wanted to be the best fighter pilot this country ever had, and Hick wanted to design the best electronics system in the world.

"If a computer problem cropped up that Hick couldn't isolate and correct from the ground, he'd go up with me to study the problem firsthand. He called it his on the job training."

Logan's tone grew hoarse, and he stopped talking for a while. Most of his memories of Hick were good, but he'd avoided thoughts of their work for a long time. He wasn't sure if he could tell Dee the whole story.

She realized why it was hard for him to discuss Hick. Logan suffered the guilt of surviving the same accident that had claimed the life of his best friend. It wasn't an unusual occurrence, but it was especially traumatizing. She wanted to make it easier for him to recount the details.

"Hick was the fatality in the crash you mentioned earlier?" She softly supplied the admission he couldn't articulate.

Logan closed his eyes, and his jaws clenched with tension. "Yeah," he said again. "There was a problem with the computer's fuel pressure readouts. We all thought it was minor, but it was driving Hick crazy because he couldn't pinpoint it."

"So he flew with you?"

Logan jerked himself to a sitting position and raked all his fingers through his hair. "It was just a damned test flight, nothing special, nothing dangerous," he argued with heat.

"We were getting ready to come in for a landing when the explosion happened. I didn't know what the hell was going on. One wing burst into flame and the plane did a dive. I was able to stabilize it again, but the cockpit was filling with smoke, and I couldn't read the instruments."

Once he started explaining, his words came in an angry rush. "Hick was ignoring the fire and cussing the computer. The ground crew and our C.O. were screaming for us to eject, but I couldn't go without him, and he was more worried about solving the damned electronics problem."

Logan covered his face with his hands as he relived the horror of those few minutes. He'd wanted to hit the ejection button for both of them, but Hick had pleaded for a few more seconds. Those seconds had cost him his life.

"I should have pushed the damned button and argued with him after we hit the ground," Logan declared fiercely. He turned tormented eyes on Dee. "I remember reaching for the switch, but there was a second explosion, and I don't remember anything after that until I woke up in the hospital.

"It's not remembering that drives me crazy," he rasped. "It's the damned unanswered questions. Why was I ejected and not Hick? We both should have gone. Did I do something wrong? What caused the first explosion? What else could I have done?"

Dee didn't have any of the answers, but her tone was softly sympathetic. "What did the Navy decide?"

He shook his head. "The investigators blamed the crash on a malfunction of the electronics system. They claimed the first explosion and fire caused extensive electrical damage and short-circuited the backup systems. That plane had been plagued with problems. That's why Hick was so frustrated. He couldn't figure it out."

"So why do you blame yourself?" Dee asked gently, knowing that he'd lived with guilt for a long time.

"I could have saved him," he argued, eyes burning with anguish and self-disgust. "I could have ejected both of us before the second explosion. Then he'd have had a chance."

"Maybe," Dee countered, "but I don't think so. I'm a fatalist. I believe that a person dies when it's their time. Maybe nothing you could have done would have saved Hick. It was his time."

"No!" he argued harshly, raking his hands through his hair again. "He was too young, too good, with too many problems to solve."

Her eyes filled with tears, and she quickly blinked them away. She felt the pain of his loss, but she didn't want to compound his anguish with her own. She wanted him to let go of the guilt.

"Don't you think you've punished yourself enough?" she asked quietly. "You gave up the work you loved, and you've mourned for your friend, but it's time to let go of the past. You can't keep blaming yourself for a freak accident. You had every right to survive."

"Did I?" he asked roughly, his silvery gaze riveted on her face.

"You're a survivor," she insisted. "You lost your best friend and your dreams were shattered, but you didn't crawl in a hole and hide. You're strong and healthy and leading a productive life."

Her words were a salve to his soul, but she still didn't know what a coward he was. Logan didn't know if he could explain his fear of flying, but he wanted her to understand why he'd been so intimidated by her career.

Dee's gaze never left his as he stretched out on his back again and covered his face with his forearm. She studied his prone form and tried to imagine what it would be like to survive a crash that claimed someone you loved. She'd had a couple of scares in the air, but nothing too serious. Sharla's emergency landing in an ice storm had been frightening enough, and she hadn't been badly hurt.

"How badly were you hurt?" she forced herself to ask.

"A concussion and a few broken bones," he dismissed as unimportant. "I healed except for some nerve and tissue damage. The doctors said

I'd never recover the full strength and reflexive action I needed to fly the fighters, but it didn't really matter. I was too damned scared to get into the cockpit, anyway."

There. The truth was out. He'd said the words. He was scared, too scared to take the controls of another plane. Too scared to revive the old dreams. Too scared to accept the fact that the woman he loved was a pilot.

"You haven't flown since?"

"Never," Logan said on a growl. "By the time I was out of the hospital, I was up for promotion and reenlistment. I refused both. I walked away and never looked back."

A few years later, he'd climbed into the cockpit of a friend's plane. The fear had still been so strong he could taste it. He'd broken out in a cold sweat when the memories washed over him, and his hands had shaken so badly that he couldn't grip the controls. Except for the simulator, he hadn't tried since.

Dee imagined his resignation had taken more courage than most men could boast. She knew Logan's superiors wouldn't have allowed him to resign his commission without a battle. She was sure they'd submitted him to dozens of counseling sessions. Psychologists and other well-intentioned professionals had probably hounded him. Then he'd had to come home to his family, feeling like a failure.

As the silence stretched between them, Logan wondered if he'd shocked Dee with his admission. Women had always chased him while he was a flyboy. It was an accepted fact of life. There would always be women who were impressed by the uniform, but uncaring about the real man beneath it. Men they perceived as daring and fearless impressed women.

He hadn't been short of feminine attention since settling down on the farm, but he'd made sure no one got close enough to cause heartache. Until Dee. Her sweetness and sensitivity had slipped past all his defenses. He'd fallen fast and hard, but how could she want a man who confessed to being a coward?

He was a harsh judge of his own strength. Dee had met a lot of pilots in her life; military, commercial, and privately licensed. But she'd never met one with the courage to train as a fighter pilot. It took a special breed of man with special skills to meet that kind of challenge. Logan was no less a man for having grasped, then lost his dream.

There was tension in every line of his body, and she badly wanted to comfort him. She didn't know if he'd reject her efforts, but she had to try. Shifting to her knees and sliding closer to him, she laid a hand on his thigh and splayed her fingers in a gentle caress.

Logan's muscles bunched, and a low moan tightened his throat. Her hand burned him through the layer of denim and sent heat spiraling through his body. It was like stepping close to an open fire after battling a numbing coldness. He didn't want sympathy, but be didn't have the strength to resist anything she wanted to give.

He held himself rigid while she leaned over him and began tugging his shirttail from the waistband of his jeans. When she pressed a soft kiss on his stomach, he clenched his teeth in sweet agony. As she scattered more kisses over his abdomen, he reached for the back of her head with both hands, slowly unwound the tight braid, then combed her thick locks with his fingers.

"Dee!" he murmured gruffly. Her tenderness and understanding were his undoing. Her kisses eased his pain and proved she wasn't disgusted by his story. He wanted to pull her completely over him, but she wouldn't be rushed.

She unfastened his shirt from the bottom, button-by-button, kiss-by-kiss, until she found the nipples hidden in tight curls. When her warm, wet tongue touched the first one, his whole body jerked, and blood surged in his loins. Then she gave equal attention to the other nipple.

He clutched her hair in his fists and guided her head upward until he could lock his mouth with hers. Their lips met, hot, hard and wanting. He wrapped his arms around her and pulled her on top of him while their tongues touched and entwined.

They shared a long, deep, ravenous kiss while each absorbed the feel of the other. Dee was pliant as she pressed closer, eager to feel every hard angle of his body. At the feel of his arousal pressing against the softness of her thighs, she undulated her hips in blatant demand.

Logan broke off the kiss just long enough to release a low groan and scatter heated caresses across her face. Then he captured her lips with increased fervor. Dee returned his kisses with a matching need.

He had to touch her. He had to feel her skin against his own. Without easing the pressure on her mouth, his hands slid over her back and then under the hem of her blouse. He didn't waste time with buttons, but pulled it off her arms and over her head. In another instant, his fingers found the clasp of her bra and he tossed it aside as well.

Combined moans of pleasure swirled in their mouths as her bare breasts were crushed against his chest. Logan clutched her close for a minute, and then lifted her just far enough to brush her nipples across his own.

The pleasure was unbearable. Dee's sultry eyes met his smoldering gaze and heat throbbed low in her body. A groan of need rumbled from Logan as his chest rose against hers. Every nerve in her body sang with awareness.

He wanted her more than his next breath. He had to be a part of her, to bury himself as deeply inside of her as possible. The need was more than physical, more than carnal, more than necessary.

"Let me love you," he pleaded in a shaking voice. It might be a little late to offer her protection, but he'd promised himself to never put her at risk again. "I promise to protect you."

In response, Dee dipped her head to steal another kiss. At the same time, her trembling fingers slid between them and found the buckle of his belt. A low sound of need quaked through him, and every muscle in his body tightened.

He wanted to take his time, to savor her sweetness and beauty. He wanted to drive her crazy with need, to kiss every soft inch of her body, but his own desire was too fierce, too long denied.

"I want you too much," he apologized in a raw tone. In another instant they were both freed of confining clothes, and he turned to pull her beneath him.

"Never too much." Dee's breath caught on a sob as the hot, heavy weight of his body fully covered her. Blood pulsed through her veins in a heated rush, and she arched her hips against him in demand.

It took only seconds for Logan to use the protection he'd promised. Then his mouth caught hers again. His tongue plunged through her lips in greedy demand. A soft cry caught in her throat as he clutched her hips and joined their bodies in the same commanding fashion.

Birds sang and a gentle breeze rustled the branches of the willow tree. Sweat glistened on their bodies moments later when their passion was spent. Logan continued to hold Dee close as their breathing slowly returned to normal.

She was overwhelmed by sweet sensations; the satisfaction he'd given her, the sun and breeze on her bare flesh, the softness of the grass beneath her and the feel of his big body next to hers.

There was no guilt or self-recrimination. She loved this man and had no qualms about entrusting her body and soul to him. Now that she fully understood why he'd rejected their love, she could cope with any problems that arose in their relationship. Logan might not be ready to propose marriage again, but he loved her. She was certain of that.

She could wait. There was no need to make hurried decisions about their future. They needed time together. She knew their love would blossom given time and opportunity.

Even though his body was temporarily sated, Logan wasn't ready to release Dee yet. He brushed kisses over her throat and neck while he asked, "Was that a serious promise to give me all the loving I wanted?"

"Uh-huh," she murmured, eyes closed, as she enjoyed his caresses.

His body throbbed to life again at the sexy softness of her reply. He might not deserve her unconditional trust, he might never be totally worthy of her, but he wasn't fool enough to refuse whatever she was willing to give. In return, he would give her everything he had to give. He'd see that she never wanted for anything.

"I'm a greedy man," he reminded, nibbling on the pulse at the base of her throat and feeling her tremble in response. "It might not be an easy promise to keep."

Dee found the strength to lift her arms and cradle his face in her palms. Her lashes rose, revealing slumberous eyes filled with emotion. "Are you trying to discourage me?"

"Hell, no!" came his gruff reply. His eyes darkened as he recognized the depth of commitment she was offering. He should be exultant, but he was wary. She was still a pilot, and he still hadn't conquered his fears.

"Does the promise come with strings?" he forced himself to ask. The future was too unpredictable.

Dee continued to gaze at him with unflinching faith. "None."

Logan pulled his head from her grip and smothered a groan against the cushion of her breast. He turned his head and sucked a nipple into his mouth, flicking it with his tongue until it was engorged and throbbing. Then his thumb replaced his mouth while he gave the same attention to the other breast.

She whimpered and sunk her fingers into his hair as he swiftly brought her body to an aching state of arousal. Arching her back, she lifted her hips and rubbed herself against him in wanton invitation.

Logan made a sound that expressed his pleasure, but this time he didn't intend to hurry. He wanted to savor every inch of her responsive body. He lingered over her lush breasts and then expanded his caresses.

Dee quivered in his arms. She'd promised him all the loving he wanted, but the promise had been a selfish one. She wanted him just as much as he wanted her — maybe more.

*F*or the next few days, they existed in their own private world. They went about their normal routines, they exchanged conversation and interacted with other people, but their thoughts were focused on each other and the next opportunity to be alone.

Neither got much sleep, yet they didn't complain. Their nights were filled with soft words, soft caresses, and insatiable hunger. He didn't blatantly take her to his bed. He didn't want her to be embarrassed or uncomfortable with the situation.

He came to her each night after the house was quiet, and left her before dawn each morning. Whenever they found themselves alone, they stole kisses. They didn't really know or care if the other members of the household and staff were aware of the change in their relationship.

Dee welcomed him when he came to her. She blossomed in the warmth of his attention. Sometimes she met his passion with enchanting innocence; sometimes with wanton eagerness. She kept her promise and gave him all the loving he wanted, but made no further demands.

Logan fell more deeply in love every day. He hadn't thought it possible, but it happened. Each time she smiled at him, each time she spoke his name, each time she touched him, he fell deeper under love's spell. She stole his heart again.

Thirteen

Toward the end of the week, Dee awoke in the early morning hours to find herself alone in bed. Logan always left her before dawn, but she sensed something different about his absence this morning. She lay still for a few minutes, trying to chase away sleepiness and identify the feelings of unease she was experiencing.

A strange kind of dread settled over her. Then that feeling began to give away to fear — real, gripping fear. Her first thought was for her sisters, especially Carlie. But after a few more minutes, she realized that they weren't involved. She was picking up someone else's emotions. It could only be one other person.

Logan. He was in a bad situation, but Dee didn't immediately realize where or how he was being threatened. Still, she could feel his fear and knew she had to find him.

Jumping from bed, she quickly located a pair of shorts and a T-shirt. After dressing and slipping her feet into sneakers, she quietly let herself out of the house to make a dash for the garage. She climbed into Patti's car, and instinct directed her toward the airfield.

Logan was forcing himself to take the controls of her plane. The knowledge came to her in a rush of emotion. He was testing himself, pushing himself to face his fears. She didn't want him doing it on her account. Over the past few days they'd avoided any mention of his naval career, but she'd realized that he wasn't willing to consider a future with her until he'd put the past behind him for good.

If he never piloted another plane, she wouldn't think any less of him. He didn't need to prove anything to her. She loved him, unconditionally and without reservations.

She only wished he had as much faith in her as she had in him. Why couldn't he understand that she loved him just the way he was? He wasn't flawed in her eyes. He was strong and courageous and every inch a man. She wanted to convince him that his fears were perfectly acceptable, if not to himself, at least to her and the rest of the world.

When Dee reached the airstrip, the car lights swept across the Cessna, and she could see Logan sitting in the pilot's seat. She parked, switched off the ignition, and jumped out, noting in the silence of the early morning that the plane's engine was also silent.

He didn't say a word when she climbed into the cockpit with him, nor did he glance her way. He was frozen in position behind the controls. Dee could feel the waves of tension vibrating from his big body. His posture was utterly still and stiff, his jaw locked in a rigid line, and both his hands gripped the controls.

She wanted to do or say something to ease his tension, but she couldn't get a sound past the tightness in her throat. He was hurting. He looked so brittle that she was afraid to touch him. His pain became her pain, and she didn't know how to ease his suffering.

She wondered if this was the first time he'd forced himself inside the plane, or if he'd been making a habit of punishing himself with his own fear. It didn't matter now. She was here and she intended to help him through it.

Fastening her seat belt, she glanced over to make sure his was secure. She forced herself to remain calm as she put on her headphones and made routine preparations for take-off. She and Butch had refueled the plane and done a safety check the previous night after his training flight. There was nothing to stop them from flying.

She was going to go through the motions Logan couldn't bring himself to do. The Cessna was equipped with two sets of controls for training purposes, so she could do all the piloting unless he took over. If he objected, she'd stop immediately. If not, they'd be past the first hurdle.

The plane's engine flared to life at her touch. The engine rumbled with its familiar trembling force. Logan didn't move or speak. Dee couldn't bring herself to look at him, but she watched his knuckles turn white as he tightened his grip on the controls.

As slowly as possible, she coaxed the plane forward in a sweeping turn and then began to taxi down the runway. She was tense and ready to cut the engine if she heard even the slightest protest from him. When he didn't make a sound, she picked up the necessary speed to lift them off the ground. Once airborne, she turned the nose of the Cessna eastward over Bradford property and toward the horizon.

The sky was turning pink in celebration of a new dawn. It had been a long time since Dee had flown directly into the morning sun, greeting the day from an incomparable prospective. It was a heady experience that never failed to enthrall her. She hoped it was something Logan loved, as well. There was always a chance he could conquer his fear and wipe out the bad memories by re-experiencing the simplest joys of flying.

The sun crept higher, turning the horizon into a kaleidoscope of gorgeous colors. Mother nature was putting on a spectacular show. Dee halted the plane's ascent and leveled off at a few hundred feet. The Kentucky terrain below them shimmered in the first rays of sunlight, while the giant orb launched itself into the sky.

For a few breathtaking minutes, Dee forgot everything but the incredible beauty of the horizon. She felt a renewed sense of wonderment. Somehow, all human endeavors paled in significance to such unmatched glory.

Gradually, as the sun rose higher, the brittle tension in the cockpit lessened. Her grip on the controls relaxed, and she felt some of the tightness easing from her body. Logan's knuckles were no longer white with strain. She dared a glance at him and noted a significant relaxing of his profile. The tension and fear that had held them both captive was lessening. She knew he was slowly coming to terms with the demons that had plagued him for so long.

She could feel his relief when a swell of elation began to replace the self-doubt he'd suffered for too many years. Beneath all his insecurity was a deep-seeded love of flying that was finally making an encore in his life.

A wild thrill swept through Dee as she realized that he was conquering his fear. He would be all right. In a flash of brilliance, the sun was incinerating the doubts and fears that had held him prisoner for so long. The fact that she'd helped him made her feel humble, yet proud.

All he'd needed was to get past the initial terror of taking to the air. She'd helped him do that. A wave of pure joy washed over Dee, thrilling her with their success. What was equally incredible was that she shared the joy with Logan, and that she could feel his spirit soar.

When he finally broke the silence, his voice was thick with emotion. "I'd like to take the controls."

Her chest tightened with pride and her smile for him was beautiful. She made the necessary adjustments and then dropped her hands in her lap.

"You've got it," she whispered.

"You're not afraid to let me pilot?" he asked, his tone still rough.

"I trust you with my life," she stated simply. You are my life, she added to herself.

Logan felt a lump rise in his throat, and he had to blink away the sudden dampness in his eyes. She trusted him and for the first time in years, he trusted himself. He felt whole again. Strength and confidence surged through him as he took control of the plane and all lingering fears diminished. He took a deep breath to ease the tightness in his chest.

In a matter of minutes Dee had given him more than he would ever be able to explain, more than he could ever thank her for, more than any man had a right to expect — her unequivocal faith in him.

His eyes were glued to the rising sun, but his tone was low and gruff when he next spoke.

"Do you have any idea how much I love you?"

Her heart swelled with emotion, her chest tightened and tears momentarily clouded her vision. She knew he loved her, he'd shown her in a hundred ways, but this was the first time in months that he'd given her the precious words.

"Not half as much as I love you," came her husky reply.

Logan slowly altered their course so that the brilliance of the sunshine wouldn't blind them both. The thrill of piloting the plane was too intense to describe, yet it didn't compare to the wealth of emotion generated by the woman at his side.

"I love you more," he insisted. This time a confident, teasing note altered his tone,

"I love you more," she countered, accepting the verbal challenge.

"Want to argue about it?"

"For a few years at least," she teased, her tone light, but her meaning clear.

Logan's chest constricted. He didn't want her for a few years or even a few decades. He wanted her forever. Now that they'd destroyed the last barrier between them, he wanted a promise for the future.

"How about for the rest of our lives?" he asked in a deep, serious tone. He didn't even breathe while waiting for her reply, and he couldn't look at her. He wasn't sure he'd survive if she refused him.

Dee's heart began to pound with an intensity that stole her breath. What was Logan really asking her? Was he asking for a long-term commitment? She wanted the words.

"Is this a proposal of marriage?"

"'Til death," he managed, suddenly taut with tension of a totally different kind.

She desperately wanted to agree, but they still hadn't discussed her career. Kentucky was a long way from Prescott Air Service, and her career had caused a major rift between them.

"I'm still a professional pilot," she reminded softly.

That didn't bother him now. They could work out some sort of compromise. He'd been planning for a long time. "Why do you think I had an airstrip built on my property?" he asked lightly.

Dee's eyes widened and fastened on the big man beside her. For the first time since they'd become airborne, he turned his head and their gazes tangled.

"You did that for me?" she asked in amazement.

"I love you," he told her with his voice and the silvery brilliance of his eyes. He grasped one of her hands and brought it to his lips. After pressing a warm kiss to her palm, he placed it on the controls beneath his own. Then he turned his eyes to the sky again.

"I knew flying would always be an important part of your life," he explained, "so I had to make it a part of mine again."

Dee's chest was so tight that she could hardly breathe. Tears spilled down her cheeks. Logan had done that for her. He'd fought his own demons because he loved her.

He could have walked away from her and never looked back. He'd chosen to fight for what he wanted, even knowing that it would cause him the agony of coming to terms with his past. She felt a rush of guilt at having thrown that love back in his face by allowing him to believe she'd aborted their baby. Silently, she pledged to make it up to him by giving him her love every day for the rest of their lives.

Aloud, she managed to whisper, "Do you know how much I love you?"

"Not as much as I love you," he teased again, then threw her with an unexpected question. "Do you think there's any chance you're pregnant?"

"Why?" she asked warily, hoping that it had nothing to do with his proposal.

Logan turned to her again, his eyes gleaming with wicked delight. "I've got an urge to do a few maneuvers, but I can wait if there's a chance it might upset you."

The incredible beauty of his eyes made Dee's breath catch and her heart ache. For the first time since meeting him, she was getting a glimpse of the irresistible daredevil he must have been before the crash had changed his life. It made her giddy with excitement and proud to claim his love.

"I don't think I'm pregnant," she told him. She didn't feel pregnant. "But I want you to know that I wouldn't have minded one little bit. I've been thinking a lot about having your baby, and I like the idea. I like it a whole lot."

Logan's stomach muscles knotted and his throat went tight. He devoured her with his eyes. They were filled with pride, possessiveness, and an ever-present hunger. She was everything he'd ever wanted in a woman, and so much more.

"We'll work on it," he promised with a gruff tone and glittering eyes. "Just as soon as my ring's on your finger."

"That suits me fine," she teased, stretching to press a kiss against his lips. "Now how about those maneuvers? I'm not confident enough to orchestrate them myself, but I like to ride along."

Logan flashed her another devilish grin, lifted her hand to his lips, and then placed it on his thigh. He returned his hands to the controls; his gaze automatically checked the instrument readings. Satisfied that all was well, he began to take them on a slow, easy roller coaster ride in the air.

He chuckled with deep satisfaction as the Cessna climbed, then dove, then rolled gently at his command. He hadn't forgotten anything about flying. He hadn't lost his touch. It all came to him as easily as climbing on the back of his horse, but with a great deal more satisfaction.

After he'd temporarily sated his need for controlling the plane, he returned to the sky above Bradford Bluegrass and did an aerial pass over his property. He noticed a small crowd near the hangar.

"I think you've attracted an audience," said Dee.

"They're probably more than a little shocked."

"Shocked, but pleased, I imagine." Dee knew that Mattie and Patti had been aware of his problem. She imagined that Jake had also been aware of it. They couldn't know that Logan was doing the piloting, but just the fact that he was in the cockpit would signify a lot.

"Do you suppose I should take it down?" he asked, sounding very much like a little boy who knew it was time to put away his toys, yet wasn't anxious to stop playing.

"I suppose," she teased.

Logan guided the Cessna through another slow, gentle roll over the airfield, then turned back and aligned the plane with the end of the runway.

"Want me to take it down?" Dee asked.

"What's wrong?" he chided. "I thought you trusted me with your life."

"I do."

"But you're willing to bail me out if I lose my confidence?" he supplied.

"You bet."

They shared a look filled with supreme love and understanding. "We make a pretty good team, don't we?"

Her grin deepened. "You bet."

He reluctantly turned his attention to landing the plane. It had been a very long time for him, and the Cessna wasn't anything like the fighters he'd flown, but he still managed to set it down with a minimum of bouncing.

As soon as he'd taxied to a stop, he cut the engine and turned to Dee. She felt the waves of emotion flowing from him.

"Thanks," he said with a wealth of feeling in the one short word.

"You're welcome," she said, loving the deep satisfaction etched in his features. "I'll let you thank me properly when we don't have such a big audience."

Logan's laughter was husky, deep-throated, and filled with masculine pleasure.

"That's a promise."

By mutual agreement, they climbed from opposite sides of the plane. Logan's feet had barely touched the ground before Patti launched herself into his arms. "You did it! You did it!" she cried in excitement. "I knew you could!"

Logan hugged her close while shooting a glance at the others. Everyone on the property had come to watch the show. Mattie was mopping her eyes with her apron. Jake was sporting a broad grin, and Butch's eyes were lit in awe. The other hands stood back a distance, but looked just as impressed.

He tucked Patti under his arm and clasped the hand Jake had outstretched to him.

"Congratulations. That was some kind of flying."

"Kid stuff," Logan teased, "but it felt damned good."

"How come you learned to do all that, and I'm just plugging along?" Butch wanted to know, the self-derogatory question bringing a round of laughter.

"I'll explain later," Logan promised. Then his eyes were homing in on Dee.

She stood a few feet away, her eyes for him alone. Her heavy hair was tumbling over her shoulders in disarray that she rarely allowed outside the bedroom. Her face was flushed, glowing, and filled with so much love that it made his heart stop and then race. The look that passed between them had Patti stepping aside. Everyone else backed up a few steps.

"I don't think you ever answered my question," he said to Dee.

"I think you need to be a little more specific," she replied breathlessly.

"Will you marry me?"

There was a collective gasp. Dee's breath caught at the adoration in his eyes. "Anytime, anywhere," she replied softly.

A rousing cheer went up as he caught her in his arms. Despite the audience, he found her mouth with his and kissed her deeply and possessively.

Her arms slid around his neck, and he drew her closer. The softness of her body excited him, as always. Her sweet, womanly scent intoxicated him. He never seemed to be able to get her close enough. He never seemed to get enough of her heady kisses.

She was a dream come true. His dream. His woman. His only love. He silently vowed to cherish the gift of her love for eternity.

Dee's arms tightened and the rest of the world melted away. She wasn't a mind reader, but she was a receptor of deep emotion, and she felt the incredible strength of Logan's commitment. Nothing was ever going to tear them apart again. Whatever the future held, they could handle it together. Their love was that strong, that true, and that special.

Loving Carlie

One

The old-fashioned chapel on the Prescott family's Virginia plantation was an ideal setting for the late September wedding. The sanctuary, decorated with enormous bundles of multi-colored roses, was small, yet perfect for the intimate celebration. Three sets of candelabras glimmered at the altar, each representing one of the Prescott triplets; Sharla, Darla and Carla. Though only two of the sisters would be exchanging vows, they were accustomed to doing everything in threes.

Strands of gossamer lace adorned the ends of every hand-hewn wooden pew, the drapes drawn into an arch that supported more candles. A late afternoon sun shone through aged, but beautiful stained glass windows, bathing the room in a kaleidoscope of muted colors.

When Carlie stepped through the doors from the vestibule, her breath caught in her throat and her pulse thrummed through her body. She was immediately caught up in a dreamy, romantic mood; transported into a wonderland of sensual pleasure. The smell and beauty of the sanctuary enveloped her, swirling around and inside her, stimulating nerves that were already hypersensitive.

Performing her duties as Sharla's bridesmaid, she took her first halting step down the white-carpeted aisle. She'd promised not to rush, so she inhaled a deep, calming breath. Forcing herself to take the slow, measured steps of a traditional wedding march, she soaked up the glorious atmosphere like a sensual sponge.

Focusing forward, her eyes rested on the three men standing to the pastor's left. They all looked tall, broad shouldered and incredibly handsome in their dark tuxedos and pristine white, pleated shirts.

Sharla's groom, Reed Connors, nodded to her as their gazes met. He appeared composed and confident as he offered an encouraging smile. He and Sharla were deeply in love and they'd soon be man and wife. Contentment etched his features.

Next her gaze met with the face of Darla's new husband, Logan Bradford. He also had the look of a deeply contented man. A justice of the peace had married him and Dee, but they planned to renew their vows today following Sharla and Reed's exchange of vows.

Lastly, her gaze met with the deep blue of Michael Trehearn's eyes, and her steps faltered. Heart fluttering and nerves jangling, she looked into his dark, brooding features. There was nothing relaxed or easy about his expression as his gaze locked with hers. The playful, brotherly affection she'd grown accustomed to had been replaced by an emotion so strong that it momentarily stunned her. He gave her a brief, challenging glimpse of pure sexual hunger, and then abruptly smoothed his features into a calm mask.

Carlie's lungs constricted, her pulse racing as blood pounded in her ears; nearly deafening her to the rhythm of the organ music. Michael rarely showed her anything but an amiable, supportive façade. That he would do so now left her feeling rattled. She immediately dragged her gaze from him and forced herself to concentrate on the rest of her procession, even while her senses whirled.

She was far from innocent, yet still not very sophisticated in the ways of men like her ex-brother-in-law. Michael was normally all teasing charm and machismo. They had quite a history and had spent a lot of time together these past few weeks, yet he'd never given her an inkling of stronger feelings. He'd never hinted at wanting more from their relationship. She must have misread the message in his eyes. It had to be a misunderstanding on her part, just a bridesmaid's version of wedding jitters.

As she took her place to the right of the pastor, she fought to calm her nerves, and then turned to watch Dee step through the vestibule doors. They'd chosen the same style of bridesmaid gowns, but in different colors. Dee had chosen a dark turquoise while her choice had been a deep shade of red. The second born of the Prescott triplets looked gorgeous in her off-the-shoulder turquoise silk gown.

Though identical in looks, Carlie had never felt half as beautiful as her two siblings. Dee had an inner radiance that warmed everything and everyone who came in contact with her. Sharla, the eldest by mere minutes, also had a magnetic personality and supreme self-confidence that enhanced her physical attractiveness.

The triplet's allotment of self-confidence seemed to have been divided between the two oldest. Carlie knew she was sadly lacking in that department. She'd never believed herself a complete equal in the triplet triangle, though she'd fight to the death to protect either of her sisters.

Once Dee had taken her place beside Carlie, the organ music swelled into the bride's processional. The congregation rose in unison and turned to watch as Sharla entered, escorted by her father. Bear, as he was affectionately called, looked big and burly and proud enough to pop his buttons.

A collective murmur of awe greeted the bride. Sharla looked like a storybook princess in her layers of silk on satin. Her gown had a high neckline, long lacy sleeves, a snug bodice and full, flowing skirts with an extended train. She'd chosen to wear a traditional veil, and Carlie's eyes began to water at the sight of her. She said a silent prayer that her sister's life would always be filled with love and happiness.

When Sharla reached the altar, she handed her bouquet to Dee, and all attention turned to the bride and groom. After a brief prayer, Bear placed his daughter's hand into Reed's, and then took his place beside his wife. Mama Belle, a true southern belle, dabbed her eyes with a hankie and smiled through a sheen of tears.

The exchange of vows was short, but Sharla and Reed's voices were strong and sure. The couple lit a unity candle and then returned to their positions before the altar while the organist played a special musical selection for them. More tears gathered in Carlie's eyes at the hauntingly beautiful words of the love song, Cherish. She couldn't imagine what it would be like to have the love of a man who would cherish her in such a way, but the melody and lyrics made her long for the impossible.

When the last notes had faded, there were more than a few sniffles to be heard in the chapel as the ceremony proceeded. Dee handed both bouquets to Carlie, then turned and placed her hand in Logan's. They quietly recited their marital vows, the depths of their commitment to each other unwavering.

By the end of another set of vows, it was all Carlie could do to hold back a racking sob. Her eyes swam with tears, turning the ceremony into a shimmering, surrealistic scene. She was truly happy for her sisters, yet she felt a deep, choking sense of loss. She wanted only happiness for them, yet today marked the end of an incredibly special relationship they'd shared for 25 years. Their lives were being forever altered, and she'd be so very much alone now. A giant fist clutched her heart, and she ached with loneliness even while surrounded by family and friends.

As the pastor introduced both couples to the congregation, a wave of applause shattered the solemnity of the moment, and Dee turned to her with a worried frown.

Too late, Carlie realized that Dee had sensed her emotional turmoil. Dee's extraordinary powers of perception made her intensely aware when her siblings were hurting. Carlie swiftly suppressed her own chaotic emotions and projected a rush of warmth and positive energy toward her sister.

"I love you," she whispered as she returned her sister's bouquet. Dee's expression relaxed into a satisfied smile and then a fierce hug. Carlie repeated the process with Sharla until everyone was ready to make the return trip down the aisle.

Reed and Sharla went first, followed more slowly by Dee and Logan. Then Carlie stepped forward to accept Michael's outstretched arm. She deliberately avoided looking him in the eyes. Her emotions were too raw, her nerves too frayed to cope with more complications right now. Judging by the zing of electrical current that skidded up her arm at the contact, Michael had just become a serious complication. Her heart raced at the thought. Her stomach muscles clenched as he pulled her close to his side. The heat of him warmed her flesh, and the scent of him filled her nostrils. Blood pounded heavily through her veins, but she credited it to her fragile emotions.

She didn't need this kind of aggravation, she insisted, silently scolding him as well as herself. She would not become another of Michael Trehearn's conquests just because he was between women or feeling dejected by Sharla's marriage. She had no intention of becoming the playmate of the month. She'd always had a special place in her heart for him, but she never doubted that he was a lady's man with a roving eye.

Her brief, disastrous marriage to his big brother had been a nightmare from beginning to end. Hadn't she learned her lesson the hard way about the Trehearn mentality? It didn't bear repeating. A shudder ripped through her at the thought, and she hardened herself to any involuntary responses.

Michael stretched out on the chaise lounge and crossed his arms behind his head. He studied the glistening water of the pool while he retraced the events of the evening. The wedding had gone well, the reception enjoyed by all. There'd been an abundance of food and a free-flowing fountain of champagne. The wedding party and guests had enjoyed every minute.

Belle had been in the height of glory; ever the gentile lady whose southern hospitality extended to one and all. Bear had been his usual good-natured self, doting on his wife and daughters. Who wouldn't? They were beautiful, intelligent and independent, yet utterly feminine.

All the newlyweds had seemed euphoric. Reed and Sharla would be gone for a month-long honeymoon to the south Pacific. A dream of a vacation that they both deserved. Logan and Darla planned to spend a week in Florida, and then return to their Kentucky home. They'd all been teeming with excitement. It had been after midnight before both couples had taken their leave.

Now it was nearing two a.m.. He'd been invited to spend the night at the Prescott mansion, but he was too restless to sleep. It wasn't hard to understand the source of his restlessness. Carlie. He'd badly miscalculated her reaction to his simmering need. He shouldn't have let her glimpse the depth of his desire, but seeing her walk down that aisle had sent his senses into overdrive. It had tapped into a gut-deep well of need, and his reaction had been fierce.

He wanted to kick himself for panicking her. She'd reacted just as he'd feared and had dodged him all evening. Even though he'd bullied her into sharing one dance, she'd kept herself rigid in his arms and chattered nervously about nothing. He'd spooked her but good.

He didn't blame her for being wary. He wasn't the least bit comfortable with the burning attraction he felt for her, either. He wished he could appease the hunger with another woman, any woman, but he knew better than that now. Sometimes he wished he'd never met her, never fallen in love with her, and never introduced her to Bill. Then he wouldn't have lost her to his brother, wouldn't have had to stand aside and watch him destroy her fragile confidence and her faith in men.

Water under the bridge, he thought, as he stared at the lights glittering just below the surface of the pool. He couldn't change the past. He had no desire to suffer through loving anyone again. But he desperately wanted to make love with Carlie, if for nothing else but to get her out of his system once and for all. She obviously didn't share his feelings or she wouldn't have given him the cold shoulder tonight.

Michael watched as the lighted windows of the mansion slowly went dark. The family had retired to their rooms earlier, but he'd decided to do a few laps in the pool. He needed to burn off some powerful physical frustration. As the balmy night air wafted over his damp body, his blood finally began to cool.

Then Carlie appeared, as though his longing had conjured her. She stepped from the darkened patio onto the pool deck. Bathed in moonlight, her blond hair, pale skin and blood-red dress became beacons of color against the night sky. Damn, but she looked hot in that red. Heat surged through him again in a rush of primitive hunger, warming his cooled flesh.

He was too deep in the shadows for her to see him, but his muscles went tight as he watched her move closer to the pool. She raised an arm and sipped at a flute of champagne. She'd been sipping all night, but he didn't know how much she'd actually had to drink. He'd never seen Carlie drunk, so he watched carefully for any reckless, telltale actions.

His gaze followed her movements as she tilted her head back and swallowed the last of her drink. The pale, creamy flesh of her neck and shoulders riveted his attention. He wanted his mouth on her long, slender throat; on the enticing cleavage of her breasts. He wanted his mouth and lips and tongue on every inch of her body, from head to toe. He swallowed hard, watching and wanting her with every fiber of his being. The need to touch and taste and sate himself in her was so intense that he shook with it.

After setting the empty flute on a nearby table, she lifted her arms and began to pull the pins from her upswept hairdo. Every nerve in Michael's body sprung to life. Pleasure warred with common sense. Part of him wanted to see her strip and dive into the water. Another part of him wondered if she'd had too much to drink.

Calm down, he mentally warned himself. Either way, he'd be close to offer protection. In the meantime, he'd just enjoy watching her every sexy move.

Hairpins fell to the concrete and Carlie slowly shook her head, loosening the heavy tresses until they swung to her shoulders. The blatantly sensual action sent the blood pooling in Michael's groin. The desire he'd kept in check for so long suddenly throbbed into a full-fledged erection. It strained against the thin covering of his boxers. He pressed a palm against it, but that didn't ease the aching need.

He continued to watch, mesmerized, as Carlie reached behind her for the zipper of her dress. A gentleman would have stopped her right then, but all thoughts of chivalry vanished as the silk slowly loosened, then drifted down her body, baring full, rounded breasts with fat, rosy nipples.

His breath got caught in his throat, his pulse throbbing in his loins as her gown slid past her narrow waist. It hitched briefly on rounded hips and he tensed even more. Then she did a gentle little shimmy that sent the dress downward and his blood pressure skyrocketing.

She stepped over the puddle of red silk and moved closer to the shallow steps of the pool. His gaze riveted on the soft sway of her breasts and heat surged through him like a lightning bolt. Then he glanced down to the tiny triangle of red cloth at the juncture of her thighs. The part of him that desperately hungered for its feminine counterpart strained against confinement, surging and throbbing with demand.

Tonight, she was his and only his. No more games. Forget the past and all the emotional baggage. He'd already waited an eternity, wanted for even longer. Tonight the wanting had become a desperation that transcended the physical. He'd make her want him. He intended to have her.

As she took the first step into ankle-deep water, he rose from his chair, alerting her to his presence. She halted, staring in his direction until he moved close enough for her to recognize him. He thought he saw her shiver, but she didn't make any attempt to cover herself. That alone convinced him she must have had too much to drink.

She stood proud and beautiful as he approached. "Michael."

His name sounded breathless and unbelievably sexy off her lips. It rolled over his body like a velvet kiss, making him tremble like the inexperienced teenager he'd been when they first met.

"Carlie." He returned her quiet greeting, his tone declaring a wealth of desire he no longer wanted to deny.

She glanced at the water, then back to him. "You've been swimming?"

He nodded, wanting to feast on the sight of her, but unable to drag his gaze from her delicate features. She searched his face and they stared at each other for a long, pregnant moment. Then she shifted her attention to his chest and lower. Michael felt his erection pulsate at the intensity of her perusal.

"The water's warm, but you've had a lot to drink," he cautioned.

She didn't argue the point. "I'm not going to swim. I'm just too keyed up to sleep, and I thought the water might help me relax." She took another step deeper, the water to her knees.

Michael stepped into the pool beside her. He went down all four steps until he was waist deep, then he reached out his arms for her. Carlie hesitated briefly, staring into his eyes for a long minute before she slowly slid into his embrace. His flesh was cool, and the warmth of her breasts seared him. Her nipples were hard and hot, poking him and sending fiery surges of sensation throughout his body.

The arms she clasped around his neck were soft, warm and supple. The feel of her body against his brought every nerve ending stinging to awareness. His legs trembled, and he knew he had to get a grip. He locked his arms around her waist, turned and sat down on a wide step, easing them slowly deeper. Then Carlie's soft thighs were straddling his lap, and he felt the heat of her body pressing against his arousal. He accepted her weight with a guttural moan of satisfaction.

"You're exquisite," he whispered roughly.

She hesitated briefly, and then seemed to come to a decision. "You say that to all the women." She chided, but didn't withdraw. Leaning forward, she began to nibble on his chin. His body sang with pleasure. She wasn't going to fight the attraction any more, and fire licked through him at the knowledge.

At first, her teeth nipped him with gentle reprimand, but then her lips began a tentative exploration of his cheeks and jaw. When she lapped at his skin with her tongue, Michael moaned. He closed his eyes as he savored the moist caress while denying her accusation.

"There are no other women."

She made a disbelieving sound, but he wasn't interested in squabbling with her. He had better things to do with his mouth; like scattering kisses along the smooth sweep of her jaw line, down her throat and across her neck. She smelled of roses, and he inhaled deeply, intoxicated by her scent. Her taste was as sweet and delicious as he'd known it would be. His heart nearly exploded in his chest when she captured his mouth with her own, offering him her tongue in a deep, exploratory kiss.

She tasted of champagne and forbidden fruit. She kissed him with uncharacteristic abandon, but he was too far gone to complain. He returned her kisses with swiftly mounting passion. He suspected she'd drowned her inhibitions with alcohol, but he didn't want to think about right or wrong or the possible consequences of making love to Carlie at her most vulnerable.

Michael knew she was hurting, even though she'd made a valiant attempt to play the swinging single tonight. Her safe little world had shattered with her sisters' wedding. He ached for her, but was glad something had finally forced her out of her safe little cocoon. She was emotionally and physically vulnerable, and he was too needy to resist for both of them.

"Trust me," he ground out against her mouth as they gasped for breath. "I swear I'll satisfy all that pent up desire," he promised, pressing hard little kisses against her lips before thrusting his tongue deeply into her mouth.

He wanted her with a desperation that superseded conscience and concern. He'd wanted too long, hungered too fiercely to rebuff the long-awaited fantasy. When she began to boldly suck his tongue, his body bucked, his hips arching upward to seek more of her heat.

Tightening his grip on her slim body, he clutched her closer. He wanted to hold her and kiss her for hours, but their bodies were both straining for deeper satisfaction. Dragging his mouth from the sweet seduction of hers, he leaned back slightly, pulling her further up his chest. Then he spread hot, hungry kisses across her neck and shoulders before lifting her high enough to target her breasts.

"Michael!" she cried out as he captured a taut, pouting nipple with his mouth and bathed the hard bud with his lips and tongue.

He loved the deep, throaty sound of his name on her lips; loved the way she moaned and arched her back to give him better access. He loved the way her hands locked in his hair, her fingers clutching and drawing him closer. He loved the ripe softness of her breasts and the diamond hard stiffness of each nipple as he teased and tasted.

The evidence of her arousal escalated his need to a fever pitch. His body was on fire, his erection throbbing with impatience, but he wanted so much more from her. He wanted to make sure she'd never forget his personal brand of satisfaction. He fought to contain his own desire while driving hers even higher. Sliding a hand over the curve of her hip, he let his fingers explore the softness of her thighs and then dipped them into her sexy panties.

The nipple in his mouth grew more taut. He felt her keening moan as it rumbled from deep in her throat. Fire scorched him everywhere their bodies touched, and he had to drag his mouth from her breasts long enough to draw in a calming breath. Fighting for control, he stroked the sensitive flesh beneath the damp silk until her grip on his hair grew painful. She rocked against him in feminine demand, and he increased the pressure and tempo of his caresses while sucking at her breast.

Her fire burned him, stroking his passion higher as he stroked her higher. When he felt her muscles start to contract, he tipped his head and watched her face as she reached the pinnacle. Her body shuddered, her grip on his hair relaxing as her features took on an expression of sublime satisfaction. His lungs contracted and a hard fist locked around his heart. She was the most incredible woman he'd ever known, and it humbled him to know he could not only arouse, but give her such pleasure.

Michael gathered her close as she went limp. She was all woman, all soft, shapely woman in his arms, trembling in the aftermath of release. He held her close and gently rubbed her back while she came down from the physical high. He adored her, but he wasn't fool enough to believe the physical satisfaction would lead to something more. It was enough right now to have breached some of her protective armor.

Carlie mumbled something against his chest. He couldn't make out the words, but he grumbled when she started to shift off his lap. Then he felt her hot mouth on his chest and eased his grip. In response, she found one of his nipples and tugged at it with her teeth, sending a shudder over him.

"Easy, sweetheart." His voice was gruff, his throat tight and his body strung taut. "I don't have any protection with me." As badly as he wanted to sink himself in her heat, he wouldn't take that kind of risk.

She either didn't hear his rough whisper or chose to ignore it. Sliding further down his body, she explored him by licking, sucking and kissing until he was a trembling mass of need. When she teased his naval with a stabbing tongue, Michael shifted restlessly. Throwing his head back, he stretched his arms behind him for support. He gazed at the star-studded sky and tried to concentrate on something besides her seductive caresses. His control hung by a thread, but he refused to embarrass himself by losing it.

Then she slid further into the shallow water, tugging his boxers down and freeing his straining erection. A strangled groan escaped his throat; his whole body clenching as she slid underwater and took him into her mouth. Her hair splayed and floated just on the surface of the water while her lips, teeth and tongue caressed him with arousing thoroughness. The contrast of cool water and feverish flesh sent waves of sensation washing over him. Too soon he lost the battle for control, his body convulsing in a rush of spine-tingling release.

For a few minutes, he couldn't think or breathe or so much as twitch a muscle.

He couldn't do anything but feel.

From somewhere he found the strength to reach out and drag Carlie up his trembling body. She crawled over his chest, leaving a trail of cool, wet kisses along the way. Then she buried her face in the crook of his neck while they both fought to control their staggered breathing.

"You're amazing," he whispered against the dampness of her hair. He smoothed some of the water from the thick tresses with one hand, but kept the other arm securely locked around her.

She made a noise of disagreement, but he shushed her. He wouldn't allow her to belittle herself. His brother had done a number on her confidence, but Michael thought she was perfect.

The air felt good against Michael's heated flesh, but as their bodies cooled, Carlie began to shiver. He wrapped her in his arms and held her tightly. When strength returned to his muscles, he pulled his legs from the water and slid up to the deck.

"How about an invitation to spend the night?" He murmured into her ear, hoping, while bracing himself for rejection.

"My room's warm and comfy," she replied huskily, nibbling on the vein in his throat.

Goosebumps that had nothing to do with the air shivered over Michael's body. His chest heaved in relief while his blood began to pump with renewed arousal. He wanted more. The next time they made love, he wanted it to be in a bed, with protection and the freedom to claim her in the most basic fashion. He wanted to make her a part of him. He wanted to be a part of her.

"Grab your dress," he suggested gruffly, rising to his feet and pulling Carlie with him. She swayed slightly when she leaned over to get her gown, and he quickly swept her into his arms. He moved toward the lounge chair and had her grab his tuxedo trousers, as well. She clutched their clothes, and he tightened his hold on her. For a long minute, they stared at each other, each searching, but wary. Then he carried her across the patio toward her private suite of rooms.

"Bathroom?" he asked once they'd entered her dark apartment.

Carlie tossed aside their clothes and pointed past the living room toward her bedroom. Michael carried her through both rooms to a small bathroom on the other side. She reached for a switch and bathed them in light. Surrounded by the scent and feel of her, he sucked in a deep breath and held her gaze. Relief washed through him at her calm expression. She didn't seem alarmed or annoyed by his actions, just oddly curious. Most importantly, she wasn't denouncing what they'd just shared. He knew she didn't think him capable of a serious relationship, but he wanted the chance to prove her wrong.

"How about a shower?" he asked, dropping a tender kiss on her lips.

She opened her mouth and invited him deeper, coaxing his tongue with the teasing flick of hers. He moaned, responding immediately; and thrust deeply to savor her taste and texture. He couldn't believe how fast she made his head spin and his blood boil. His desire, just sated, surged to life again. He wanted more, but was determined to take it slow and easy, to take pleasure in every second.

He broke off the kiss long enough to let Carlie slide down his body, and then he quickly adjusted the water taps before pulling her back into his arms for another kiss. Her body was a perfect fit against his, her breasts pressing against his chest, her hips nestling in the cradle of his thighs. She felt exquisite and tasted even better. They kissed, their desire steadily escalating as steam swirled around them like a lover's cloak.

"Shower," he muttered against her mouth, trying to check his passion before it raged completely out of control again.

In response, Carlie writhed against him in impatient feminine demand. She locked her mouth on his and kept her arms locked around his neck. They kissed, slow and long and deep, until they were forced to drag air into tortured lungs. In the next instant, he'd shed his boxers and rid her of the tiny panties.

Chest heaving, muscles clenched, Michael slid a hand under her rump and lifted her against him while he stepped into the shower stall. The spray pounded his back as he backed her against the wall, protecting her from the worst of the water's sting. He grabbed her hands and drew them over his shoulders, putting a little distance between them. Then he reached for some nearby shower gel and filled his hands.

He watched Carlie's expression as he smoothed the slick, soft soap over her cheeks and down her throat. Her eyes dilated when his hands cupped her breasts, weighing them in his palms. He kneaded the incredibly soft flesh, using this thumbs to tease the nipples while watching her features tauten with arousal.

"You like that?" His whisper was rough.

"Mmm . . . " she murmured, tipping her head backward and closing her eyes.

"Don't," he growled softly, insistently. He tugged at her nipples. "Don't shut me out. Let me see you."

Carlie lifted her long, spiky-wet eyelashes and stared directly into his eyes. His heart thudded in a heavy cadence. Heat and desire spiral between them like a rapidly escalating storm. Shifting to let the water wash the soap from her breasts, he went down on his knees to take a nipple into his mouth.

She trembled violently. Matching shudders racked his body. Rolling first one nipple and then the other with his tongue, he took his time adoring every feminine inch of her. He licked water from her navel and scattered kisses over her abdomen. When his caresses settled between her thighs, she made a harsh sound of excitement and dug her nails into shoulders.

"Michael! I've never. . . "

Deep, male satisfaction arced through him. Carlie was the only woman who'd ever made him feel savagely possessive and territorial. He'd nearly lost his mind when she married Bill. He'd learned to live with the fact, but he desperately wanted to give her something more special than she'd ever known.

He braced them both with his forearms bracketing her hips, and then shifted one of her legs over his shoulder, wanting to get even closer. She anchored herself with fists full of his hair while he adored her with his teeth and tongue until she quivered and moaned in satisfaction.

As her body went limp, Michael held her in his arms until she quieted again. He didn't think he'd ever tire of having her so close. She felt incredible.

When the water began to cool, he let go of her long enough to shut off the taps. Next, he treated them both to a slow towel drying with soft, fluffy towels. Carlie's damp hair had the look of dark gold. Her eyes glittered with a hazy, sensual pleasure. Her skin held a blushed, rosy glow that enticed him to touch and taste some more. Her lips looked so kiss-swollen and irresistible that he had to stop every few minutes and pamper them with his mouth.

The whole process had him rigidly aroused and needy long before he carried her back to the bedroom.

"Please tell me you have a condom stashed around here somewhere," he begged gruffly as he deposited her onto crisp cotton sheets.

Carlie smiled, then nodded toward the bedside stand. Michael left her long enough to switch on a small lamp.

"There are a couple in the top drawer, but they're old. I don't know how safe they are," she murmured.

He pulled open the drawer and ran a hand through the contents until he found the small packets. The familiar style and packaging had him stiffening. He shot a glance at the exquisitely naked woman stretched out in bed.

Keeping his tone carefully neutral, he asked, "How old are they?"

Her beautiful eyes stared directly into his, her expression slightly challenging. "They were Bill's."

Every muscle in Michael's body clenched with fury. Resentment raged through him with a force that shattered his breath, bombarding him with a rush of fierce, unexpected emotion. Jealousy, vicious and blinding, reared its ugly head and destroyed his arousal in one swift, electrifying jolt. He crushed the condoms in his fist, needing an outlet for his temper and feeling like ripping something to shreds. Then he strode to the bathroom and flushed them down the toilet. After taking some deep, harsh breaths, he mentally warned himself to get a grip. He lectured himself as he returned to the bedside, but the tremors still shook his body.

"That was stupid." Carlie whispered softly, her gaze raking him with gentle reprimand.

He agreed. Flushing the evidence of Bill's existence in her life wouldn't solve a thing. It only ensured that they couldn't make love tonight. He'd penalized himself, but his reaction had been prompted by emotion, not common sense. The thought of his brother making love to Carlie made him physically ill.

He clenched his hands into fists at his sides, wishing for something else to crush. Something to stem the flow of his frustration. "Stupid, but necessary."

"You can't change the past, Michael," she whispered, pulling a sheet over her slender body.

The action caused another surge of primitive emotion. He hated for her to put barriers of any kind between them, yet he knew better than to crawl into bed with her. He felt too raw, too needy, and too vulnerable. The desire to claim her in the most elemental fashion was too strong.

"I don't have to dwell on it, either."

"There's no need to feel intimidated by your big brother's legendary prowess," she mumbled, her eyelids drooping.

Michael stared at her in disbelief. He was trembling with frustration, and she was taunting him? Worse yet, she was conking out on him.

Carlie's body went completely slack, her voice fading as she drifted toward sleep. "It's no contest," she murmured. "You were incredible."

The softly spoken words were a balm to his badly bruised ego. Her compliment calmed him some until he remembered all the champagne she'd sipped throughout the evening. How much had she actually drunk? Was it just the alcohol talking? Had it been responsible for her feeling so incredible?

The thought had him clenching his teeth so hard his jaw threatened to snap. He paced across the room, snatched up his trousers, and shoved his legs into them with far more force than necessary. The hell with his wet boxers. He'd leave them as a reminder in case she tried to deny what they'd shared.

On Sunday afternoon, Carlie woke to her first experience with a hangover. She took aspirin, but they refused to stay on her stomach long enough to help. The pounding headache and bouts of dry heaves did little except keep her mind off Michael. At least for a few minutes of each hour. Despite parts of her body feeling battered by the effects of alcohol, other parts throbbed with the memory of his remarkable loving.

Bill might have a reputation as a great lover, but he couldn't hold a candle to his baby brother. All she'd ever shared with her ex-husband was fast, furious sex. Making love with Michael could very well have spoiled her for any other man. His sensitivity and slow, thorough loving had been incredible.

And she'd told him that. She vaguely remembered telling him he'd been incredible. A blush warmed her whole body every time she thought of it; of the intimacy. Michael had explored her from head to toe with a thoroughness that shocked, yet thrilled her. It had been a horrendous mistake to encourage him, yet Carlie knew she would always treasure the memory.

Once the bridal parties and guests had left the house last night, she'd felt more alone and bereft than she'd ever felt in her life, and that was saying a lot. Michael had filled the horrendous void. He'd filled the emptiness in her with enough passion to make her feel wanted and needed; alive and sexy and special.

She'd wanted more. She'd wanted to spend hours exploring his buff, gorgeous body. She loved the steely strength of muscles beneath firm, masculine flesh. She loved the way his masculine hardness coupled with her feminine softness. With the help of several glasses of champagne, she'd managed to ignore all the doubts and simply enjoy. She'd fantasized about abandoning herself to a man who knew how to treat a woman. Michael had certainly filled the bill. Though they hadn't actually had intercourse; they'd certainly made love.

He'd been her first and last one-night-stand, she mused, but he'd been a perfect one. With the wedding over, he'd disappear from their lives for a while. He'd followed in his brother's footsteps and become a commercial pilot, so his normal schedule kept him criss-crossing the country. She wouldn't have to worry about facing him any time soon. By the time he showed up again, Saturday night's events would be old history.

She'd gotten him out of her bed by gently bruising his ego. Now she just had to find a way to get him out of her mind.

Two

By Monday, Carlie had recovered from the stress of the wedding and the physical effects of too much champagne. She felt rested and ready to face her hectic schedule. As cargo hauler for the family air service, she'd been especially busy since the horror of September 11. Their customer base had tripled with people who didn't want to risk using the bigger airlines. Now that Sharla was honeymooning, they'd be more understaffed and overworked.

She showered quickly, wondering how long it would take to wipe out the memory of Michael sharing the same small space. The memory of his intimate seduction kept intruding on her thoughts; nagging her with too-vivid images and not-so-easily dismissed responses to those reminders. She actually ached with longing, a totally new and unwelcome circumstance for her.

A touch of makeup and a couple twists of the curling iron completed her morning ritual. She and her sisters had been blessed with thick, easily managed hair. Her's swung to her shoulders in a smooth curtain. As long as she kept it and the wispy bangs professionally trimmed, it didn't require much time or attention.

Within an hour of waking, she'd dressed in her standard one-piece jumpsuit and headed for the Prescott family airfield. There was just a nip of autumn in the air, and she inhaled deeply. The sun was already shining brightly, so they were in for another warm, brilliant day. Just the thought improved her spirits.

As she crossed the tarmac toward the main hanger, she caught glimpse of her dad deep in conversation with younger, slimmer dark haired man. A frown creased her brow. The second man had his back to her, but he was wearing the familiar Prescott flight suit. All the little hairs on her body began to tingle as the man slowly turned at her approach. Her stride slowed.

"Good morning, daughter," teased Bear. They had a long-standing joke about him not being able to tell the triplets apart, so he greeted them all as daughter.

Carlie stepped closer and gave her dad a kiss on the cheek. "Good morning, Daddy. She greeted the other man with wariness. "Michael." A slow heat coiled through her as his gaze lingered on her features. Her skin tingled with remembered sensations. She did her best to ignore the sensual jolt of facing him for the first time after what they'd shared.

"I thought you were long gone. Why the Prescott flight suit? Did the airline lose the rest of your luggage?"

Even before her dad could explain, a frisson of alarm started swirling through her body. Her eyes widened as she stared at Michael. His jaw tightened at her reaction.

"Mike's agreed to help us with the backlog of flights," explained Bear. "He's a godsend with business so hectic and Sharla gone."

Carlie withstood Michael's penetrating gaze without flinching, but the tension between them escalated another notch. She could tell that he wanted her to be happy to have him aboard. She wasn't.

"That's nice, but we're not in the same league as your commercial employer. There's no way we can match your regular pay or flexible schedule."

"I don't' have a regular pay," he explained coolly, his eyes watchful. " The airline laid off more than half their staff and the other half had a lot more seniority than me. I was facing the unemployment lines until Bear offered me a job."

Panic clutched at Carlie's throat, nearly strangling her. She fought to drag in air and deal with the unexpected shock. She knew they desperately need help, but the idea of working with him every day was just too much to handle. She'd thought he would conveniently disappear from her life. How in the world would she cope?

"Mike's going to fly Sharla's schedule with a mix of short charters and the big cargo plane since you prefer the smaller one. It won't be as big as he's used to handling, but it's close enough that he shouldn't have much trouble adjusting. He's getting ready to take it up, but I wanted you to tag along the first time," said Bear.

Carlie felt another instant of panic. She didn't want to be crammed in a cockpit with Michael. Not today, not ever. Her body was still too sensitive to the sight of him, the sound of his voice and the attraction that fairly sizzled between them even in the cold light of day.

"Don't I have my own flight scheduled this morning?" she demanded.

"Since you're early, you've got an hour or so. That's plenty of time to make sure Mike is comfortable with the cargo bus. We just finished the pre-flight check, so it's ready to roll."

Carlie licked her lips. She wanted to offer more arguments, but nothing sane or practical came to mind. Bear took their agreement for granted and headed back into the hangar, leaving them alone.

"I take it you're not too pleased to have me on staff," said Michael. "Had you hoped I'd disappear like a bad headache?"

More heat crept up her neck, and she had to shift her gaze from the intensity of his. Too easily, he read her thoughts. He was altogether too wise and knowing when it came to women and their reactions. She was woefully inept when it came to dealing with men, especially one as experienced as him. The disadvantage fueled her frustration.

"Saturday night was a mistake," she finally managed, though her voice lacked conviction. Turning, she strode toward the plane they needed to board, mumbling to him over her shoulder. "We were both a little too drunk and feeling especially needy. We gave in to temptation, but that's the beginning and end of it."

"Just for the record," he injected as he followed her across the tarmac. "I wasn't the least bit drunk. I knew exactly what I was doing every second I spent with you. We were dynamite together, and I'm not interested in brushing it off like it never happened."

Heat curled through Carlie like smoke, sneaking into every secret crevice. Her pulse quickened and so did her stride. His tone and words reached deep inside of her and she felt her senses responding to the husky reminder of what they'd shared. Her hands grew damp, the rest of her body flushed with arousal.

This wouldn't do. Not at all. She couldn't work with him and get aroused every time he spoke to her. There had to be a way to call a halt to the situation before it got too far out of hand. She had to find a way to get their relationship back on a strictly platonic level.

"You've met the challenge, Michael, and came out ahead. You got what you wanted and now the game's over," she insisted as she stopped and stared directly into his handsome face. "I've never been anything more than a trophy in your ongoing rivalry with Bill. You're both too self-centered to give a damn about what I really want, and I'm taking myself out of the competition. I'm not playing anymore."

For an instant, he seemed too shocked to respond. Carlie turned and started to climb into the passenger side of the cockpit, but Michael grabbed her and whirled her around to face him again. She felt the anger coursing from his body to hers, and felt a brief instant of panic. Then she stiffened her spine. No man would ever physically intimidate her again.

"You are way off base, lady." His tone was a dangerously low growl. She shifted from his touch, relieved when he didn't try to overpower her.

"Don't throw my brother or his inadequacies in my face, and don't think I'll let you wedge him between us. I was interested long before you met Bill. You're the one who created the competition."

She couldn't believe he had the nerve to chastise her after all this time. He hadn't done or said anything to keep her from marrying Bill. He'd seemed almost happy to be rid of her. "You're saying I'm at fault for picking the wrong brother?"

"It sure as hell wasn't my decision," he snapped.

"You sure as hell didn't challenge it then."

"What should I have done? Grovel? When you were all dewy eyed and panting after the older, more experienced brother?"

Carlie gasped at the insult, even though it held some truth. She wanted to argue that she hadn't been ridiculously stupid, but they both knew better. Much to her shame, she'd been head over heels in lust with Bill; his looks, his charm and his reputation. She'd been in love with the idea of marrying the superman she'd thought him to be. It embarrassed her to remember how naively ignorant she'd been.

"His sexual prowess had nothing to do with it."

"Sure. That's why you never gave me a second thought after I introduced the two of you. The hell with competition. There was none."

Carlie blushed because she knew he was right. She'd treated him badly back then, but she'd never realized he held a grudge. He'd always offered her friendship and respect, if distantly. It hurt to learn the truth; that he harbored such negative feelings toward her all these years.

"So Saturday night was your chance to get even?" she asked, hoping he'd attribute the tremor in her voice to anger. "Instead of being a trophy, I offered a little vengeance?"

Michael glared at her and swore viciously. She took a step backward. Never having been the receiving end of his temper, she wasn't sure what to expect. His brother hadn't hesitated at physical abuse.

Noting her reaction, Michael reached out a hand, which she quickly dodged. His expression turned even more grim.

"I don't hit women," he snarled.

"I'm glad to hear it," she whispered. Her throat clogged with emotion as lingering fear, regret, and frustration churned inside of her.

She couldn't know what she looked like at that minute, but either her tone or her expression drained the anger from Michael. He turned, raked a hand through his hair and sighed deeply. When he confronted her again, his features were a mask of control.

"I am not my brother," he said, enunciating each word slowly and carefully. "I may not be Mr. Perfect and I have my own faults, but I won't be held responsible for his weaknesses. I've never hit a woman in my life. I'm not the womanizer you think I am, and I'm not competing with him for anything. Got that? Nothing. What's between you and me is strictly between you and me. He has nothing to do with it."

"Then why did you get so angry when you found his condoms?" she asked in a wary whisper.

Michael dragged his hand through his hair again. Carlie watched the thick, inky waves part and then curl back into natural order. Her fingers tingled with remembered sensation, but she shoved aside the memory.

He didn't look at her when he replied. "Because I was as jealous as hell, okay? It didn't matter whether they belonged to Bill or some other man."

Bill had been the jealous sort, too. He hadn't loved her, but he'd considered her his personal possession. If another man flirted with her or showed too much interest, he'd been livid. He'd blamed her and directed his anger at her. Michael had taken his anger out on the condoms, but she had to wonder if she'd take the brunt once he tired of smashing inanimate objects.

"So the anger had nothing to do with your brother?"

"Only by bringing him between us when that's the last thing I wanted," he said, facing her again.

Carlie took a slow, deep breath. She needed to get some control over her haywire hormones and try to think more clearly. There was no doubt about Prescott's need for another pilot and Michael was more than qualified. If they were going to work together, they had to find a way to get past their personal problems and reestablish a nonphysical relationship. She needed to get tough and professional, but she heard herself saying:

"You could have used the condoms to wipe him completely out of our lives."

He stared at her for a long moment, gauging her seriousness. "If I believed that for a minute, I'd tear up the plumbing and salvage the damn things."

The fierce sincerity of his comment brought a genuine smile. She offered it to him in the way of an olive branch. "I don't know how effective they'd be after a dip in the sewer."

His expression softened, too, and a humorous gleam entered his eyes. "You were passing out on me anyway."

"I was not."

"Yes you were. You did."

Carlie lifted a haughty brow, knowing he was right yet refusing to let him win the verbal battle. "Are you going to fly this thing today or not?" She turned toward the cockpit, but Michael stilled her again with a touch on the arm. His expression had gone from light to darkly intense again in the span of seconds. It took her a moment to absorb the change. Then she understood with his next question.

"Are you still in love with him?"

Her heart thudded at the intimacy of his query. She didn't love Bill. What she'd felt had been lust and a big dose of hero worship. He'd quickly taught her the folly of thinking him a hero, but she didn't want to admit that. She didn't want to encourage Michael, nor would she lie to him. It was hard to know how to respond.

Her hesitation made his expression go grim again.

She'd planned to alienate his affections, but perversely didn't want anyone to think she still had feelings for her ex-husband. "Our marriage is history. It has been for years."

His tone didn't soften. "That's not what I asked."

"I'm not in love with anyone," she finally snapped with impatience, wondering why she felt guilty about angering him. It wasn't her job to keep him happy or make him privy to her innermost emotions. "I don't want or need a man in my life. I tried to make that clear, but you deliberately ignored me. It's not my fault if you don't like what you discover."

"Oh, I like what I discovered, all right," he insinuated smoothly.

"Right up to the part where I found the condoms and you passed out. Maybe we should just forget that part and pick up where we left off in the bathroom."

Carlie's breathing faltered at the reminder. "Maybe we'd better get to work if we're going to get anything done today." She turned abruptly and climbed the ramp into the plane. Michael followed, brought the ramp into the belly of the plane and secured it. In a matter of moments, she'd settled into the co-pilot's seat, and he'd taken the controls.

The flight was brief but tension-filled. She tried to concentrate on the brilliant blue sky, the beautiful patchwork world beneath them and the functioning of the plane, but her concentration shattered every time she glanced at Michael. His hands fascinated her, so confidant, so strong and sure. He asked an occasional question, but his attention never wavered from the job.

This was an aspect of his life that she'd never really considered. She'd known him as a high school pal, a flirtatious rogue, and a teasing brother-in-law. Saturday night, she'd gotten a sample of him as a lover, but she really didn't know much about the man beneath the charming façade.

His piloting skills were exemplary. It didn't surprise her that he was certified to fly a variety of aircraft. He seemed as comfortable with the controls as Sharla, and she was one of the best. Sharla's natural affinity with planes was rare, but Michael had the same extraordinary connection with the aircraft.

She assumed he'd become a pilot to follow in Bill's footsteps because they'd always been so competitive. She'd never given him credit for being a talented professional in his own right. Nobody could be as accomplished without dedication and a passion for their work. It offered new insights to his character. He was an intriguing, complex man. One she realized she didn't know at all.

Carlie knew her own skills were competent, but not exceptional. That's why she preferred piloting cargo rather than people. She didn't want the responsibility of passenger's lives in her hands. It made her all the more awed by Michael's ease in handling the plane. By the time he brought them back to the airstrip, she knew the commercial airline's loss was Prescott's gain. Despite the emotional upheaval he'd caused her, he'd be an asset to their staff.

Once they'd touched down and unfastened their belts, he turned to her, his expression solemn.

"Did I pass inspection?"

Carlie dropped her gaze to the earphones in her hands. "I don't have Dee's teaching skills, but I'd say you passed with flying colors."

"So you don't mind if I work for the family?" he asked, lifting her chin with a gentle finger and forcing her to look directly at him.

"We badly need help. Bear's licensed, but his health isn't great."

"That's not what I asked. You have a habit of dodging direct answers to my questions."

He was pushing again. Forcing her to verbalize her feelings and impressions. He didn't want her hedging. Wouldn't allow her to hide behind her safe little wall of detachment.

The tension shimmered around them, adding to the heat of the small cockpit. "You're a good pilot and an asset to any company. I'll be happy to have you aboard as long as we don't confuse our professional lives with our personal ones."

His eyes were the most incredible blue, she mused, a rich shade that rivaled the clear blue of the sky. The color seemed to deepen while she stared into their beautiful depths.

"I know how to separate my professional and private lives. I'm willing to keep things in perspective if you're willing to admit we have a very personal relationship. Not just a one-night-stand to be forgotten," he insisted gruffly.

Carlie cursed the blush that swept over her neck and cheeks. She dropped her lashes to conceal her eyes and hoped he couldn't feel the tremor passing through her. Too easily, he'd guessed her intentions. She wanted to deny it. She wanted to pretend nothing had changed between them, but it was impossible. Especially with her body quivering at his touch.

"I think we'd be wise to forget Saturday night."

"Do you?" he asked softly, huskily.

He drew her close and brushed his lips across her mouth. It was the lightest of caresses, but they both trembled at the contact.

"I think you're lying to yourself if you believe we can ignore this," he said, his warm breath mingling with hers.

"Exploring it can only lead to trouble," she warned. "And I can't handle the distraction while I'm working."

Michael leaned back and gave her some room. "Agreed," he said, his tone still a little rough, but firm. "We keep it strictly professional here at the airfield."

And everywhere else? She wondered, but didn't ask.

He answered for her. "Tonight, I volunteer to cook dinner. It's time we got to know each other again. How about you come to my place?"

Carlie was torn between desire and wariness, but desire won. "What are you cooking and where is your place?"

He grinned, a totally male, totally devastating grin that deepened the grooves in his chiseled cheekbones. "I'm grilling steak, and I'm your next door neighbor."

She frowned. There weren't any hotels or apartments within miles of the Prescott's plantation home. None of their neighbors were likely to take in renters. "Neighbor?" she challenged.

"Your parents offered me Dee's apartment until I can sell my condo and find a place near here."

Her breath caught in her throat. Not only was he working for the family, but he'd moved into their house. She and her sisters had separate apartments within the sprawling old mansion. They were on the opposite side from her parent's living quarters, but nestled side by side. Michael's temporary quarters adjoined hers.

When Carlie returned home later in the evening, dusk was falling. It had been a long day. She hadn't seen Michael since they parted earlier in the morning, but she'd gotten a report about his progress. He'd handled Sharla's schedule without a hitch. Her mother and dad were immensely relieved. She wanted to berate them about making all the arrangements without consulting her, but knew her complaints would seem petty.

Her parents didn't know that her brotherly affection for Michael had undergone a drastic change. To what, she wasn't even sure herself. All she knew was that her body throbbed with warmth whenever she thought of him. He'd offered her a world of sensuality that she badly wanted to explore. She'd decided to turn over a new leaf, throw caution to the wind and take pleasure where she could find it. The hell with being sensible and celibate.

By the time she'd showered and changed, her body was humming with anticipation. She'd convinced herself to enjoy his sexual offerings without worrying about deeper commitment. Michael wasn't looking for long-term relationships, so she didn't have to concern herself with that. There was no reason they couldn't share a flaming affair for as long as it suited them both.

The smell of charcoal finally drew Carlie to the enclosed patio that extended along the entire west side of the house. She stepped into the muted shadows of Japanese lanterns, and slowly approached Michael. He stood at the grill, looking casually elegant in tan slacks and a white knit shirt that highlighted his dark complexion. Her heart stuttered as he lifted his head and greeted her with a slow smile.

His voice was low and warm with welcome. "Hey there, neighbor."

Carlie gave him a smile. "Hey there, yourself. The smell of the grill has my stomach growling."

"You're too easy. I just started the steaks."

"Doesn't matter. I'm starving, and I like mine medium rare, please. What else is on the menu?"

Michael's deep chuckle rippled over her like a caress. She stepped out of the shadows and into the brighter light at his end of the patio. Then she took a minute to absorb the sight of him. His hair glistened from a recent shower, looking blue-black with just enough wave to make her fingers itch. His handsome face and welcoming expression made her heart flutter with increased excitement.

"Don't be shy," he teased, slapping the meat on the grill. "I know you're only here for the free food."

"I confessed that I'm starving."

"It's pretty simple fare. Some rolls fresh from the bakery, a little cheese, wine and steak."

"Sounds a whole lot better than microwave pizza."

He grimaced, and she laughed.

"Anything I can do to help?"

"You could pour us some wine. There's not much else to do. The steaks will be ready in a couple minutes."

Carlie entered the small kitchenette of Dee's apartment and poured chilled wine for each of them, then carried it back to the patio. She held a glass out to Michael. He captured her wrist, lifting her arm along with the drink and pressing a kiss against her skin before taking a sip of wine. The brief caress sent a tingle of awareness coursing through the rest of her body. Her heart began to pound heavily in her chest as the blood sang through her veins.

Their gazes met and locked. Carlie recognized the taut hunger in his features because she felt it in every pore of her body. For a long moment, all they could do was stare at each other with a need that seemed to intensify with every heartbeat. She told herself that the craving was perfectly natural. They were two healthy adults who knew what they wanted, and there was no reason to deny it.

"You're looking especially beautiful tonight," Michael said, sipping wine but keeping his attention focused on her.

Normally, Carlie would have made some disparaging remark about her looks, but not this time. Nor did she worry about how often he might pay the same compliment to other women. He made her feel beautiful, so she basked in the warmth of his flattery.

"Thank you." She'd worn a aqua patterned sundress with a peasant neckline and a flowing skirt that fell to her ankles. It wasn't fancy, but the soft silk fabric made her feel feminine and sexy.

"I suppose you know how well that color suits you," he said.

She laughed and shook her head. "I wouldn't have given it that much thought, but I'm sure Mother did. It was a gift from her. She loves to shop and swears her daughters are missing some elemental female gene because none of us likes to. I'm not crazy about all her choices, but nothing she buys could ever be considered inappropriate."

"Belle's a woman of excellent taste, no doubt about it," he teased. "But just for the record, I don't think you're lacking anything in the feminine department."

The low timbre of his voice sent another quiver over Carlie. She gave him a demure thank you and dropped her lashes to conceal her eyes. Too easily, he made her head spin, her flesh tingle and her pulse quicken. Not with his compliments, but with the deep sincerity of his tone. She didn't how often he used the seductive tactic; it was incredibly effective on her.

"I think our steak has reached the medium rare stage. It's not oozing anymore. Are you ready to eat?"

"Absolutely. It smells great."

Michael dished up the meat and they moved to the tiny table in the kitchen. The place settings were laid out and the rest of the food ready to eat. A cinnamon scented candle added an erotic fragrance and romantic glow to the room. They ate slowly, enjoying the meal and a compatible talk about their busy day.

Everything tasted delicious. Carlie couldn't remember ever enjoying a simple meal so much. The years fell away as they reestablished a rapport that had been stifled for too long. She'd forgotten what good company Michael could be and how much they had in common. They'd always enjoyed similar books, movies and pastimes. They argued about a few political issues and favorite sports teams, but it was good-natured bickering. Conversation flowed as freely as the wine until she was feeling relaxed and replete.

"You cooked, so I guess I should offer to clean," she teased, giving him a slow, lazy smile.

"Forget the dishes," he insisted, rising from the table and taking her hand. "I'd rather have you in my arms."

The warmth and strength of his grasp sent a current of electricity through her body that heated her blood. He led her into the living room, and she expected him to continue to the bedroom, but he stopped in front of the entertainment center. After switching on the stereo, the room filled with haunting melody that quickly seeped into her body. Then Michael pulled her more fully into his arms.

Carlie sighed with pleasure as she was pressed against him from chest to thighs. He was hard and warm and so very male. She immediately felt the hard ridge of his erection and nestled closer. Her breasts, already full and sensitive, grew tight with need. Her nipples puckered, spearing him in silent, feminine demand.

"Damn, you feel good," he whispered, the heat of his breath teasing her ear as he pulled her even closer. He rocked his hips deeper into the cradle of her thighs.

She didn't comment, but wrapped her arms tightly around his neck and let him lead her around the room in a slow, hypnotic circle. Their bodies swayed as one, every tiny move heightening the sexual tension to an almost unbearable level. Every inch of her body was alive with sensation and throbbing in anticipation. She wanted more of the kind of loving he'd offered her on Saturday. Lots more.

It might be foolish to crave such total abandonment. It was out of character for her, but she was way past the point of protest. Her body hummed with an excitement that this man had created and only he could appease.

She made a small sound of protest as he dragged her arms from his neck, but she snuggled closer when he shifted them to his waist. The new position gave him free access to her throat and shoulders. He took advantage by scattering hot, open-mouthed kisses over her bare flesh. Carlie moaned and tilted her head backward, feeling her skin sizzle with sensation. In response, he slid the neckline of her dress down her arms, baring her breasts to his ravenous mouth.

The music continued to flow around them, but their dancing became a whole new kind of erotic mating ritual. Her hands slipped further down his body to grasp his tight buttocks. As he sucked one nipple deeply into his mouth, she arched her back and mewed with pleasure. She clutched him closer, rubbing herself against the evidence of his arousal, straining toward the part of him she most desperately wanted.

"Carlie!"

His hoarse cry excited her beyond belief. She slid her hand between their bodies and fumbled for his zipper. Suddenly impatient to complete their union, she struggled to release his straining flesh.

"Protection," he reminded gruffly. He reached into his pocket and handed her a packet before carrying her to the nearest chair. He sat down with her straddling his lap.

Carlie managed to secure the condom, thrilling at the deep masculine groan her gentle fondling produced. Then his hands were sliding up her thighs, lifting her dress and making her forget everything but his touch.

"Kiss me," he begged.

She took his mouth with a ferocity that surprised them both. The kiss was hard and demanding and fiercely passionate. They took turns sucking tongues and dueling with each other for deeper, stronger contact. Their bodies trembled with desire until Michael shoved aside the last barrier between them and impaled her on his straining flesh. A mutual groan rumbled from their chests as their bodies bonded in the most elemental fashion. For just an instant, they stilled, mouths parting to drag in air, their bodies adjusting to the intimate coupling.

Chests heaving and limbs trembling, they stared into each other's eyes. She licked her lips and that seemed to snap Michael's control. His hands tightened at her hips, his body bucking with impatience. She gave him a smile, dropped her mouth to his for another deep, wet kiss and began to rock against him in agonizingly slow movements.

He allowed her to maintain control until she trembled on the verge of release. Then he gripped her hard, thrusting faster until they both careened over the edge.

Carlie cried out his name as pleasure spiraled upward through her body, tightening her lungs, her breasts, her nipples; and downward, stiffening her legs and curling her toes. Then all the strength flowed from her limbs, and she collapsed against his chest. He hugged her close as their bodies shuddered with pleasure.

The scents, sounds and feel of their loving were indelibly recorded in her memory in the following minutes while they struggled for air. Michael's fingers tangled in her hair, gentle and caressing. He pulled her still close and nuzzled her neck, then whispered in her ear. "Thank you."

The husky earnestness of his tone melted away more of her emotional armor. For years, her heart had been a tight little rosebud, protected by layers of invisible barriers. Now the petals were gradually opening to allow him closer. She buried her face against the dampness of his throat and murmured her contentment.

"This isn't exactly what I had planned." He continued to whisper in her ear.

"Is that a complaint?" she challenged softly.

She felt as well as heard his chuckle. "No complaints from me, lady." He splayed a hand at her back and stroked her spine. "I just wanted everything to be perfect. I wanted to wine and dine and dance."

"We did that."

He went on without acknowledging the comment. "I wanted to woo you into my bed, not drag you to a chair and ravish you."

Carlie smiled to herself and wiggled in his lap. The strength was beginning to return to her body, and she felt a renewed surge of desire. Her hands were flat against his chest, so she began to pluck at his nipples while locking her mouth on his neck. When she sucked hard and strong, he began to harden, too.

"This isn't safe," he growled, his tone low and intimate.

"Then you'd better woo me to your bed," she admonished.

His arms tightened around her and he began to move, but they were startled to stillness by the sudden ringing of the phone. On the table to the right of the chair, it was way too close and too loud to ignore.

Michael swore, and Carlie chuckled.

"Let your machine answer," she teased, nibbling on his lips.

He grumbled, returning her kisses until his outgoing message was played and a similar masculine voice responded.

"Mike, it's Bill. If you're there, pick up the phone."

At the sound of her ex-husband's voice, an involuntary shudder coursed through Carlie. His intrusion was like being doused with ice water after soaking in the sun. The shock was both physical as well as emotional, making her want to withdraw into a protective mode. She would have climbed off Michael's lap, but he held her tight and punched the button.

"What's up?" he asked, his voice none-too-welcoming.

His brother's reply wasn't much warmer. "Have you got me on a damned speaker phone? Pick up the receiver."

Bill's arrogance never failed to amaze her. It was just like him to demand instead of requesting, she thought, but she didn't comment. Nor did she relax.

"My hands are occupied," Michael told him. His fingers caressed her hips, but his arms held her tight enough to prevent her from moving off his lap. "Either talk this way or call back later."

Bill groused, but continued. "I'm calling about Mom and Dad's anniversary. Their fiftieth is coming up at the end of October, and we're throwing a dinner party. Just family and a few close friends, but I wanted to make sure you'd be there."

Carlie felt Michael's stare and looked into his eyes. She didn't know what he was searching for, but she kept her expression carefully guarded

"I just started a new job and the schedule is tight, but I'll see what I can do."

"That's why I called," Bill insisted impatiently. "So that you can clear your schedule. I can't believe you went to work for Prescotts. Hell, there are dozens of other opportunities for a pilot of your caliber. I know things are tough right now, but I'm calling in favors to line up interviews for you."

"Don't' bother. I don't have any plans to look elsewhere," said Michael, his tone taking on a hard edge that warned the decision wasn't open to discussion.

Bill wisely dropped the subject, but Carlie assumed it was a sore one for his whole family. They would hate having Michael work for the enemy. She could hardly believe it herself.

"I'll see you in a few weeks. Don't disappoint Mom and Dad."

The connection was abruptly severed, and Carlie felt the tension radiating from Michael. This time when she moved, he didn't attempt to stop her. She rose, stepping away from the chair while she tugged her dress back into place. He rose more slowly, and then excused himself for a few minutes. By the time he returned from the bathroom, she was ready to leave.

"It's getting late," she said. "We both have a busy day tomorrow, so I'd better get back to my own room."

He studied her expression for a few minutes, and then said, "Go with me."

She didn't immediately understand, but when his invitation registered, her mouth dropped opened in shock. "You mean to your parents house? For their anniversary? You have to be joking."

His jaw went taut. "I'm not joking. I want you to go."

"Why? You know I'll never be welcomed by Bill or the rest of his family."

"They're my family, too."

"Do you think I've forgotten that for even a minute?" she insisted, becoming immediately defensive. " It's the same family that blames me for not being good enough for their first born, that blames me for the only divorce in Trehearn history. The same one that blames me for having him arrested on assault charges. Which was another unpleasant first for the family."

"Their attitudes have changed," he defended. "Especially since Bill attacked you. Mom and Dad went to counseling with him and they understand better now. They'd like a chance to make things right."

Carlie was shaking her head, refusing to believe it. His parents heralded from a long line of social snobs. They could trace their roots back to the Mayflower, and they'd never forgiven her for not being the perfect, malleable wife. Even if they were willing to forgive and forget, she wasn't sure she could. They'd made her life pure hell during her short marriage. Her self-esteem had been brutally damaged.

"It won't work, Michael. We're fools to even flirt with the idea. There's just too much emotional baggage, and there's no way we can ever have a serious, long-term relationship."

He flinched as though her words struck him a physical blow. She'd never seen his expression more grim. His jaw was rigid, his mouth a tight, disapproving line. He glared at her with narrowed, challenging eyes.

"Then what would you call tonight?" he wanted to know, his tone angry and demanding. " Just a game? A casual fling? You think either of us can walk away from it? If you can, you're a helluva lot stronger person that I am."

"It's just sex," she issued the edict she'd been repeating to herself for days. "We're two healthy adults with normal physical desires. There's no reason we can't enjoy each other's company without strings."

"In other words, I'm good enough to relieve your frustration, but not good enough to warrant any other type of commitment. That's what you're saying?"

Carlie felt all the color drain from her face. Put that way, her little edict did sound petty, selfish and really horrible. "You're saying you want more?" The idea sent panic scurrying along her nerves. "Why? Men are supposed to love relationships with no strings attached."

Michael raked all his fingers through his hair in frustration, turning his back to her. He paced the small living room. "Hell, I don't know what I want, except that I don't want you constantly comparing me to my brother. I don't want you measuring our relationship by the bad experience with him."

"I don't know if I can measure any relationship without taking that into consideration," she said, her tone soft, but insistent. "It's too much a part of me. If I haven't learned from my mistakes, then what's to prevent me from repeating them?"

Michael faced her again. "I don't know, either," he said. "But I don't like being labeled a mistake waiting to happen."

It wasn't fair, of course. She knew that. But one lesson she'd learned well was that life wasn't always fair.

*T*he next few days passed in a whir of activity. Their schedules were so heavy there was little time for anything but work from dawn to dusk. As soon as one charter was completed, they took short breaks and headed out on the next. Carlie rarely saw Michael at the airfield because they came and went at different times. When their paths did cross, they were polite, but distant, each still licking the newly inflicted wounds.

Meanwhile, Carlie was hurting. She wished she could crawl back into her protective armor, but it wasn't that easy. Michael had destroyed her defenses and exposed her needy heart. She just didn't know how to deal with all the confusion he'd uncovered. He'd eased the terrible loneliness, made her feel beautiful and desirable, but left her feeling more vulnerable than she'd felt in years.

She wanted a chance to explore their attraction, yet she didn't know if what she wanted was emotional or just physical. Her body craved his touch. The ache was all too real and all too fierce. Was she asking for more heartache by even considering a serious relationship?

Her thoughts were filled with him, but she didn't know how to make amends without making a fool of herself. She needed to apologize. In blaming him for his family's problems, she'd been as guilty as them, placing blame on the person with the least control of the situation.

Her job was the only thing that saved her sanity. Bear hired two part-time pilots to help with the workload, but her flights were demanding until they gained some experience. The schedule eventually eased, but she still went home ready to collapse each evening. A combination of work, worry and emotional turmoil added to her exhaustion. Most nights, she settled for a microwavable dinner, a shower and bed. On good nights, she'd fall to sleep without restlessness or dreams.

Three

On the following Saturday evening, Michael showered, towel-dried, and ran a comb through his hair. He pulled on a pair of jeans, not bothering with briefs or even the zipper. The only thing he needed was the condom tucked in his back pocket. Another week had passed, and Carlie still hadn't come to him. Tired of waiting, he was going to her. There wasn't an inch of his body that didn't ache for her. He went to bed each night and woke up each morning with an ache that wouldn't subside. It wasn't just physical, but the deep, burning ache of a man who yearned for his woman.

He loved her. Maybe he'd never stopped loving Carlie. He'd buried those feelings when she married Bill, swearing it was one area where they wouldn't compete. He'd spent too much time in his big brother's shadow, too much time trying to live up to his image, and he refused to let the competition extend to his intimate relationships.

But his love for Carlie wasn't the sort that had faded with time. It just simmered on a back burner of his emotions until he'd touched her again: Until he'd made love to her and felt her come apart in his arms.

He loved her eyes, her smile and her innocent charm. Bill had nearly destroyed all the innocence and optimism, but he'd caught a glimpse of it during their dinner. The evening they'd shared had brought all his latent feelings to the surface, making him want more from their relationship than he had a right to expect. His family, most especially his brother, had caused her more pain and hardship than any woman should have to suffer. He badly wanted to make it up to her.

Heading through the apartment, he plucked a bottle of wine from refrigerator and continued out the door and across the patio. A light shone through the curtains of Carlie's French doors. For just a few minutes, he watched her silhouette moving around the room. It only took an outline of her body to make his body come alive with awareness. Muscles clenched and nerves strung tighter, but he kept his knock light and undemanding.

His breath hitched when she pulled back the curtain and opened the sliding door. Freshly showered, she looked dewy and sweet and dressed for sin. Red silk. The outfit was sheer fantasy material, exposing bare, slim shoulders and arms and a to-die-for length of trim, gorgeous legs. The skimpy top had narrow straps and was barely long enough to cover her midriff. The pajama bottoms looked more like men's boxer shorts, yet there was nothing masculine about the thighs they encased.

Michael's body reacted in a purely masculine fashion. At risk of dislodging his jeans, he propped a hip against the door jam and waved the bottle of wine. If she kept studying him with her warm, turquoise eyes, he'd really be in trouble.

"Are you lost?" she asked quietly, her gaze tangling with his. He felt it warm him all the way to his toes.

"No. It's just too lonesome down there by myself."

Carlie was slow to reply, and he held his breath, his heart thundering in his chest.

"It's pretty lonesome here, too," she whispered.

The blood drummed in his ears and pooled in his groin. He allowed himself to breathe again. Maybe she'd missed him, too.

"Want to be lonesome together?"

She silently deliberated for a heart-stopping minute, then stepped aside and waved him in. The action tightened the silk across her chest, the soft fabric outlining the plump mounds of her breasts. Mesmerized, he stared at them in fascination until the nipples beaded. Now his blood roiled through his veins and pulsed in his erection. His jeans slid precariously lower as he stepped into her apartment.

Carlie closed the door and drew the blinds. Then she took the bottle from his hand and placed it on the table. Without another word, she curled a finger into one of his belt loops and tugged him into her bedroom.

Michael didn't offer any resistance. His pulse was pounding in his ears with a deafening roar; blocking out everything but the sight, scent and feel of his lady as she rid him of his jeans. Her touch soon had him trembling. It was incredibly soft, making him incredibly hard. His knees went weak.

When he could no longer stand her gentle assistance, he lifted her onto the bed and stretched out beside her. Then he enjoyed the pleasure of sliding the silk pajamas from her satin-smooth body. Her skin was softer than the silk. He wanted to touch and feel and taste every inch, so he didn't waste any time.

His mouth found a pouting nipple and he lapped at it with his tongue. When it beaded, a shaft of desire shot through him, and he sucked softly on the tight knot of flesh. Her responsiveness fueled his hunger until he was sucking more greedily. Carlie's soft moans urged him to bring the other nipple to matching attention. Her hands stroked his hair and then his shoulders; her touch growing increasingly restless.

Her body began to undulate slowly against his in feminine demand that quickly threatened his control. No other woman had ever challenged his control the way she did. The smell, feel and taste of her shot his good intentions all to hell. He promised himself to go slower the next time. But first, he needed to stake a claim. A very personal, intimate claim.

He slid over her body, settling into the cradle of her thighs as she eagerly made room for him. Then he plunged his tongue into her mouth at the same time he plunged into her welcoming heat. Her moans echoed his, and he knew there'd never be a greater satisfaction than making love with Carlie.

*F*or the next few weeks, they continued to work together in the daytime and sleep together at night. Sometimes they slept in her bed and sometimes in his, but always in each other's arms. Their need for each other grew deeper even though Carlie was afraid to trust her feelings. Her belief in happily-ever-afters had been destroyed at an early age. She couldn't trust her instincts, so she didn't expect the relationship to last. She feared Michael would tire of her, just as Bill had done. It wasn't fair to compare the two brothers, yet she didn't know how to stop.

She'd felt the same strong desire for Bill in the early weeks of their marriage. Their physical relationship hadn't been nearly as satisfying, but she'd been much younger and less mature back then. She'd thought their love would survive long-term, yet she'd been wrong. How could she trust her instincts now? How could she ever be sure?

Bill had called her juvenile and clingy when she'd tried to salvage their marriage. He'd acted jealous and possessive, yet she'd always believed his abuse stemmed from disrespect and loathing. She couldn't bear the thought of that happening with Michael, so she kept her emotional distance and unconsciously prepared for the worst.

"How about having dinner with me?" asked Michael. "And not just your place or mine, but a real night on the town? Are you too tired?"

They were strolling home from the airfield after another hectic week. Their arms were locked around each other's waists and the warmth of his embrace made Carlie feel secure. His words had the opposite affect. She immediately wondered if he was tired of spending time alone with her. As soon as the thought popped into her head, she shoved it out, battling her own low self-esteem, but the niggling doubt remained.

"I'm tired, but a shower will do wonders, and you know I never refuse a free meal. How dressy are we talking?"

"I have a friend at the Tower Restaurant, so I can get a last minute reservation. How's that sound?"

"Mmm . . . they have the best stuffed mushrooms. Just the thought makes my mouth water."

They'd reached the patio leading to both their apartments and Michael walked her to her door. Out of sight from the rest of the house, he took her into his arms and gave her a long, lingering kiss. Carlie wrapped her arms around his neck and leaned against him, loving his hard warmth. She returned his kiss with fervor. It was always the same, every time they touched or kissed, the hungry need kept intensifying.

When they finally drew apart, they were breathing roughly. He pressed his forehead against hers, nudging her stomach with his lower body. "I missed you today," he murmured against her cheek.

"I missed you, too," she whispered, brushing her lips lightly across his.

"I don't suppose a shared shower would be very productive, would it?"

"Hmm. . . depends on what you call productive."

"As in getting ready for dinner as quickly as possible."

"Then, no, I don't suppose it would speed us along."

Michael's stomach chose that minute to growl. They both laughed, and gradually drew apart. Then Carlie gave him another quick kiss and they headed to their respective apartments.

*T*he restaurant was one of Carlie's favorites with a Polynesian décor, soft music and muted lighting. Their table was tucked into an in cozy little alcove. The food, wine and service were exceptional, the food delicious. After dinner, they ordered cappuccino and shared a decadent dessert. By the time they'd finished eating, she'd fallen deeper in love with Michael.

He made her feel so incredibly special. He treated her with respect, deferring to her about preferences rather than trying to make decisions for her. He was always attentive, and his gaze never roved when they were together. He listened as though her every word was of great importance, and she felt the same about him. His slow, sexy smiles were for her alone. He touched her often with gentle caresses to her hands or face.

Their date became an intimate party for two with secret touches and smiles filled with promise. Even though they lingered over coffee, neither would deny the desire to be home in bed. No matter how often they made love, the need just kept growing.

Carlie had almost convinced herself that their relationship had a fighting chance, and then Michael produced a velvet ring box. She gasped as he opened it to show her a beautiful diamond solitaire. Panic clutched at her chest, then spread to her throat, nearly strangling her. Her eyes widened, shadowed by fear. The thought of marriage, and possibly another dismal personal failure, scared her to death.

She felt his steady gaze watching her face for reaction, but she couldn't seem to alter her shock. She was frozen with fear, barely able to move or breathe.

"I guess I don't have to pop the question," he declared in soft resignation. "Your expression says it all. I didn't realize how horrifying a marriage proposal might seem. I thought you were falling in love along with me."

His tone held a ring of defeat that made her feel guilty. Already, she'd disappointed him. How badly might she disappoint him if they were married? She dared to look at him then, but her eyes were too misty to make out his expression. "I'm sorry. You just took me by surprise."

"Obviously," he countered. "Do you have any desire to try it on or do you hate my choice of rings?"

"Oh, no, Michael! It's gorgeous." Her fingers trembled as she took hold of the box. She pulled the marquis cut diamond from his velvet cradle and watched in fascination as it sparkled. "I just don't know if I can accept it."

"You don't have to make any decisions tonight. I didn't mean to rush you, but I thought it was time to let you know how I feel. I'd hoped that you'd change your mind about going to my parents' party, and I wanted you to go as my fiancé."

Carlie's first thought was that he wanted to present her either as a trophy or an affront. Then she quickly chastised herself for such uncharitable thoughts. She didn't believe he was that cold hearted, yet neither could she believe that he was serious about marriage. They'd never discussed a long-term relationship. They'd been careful not to make plans beyond one day at a time. He'd never seemed the type who wanted permanency, and the suddenness of his actions put her emotions in turmoil.

When she didn't say anything else, he reached across the table and took the ring from her unsteady grip. Then he held her left hand in his right and slowly slid it over her ring finger. The fit was perfect and the ring nestled as though it belonged. A huge lump formed in Carlie's throat.

Her eyes were awash with tears when she lifted her gaze to his again. She blinked, but still couldn't focus.

"Leave it there for this evening, okay?" His voice sounded so rough that she wanted to read his expression. She swiped at her eyes and blinked again, but by then, he'd schooled his features in a detached mask. She felt horrible for disappointing him, and even more horrible for not trusting her own heart.

"Let's go home," she urged quietly.

"Just sex and no strings?" he asked, his tone low and accusing.

Carlie wanted to cry. She felt like screaming and sobbing at the injustice of it all. She hated herself for not having the strength to accept what Michael was offering, but she silently promised to make it up to him in bed. There, at least, they were perfectly attuned to each other. Anytime they made love, she felt cherished and safe. Facing the future and Michaels' family was what terrified her.

The trip home was made in relative silence with each of them lost in troubled thoughts. Michael walked her across the patio to her apartment door and stayed close until she'd unlocked it. When she stepped inside, he didn't follow.

"You're not coming in?" she asked.

He stood in the shadows. Carlie couldn't see his face, but she could feel his tension in his voice. "I'd better not."

A sick sense of dread settled in her stomach. "So I'm being punished?" she whispered roughly. "If I don't accept your proposal, I don't get to sleep with you?"

Michael quickly narrowed the distance between them. He pressed her against the door with the length of his body and cupped her face in his hands. His eyes, though shadowed, seemed to bore into her soul.

"This isn't about competition or control. I've told you over and over that I'm not like my brother. I don't want your unquestioning obedience," he nearly growled. Then his tone dropped to a husky, coaxing softness. His thumbs began to caress her cheeks.

"I love you with all my heart. I know now that I've always loved you. I never stopped loving you even though I lied to myself and buried those emotions for a lot of years. I want you to accept me for who I am, love me and be my wife. I want the whole package; total commitment with marriage, and babies and rocking chairs in our old age."

Carlie swallowed the tears gathering in her throat. His words instilled a strange kind of panic in her. She was afraid he wanted more than she was capable of giving.

"I was wrong the first time I took that risk," she whispered. "The failure nearly destroyed me. How can I be sure now?"

Michael pressed a gentle kiss on her lips and stepped away from her. She immediately felt cold and abandoned.

"Love doesn't come with guarantees," he said. "We're both experienced enough to know that by now. It's either there or it isn't, and your fear of commitment is a pretty good sign that your feelings for me aren't as strong as mine for you."

She made a sound of denial, but he abruptly interrupted.

"I thought I had a chance to wipe Bill out of your heart and your mind, but apparently I don't have what it takes. If what you feel for me isn't strong enough to overcome your doubts, then it's better that we go our separate ways."

Carlie trembled, her pulse going haywire as she considered what he was suggesting.

He reached out and cupped her cheeks as though he couldn't stand to be near her and not touch her. His eyes were dark and brooding as he studied her upturn face. I'm flying to New York in the morning. I'll check into some other job possibilities and try to get out of your life again."

She drew in a rough breath. "You want to leave for good?"

"It's probably best for both of us, and there's no sense delaying the inevitable. Sharla will be home tomorrow; you have good part-time help, and won't need me as much. Better to make a clean break now."

With that, he was gone. Carlie watched through a haze of tears as he continued along the patio to his own door. He didn't look back, just disappeared inside without another sign that she existed. It hurt so much. Her heart and lungs constricted in pain and her breath came in strangled little gasps.

He hadn't even bothered to issue an ultimatum, he'd just decided she didn't care enough and given up on her. He wrongly assumed that she still loved Bill. Anger and annoyance warred with pain of loss she wasn't sure she could survive. Apparently Michael didn't have any more faith in her than she'd shown in him. Maybe they were better off to call it quits before they did permanent damage to each other.

Turning, she stepped inside her apartment and locked the door. Heading straight for bed, she shed her shoes and clothes along the way. Then she crawled naked under the covers, shivering at the cool slide of cotton and even more chilly emptiness.

*L*oud knocking at her door woke her on Saturday morning. After a restless night of tossing and turning, she moaned at the disturbance. The sun shone through the window, catching fire on the diamond on her hand. The sparkling stone made her think of Michael and she immediately jumped from bed, grabbing a thin robe to wrap around herself. She hurried to the door in hopes to find him there.

Instead, she found a whole collection of unexpected family members. Reed, Sharla, Dee and even Logan stood on the patio. A rush of joy filled her at the sight of them, but their worried expressions kept her from squealing in delight.

"What's wrong? Belle? Bear?"

"No, no," insisted Sharla. "Reed and I just touched down at the strip at the same time Dee and Logan came in. Nothing's wrong with Mother, Daddy or the business."

"Then what? I know you and Reed were due home today." She turned to Dee, "Did you guys just show up to see the honeymooners?"

"Not exactly," Dee said.

Logan explained. "Dee had a restless night. She was worried about you, so we finally gave up trying to sleep and flew over here."

Carlie sighed heavily, running the fingers of one hand through her tousled hair. She belatedly realized how bad she must look and that Dee would be picking up on her emotional trauma. Dee had always been super-sensitive.

"I'm sorry. It's nothing. Just a bad patch I'm going through. I should have called and let you know not to worry."

"There's more," said Sharla.

Carlie's stomach rolled. Her thoughts flew to Michael. "What?"

"There's been an accident," added Reed.

"No!" Carlie screamed in response, startling them all with her vehemence. "Don't tell me Michael's involved. Please, God, don't tell me Michael's been hurt."

The mix of expressions on everyone's faces had panic surging through her body. She began to quiver and her throat went raw. She wrapped her arms around herself in defensive reaction.

"We're not sure of anything yet," Sharla hastily explained. "All we know is that Michael piloted the Cessna to New York to pick up Bill. Then the two of them headed upstate toward their parents' place. There was some sort of problem and the plane went down."

"No! No! No!" Carlie was screaming and shaking her head in denial. Her breath got trapped in her throat until only harsh gasps escaped.

"They didn't crash," insisted Dee. "They had a forced landing and a lot of trouble, but the plane survived."

"The plane? What about Michael and Bill?"

She didn't like the looks that her sisters exchanged. "What about Michael?"

"We don't know," said Reed "We haven't been able to get any confirmation. All we know is that one of them walked away and the other was life-flighted to the nearest hospital."

Carlie slapped a hand over her mouth to stifle a scream of fear and rage. Then she turned frantic eyes to Dee. She grabbed her sister by the arms, clutching her in panicked reaction. "What do you think? Please tell me what you're feeling and that he's all right." She held her breath, praying her sister could offer more insight.

But Dee was shaking her head. "I just don't know, Carlie. I wish I could tell you more, but all I'm picking up is your distress. I sense pain and confusion, but I'm not sure which brother is suffering."

Carlie whirled around and headed for her bedroom, yelling over her shoulder as she dragged out clean clothes. "How soon can we get there?"

Sharla answered immediately. "Papa Bear is doing a pre-flight check on the charter plane. I'm rested enough to pilot. We can leave as soon as you're ready." There was no question that her sisters and their spouses would accompany her. Somewhere in her frantic thoughts, that added a bit of comfort. No matter what she had to face in New York, she wouldn't be alone.

It was the longest flight of Carlie's life. She sat in the tiny seat of the plane starring out the window, fighting to keep terror at bay, alternately swearing and praying. At first, everyone tried to distract her with small talk, but they'd finally given up the effort and grown silent. Nobody could console her as long as there was a chance that Michael hadn't survived that emergency landing. She thought of all the things that could go wrong, all the ways a pilot could be trapped or hurt, all the horrible damage that could be inflicted on the human body by pounds of metal and pressure. Her chaotic thoughts frightened her even more.

The diamond on her ring finger kept winking in the sunlight, shooting blue sparks and drawing her gaze. She stared at it until her eyes watered. Its brilliance reminded her of Michael's eyes, of his declaration of love, and the way she'd dismissed his proposal without offering him hope. She'd been angry by his actions last night, but she realized now that she hadn't given him much reason to believe they had a future. Had he walked away in hopes of forcing her to make the next move? Had he been offering her a way out, but hoping she wouldn't accept it?

After a month of incredible intimacy and insatiable loving, she hadn't even given him the benefit of the doubt. She could have argued. Could have followed him to his room and insisted he give them more time. She should have shown him how important he was to her, not just the physical attraction they shared, but the love that was so strong it frightened her. She should have done something, anything to make him understand how much she cared.

Now it could be too late. No! She shoved that thought to the back of her mind, refusing to believe she wouldn't have a chance to make it up to him. She'd already wasted too much time denying the facts. They were made for each other. They were true soul mates even if she'd gone astray in her teens and made a stupid decision. It couldn't end this abruptly, this permanently. She couldn't bear to lose him. He made her whole. He completed her in every way. Why hadn't she had the courage to confess that love to him?

Carlie silently thanked whoever had the forethought to have a car waiting for them at the small airport near the hospital where the Trehearns had been taken. The drive was short, and her nerves continued to fray. She kept lecturing herself to stay focused, remain in control, be strong and ready to handle whatever she found waiting.

She wanted Michael to be alive and well, but she'd settle for just alive and able to communicate with her. Whatever physical damage he might have suffered could be dealt with as long as they were together.

Their small entourage entered the hospital through the emergency door entrance. Dee grabbed her hand and gave it a reassuring squeeze. Carlie offered her a brief smile of thanks. Her family's support enveloped her in a strong, invisible shield against any trauma she might experience, just as they'd always done in the past. Their support gave her strength as they walked the corridor toward the neon waiting room sign.

Once there, Carlie immediately focused on the Trehearns. Her ex-in-laws and a few other people she didn't know were gathered around Bill. He looked dirty and bruised with a stark white bandage on his forehead. The sight of him halted her in her tracks. Her brain whirled with the implication. If he was all right, then Michael had to have been the one who'd been badly hurt, maybe killed.

Carlie felt all the blood draining from her face. She wrapped an arm around her waist and pressed her other hand to her mouth to stifle a cry of horror. The wounded sound she made drew everyone's attention and all eyes riveted to her. With their usual stoic expressions in place, she had no way of knowing what to expect.

"Michael?" she managed a hoarse cry. "Where's Michael? I want Michael!"

She felt her sisters shifting closer in a protective effort to comfort her, but then she heard a voice to her right. A voice as familiar as her own heartbeat.

"I'm right here, baby," he said.

Carlie turned and saw Michael for the first time. He looked as dirty and bruised and Bill, but he was walking toward her with sure, strong strides. She swiftly scoured his body for injuries, but other than some iodine, he didn't appear to be hurt.

She turned and raced toward him, halting an instant before they touched. "You're okay?" The words barely slipped past the tightness of her throat. "I won't hurt you?"

In response, he opened his arms and scooped her against his chest. She threw her arms around him and clung with a desperation born of fear and gratitude and desperate love. They clutched each other tightly, holding and rocking and finding reassurance in the fact that they were alive and together again.

Carlie couldn't stop the shudders racking her body. She just clung to Michael, drawing strength from his hard warmth. When she could speak again, she whispered in his ear. "I've never been so scared in all my life!"

"It's okay, sweetheart. I'm all right. The plane's badly damaged, but we're going to be fine."

"They told me only one of you survived."

Michael's grip on her tightened even more. "Bill was unconscious when the paramedics reached us. At first, they couldn't find a pulse, and we didn't know how bad his head injury was, but the doctors said it's just a concussion. He'll be fine after some rest."

Carlie nodded, glad Bill would recover, but eternally grateful that Michael had escaped serious harm. She burrowed her face into the curve of his neck and inhaled deeply. The feel and scent of him as well as the tightness of his grip gradually calmed her shuddering body.

"I love you so much," she told him with deep sincerity.

"You had a scare," he reasoned, his tone telling her that he wouldn't hold her to the emotional declaration.

Carlie didn't want him dismissing her feelings as carelessly as she'd dismissed his last night. She never wanted that kind of misunderstanding between them again.

Pulling back slightly, she looked him directly in the eyes. Her voice was strong and sure when she spoke. "I was a coward and a fool last night. I've been a coward for a long time, but I'm not a total fool. I love you with all my heart. If anything had happened to you, I would have shriveled up and died."

Michael made a rough sound of rebuttal, but she pressed her fingers against his lips. Her gaze locked with his, her eyes a window to her soul. A soul that belonged to him as surely as her heart.

"Maybe it took a bad scare to drum up the courage to say the words, but I know what we have is real and lasting. I love you with all my heart. Whatever challenges we face, we'll face them together. I swear that I want the same things you want; a lifetime commitment. I want marriage, babies and that rocking chair on a porch when we grow old."

Michael's beautiful eyes glistened with tears, and Carlie thought her heart would explode with joy. He blinked and looked away to hide the reaction, but she knew he felt it as deeply as she did. She clutched his face in her hands and drew his head down, locking her lips on his in a fierce, hungry kiss that only began to express the churning emotion. He gathered her closer and returned the kiss with a fervor that caused a rumble of reaction throughout the room.

Only then did the two of them remember they were in a public place surrounded by people. Carlie's blush was part excitement from his kisses and part embarrassment from an audience. He gave her a roguish grin, and slowly turned toward the others.

Keeping one arm around her, he reached the other out to shake hands with Logan and Reed as everyone exchanged greetings. Carlie stiffened a little as they approached his family, but his parents greeted her with unexpected warmth. Their easy acceptance of her in Michael's arms went a long way to relieving her misgivings.

Bill was cool, but not hostile. He obviously wasn't feeling very well, and he just as obviously being fussed after by a woman Carlie had never met. The other woman, introduced as Bill's friend Delores, greeted her with polite reserve. She hoped the two of them were an item, and that neither gave her another thought. All she cared about was the man by her side. .

After a round of introductions, Margaret Trehearn turned to Michael. "Is it all right to go home now?"

"Everything's taken care of and we can leave whenever you're ready."

Carlie belatedly remembered their anniversary. "You aren't getting a very good start to your celebration, are you?" she asked.

"It's not exactly what we planned," said Stan Trehearn, offering her a gentle smile, "but having our sons safely at our sides is the best gift we could ask for."

"Amen to that," whispered his wife.

"Margaret?" Stan held his arm out to his wife, and then turned to the Prescott family. "You're all more than welcome to spend the night at our place. There's plenty of room and more than enough food."

Sharla quickly replied that she wanted to get back to Virginia before nightfall. The others added their thanks and apologies.

Michael looked down at Carlie, and her gaze steadily met his. "You'll stay for the rest of the weekend?"

She gave him a slow smile, her eyes promising that she'd learned her lesson. She wouldn't risk what they shared. It was too precious, too rare. Nor would she let her doubts jeopardize their relationship.

"If you still want me." Her words held an unspoken question.

He brought her left hand to his mouth, pressing a kiss against the ring he'd placed there less than twelve hours earlier. "I love you," he said, his voice was steady and sure, his eyes a deep, turbulent blue.

And there, in front of their families, she returned the words with heartfelt devotion. "I love you more."

"And trust me?"

"Totally."

While the others slowly made their way down the hall, Michael took Carlie into his arms and sealed their vows with a long, lingering kiss.

Epilogue

Eighteen months later....

"We have a secret."

Dee teased her family from the circle of her husband's arms. Logan hugged her tightly and pressed a kiss on her hair. She couldn't see his face, but she knew he was hiding a smile.

The triplets and their spouses were gathered in the living room of the Prescott mansion. They were celebrating their 27th birthday with their parents, and had just finished a southern style dinner complete with cake and homemade ice cream. Contentment had settled over the room.

Sharla was sprawled in an easy chair with Reed sitting on the floor between her legs. Carlie and Michael shared the sofa, snuggling close. Bear was tilted back in his favorite recliner, and Belle had settled into her bentwood rocker. The two were never happier than when surrounded by their family.

At Dee's declaration, they all turned their attention to the loveseat where she and Logan were cuddled close. One of his big hands rested on her swollen stomach.

"You learned the baby's sex today, didn't you?" Belle insisted. "You had the ultra-sound."

"I thought you didn't want to know," said Carlie. She rested her cheek on Michael's chest. He had one arm draped over her shoulder and their hands were intertwined. They couldn't be close without touching.

Sharla idly ran her fingers through Reed's hair as she questioned Dee. "It's a girl, isn't it? Reed's so sure it's a boy, and we've got a friendly little wager riding on it."

"You're right," put in Logan. "We're having a girl."

Sharla squealed her delight and tugged at Reed's hair, demanding money.

"Don't be too quick to claim your winnings," injected Dee. "Reed's right, too."

A pause followed her quiet comment and then an explosion of reaction.

"A boy and a girl!"

"Twins!"

"Oh, my!"

"I'll be darned!"

"Wow, congratulations, I think."

When the exclamations of surprise had quieted, Logan prodded Dee to reveal the rest of her secret.

"There's more?" asked Carlie.

"Actually, we found out we're having one girl and two boys." She felt a blush warm her cheeks; a blush of happiness and anticipation.

"Triplets!" Everyone yelled in unison, their voices ringing with amazement.

"Triplets! I can't believe it. They're supposed to skip our generation!" insisted Sharla.

"Well, apparently they didn't skip very far," said Dee.

"Good grief!! What will you do? How will you cope? Are the babies okay? Are you scared witless?" Carlie wanted to know.

"We're still a little overwhelmed by the news," put in Logan. He and Dee shared a special smile of love and devotion. "The babies are fine, and we'll treasure them just like Bear and Belle do their triplets."

Belle nodded serenely, and then dabbed tears from her eyes.

"And we've already decided that their aunts, uncles, and grandparents are going to have a major part in their upbringing. We'll need all the help we can get," said Dee. "Luckily, the family has a few good pilots who can make regular trips to Kentucky."

Her comment spurred another round of laughter and more questions.

Michael's hand slid to Carlie's flat stomach.

"Don't even think about it," she muttered. "I thought I was ready, but I might have to reconsider after this little surprise."

His low chuckle teased her ear. "We'll wait until you're ready, but we can still practice, can't we?" he whispered.

Carlie gave him an intimate smile. "I guess that would be okay."

"Okay?" he challenged. "Just okay?"

"Quit whispering over there," said Sharla. "If you have secrets, we want to hear them."

"Then they wouldn't be secrets, would they," Reed argued just to get a rise out of his wife.

"You know I don't like secrets," she told him. "You and your fellow marshals are always keeping secrets. I think it should be a federal offense for husbands to keep secrets from their wives."

His voice dropped too low for anyone else to hear. "Then I should probably tell you about my test results, shouldn't I?"

Sharla grasped his head and tilted it until she could look him in the eyes. The rest of the family continued to bombard Dee with questions, but she blocked out their conversation and gave him her full attention. "What test results?"

"The fertility test I had done."

Her mouthed dropped open, but she could find no words to respond. They'd assumed it was impossible for them to have a biological child together. They'd agreed to wait another year or so and check in to adoption. Because of that, they'd never worried about birth control.

"Seems I'm not shooting all blanks." His tone was light, but his expression held a wealth of emotion. "It might not be easy for you to conceive, but it's possible."

Sharla's eyes and mouth widened even farther. Reed nuzzled his face against her stomach, and she clutched his head with both hands. "Ohmigaud!" she finally managed, nearly hyperventilating.

"Now who's keeping secrets?" demanded Carlie, drawing everyone's attention to them.

Sharla merely stared at her, totally lost for words. All she could think about was triplets. Three of everything. Triplicate. Her gaze skipped from Carlie to Dee and then back to Reed again.

"Happy Birthday, Sweetheart," he said in a voice rich with amusement.

"Happy, happy, happy birthday," echoed Papa Bear.

Printed in the United States
5826